A novel by Bryan Zepp Jamieson
© 2014, All rights reserved
ISBN-13: 978-0-692-23891-2

Thanks to William Shakespeare for the use of his sonnets, and to Joni Mitchell for lyrics from "Urge For Going", Copyright 1972, Asylum Records.

Printed by Lulu Books

Electronic Versions are available at:

www. http://icefallsfnovel.webege.com/

This page intentionally left blank.

Of course, the page exists in a superposition of states, blank or not blank, until you actually look at it and determine that there has been a wave function collapse, and this page is, in fact, not blank using the most literal interpretation of the word 'blank'.

That leaves the matter of intent. If the page was intentionally left blank, and was, when you opened it, actually blank, then there is no quandary about intent. However, it does violate the premise of a superposition of states, which call for an element of randomness. Therefore, the question of whether the page itself actually exists must be called into question.

If the page was not blank, and existed, then the intent of the writer is a paradox, since the stated intent was that the page be blank. If you are reading this, the writer was incorrect. If it is not here and you are reading this, then it is you who is incorrect. I suggest reopening the page until you get it right.

Interesting universe we live in. Let's go explore it.

Foreword

This book in large measure owes a debt to Allen Steele and his *Coyote* trilogy. If you've never read them, you are in for a treat. It's Allen Steele at his best, with engaging and believable characters, a strong plot, and an intriguing world. My idea to build my own interstellar colonization story comes from Mr. Steele's opus, and the discerning reader will spot some similar plot elements along the way. Despite those points of commonality, this story is entirely my own.

I re-read Mister Steele's trilogy in spring of 2012, and enjoyed it even more on the second reading. But the meteorology and cartography of Coyote didn't match what I would have done if I was building a world.

So what would I have done?

I would build it with lots of water, and a much warmer climate. This allows greater variety, not just in the weather, but in the biology of the planet. I would have it behave like a moon orbiting a gas giant. And, just for the sake of the challenge, I wouldn't have any dangerous native life. I wouldn't have the colonists live like 18th century Americans; they arrive with incredible futuristic technology, and there's no reason they shouldn't keep it.

At that point, I had my world, and the germ of my story.

After a few weeks of considering and discarding dozens of plot ideas, I learned exactly how the story would end. I even had about half the sequel plotted out. Yes, there will be a sequel. For those who hate cliff-hangers, this isn't that type of story. There are unresolved plot elements, and it clearly ends on a "to be continued" note, but it's not a cliff-hanger.

Acknowledgments

Fractal Terrain III, for the maps. The story was written on a Hewlett-Packard computer, in Ubuntu 12.04, using Libre Office 3.5 for the raw manuscript, and formatting for printing in Windows 7, using Microsoft Word 2010. The cover design came from a stock image of a crescent Moon, combined with special effects courtesy of Corel Photo Impact 12 and Corel Draw X6. Typesetting for the paperback edition was done throughout in Garamond 11 point. The e-books are in Arial. The title of the book in in Milano Letter.

Wikipedia and Duckduckgo combined brought the universe to my fingertips, as they do for all of us, and I put in quite a bit of time getting nollij I probably should have had back in high school.

Research for the novel took me to such places as Sol Station (where I leaned that nu Phoenicis would be a good destination for the star ship). I'm not the first to 'visit' that star system; Google 'Furuha'.

Many deep thanks and love to my wife, Paris, whose unstinting support and willingness to wade through watching for spots where my ability to conjugate a simple declarative sentence deserted me. Copy editing is tedious trudge work, and her willingness to do it made for a much stronger book. And thanks to my beta readers, John and Jim, and all the folks at Scribophile who took the time to critique the first 15 chapters of the book. They brought decades of discerning reading to the fore to tell me why my book utterly sucked, and what I needed to do about that.

I'm sure there are errors and omissions remaining, but those that remain are entirely my responsibility. Hopefully I don't have any errors of the Calvin and Hobbes "Bats Aren't Bugs!" variety.

The Crew of RESS Phoenix

Admiral Daniel Elias Vargas, captain of the RESS *Phoenix,* born in Torreón, Coahuila, The Americas.

Commander Sean Sheffield, born in Manchester, Great Britain, Royal Europe.   First Mate, RESS Phoenix and Surveyor

Commander Alan Trapp, born in Heidelberg, Germany, Royal Europe, the Chief Medical Officer, physician, hospital administrator

Chief Petty Officer Nate Harlen, born in Vancouver, Oregon, The Americas. Crew chief

Commander Gordon Lassiter, Born in Wellington, New Zealand, China Union, Chief Technical Officer (2)

Lieutenant Commander Etienne Sorlund, born in Ypres, France, Royal Europe, Chief Navigations officer and Helm Operations Paleotology and Paleo-botony

Lieutenant Commander Jeanine Barney, born in Brisbane, Australia, China Union, navigations and Imprint requisitions, Nucleonics

Commander Apunda "Scotty" Boitumelo, born in Yaounde, Cameroon, African Union. Chief Engineer

Commander Madelyne Isaakson, born in Krakow, Poland, Russian Federation. Head of maintenance, Architect

Lieutenant Commander Doctor Ian Spencer, born in Bristol, Great Britain, Royal Europe. Second in command of medical, ship psychologist, Animal husbandry

Midshipman Michael Matthews, Horticulturalist

ABS Matthew Bissont, engineering, Toxicology

Midshipman Virgil "Red" Farnsworth, in Manchester, Great Britain, Royal Europe. Maintenance, ROV wrangler, Charliemeister, Horticulture

ABS Günther Brülow, born in Bonn, Germany, Royal Europe. Maintenance, soil analyst, explorer.

ABS Davis McDonald, born Pretoria, South African Province, African Union, Electronics, construction

ABS Tim Simmons, born in Johannesburg, South African Province, African Union. Physicist

ABC Sam Buchanan, born in Atlanta, Georgia, The Americas. Heavy equipment drilling

ABS Adelena Conti, born Acona, Italy, Royal Europe. Microbiologist

Lieutenant Susan Bartlett, Ottawa, Ontario, The Americas. Comm operations, horticulture

Lieutenant Commander Jan Steinberg, physician, born Essen, Germany, Royal Europe. Epidemiologist, pianist.

Lieutenant Ian Mann, born Gillam, Manitoba, The Americas. Requisitions, shuttle pilot, xenobiologist (2)

Lieutenant Andre Morley, born Paris, France, Royal Europe. Climatological studies

ABS Ann Forster, born Diani Beach, East Africa Province, African Union. Botanist

Colonists

Jim Hartnell, xenobiologist

Rudy Harlen, engineer

Maureen Spencer, wife of Ian Spencer, large-animal vet

Jim Spencer, 16 year old son (at time of launch) of Ian and Maureen Spencer. Cat lover.

Sylvie Spencer, 14 year old daughter of Ian and Janice Spencer. Cat lover.

Rebekah Cohen, farmer

Asuka Tsuchishima, exobotonist

Aaron Kessler, geologist, computers

Cyril Voss, architect, urban planner

Earthers

King Edward IX, Sovereign of Great Britain, President, European Federation

Percival C. Siddons, Operations Manager of Dry Dock, Dry Dock Captain of RESS Phoenix

Jefferson Handling, Imprint technology

Rafael Vargas, father of Dan Vargas

Douglas Reeman, 20th century author of *Captain Richard Bolitho, RN*

Gustavo Bécquer, Commander, Gabon Space Facility

NOTES FROM THE CREW LOG OF RESS PHOENIX:

Nu Phoenicis (Phenu PhoenicisHD 7570+5 var49 Yellow-white dwarf) is a main sequence (F8) dwarf star in the constellation Phoenix. It is similar to the Sun, although somewhat more massive and luminous. At an estimated distance of less than 49 light years, this star is located relatively near the Sun.

Based on observations of excess infrared radiation from this star, it may possess a dust ring that extends outward several AU from an inner edge starting at 10 AU. This is very similar to the rings of Saturn but on the "sun'

Nu Phoenicis 4 (Name to be chosen by captain.)

Simply called "The New World", this planet is regarded at being by far the better of the two planets capable of supporting life from earth. The average temperature is about 20C, the rotational period is an amazing 24:01 hours, and it has an axial tilt of about 22 degrees, and has about 65% water coverage. The atmosphere appears to be about 17% oxygen and 90% nitrogen. Spectrographic analysis, while obviously imprecise at 49.3 light years, suggests the possibility of chlorophyll-based life.

There is no evidence of any broadcast activity, which suggests that there is little in the way of developed civilization, or indeed intelligent life at all.

Nu Phoenicis 8 Cueball

Nu Phoenicis 8 is terrestrial planet, furthest of the eight planet system and about 9.4 Aus in distance. While observation suggested an atmosphere and water, it was never considered seriously as a suitable locale for habitation, and in-system telemetry bears this out. The planet appears to be nearly completely enveloped in water ice, with the exception of a dark band along the equator. It has been speculated that this dark band may be the shadow from rings orbiting the planet (unlikely, in this writer's opinion) or an area that is free of ice. The nature of the band remains unknown, as telemetry showed the average surface temperature to be between minus 100 and 150 centigrade, significantly colder than Antarctica. The planet has been dubbed "Cue Ball".

Nu Phoenicis 2/1 Hō-ō One

Hō-ō One is the first moon (of about 20 significant moons) of the planet Hō-ō, which is the second planet out from Nu Phoenicis, re-dubbed Zhar-Ptitsa (Fire Bird) by some of the crew. The firebird imagery used for the star and its system of planets and moons come from the fact that it was part of the Phoenix constellation, visible in the southern hemisphere of Earth.

Hō-ō is a ringed gas giant. Typical of its class, it has an atmosphere comprised mostly of hydrogen and helium, with no discrete surface. The rings are composed mostly of water ice, floating bergs ranging in size from a half meter to 250 kilometers. The rings have a high albedo, which helps explain why they don't simply melt and disperse.

Hō-ō is at 1.2 astronomical units from Zhar-Ptitsa, a distance considered to be too close for human habitation. However, there are mitigating factors that make nearly 10% the existing land mass suitable for human colonization.

Hō-ō One has an average rotational period of 23.6 hours, and a surface gravity of .77. It revolves around Hō-ō once every 10.2 days, and has effectively about a thirty degree axial tilt in relation to the mother planet. It orbits in the same plane as the rings, and the large majority of other moons that Hō-ō has.

However, Hō-ō itself has an axial inclination of nearly 30 degrees, and combined with its orbital period (c. 440 days) suggests that seasons will not only be longer, but more extreme than is found on Earth.

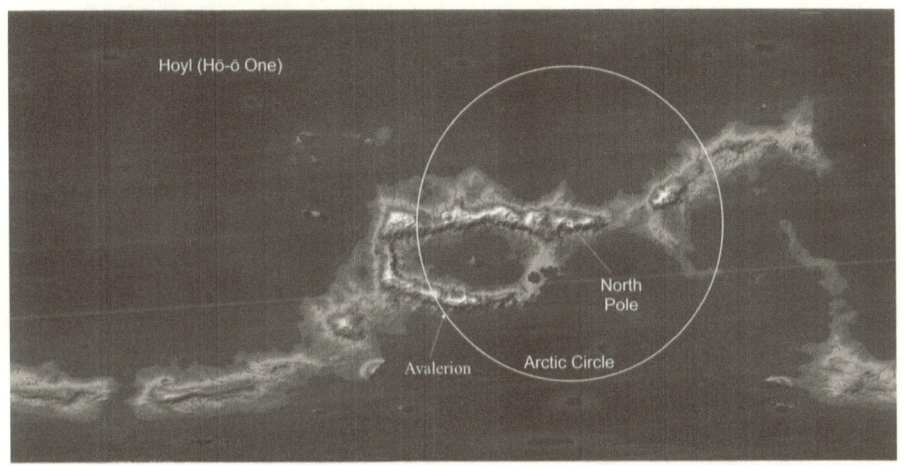

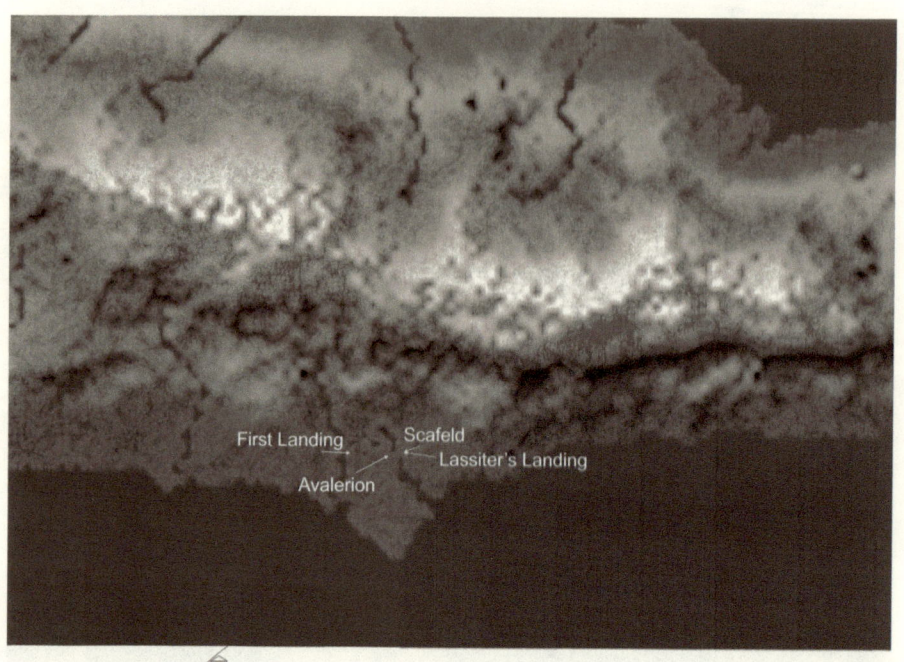

First Landing
Scafeld
Lassiter's Landing
Avalerion

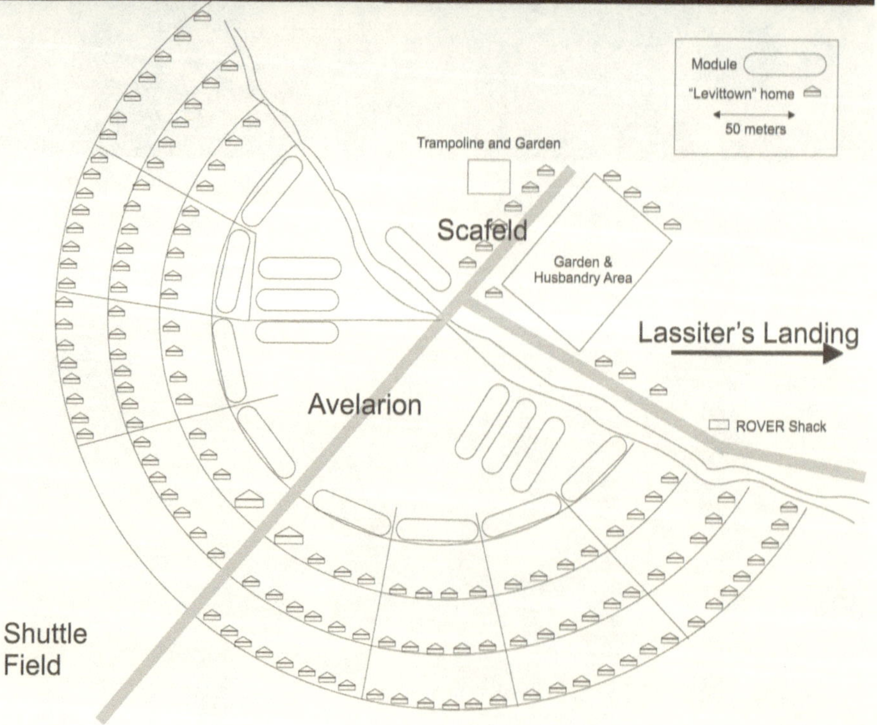

Module

"Levittown" home

50 meters

Trampoline and Garden

Scafeld

Garden &
Husbandry Area

Lassiter's Landing

Avelarion

ROVER Shack

Shuttle
Field

Table of Contents

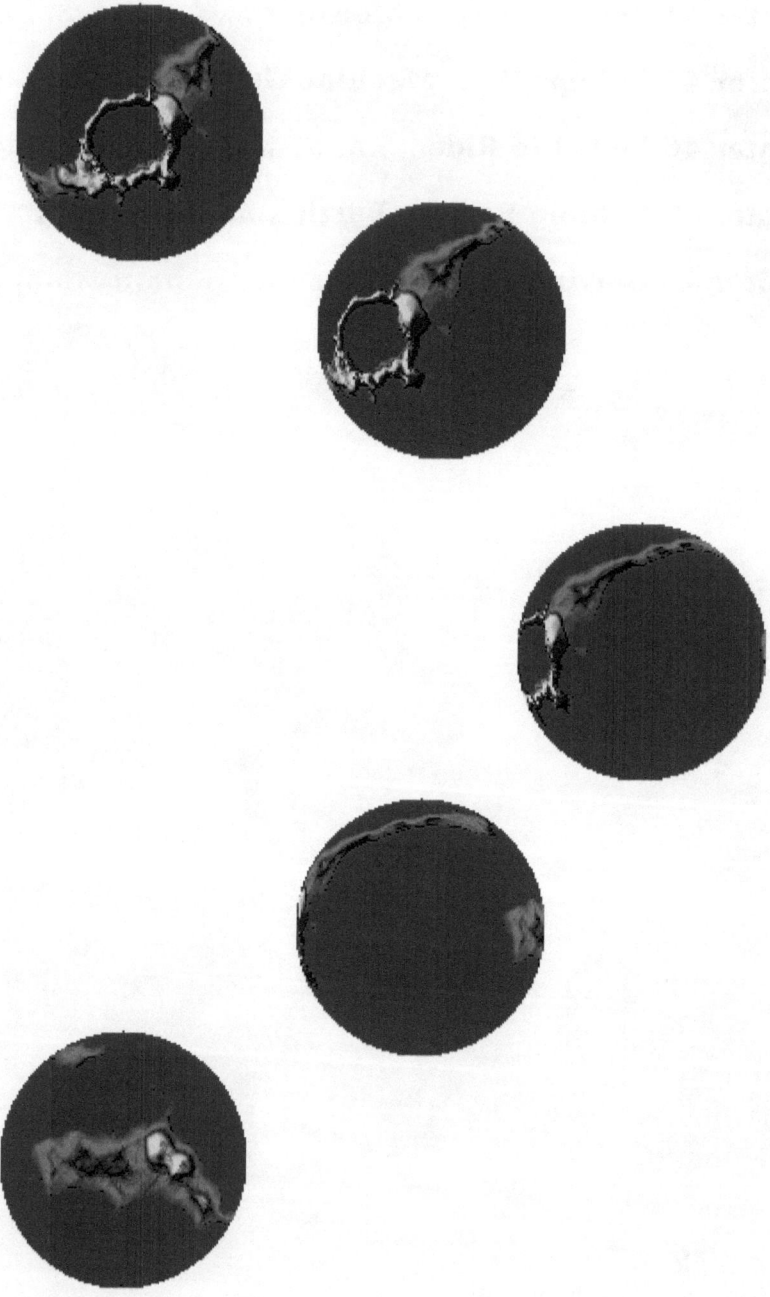

Part 1
Leave-Taking

Chapter 1 Leave-Taking

CAPTAIN VARGAS knew it wouldn't be good for morale if he looked at his first officer and burst into laughter.

Sean Sheffield didn't have much of a sense of humor, but humor was not a vital feature for a second-in-command.

Thirteen other senior crew members were Velcro-walking in an awkward cluster with them, and they, too, were almost naked and, except for eyelashes, completely hairless. Worse, their skins were a variety of odd colors because the same treatment that cost them their hair also peeled the top layer of dead skin cells. They all wore Velcro mittens and booties which someone in the echelons decided needed to be a fluorescent shade of pink.

Admiral Daniel Elias Vargas, captain-to-be of the *RESS Phoenix*, never imagined taking command of a star ship in quite this manner. He envisioned a formal military uniform, with a snappy beret and a few discreet insignia telling of elevated rank. Or maybe not so discreet; occasionally a little bragging was justified. Cheering crowds would watch as, with considerable but understated determination and courage, he led humanity to the stars. A marching band, even the lousy one his high school had, wouldn't be out of line.

Instead, he was in an opaque yellow tube, hairless, parboiled, and bouncing lightly off the walls of the access tube in micro gravity and sickly yellow light like a pink bald bunny rabbit. Between the lack of gravity and his motions, his penis was waving about like a mad conductor's baton. Man's first step to the stars was an undignified comic hop.

He especially took care not to look at the ship's engineer, Apunda "Scotty" Boitumelo. At one hundred and eighty centimeters and with ebony skin, she was the one person in the group who didn't look utterly ridiculous. In fact, she looked pretty damned hot, and the last thing Vargas needed at that particular moment was an erection.

At the age of forty-six, Vargas, recently retired as a brevet admiral, was remarkably young to be commanding something like the *Phoenix*. Striking green eyes offset his broad Indio features, and a perpetual smile belied a keen and decisive mind. He was there, in part, as a result of a political compromise. Despite that, he was suited for the job. He was a veteran, a war hero, and a tactical genius. Or so his publicity releases said. He was happy to just be a veteran.

At least the cheering crowds couldn't see him now. At least he was an even brownish-pink. Poor Sheffield had come out blotchy, a mix of pink and old ivory. He looked less like the top line officer than custard gone bad. At fifty-three, Commander Sheffield usually had jet black hair, cropped short, and a perpetual five o'clock shadow common to the type of Briton known, inaccurately, as 'black Irish.'

The yellow light didn't improve matters.

Keeping his mouth firmly in a straight line, eyes resolutely forward, Vargas moved toward the final airlock separating the *Phoenix* from the vast Dry Dock in which she reposed. Once on board, he hoped his captain's instincts would be more firmly in charge of his sense of the ludicrous.

The endless ceremonies saluting the fifteen hundred who were leaving for the *nu Phoenicis* system had come to a merciful end five days earlier with an audience from inside the quarantine tent with King Edward IX. Still, the most sober and ritualistic moment lay ahead, an hour and twelve minutes away, when the gigantic ship began to ease slowly out of Dry Dock. The next big moment would be three hours after that, when the massive main engine exploded into action, driving the ship to eighty-seven percent of the speed of light over the next three hundred and sixteen days.

Fifteen years earlier the European Ministry of Space had rather diffidently asked if anyone was interested in being on board the first interstellar ship. There was no ship, no place to build it, and no feasible way of getting to the stars, and they still got hit with nearly a million applicants. Daniel Vargas, still just an Air Force ensign, was one of them. He never really had any doubt he would secure a berth.

Vargas officially prepared for this day for over three years, and unofficially since he was ten years old. It still didn't seem quite real. Even the notion of going to a different star system had seemed firmly in the realm of science fiction just fifteen years earlier. Indeed, as captain of a warship during the China-Americas war, Vargas knew he only had a small shot of even being alive for the launch date. A survivor of eight engagements, he knew he was due to lose one. Space battles didn't leave survivors on the losing ship. You won, or you were dead. It was that simple. Winning was often a matter of pure luck – or nearly prescient tactical skills. Vargas had plenty of both.

Luck came in. The war ended just as Vargas and his crew was jockeying to begin a ninth battle.

Vargas entered the war as a midshipman, and at the end he was a young decorated captain on track for the admiralty. His career arc suggested five years in the admiralty, capped by a year on the Joint Chiefs of Staff, and then a happy and young retirement. He first joined the military because life in depression-ridden Coahuila offered little beyond a backwater life surrounded by grinding poverty. Because that same paranoid government kept them in poverty, they kept them under constant watch. Vargas couldn't live like that.

He qualified for Officers Training as much to escape the cameras and microphones as to escape the privation of the Americas' wastelands.

In peacetime, he would have retired after thirty years as a commander, with a parting gong to a titular captaincy, but the war, came along with great hazards and fast promotions. At the end, Captain Daniel Vargas was a war hero who never once saw the faces of his enemies, and the Americas government was looking for a hero. A young soon-to-be Admiral from a glamorous and fantastically dangerous branch of the military, and the Americas' only 'space ace', Vargas fitted the bill perfectly. That he had advanced degrees in math and science was a nice bonus, too. Vargas never understood the mindset that appreciated education and intelligence whilst clearly understanding neither, but he wasn't about to discourage politicians who thought, "Him gots brains. Smart!" was a good thing. It was a very good thing for the job in question. That the politicians accidentally picked someone who actually had the education and the brains to use it was a happy coincidence.

European, African and Russian planning of the giant ship that became the *RESS Phoenix* began over twenty years earlier. The craft started out as little more than a 100 meter long glorified shuttle, but as humanity's fusion-fueled abilities to move ever larger objects into orbit grew, so did plans for the ship. it was redesigned from stem to stern, given a whole new propulsion system, and was envisioned for three different star systems before its builders finally settled on a faint, yellowish star not even visible from Europe and Russia. The final plans included a monster engine, one so big there was no way to test fire it. It was a testament to the boundless optimism of the designers that such an engine was built.

Then war broke out.

Things might have stalled indefinitely, but then, after just six months, China unexpectedly sued for peace.

When the Americas won their pointless war with China, they found themselves with accelerated space technology—in particular, a new and better fusion drive. That freed ships from many of the dictates of orbital mechanics and won the strategically minor but emotionally-loaded space war.

It could provide constant thrust capable of getting a large ship to near light speed in less than a year, and forced yet another revamp of the starship plans,

The Americas also enjoyed a vast post-war economic boom that left the treasury flooded with money.

Europe and Africa had smaller, inadequate launch facilities, and needed the Americas' vast Dry Dock facilities in geosynchronous orbit.

The half-built ship would still be as big as when the designers envisioned taking six thousand people four centuries to reach the nearest likely star system. But with an anticipated travel time of twenty-six years ship's time instead of 400, a smaller complement seemed reasonable.

The Americas were willing to join the effort, but at a price. They would ante up a third of the cost, full access to Dry Dock, the schematics for the fusion engine, and the latest in Imprinting technology. In return, they wanted the captaincy of the vessel, and a fifth of the crew membership. They also wanted naming rights for the starship and any habitable planet they colonized. Here, a compromise was reached. The vessel would be named for its destination, and the Americas could tell their population it was named for an Americaner city destroyed in the war. As for naming the planet, the Captain would be given a list of names from which he could choose. Thus Vargas had, both on his data pad and on actual paper in his duffel, a list of names including Columbia, Plymouth, Jefferson, Gingrich and, somewhat mysteriously, Akron.

Commander Sean Sheffield was the man who most likely would have been captain had it not been for the Americas' demands. If it bothered him, he gave no sign. He glanced over at Vargas and said quietly, "I just realized we've seen our sun for the last time."

"With luck," Vargas replied. He grinned at Sheffield. "But we will have telescopes. You can look back from *nu Phoenicis* and see what the Sun was doing forty-eight years earlier."

"A bit late to be looking back."

Vargas conceded the point with a nod. He glanced at his ranking officer. Despite the solemnity of his words, Sheffield had an excited glint in his eye, and his cheeks were missing their usual pallor. The corner of his mouth was twitched up, a reluctant grin.

The group reached the airlock, and with a faint sigh, it cycled open. Vargas felt his ear drums tingle from the slight overpressure from the ship side. A light changed to green, and the group moved into the chamber.

Human behavior in airlocks was the same as it was in elevators. During the ninety seconds in which it equalized, everyone stared at the upper walls, lost in their own thoughts.

Vargas thought about his audience with the King of England. Edward the Ninth and Vargas could have been twins, with short dark hair and neatly trimmed beards. They were of an age, this forty-two year-old starship captain and historic monarch, and Vargas felt an instant kinship with the soft-spoken man who was burdened with remote grandeur. He wondered if Edward had looked at him and thought of the Mark Twain novel. The King had smiled and whispered, "I wish I could be going with you. I would trade. . . " The King shook his head. "You're leaving a very sorry Earth, you know. I'm very much concerned you may be humanity's last best hope."

Vargas took a deep breath. He could get away with contradicting the monarch, but only if he appeared to be agreeing with him. "Majesty, under your wise leadership other ships are being built. And this is hardly the first time humanity as found itself in such dire straits."

The King's gentle tone robbed his words of impatience. "I know that as well as any man on Earth. But this time. . . Admiral, I will breathe easier once you are on your way." Vargas had given the King a sharp glance, wondering what he meant. His Majesty then said some things that shocked Daniel Vargas. They weren't the words of a King to a visiting heroic explorer, but rather words of one careworn leader to another, peers in the eyes of the other.

The King, waved a royal flourish and stood. The audience was over.

Vargas left feeling considerably subdued, and even more keenly aware of the stakes of his mission. The population of Earth told the tale of the past two centuries, beginning with the Flare and then the Vast Depression. Humanity's numbers had fallen from nine billion to just under one billion, and only fifteen percent of the land area, mostly coastal, remained habitable. *Phoenix* represented humanity's last great hope for a bright future. Or any future.

The airlock opened to the *Phoenix*. Crew hovered at the ready, ship's tunics in hand. Vargas felt relief. Nudity didn't bother him, but missing the scant coverage of body hair changed nudity to nakedness.

He floated in the cleanest environment it was possible for humans to create. Humanity might avoid bringing most of its communicable diseases along, or so the theory went. Vargas reserved judgment, but allowed that it would be nice to never get any more colds or flu. About two dozen would-be colonists who had spent years in training and preparation were scrubbed at the end because they had the horrible misfortune to catch a cold in the final month.

If their destination world had life of its own—and the presence of oxygen in the atmosphere made that likely—then they might reduce the potential for disastrous contamination. Of course, the situation wasn't reciprocal; the planet might well poison or sicken them.

Clothed in the light ship's crew uniform, Vargas began to feel a bit more like a starship captain. Most of the rest of the line officers, now clad, floated off to their various duties. Only Sheffield and a few of the other bridge officers remained. A small balding civilian, anachronistically bespectacled and balding, drifted in front of him with a clipboard. "Welcome aboard, Commodore. Are you ready to relieve me?"

Vargas resisted the urge to return a salute which hadn't been given. As chief of Dry Dock operations, this civilian, Siddons, was titular captain of the vessel until relieved. In the Navy, where rank was everything aboard ship, the custom made sense. Vargas had heard tales of fleet officers who lost track of what their ranks were while visiting ships. In civilian life it seemed silly.

"Is everything in order, Captain?

Siddons awkwardly stiff armed the clipboard, with a thick sheaf of flimsies in front of him. They trembled in his shaking hand. Didn't they believe in data pads? With his other hand he grabbed a handhold to prevent himself from reciprocal drift backwards. "Here are the final inspection results, Admiral." Clearly for the moment the weight of human history and future hopes weighed heavily upon the shoulders of one Captain Percival C. Siddons, Provisions Administrator and Earth's first starship captain. Not that Siddons, whose primary duties revolved around the smooth functioning of the loading of materiel into *Phoenix* rather than actual construction of the ship, had spent much time on board prior to this week. Vargas studied the sterile sheets in order to hide a smile. He thought all the formalities were done with.

The results on the clipboard were just a formality. Over the past three days, during final decontamination, a steady stream of reports, the ones on this clipboard, streamed into Vargas' data pad. His inspection was cursory. "Very well, Ser, I relieve you."

Siddons snapped off a smart British-style salute, spoiled only by the fact that, holding the clipboard for Vargas with his right hand, he awkwardly did so left-handedly, rotating slowly rightward. Vargas cocked an eyebrow, decided this was not the time to lecture the man on etiquette.

"The hopes and prayers of all humanity go with you, Captain. God speed."

Three different ranks in fifteen seconds. That had to be a record. Civilian bureaucrats shouldn't play at being members of the military. Vargas put on a look of well-practiced modest pleasure. "Thank you, Mr. Siddons. Perhaps you will be on one of the future ships."

"All due respect, Captain, but the wife likes Kalaallisut, where God intended men to be."

The name brought an image to Vargas' mind of deep conifer forests and snow-capped mountains. He had visited Greenland as a military dignitary and for cold weather training several times, and loved the cool freshness of the place. He felt a pang, and realized his goodbyes to Earth weren't emotionally complete.

With that, Siddons turned on his heel and almost marched to the airlock. The last of his crew were already in with him, and the lock cycled for the final time.

Sheffield glanced, making sure the airlock doors were closed. He gave Vargas a look of mock concern. "That was the man responsible for our provisions?"

Vargas did smile at that. "Yes, and pretty much everything else that came on board."

"I wish we had more than an hour before we light this candle. If he's usually that nervous, it could get mighty hungry in here."

Vargas chuckled. He knew that Sheffield and Siddons had worked together closely over the past month, ensuring everything they needed was right where it needed to be. "Let's go see what the bridge is up to."

Phoenix had lifts, but in zero gravity, such devices were universally seen as annoying and wasteful vomit comets. Accelerations comfortable in one gravity were disorienting to even the most seasoned orbital monkeys, and so the group, without conferring, elected to simply float up the ugly, but spacious corridors to the bridge.

The unreality Vargas had been feeling dissipated as the team entered the bridge. It was identical to their training module in every way save only for the lack of gravity. All previous space craft had cockpits rather than bridges, with up to four seats closely enveloped by controls and readouts. This was a true bridge, with twenty-five stations, a curving bulkhead filled with screens and throne-like in the center, a captain's chair with God Console. There was even a wardroom behind and adjacent that served as bridge mess. It was a thing of beauty, a science fiction dream with huge curved screens encompassing nearly half the area and controls and readouts for every function on the ship.

The bridge would be unoccupied and dark for nearly all of the flight, save for the occasional little cleaning Charlie.

Vargas strapped into his seat and a sense of competent familiarity descended. He had done this hundreds of times in the simulator, facing everything from misfiring thrusters to containment breaches and even alien encounters (friendlies, fortunately). He glanced around the bridge, sensitive to the slightest element that might be out of place. Even the ship's air had been faithfully replicated in the simulator. He found himself settling into the routine that should take him through the three hours needed to clear Dry Dock and attain a safe distance before firing the main engine.

The Captain's God Console kept him apprised of launch status, and his data pad was given over to displaying status of Dry Dock in relation to the launch. The entry tube his party came through had uncoupled from the ship and in about fifty-eight minutes the last of the brackets holding her steady in the vast artificial cavern would be released. The brackets, not particularly sturdy given the size of the masses they connected, were enough to overcome microscopic gravitational perturbations that might otherwise cause the ship to bump against the side of the containment structure. Even at a few millimeters an hour, the inertia involved a ship of over sixty million tons and Dry Dock's not-inconsiderable three million tons would ensure considerable damage.

The trickiest part of the entire flight mission would be the first 1,650 meters. *Phoenix* would accelerate slowly, easing up to a rate of about fifteen centimeters a second over a half hour. Dry Dock would have its own engines going to avoid being pushed backward and thus out of geosynchronous orbit until *Phoenix* was clear. For those three hours, the bridge and Dry

Dock would be watching the clearance parameters with intense care. The ship had roughly three meters clearance on all sides, and protocol allowed it to drop to a minimum of two meters before a corrective firing would be needed. Lateral motion at no point was permitted to exceed fifty micrometers a second, which meant the first three hours would require precision. The hundreds of small directional rockets—most of which might never be needed again after the first three hours—were finely adjusted, but there was always some margin of error. Computers would handle most of the responses, dealing in levels of angstroms per microsecond, but close human supervision was still deemed utterly necessary.

Once clear, it was just a matter turning the ship enough for the backwash to miss Dry Dock, accelerating at one gravity, putting almost everyone into hibernation, and spending the next twenty-eight years flying the biggest artificial object humanity had ever created nearly fifty times faster than humans had ever gone before to a different star fifty light years away.

Everyone would be holding their breath as the engine was brought up to full thrust. Built *in situ*, there was no way to test it without ruining dry dock. Firing it outside Dry Dock was even less feasible; even a few minutes at half thrust would result in greater inertia than the entire fleet of shuttles and tugs could overcome. Mock-ups of the engine, built to 1/20th scale, had been tested on Earth and in orbit, and yet smaller versions were on the shuttles and tugs. They all worked perfectly.

Now, getting to *nu Phoenicis* after all that – that was the easy part.

A yellow info flag appeared on his data pad. The communications room on the Dry Dock passed along the information that hostilities had just broken out between the African Union and India. There had been a missile exchange, and the ruins of Bombay were believed to have suffered extensive damage. Dry Dock was advised not to accept any ships from either side.

Vargas impatiently cleared the advisory. Like much of the crew, he had watched world video as a way of passing time in the confinement of decontamination, and the outbreak of war came as no surprise. And Bombay was already a ghost town these days. It wasn't a major story. At this point, global politics – even a nuclear war – meant as little to him as Little League scores from Topeka. Still, Vargas would feel a lot better once they had several light minutes between himself and Earth. He reflected uneasily on the thoughts the King had vouchsafed him a few days earlier. His Highness had the dreadful aspect of a leader who saw another war as inevitable.

In their private meeting, the two men, so much alike in temperament and intelligence, had gazed at one another across a chasm of birthplace and birthright and found a mutual liking. Vargas knew he and the King were the same age, and close up, he was shocked at the weary lines the King's face wore.

"If this conflict comes," the King had said, "you'll be well away and might be humanity's sole hope."

For a moment, Dan Vargas felt the weight that rested on the King's shoulders every day of his life. What a terrible responsibility!

The King continued, "Tell me. You are a decorated hero of your country's war with China. Will you be taking your medals with you?"

Vargas hesitated, slightly confused. "I placed them in the hands of the Smithsonian for future display. They just didn't seem to be something that belonged on this mission." His own government remained unaware he had done that.

"Good," the King replied, nodding. "I would hate to think we were sending the ship off under the command of a patriotic fool."

Vargas, caught unawares, didn't know how to respond.

"If this war comes, Admiral, it will not be glorious, or brave, or noble. It will be a catastrophic failure. It will be my catastrophic failure. I will have let down my people, and yours."

The tired King peered sharply at the young Admiral. "If I should fail, it is even more important that you must not. Take care of your people, Admiral, and God speed."

Chapter 2 First Flight

THE READOUTS SHOWED THE SHIP was now self-contained. In the forty decks behind the bridge, crew and passengers were taking advantage of the micro gravity, storing last-minute items and double checking everything else. Then for three hours, everyone would restrict their movements in order to keep the ship's distribution of weight as constant as possible. Given the fantastic mass of the hull, the arrangement of personnel and their effects seemed trivial, but the tight tolerances *Phoenix* operated under during Dry Dock departure made it necessary.

Once clear of Dry Dock, the ship would begin full acceleration, and the process of putting everyone into hibernation would commence. Twenty five six-person complements would stand watch on six month rotations, resulting in each crew member standing two watches totaling a year in length. Vargas would be on first and last watch.

The only sounds were the faint susurration of voices. Each crew member was ticking off each step on a side panel. From the God Console, Vargas oversaw every item being checked, and with the ability to see exactly what every duty post station showed, and could run a discreet double-check or override. He wasn't worried about complacency, the leading cause of error on the simulations. This time it would be the opposite, the possibility people might be overwhelmed by the sheer magnitude of what was happening.

Another yellow flag displayed in the Dry Dock window. Europe had declared war on India following another exchange of missiles between India and the African Union. Vargas tapped his armrest thoughtfully, eyes involuntarily moving in the direction of Earth. The unblinking glass eyes of the media had shifted focus away from the launch to the blossoming war. He felt irritation at the distraction, and then a slight sense of shame at his pettiness.

Outside feeds to the ship were severely limited to spare the crew and colonists the distraction of the ongoing media frenzy.

He thought the restriction reflected excessive caution by the RESS bureaucrats in Gabon, but was grateful for the block.

The overhead lights blinked to blue and back, indicating thirty minutes until they began creeping out of Dry Dock. Sheffield glanced over from his console. "Everything's optimal, Captain."

Sheffield's tone changed. He snapped to Sorlund, the chief navigator, "Get me a trajectory on that." Vargas flashed a data pad question mark to him. Sheffield switched to voice mode on the data pad. "We have an unexpected launch. Given the situation down there, we're monitoring."

Vargas flicked open his navigators' window. An outline of the Dry Dock appeared, nearly two kilometers in length and one half kilometer in diameter. Them. At the bottom was a curved line, representing Earth. Telemetry showed the launch had come from The Americas. Vargas felt himself tense. His nation was involved in the war now.

A private message from Sheffield popped up. "Americaner missile. Aimed at India?"

Now worried, Vargas acknowledged. If the Americas attacked India, would India retaliate by firing on the Americas' most prized possession—the Dry Dock? Suddenly the situation below didn't seem remote.

Sheffield stood directly behind Sorlund and pointed at his display, asking him something. Vargas pulled up Sorlund's display on the God Console and frowned. It was a high arc for a ballistic missile. In fact, it looked like it was headed for orbit. Vargas watched as Sorlund tapped inquiries in. By the time the projected path came up, Sheffield was standing directly beside him. "It's coming here, Dan," he whispered. "And it's pulling eight Gs."

"What is it?" Sorlund brought up the specs just as Vargas realized what it had to be. It was an SDM-28, a nuclear missile capable of attacking objects in geosynchronous orbit. It was coming right at them.

"Sean, any chance that's not a nuke?"

"I don't think so."

Dry Dock didn't have any defenses. There was nothing to stop the missile from reaching them.

"Let's get out of here." Vargas unconsciously took a deep breath. "Helm officers, engage main thruster."

The men stared at him, looking stunned. "Captain?"

"That's an order, Mister Sorlund. Full thrust. Monitor yaw and pitch."

Vargas saw Sorlund give Sheffield a questioning glance. Sheffield nodded, almost imperceptibly. Wide eyed, reluctant and clearly aghast, the two crew members moved the four main controls on their panels forward.

A vibration rattled the ship, followed by a faint hum. Distantly, there was a crackling noise, and gravity suddenly returned. Red emergency lights lit one side of his data pad, and he heard a voice scream, "Captain! Your engine has engaged! Shut down! You'll destroy us! Shut. . . " The voice went dead, and the red request lights from Dry Dock suddenly changed to a neutral, accusatory gray. With a clench to the gut, Vargas realized the voice had belonged to Siddons, the last man they had seen before sealing the ship.

Vargas cut off bridge communications from below decks. The only thing that mattered now was that missile.

The ship was moving out of the Dry Dock with apparent slowness, but their speed was already greater than any they had tried in the simulator.

Another red request appeared, from one of the few people on board with the privilege of overriding Vargas' 'do not knock' data block setting. Commander Scotty Boitumelo, head of Engineering, appeared on the pad, and she looked ready to kill. "Captain, we have three injured personnel, me included. What in the fuck do you think you're doing?"

Part of Boitumelo's tunic was burned. "Scotty, we have a nuclear missile coming up our ass and need to run, right now." Apologies could come later.

There was a slight pause as Apunda's eyes widened slightly. "I can give you seventy percent more thrust. We'll pay for it. But please, send some medical personnel down here. One of my boys looks critical."

"Done. Thank you, Scotty." He called up Doctor Trapp. "Doctor, please dispatch some of your people to the engine room."

Trapp slouched, relaxed in his tunic despite the sudden gravity. Bereft of his usual beard, he looked like Doctor Evil. "They're already on their way, Captain."

Vargas intently tracked the readings on ship clearance. The ship appeared to be yawing to the port side. He rechecked telemetry. No, they were straight. He felt his weight increase as Engineering pushed the engine. His acceleration meter hovered at one point nine gravities. He heard his seat cushions crinkle in protest as his head support cuffs snapped up.

The blast of the backwash forced the already ruined Dry Dock to skew slowly clockwise. Sorlund fired the port thrusters, trying to keep the ship away. "Forward is clear!" Sheffield shouted. The bridge was a babble of voices, and lights and readouts were in a frenzy.

The ship accelerated at a little over 1.96g, near theoretical maximum, and was half way out of the Dry Dock. The much lighter structure was accelerating in the opposite direction twenty times as much. Six seconds to go. A ripping, grinding sound came from starboard. Vargas imagined the *Phoenix* breaking in two like a pencil from the mass of Dry Dock careening into her along the side of the main thruster. The main compartment would remain intact unless the engine, freed of all constraints, slammed into them. Of course, the coming nuclear explosion would make that moot.

The navigation officers, Sorlund and Barney, jabbed at their screens frantically, pushing the ship away from the dock bulkhead. Vargas fancied he could feel little wavelets of lateral motion, and then realized that had to be imaginary. Indicators showed pressure loss in modules, breaches, or contents shifting. A dissonant chorus of alarms filled the air.

The scraping resumed, the top of the ship taking the brunt of it. Hands flew over screens, as the navigators desperately tried to realign the massive craft. *Phoenix* dwarfed the mightiest of all sea-going vessels, and was no more maneuverable. Sparing a quick glance up, Vargas saw red flashing from many screens.

Now the right side of the Dry Dock was slewing away from the side of the ship wildly. Fighting panic, Vargas pounced on the port controls, ready to override. He stopped, puzzled. The left wall was stable in relation to the ship, even drifting away slightly.

Horrified realization hit. The Dry Dock was breaking apart from their back thrust. If the damage from the heat and backwash weren't enough, the whole assembly must be a superheated hell by now. Anybody still alive would not stay alive for long. He felt himself reaching for the rosary he had stopped carrying as a teen.

"Clear!" Sheffield pounded the console savagely. He turned, looked to Vargas. "Captain?"

"Steady, forward full thrust. We're not in a nosedive toward the planet, I hope."

"No Ser, but we're definitely not going the right way if we want to get to *Phoenicis*."

"We'll deal with that later. Where's that missile?"

"Sixty-two seconds from where Dry Dock was."

Was? "Where will we be then?

"A hair over thirty-eight kilometers away." Vargas considered the standard payload of the SDM-28. That was survivable. Maybe.

Vargas looked over the God Console. He paged Engineering. Commander Isaakson, Head of Maintenance, answered. "We're still assessing damage, Captain. No loss of pressure in populated areas. Engine OK, a few side thrusters damaged. No way to visually survey the area—the cameras got scraped off, too. Fire reports from Engineering – our injuries – but apparently out now."

"What's going on with the electronics?"

"No idea, Captain. Every time they futz out, the indicators futz out with them. I think it's something off board."

"How is that possible, Madelyne?"

Isaakson shook her head. "Ask me later. The good news is the main hull is intact. Took some gouges, but there's no sign of water loss." Vargas nodded and turned to his other readouts.

He pulled up a rear image. The Dry Dock sides glowed yellow and red, pulled apart like a wishbone, heat waves dancing over much of the rear area, and the entire huge assembly was slowly turning clockwise and receding rapidly.

In less than ten seconds, Vargas had destroyed something it took his country trillions of dollars and thirty years to build.

"Ten seconds."

There was nothing to do. Most of the people on the bridge stared fixedly at their consoles, some tracking the missile, some just listening, eyes wide, to the ominous creaking and grindings of the abused ship.

There was a flicker like summer lightening. Sorlund spoke into the dead silence. "It detonated."

Barney swiveled around. "Is that all?"

Sheffield glanced over at the navigation officer. "What were you expecting, Ms. Barney? A loud bang?"

Just then, there was a loud bang. Everyone on the bridge jumped at once. The deep resonant harmonics lingered. "What the hell was that?" Vargas demanded.

Sheffield's fingers flew. "Debris from the Dry Dock, I think. Hit us topside, oblique."

"Any damage?"

"Cosmetic, I think. Nothing on the sensors. Wait." Sheffield tapped pop-ups. Pressure drop in a couple of modules.

"Any more coming our way?"

Sheffield tapped. "No. Um, no sign of Dry Dock. It's gone. Wait. . . no, it's there. Damn, my readings are fading in and out."

Vargas nodded. Between the nuclear explosion and the interference from the fusion drive, it was a wonder they could see anything at all. His own rear view screen had gone dark.

Sorlund spoke up. "Should we go back, Ser?"

Everyone on the bridge wore the same what-are-you-crazy expression. Vargas didn't feel any need to answer the question.

"Mister Sheffield, get on the horn and let the passengers and crew know we were forced to take evasive action but we don't expect to have to. . . "

"Another missile, captain." The expression on Sorlund's face reminded Vargas of a frightened horse.

"Belay that, Mister Sheffield." Vargas looked at his God Console. The missile had just cleared the planet's horizon and was coming right up their tail. Fast response by the bridge. Good.

"Where's it going?"

"It is on an intercept."

No need to ask with whom. "Three degrees to port. I want a minimum target profile." Figures jumped up from Barney indicating the trajectory. He sent back a correction.

"Captain. . . "

"I know. The ship's not designed for it." Vargas' eyes flicked from the readout to his second-in-command. He lowered his voice so as to not be overheard. "We're dead if we don't." Sheffield, looking grave, nodded.

Vargas studied the readout. The ship only needed to yaw to starboard three degrees to line up, but *Phoenix* handled like a drunken cow. They would need full power from every thruster they had to turn that far that fast.

"Ser." The ship actually groaned as all thrusters on the starboard forward fired and the surviving thrusters on port aft and the bridge lights flickered alarmingly. *Phoenix* wasn't meant to maneuver laterally while under full thrust. What structural damage was being aggravated? *Phoenix* had water in the hull, about one point three meters wide at any point, and under one point nine gees, the pressure down by the bottom of the main life section would approach three hundred atmospheres, a figure that made engineers tremble in fear. But the main hull was modular, and the special hull only enveloped the living areas of the ship, the first two hundred meters. But being modular meant if it had to maneuver under acceleration it could break up. Vargas strongly hoped it wouldn't do that.

"It's matching course."

"Steady." Vargas expected a smart missile. In fact, he was counting on it.

"Five minutes to intercept." Sheffield knew what Vargas needed. "We're at mid-point for minimum target profile." The firing order of the thrusters reversed, sending a faint shudder through the ship.

The ship had come about one and a half degrees, and now had to be trimmed so it would stop yawing at the required three degrees. Minimum target profile meant that the ship was presenting the smallest possible profile, making itself as small a target as possible. It also meant the ship running directly away from the missile. The readouts made it clear they couldn't out-run it, but that wasn't what Vargas was trying to do.

Vargas could hear faint creaks and groans that had never been part of the simulations. *Phoenix*, separated from the fusion engine by three hundred meters of vacuum, was supposed to be quiet under power. However, she wasn't designed for this sort of lateral torque. The ship protested the treatment. Vargas resisted a mad impulse to have the God Console a reassuring pat.

"At minimum target, give me every bit of thrust you can." In theory, *Phoenix*'s engines could deliver almost two full gees of acceleration. "Make sure we're running away from that beast as fast as we can."

Scotty's voice sounded stressed and blurry, but she didn't argue. "Full acceleration, Ser." Vargas looked at his acceleration readout. It would only change from 1.96 to 1.98. Well, every bit helped.

The lights flickered again and screens posterized for a moment, strange colors rippling across them. Frowning, Vargas looked again at the acceleration readouts. Whatever was giving the electronics fits wasn't affecting engine operations.

"Four minutes." Sheffield, defying the double gravity, came to his side and pointed to the console where Sheffield's own panel was showing. "That's our thrust. And that's the estimated mass and profile of your bogey."

"Can you get an intersect curve on that?"

"It'll just be an inverse square calculation. I can't vouch for its accuracy."

"It won't matter. We're committed. I just want an idea of when the ETA begins to change."

Tap. Tap. "I make it twelve seconds for closest approach."

"Twelve seconds? How far will it be?

"About one point eight kilometers."

Vargas put a hand over his mouth, squeezed his upper lip. "Let's just hope they aren't using a proximity sensor." Sorlund looked startled. At that distance, they wouldn't have a hope of surviving the blast.

A surreal silence descended on the bridge. By now everyone had figured out what the strategy was, and watched the count-down clock that Sorlund thoughtfully provided. It blinked, and all the screens wavered.

"Minimum target profile achieved."

"Steady, everyone." He felt himself wanting to rock back and forth in an absurd effort to make *Phoenix* go faster. In battle, he had seen men do that as they fled incoming missiles. He set up a real-time countdown clock next to the Sorlund one, which was based on their relative velocities.

At fifty-eight seconds the numbers began to diverge.

"It's. . . slowing, Ser."

"Relative to us, you mean? Are you sure?"

"In an absolute sense. Its main engine has shut down." Sorlund shook his head, clearly puzzled. "ETA forty-eight seconds"

It was still closing on them. It just wasn't gaining as fast.

Sheffield spoke up. "We're catching up on speed."

"About twenty kilometers, then?"

"Um. Nineteen-six. Still too close."

"It's nearly at match point, Ser."

Nobody responded. Everyone was watching the displays.

At forty-two seconds, the number paused, and changed to forty-three. "Ohmigawd," Barney muttered. Vargas could see her pressing back in her seat, an involuntary recoil.

One minute ten. Four minutes. Then a dashed line, indicating null answer. *Phoenix* was now pulling away from the missile.

Sorlund spoke up. "Range twenty-two point one kilometers." His voice was almost a whisper.

If there was a manual override, now was when the missile would detonate. The sheer force of their backwash had stopped the missile better than Vargas dared hope. The ionized hell the missile was facing may have destroyed its electronics, shielded as they were. Or perhaps it was what was causing the fluctuations. Vargas didn't know, and right then he didn't care.

Vargas let out his breath. In a few seconds they could be safely out of range. He began counting down from ten to himself, wondering what number he might die at.

He reached zero and looked at his console. Range was thirty kilometers and growing fast. It hadn't detonated. A faint fuzz of static filled the bridge, an untuned AM radio at night.

Earth's farewell to her child.

"Any more missiles?"

There were none.

Chapter 3 Full Speed Ahead

IT WAS AN ARDUOUS FEW HOURS for everyone. Vargas divided his attention between the bridge updates, and determining the amount of damage the ship and complement had taken. The electronics were still having fits, and nobody seemed to know why. The ice shield between the ship and the engine was intact. The fact that he was alive told Vargas that. Multiple attempts to contact London, Gabon, or his own government were futile.

Acceleration was cut back to one gravity. Soon they would coast and *Phoenix* could turn toward her intended destination.

Vargas intended to get *Phoenix* well out of range. The second missile would have caught them had they not deliberately trained the ship's back-blast on it. The main thruster's emitted photons were few and nearly weightless, but at nearly the speed of light they gave the missile a substantial headwind to fight, and an intense electromagnetic field powerful enough to overcome the missile's shielding.

It was a standard tactic—the only defensive tactic available for fending off a missile in space, although in this instance the power of the thrust was many magnitudes greater.

No one was killed. There were several dozen broken bones, and other, minor injuries, plus the three burned engineers who required medical treatment. Anyone unlucky enough to be hovering more than a meter above an aft bulkhead had suddenly had a floor accelerating toward them at fifteen meters a second squared.

There were two major breaches in the modules. Another piece of debris had holed the module directly behind the bridge, which saved them. That was the loud bang they heard after the first missile detonated.

That module had shuttles, designed for hard vacuum. The other breach was the Imprinter module, and was more serious. The Imprinter section, like all the other modules, was designed to detach and drop to a planetary surface in a controlled glide, and for now there would be no sure way of assuring its flight-worthiness.

Neither breach demanded immediate attention. Twenty percent of the living areas had lost power and there was a mysterious phasing in and out in the rest of the ship that intermittently dimmed lights and caused screens to flicker and fuzz which complicated repairs. Fixing it was the first order of business. Ship's engineers, maintenance and Charlies fanned out. The acting chief engineer, Isaakson, reported the engine wasn't affected, but advised against efforts to change thrust until the electronic issues were stabilized. If the wrong order got scrambled while transmitting . . . as it was, the Charlies stuttered and twitched and had to be watched closely.

A third of the thrusters were knocked out, and bridge members fed the data on those to the main computer so the navigation program could compensate. *Phoenix* would be even more unwieldy.

Many of the external cameras were knocked out. They could see forward, and along the starboard side, but nothing aft. That would be frustrating in twenty six years when they would be decelerating tail-first toward their destination. Most other types of sensors were in good working order.

After two hours the injured were sorted, and power restored to living areas. Vargas, anticipating questions about the spectacularly irregular launch, sensed a growing sense of unease, especially among the civilians. No, not civilians. His people. Time to speak to them.

He made his way to the bridge, where Sheffield had crew members devising workarounds for the damage. He pulled him aside. "Sean, can we cut the main engines yet?"

Sheffield shook his head. "Not before we figure out what's going on with our electronics, Dan. Why in hell were they shooting at us?"

"I would give my left nut for an answer to that. I'm going to address the ship, and I want you standing next to me."

Sheffield looked puzzled. Quick realization spread over his face. "You have to tell them who shot at us, don't you?"

"Where the shots came from, anyway. The people in Washington can be pretty crazy, but they aren't that crazy. I want you to feel free to answer some of the questions we get. Are you comfortable with that, Mr. Sheffield?"

"Ser." He turned to a crew member who Vargas recognized as a physicist, Tim Simmons. "Tim, have a report for me when you're done. I want to know why the electronics keep phasing out, and what we can do about it."

"Phasing out," Simmons repeated. Vargas could see the phrase had given the scientist an angle of approach to the problem. Simmons nodded. "Ser."

Vargas sat down, Sheffield standing immediately to his right. Sheffield opened the ship's rarely-used intercom, and Vargas wondered if anyone had bothered to see if it was operational. The ubiquitous data pads made it obsolete except in the Navy, where nothing was ever obsolete. This held true even on a ship where crew and command were effectively civilian at heart.

"Attention, everybody. This is Commander Sheffield. Please pause what you are doing if at all possible. The Captain will fill you all in on what has been occurring over the past three hours, and what to expect next. Thank you."

Vargas propped his data pad in front of him and regarded his image. He felt like he was shivering, pale, and wide-eyed. What he saw there was what everyone on board would see on their data pads. His image gazed back at him calmly. Conscious of his bald head, he pulled on his captain's cap, which, unsurprisingly, was loose. Too loose, and it made him look like his head had shrunk. He took it off. He licked his lips, and pushed the open button.

"Good afternoon. At 1050, we were entering the final stages of preparation to detach from the Dry Dock and, at 1400, begin our voyage. I first want to let you know that in a few hours, we will begin that journey. We're going to another star. We've finished a preliminary survey of the ship, and we're flight worthy." A cheer went up on the bridge, faintly echoed from aft. To Vargas' relief, the strange power fluctuations didn't pick right then to interfere with his 'cast.

"Some things went horribly wrong beginning at that time, and that is what I want to discuss with you.

"We received alarming reports of a nuclear exchange between the African Union and India. We do not know who fired first, or what damage was done, aside from a fragmentary report that the remains of Bombay were destroyed.

"Given the nature of the geopolitical situation, most of you are probably not surprised at this news.

"At 1058, a missile, an armed missile, was deployed. It was on the far side of the world, but the launch site appears to have been the Dakotas or Manitoba. We don't know who authorized the firing of the missile, or why. It was aimed at Dry Dock. If we didn't leave immediately, we would be destroyed in a nuclear explosion." Vargas paused to let that sink in.

"The decision to fire the main engine in the Dry Dock was entirely mine, and I take responsibility for that order. It destroyed the Dry Dock and killed everyone on board. It also did some damage to *Phoenix*, although not enough to stop the mission. The power fluctuations don't appear to be related to the nuclear explosion. Nor, as far as engineering and maintenance can determine, is it an on-board problem. Earth appears to be experiencing them, too. These ... fluctuations seem to be abating."

Over the next ten minutes, Vargas recounted the events.

"We are satisfied that we have gotten far away from Earth that we're safe from anyone else who has a mind to lob a nuke at us. So at 1400 hours, or about. . . " he glanced at the readout, "an hour and twelve minutes from now, we will ease back to zero acceleration for about fifteen hours while we get the ship pointed in the right direction, and then return to the planned mission." The lights flickered, and Vargas added dryly, "At least, that's the plan."

"To anyone who has friends or relatives on the Dry Dock, my deepest condolences. And my regrets to those who were hurt during our efforts to escape. I wish you a speedy recovery." Damn, that sounded stiff. "I'm sorry that I haven't met with you in person. We probably could get everyone into the mess hall, but we don't have the luxury of time. We need to get everyone squared away in hibernation, and the ship on her way."

Vargas squared his shoulders. Now the fun part. "Does anyone have any questions?"

His board lit up. They had questions, lots of questions.

He decided to start easy. "'We're pointed the wrong way, you said. Does that mean we're lost?'"

He nodded to Sheffield. "Commander Sheffield is in charge of navigation, so I'll let him handle that." Careful to keep his hand out of camera range, he held it palm down and made a patting motion to indicate patience. One of the civilians. A farmer. Sheffield glanced at the name that accompanied the image.

"That's a good question, Mister Aiello. No, we're not lost. We know exactly where we are, and we can see where we're going. We're off course, but it's far away, and we gone such a little way, that you wouldn't even be able to see the change in direction the *Phoenix* will go in once we start the real journey. And yes, we'll get there at the same time."

"Next question." Vargas decided to bite the bullet. "'Who fired at us and why?' Mister Matthews, all we know is the missiles came from the Dakotas or Manitoba. We don't know if the Government of the Americas was responsible, or some insurrectionist group. Speaking as a native of that country, I find it impossible to conceive of any circumstances under which Washington would want to fire at us, let alone at their own Dry Dock. We've had communications attempt to contact Chetumal Command, Gabon, or anyone on Earth. We don't know why, but we aren't getting responses. Communications are garbled, and we can't make sense of them."

Vargas took a breath. "What I tell you strains belief, but bear with me. When that nuclear explosion destroyed the remains of Dry Dock it was bright enough to cast shadows across most of Asia and Europe, and some of Africa. Certainly our engine is that bright; people ground side were advised not to stare at it for too long, especially since in daylight it wouldn't look dangerously bright. We haven't seen a single reference to it on any broadcast from any of the hundreds of sources we are trying to monitor. I. . . excuse me." Vargas paused to read a flashing red alert from Communications. "The Americas government just issued a domestic news report informing the public that *Phoenix* 'has been destroyed by a missile fired by insurgent forces.'"

Vargas looked up. Everyone on the bridge stopped, and stared at him dumbfounded. "Mister Harlen, please continue signaling to the Chetumal Center and Gabon that we have survived the attack and have deemed ourselves space worthy and plan to continue our mission." Shaking his head in disbelief, he returned his focus to his planned remarks.

"We have three breaches in two external modules, numbers two and fourteen. One contains shuttles. The other contains the Imprinter."

The God Console resembled a Japanese arcade game. Vargas picked Madelyne Isaakson, head of maintenance. Even without the hair in a severe bun and the fierce eyebrows, she was an imposing figure, with glinting gray eyes and square jaw. "Captain, The Americas have to know we're still here. They can see us. We're not that far away. Did the blasts take out our coms?"

"Our corms have been experiencing intermittent interference, but they work. As are our transponders. Since we're still only a couple of light minutes away, the space scopes can see that we're intact, and there shouldn't be any difficulty communicating."

"So they're lying." Isaakson's mouth was set as firmly as her words.

Vargas chose his words carefully. "That may be so. Almost certainly so. If they are deliberately lying, it's important to consider that they might be lying on our behalf. If insurgents fired those missiles, they might not have the capability to confirm our continued existence, and this may be buying us time to get away before any more missiles are launched at us."

"Don't they have missiles that can strike any target in the Solar System?"

"They do, but in another hour or so our velocity will exceed their maximum. In fact. . . " Vargas paused to check his readout, ". . . if we maintain acceleration for another forty-two minutes we will reach the point where they can't possibly catch us." He managed a wan smile and selected another colonist. "Ms. Kennemur?"

"Captain, is nobody responding to us? And do you trust our electronics?"

"We're listening to Earth, and what we're hearing is fractured and disorganized. We gather that the hostilities have become widespread, and that the four major powers have all become involved. If it's as bad as it sounds, I don't think anyone is paying much attention to us right now—except the people who are trying to kill us, possibly. As for the electronics, we believe it is interference from outside, possibly a point on Earth. The main engine is unaffected, and the effects seem to be diminishing as we pull away."

Vargas waited for that to sink in before he took another question. Everyone on board had spent six months saying good-bye to Earth and everyone they left behind. Home was now as far in the past as the Mesopotamian Empire. Still, everyone carried Earth with them in their hearts, a bond that could not be severed by time or distance.

"Captain, if the Americas are lying and they did attack us themselves, will you step down as Captain and let someone from Europe or Africa run the ship?" Vargas cursed under his breath. He shouldn't have picked Rudy Harlen for a question. He had the dour colonist engineer sized up as a potential troublemaker, and here he was. How did he get past the personality evaluations?

"Mr. Harlen, it is my duty to bring *Phoenix* to the *nu Phoenicis* system and establish a colony. When that task is completed, I expect the colony will want to establish a government. They may choose whomever they wish as their leader. On this vessel, however, I am the Captain, and that is not subject to plebiscite. You're also begging the question with the assumption that Americas fired on Dry Dock – Mr. Harlen, that was the crowning achievement of The Americas over the past three decades, an incredible technological feat that matched some of the accomplishments of the old United States. I can think of no sane reason for them to want to destroy Dry Dock.

"There is no sane reason *anyone* would attack us. You know that there were over a million applicants to be a part of this project, and the only opposition of note came from people who felt the cost was too high. It just wouldn't make sense for them to wait for the money and resources to be spent, the ship to be built, and then destroy us.

"Another thing, Mr. Harlen. The minute the airlock sealed behind me this morning, I ceased to be a citizen of the Americas, just as you ceased to be a citizen of Royal Europe, and all the other fifteen hundred people on board ceased to be citizens of their respective countries. We are all Phoenicians now."

Sheffield spoke up, glowering. "This is not a military vessel, but the law of the sea—or space, if you will—applies. The Captain is the Captain. Talk of replacing a Captain is mutinous. If you were a part of the crew, you would be on your way to the stockade right now." No point in mentioning the *Phoenix* didn't have a stockade. "That sort of talk will not be tolerated. If you have questions or concerns, bring them to us. But never question our right to command this vessel."

A crew member, Matthew Bissont. "Captain, Ser. A great statesman from England once said that the Americas was 'a riddle wrapped in an enigma wrapped in a mystery.' Is it possible that there was a faction in their government that didn't want us to succeed? The Dominionists, for example?"

Despite himself, Vargas chuckled. "That was Sir Winston Churchill, and he said it about Russia, the old USSR. The Americas didn't exist when he was alive. It was still the United States then. Still, if Sir Churchill were alive today, he might have said that about Washington. It's a pretty Byzantine place, as some of you have reason to know. Now, maybe there was some secret, paranoid. . . " Vargas moved his hands in front of him, trying to frame a concept that had no shape, ". . . cabal that actually wanted to destroy the mission. Some religious group who thought we were defying their notion of God, perhaps. But the people who run the government, the people who paid for much of this mission and who granted free use of the Dry Dock, saving Europe tens of trillions, they were behind us one hundred percent. As for Dominionists, they are widely hated in the Americas, as they should be. They wield no power in Washington.

"I worked closely with the people holding real power in Washington for several years, and I never had reason to suspect anything other than utter devotion to the project. The Americas came in late, and wanted to rejoin the world community after a century of isolation. It benefited the country and her citizenry." Vargas noted, with gratification, that nearly half the queue of request lights went dark. Good. He was reaching them, answering their concerns.

"Captain, what is the status of the Imprinting component?" That from one of the Imprinter techs.

"We're examining it now. It's still in hard vacuum, although as you know, the Imprinter should be able to survive that. We'll be counting on Mister Farnsworth, once it's repressurized and up to room temperature, to let us know when it's safe to run a full diagnostic." He saw the tech nod, clearly relieved. Near-space conditions alone wouldn't cause damage, and depressurization of what had been a nitrogen atmosphere. Vargas in turn took heart from the man's relaxation.

"We don't see any sign of physical damage, and the airlocks to the component are all functioning, so there's no problem with access. We'll spend a couple of days determining what sorts of repairs to the hull breach can be made. We have reason to believe the hull's exterior is pretty radioactive right now, mostly contaminated dust from Dry Dock embedded in the hull. We'll send an ROV to take a look. This debris presents no hazard to us on the inside, but our vacuum suits can only handle so much exposure.

"In any event, it's safe to say that particular reentry component will never be made fit for safe planetary reentry, especially with cargo so important. We'll figure out a work-around, hopefully before we get to *nu Phoenicis*."

A colonist spoke up. "Can we colonize without the Imprinter?"

Vargas nodded the question over to Sheffield. "Yes, Mr. Reiche, we can. Assuming a planet no less hospitable than Earth, we can make do without. It just won't be as easy."

That was an understatement for the ages.

"Captain? I know you said the radioactive debris was on the outside, but we're going to be inside for at least twenty-eight years. How much radiation will we be taking?"

"In the living areas of the ship, there is no measurable difference in radiation levels. As you know, we have a very unique hull. One hundred and fifty centimeters of titanium, a meter thirty of water, and another twenty-five centimeters of titanium. Plus two layers of lead wafered in the titanium, and then about a hundred and fifty centimeters of steel on the inside, mostly to ensure the water stays outside. Most of it was shielded in turn by the components that have the shuttles, the Imprinter, and the prefabricated colonial structures. We are measuring elevated levels there, and are determining the best way to decontaminate the hull, should it become necessary." He held up a finger. "Even if it turns out we can't mitigate the debris on the hull, we can adequately protect people who go in those areas."

Time to wrap it up. "I realize that everyone would like to keep talking about what happened, but we all have a lot of work to do, Not the least of which is to get everyone into hibernation. The ship is only designed to recycle for about a hundred people, not fifteen hundred."

That wasn't entirely true. It could keep up with the needs of one hundred indefinitely. It could go several weeks with the full complement of people awake and moving about.

Vargas felt a sudden gust of anger. Someone had forced him to kill thousands of people. He could only helplessly hope that someone would make them pay for that.

He quashed the thought. It wasn't germane right now. "People, get ready to hibernate. New worlds await. Let's go to *nu Phoenicis!*"

* * *

Vargas had one more duty to attend before the ship was truly on its way and the vast majority of the crew joined the colonists in hibernation. He, Sheffield, Alan Trapp, the CMO, CPO Nate Harlen, and CTO Gordon Lassiter went to visit the injured.

They were lucky in one way: they would do their healing in hibernation. Vargas wondered if he should be feeling more guilt about the relatively minor injuries crew members had sustained than he did about the two thousand dead left behind him.

Commander Scotty Boitumelo was one of three injured severely enough to require continued bed rest. After a quick consultation with the attending medics at the infirmary, a relieved Alan Trapp was able to let the other line officers know they would fully recover during the time in hibernation. Few environments known to humans were more sterile than the hibernation module. Healing took longer in such an environment, but was cleaner and usually more complete. In Trapp's opinion, there wouldn't even be any scarring.

The convalescents were joined by the line officers, and the thirteen other injured. Vargas spoke briskly.

"I wish I had medals to hand out. In the military, we considered it important to recognize the sacrifice and loss of anyone injured in the line of duty. It didn't matter if it was during conflict or not. If someone tripped over a mouse while on duty and broke their nose, they got a medal for it.

"It may seem silly to civilians, but the military is about shared sacrifice more than anything else.

"This expedition, while not military, has that same spirit of shared sacrifice. We all gave up the world we loved, and will most likely never see again, in order to engage in this monumental task. And, despite the turmoil of the world we just left, and thanks in part to your efforts, we have begun that task.

"I don't have medals. But I have humble thanks and gratitude. Thank you, and I'll look forward to working with all of you at *nu Phoenicis.*"

There was an awkward silence.

The group of injured glanced among themselves, and at a signal invisible to the captain, Boitumelo was selected to speak for them.

"It is very much appreciated, Captain. I understand the situation that led to the sudden engagement of the engines. I have nearly completed a report for the log addressing my concerns about damage the main engine may have taken. I strongly recommend curtailing the number of starts and stops until we have an opportunity to fabricate more replacements. Some critical fail elements have fallen to single redundancy, which is intolerable."

Vargas struggled not to smile. Injured or not, Boitumelo was an engineer above all else.

She continued, "Permission to speak freely, Ser?"

Puzzled, Vargas flicked an eyebrow and nodded assent.

"It is my intent to get you to the dojo and kick your ass for what you did, Ser. With all due respect, Ser."

"You're welcome to give it your best shot, commander," Vargas said, returning Boitomelo's broad grin.

One of the other injured engineers spoke up. "Captain, could you please at least explain to us why you fired the main engines in Dry Dock?"

Vargas hadn't realized that they didn't have access to their Data Pads in sick bay. In fact, they didn't have video screens. No wonder the atmosphere was so odd. They were wondering if the Captain had gone mad. He glanced at Boitumelo. She knew what had happened, of course, but without conferring with Vargas or at least Sheffield first, she wouldn't discuss it.

Rapidly, he explained the events leading up to the firing of the engines. The injured goggled at him, round-eyed. He saw eyes searching the faces of the other line officers, seeking confirmation.

He finished, and watched the reactions. He realized that this was an element that had been badly missing when he addressed the ship's complement. The expressions were aghast, appalled, and slightly disbelieving.

Sheffield leaned forward. "I have a question, Commander Boitumelo."

"Please feel free."

"Why are you called 'Scotty'? I'm from Manchester, not that far from the Scots' border, and I don't recognize your accent. And before you bother asking, no, it wasn't much fun being named Sheffield in Manchester."

Vargas shot his second in command a sharp glance, realizing the distraction was deliberate.

Everyone, including Boitumelo, looked puzzled. She smiled. "My accent is from Central Africa, not far from the Command Center in Gabon. I was raised to speak French as my primary language. I have never been to Scotland, although after people started calling me 'Scotty' I looked up the place. It sounds a lot like some of the tribal regions back home."

Vargas tilted his head. "So Scotty is a recent nickname?"

"Just since I was selected chief engineer for the *Phoenix*. I've no idea why people call me that. But I had a Scotch terrier dog, Scooty, as a little girl, and I liked what I read about the place, so I am happy to be called by that name."

Chapter 4 We're Not In Devon Any More

IN FORWARD 18B, A STERILE WHITE CABIN/TOMB of about six cubic meters, Jim Spencer finished repacking his personal effects duffel. Jim, tall for his sixteen years, was nevertheless classified as a dependent, one of eighty four such teenaged passengers on *Phoenix*. There was nobody under the age of fourteen on board. Two years earlier when they had cleared the first rounds of the selection process and were beginning to think they might actually get a berth on the ship to the stars, he had asked his father about that. His father had grinned and explained that if they brought small children along, and it turned out there were ferocious beasts about on the new world, the colonists might be overly tempted to use the young ones as bait.

Later, his father explained that younger children would maladapt to the extraordinary changes likely on the new world, possibly in ways that would mess them up as adults—depression, alienation, acculturation. Smelling a rat, Jim pressed the issue and his father admitted children under fourteen didn't hibernate well; about one in twenty-five died, and nearly one in ten developed severe cognitive deficiencies. Jim asked how they knew that, and his father got a funny expression on his face, and said they had done tests in the Americas, where hibernation was first developed.

Jim's father, Ship Psychiatrist Ian Spencer, also explained that his colleagues had determined that a colony with no children at all would be a stressed colony, and a "next generation" – even one of surly, hulking and sometimes troublesome teens— would be good for morale. Besides, they were old enough to mow the lawn.

Jim eyed the tiny cubicle with four white hibernation pods, each to a corner, where he, his sister, and his parents would spend the next twenty six years. Personal effects were placed in the ceiling storage bins, which he now couldn't reach until acceleration ended. The original plan called for an hour of zero-gravity during which time everything could be stored and shut down, but that was supposed to be hours ago. He should be in hibernation by now.

Did he want to leave his duffel unattended? He didn't think anyone would steal it, but he didn't want other people handling it. It had something in it that didn't exactly belong there, his personal science project. He opened the duffel, and pushed the object, a cylinder about a meter by two hundred millimeters, closer to the center, in with the clothing. He tied the mouth, and felt the duffel carefully. It felt like a regular old duffel bag. There was a solar cell tag poking out, but anyone noticing it would assume he was just keeping his data pad charged. He decided that would do. He checked Sylvie's, which also had a few unauthorized objects, and decided it was passable.

In the passageway, his sister was playing a game on her data pad. Fourteen, Sylvie was barely old enough to qualify for the trip, and one of only three kids her age. Only one of those was a boy, and from what Jim could gather, he was a dead loss in his sister's hypercritical eye. She was presently avoiding people because she was sensitive about being hairless in a ship full of hairless people. Jim considered saying that Sylvie should be less upset about the loss of her flowing red hair, but with the beginnings of wisdom, had elected to keep his mouth shut. Sylvie, also wise, hadn't mentioned that she was scouting some of the older boys, including some who weren't boys any more. She knew that even without hair, she was young and attractive.

Sylvie looked up. "How long before we go in?" She nodded to the cubicle.

Jim glanced at his data pad. "Twenty-five minutes or so."

Sylvie made a moue. "This is boring. How can a trip to another planet be boring?"

"It'll be more interesting once we're there. To us, that'll be tomorrow."

"I wish we knew more about it."

"Fifty light years, give or take. Dad was saying that back in the twentieth century, people thought that Sol was the only sun with planets. Not the scientists, of course, but the average guy in the street. Thought Earth was unique."

"Just like they all thought the Earth was flat in the fifteenth century."

Jim glanced at his sister out of the corner of his eye. She knew better. Even farmers knew the world was round because they could see its shadow on the Moon. . . he noticed a faint smile tugging at the corner of her mouth.

Sylvie's smirk widened into a smile. "You know, I think this is the first time in three months we've been able to just sit and talk."

Jim returned the smile with a grin. "Training didn't leave much room to just hang out. Cameras everywhere, and microphones. And not many places where you could just be alone."

"You figured out ways to beat the cameras, didn't you?"

Jim grinned wider. "So did you. I was watching, even if they weren't."

"Yeah, I know. But I outwitted you a couple of times, too."

"I'm sure you did. I guess the Americaners are used to this. I didn't see them trying to beat the system much."

"They would have been thrown off the program if they were caught."

Jim cocked an eyebrow—or at least tried. "What? Just for playing hide and seek?"

"Yeah. Their government figures that's hiding something."

"Hiding something is bad." Jim smiled sardonically.

"That's what they say." Sylvie tried to toss her hair, failed. "Jim? What if there isn't a suitable planet at the other end?"

"Well, I guess the Captain and others get together and try and figure out which of a dozen other systems might support life. We could even go back to Earth if we really had to, but after what just happened, I don't think anyone would want to."

"Suppose we could live there, but it isn't safe?"

"Then we try and make it safe. Remember how when we were little, we used to go for long walks in the countryside? Nothing to fear but rain. It was Devon. Safe as houses. But when the Dumnones first arrived three thousand years ago, there were lions roaming about the countryside. Big lions, what would eat you!" He snarled and made claws at his sister, who scrunched her lips to one side. "We made it safe. Or rather, the

Dumnones did. I suppose some of them got eaten in the process. Maybe dad's right, and we're just along to feed the lions."

"Stop that." Sylvie punched his arm. She glanced at the cubicle, back to Jim, and lifted an inquiring eyebrow. He nodded imperceptibly.

"I still don't get why we have to go so far. Fifty light years."

"Forty eight, actually. There's about forty stars that are closer that have terrestrial planets. At least five look like they could support life. But *nu Phoenicis* is the best of all. First, the planet we're going to is almost exactly the right distance from the star and has a temperature just a hair cooler than Earth's. Second, we can see it has water and oxygen, rather than guessing it does. Third, it's not the only water planet there. *Nu Phoenicis* eight looks to be an ice ball. We probably couldn't live there, but it might be suitable for mining operations that pollute a lot, since it probably doesn't have life."

"How would it have an oxygen atmosphere if there's no life?"

"Well, if there isn't much for the oxygen to react with. . . "

"But why not the five closer suns?"

Jim thought for a moment. If he meant to look impressive and academic, Sylvie thought with amusement, he better wait until his eyebrows grew back. Bald, he just looked like an old man with indigestion.

Jim began counting off on fingers. "First, *nu Phoenicis* is a stable star, much more so than the other ones. It's high in metallics, which we think translates to planets that are mineral-rich. *Nu Phoenicis* 4, the planet we're going to, has a very nearly perfect circular orbit and the poles aren't tilted much. That means mild seasons and steady temperatures. Fourth, the Atacama Large Millimeter/Submillimeter Array tells us there is oxygen, sugar molecules, amino acids and more involved strands that strongly suggest life." Jim ran out of ideas before he ran out of fingers. "And maybe people just liked the name," he finished lamely. "*Phoenix.*" He considered asking Sylvie why she didn't already know this stuff, decided now was not the time for a squabble.

"Have you noticed there are no cameras here? Lots of sensors all around, but they're watching the ship, not us."

Sylvie looked around with a well-practiced eye. None of the tell-tale dimples or glitters appeared anywhere. She hated the color scheme of the corridors, lavender blending halfway up to persimmon, a bland cacophony of colors designed to ease and sooth but which essentially just annoyed. What she didn't know was that her father had been the one to propose the décor for exactly the reasons of soothing and easing—and he now found that it irritated him, too.

"I know in my heart there's a planet with air and water at the other end. I hope it will be safe as Devon. And I think we'll be free of surveillance. I wonder how the Americaners will like that?" He glanced down the passageway, saw his father and mother moving their way. "Oops. Sharpish. Parental units approach."

The two stood up, pressed palms together and bowed. "Greetings, honored parents."

"Cut the crap," Ian said amicably. "Are you guys ready for the Big Sleep?"

Maureen spoke up. "I wish you would stop calling it that. I keep thinking of the Bogart movie."

Seeing the puzzled looks of his offspring, Ian said, "Old black and white movie. 'The Big Sleep.' It's probably in the library. You can access it when we get there." His inner editor chuckled. He sounded like they were getting ready to drive to grandma's for the weekend. Fifty light years. Some drive.

"Are you guys OK? Nervous? Second thoughts?" The two shook their heads. Sylvie said, "A bit nervous. The hibernation, not the trip."

Ian nodded. Sylvie knew he hadn't liked the idea of scaring his daughter, but he would never let her do this without knowing the risks. She deserved to know how much higher the risks were for her. Oddly enough, she felt the better for it.

The tell tales on the pods gave early warning if someone was in trouble. In addition to readouts on the bridge, each pod would be inspected weekly for any signs of problems the electronics might miss.

For the people in the pods there was still electromagnetic activity—some people even claimed to have had dreams—and the readouts would show signs if someone was beginning to take damage. If they were awakened quickly enough, they might be fine. It was the main reason a skeleton crew was on the almost autonomous ship during transit. Each of the 1,494 sleeping colonists would be checked once a week for evidence of neural degradation.

The ship could take care of itself. Sylvie wondered about that. Was the Captain honest about the extent of damage? She wasn't sure she believed his denials that his country was behind the attacks, either. And if the ship was impaired, did that mean the crew would have to take time away from monitoring the hibernators?

The Americaners insisted on calling it "sleeping" rather than hibernation, a facile PR ploy that fooled nobody and annoyed those who had to undergo the process. So it was a point of pride among the rest of the colonists to refer to it exclusively as hibernation. Except Ian, who liked to contrary the contrarians.

A certain number of people—it was hoped less than one in a hundred, and feared to be as high as one in fifty —would start to show degradation. Some people showed it immediately, others after several months or years. Nobody knew how many would show trouble over twenty six years. All of the crew and about a thousand of the passengers had been test subjects, and those that had problems after a week washed out – twenty-two unlucky individuals, as it turned out. Due to ethics laws, none of the children had been tested, unless the Americaners had done so, and they weren't saying. They were still angry at the world response to earlier tests they had administered on very young children, killing several of them. Sylvie privately thought those tests, horrible that they were, may have spared the colony far greater horrors had they brought along a significant number of very young children only to find many of them dead or incapable of feeding themselves. She found herself both appalled and grateful to the Americaners simultaneously.

The rest of the sample outside of the project was too small to use reliably.

Those who started to show signs of trouble would be awakened, and face the unappealing prospect of spending up to twenty-six years on board, awake and aging. The ship was designed to handle up to a hundred and fifty such unlucky individuals. Ian hoped that the next time anyone in his family opened their eyes, it would be twenty-six years from now, relativistic ship time. He would serve two six-month stints, and was likely to be awakened to deal with psychiatric emergencies.

Never mind that the ship's library had over sixteen hundred petabytes of movies, music, books, texts, and other works; nearly every work known to man that could be copied to electronic media . Thanks to the Imprinter, nearly every object created by man could be recreated, including organs for the colonists. The ship boasted a well-equipped gym and exercise area. It was, in effect, a small city.

However, to anyone facing the prospect of decades waiting for the ship to arrive, it would be an upholstered prison. The crew were encouraged to include the "Insomniacs" in crew activities when feasible. Psychiatric emergencies seemed likely.

Their data pads simultaneously beeped, informing them the ship would end thrust in five minutes, and to prepare for micro gravity.

When weight vanished, Jim drifted into the cubicle and opened the ceiling hatch. His sister cautiously pushed the four duffels up to him, and he carefully stowed them. Jim looked at his duffel, made sure the inconspicuous little light panel was facing the storage light, and then closed the panel, making sure the bright little internal light stayed on. On a ship with a fusion engine, the power needed would never be noticed even over twenty six years. He secured the hatch, double-checking the locking mechanism.

There was a wait for the hibernation technician to show up. Two hundred and fifty colonists had been trained in the rote knowledge of getting people into the pods, but it could still take a couple of hours to get everyone seen to. Ian and his family were lucky. The tech showed up within minutes. "Right," the tech said, rubbing his hands. "Who's first?" Sylvie found herself staring at a shorter, thinner crew member behind the tech. She was trying to guess gender, and not having much luck. Lack of hair and bulky puffy flight suit obscured the visual cues, and lack of gravity hid other giveaways like stance and gait. A colonist, judging from the lack of insignia.

Slightly awkwardly, the family embraced one another before stripping for the pods. Sylvie had to remind herself that he would see all of them 'tomorrow morning.'

Sylvie went first, stepping into the compartment and doffing the flight suit and underwear. Months of medical tests and practice had resolved feelings of outraged modesty. All jewelry had already been stowed, and so the tech helped glide Sylvie into the pod, carefully checked her mass and age, and began inputting the settings. In minutes, Sylvie was in hibernation.

She gave Ian a wide-eyed look as the hatch sealed shut with a sigh, one he hoped was just last-minute nerves and not full terror.

Sylvie dreamt, although she would not remember any of those dreams. As her brother and parents entered hibernation, she dreamt of playing with Jim and their cat, Tipsy. As the mighty engines engaged and *Phoenix* at last began her journey in earnest, she dreamt she had a math test, but forgot all the answers because her clothes were gone. As the ship passed the Oort cloud and entered interstellar space, she dreamt of luminescent fish swimming in gelatinous sapphire waters.

Sylvie dreamed of kittens and fields of grass and men singing love songs and raw sex and birds and fears and joys, remembering none. She dreamt until she woke up fourteen years later, still more a child than an adult.

Chapter 5 The Old Young Sea Captain

KICK.

BOUNCE.

KICK.

BOUNCE.

REPEAT ONE HUNDRED TIMES.

Dan (never "Danny") Vargas, seven, was determined to be a futbol player. Not the type of football they played in the northern states, with its funny oblong ball that couldn't roll, but real futbol, with two nets and an expanse of luminously green grass and adoring crowds of hundreds of thousands of people, all chanting "Var-gas! Var-gas! Var-gas!"

Dan painted a red square about fifty centimeters on a side on a concrete wall, and was kicking a well-scuffed soccer ball at the square from five to fifteen meters, hitting it about one in three times. A thumbtack was all that remained of an image of the net minder for a despised rival team in Mexico City.

To be a football hero was the dream of nearly every kid in the south, but few showed the determination and doggedness of Dan. Most were content to go to the hard-dirt pitches in the desert state and play rather than practice, and only a handful possessed raw talent beyond the punter stage. Few went home after the games and then spent another hour practicing boring, monotonous kicking and dribbling drills. Dan was never seen without a hackysack to practice his footwork.

Dan had a backup plan. He was going to be a captain in the navy. Not the space Navy, of course. There were no pirates or tropical islands or sea monsters or gales in space. No mermaids or old men with one eye and a parrot. No salt breezes and filthy shanties. To Dan, like most seven year old boys, space was a big nothing.

Dan's papa, Rafe, gently explained that the navy Dan was in love with was in storybooks only, and that the modern navy might have gales and tropical islands and a chance for adventure, but nothing like what Dan read about in those books.

Nevertheless, Rafe encouraged a career in the Navy. The city of Torreón was dying, a victim of global warming and industrial poisoning. The only thing of note in the bedraggled city was a twenty-two meter tall statue of Jesus, now pitted and with rivulets of lye streaming down its cheeks. Summer often saw temperatures over forty, and sometimes fifty. Many of the factories had closed by the middle of the twenty first century because word had spread that many workers were dying after five years of employ, and the mad libertarians who ran the factories refused to clean up their act. Finally the riots of '95 destroyed most of the remaining factories, leaving only the poisons in the soil and water behind, the legacy of the free market. The poverty of the flare years meant that the area would just slowly sink.

Rafe guided his son to escape rather than let Torreón slowly eat him from within. Rafe taught physics at the Institute of Technology, and so they enjoyed a standard of living that allowed them to avoid much of the heat and contamination of the wasted land. It had driven his wife, Dan's mother, to flee to the fertile and cool lands of Keewatin when Dan was five. Dan refused to go with her. She didn't like his adventure books, felt it wrong that a boy his age could read fluently in two languages.

One day Dan wanted to know why the soccer ball would curve if you kicked it toward the side, so it would spin. Rafe saw his opportunity to let math fascinate the boy.

He explained to a wide-eyed Dan about how the spinning ball created differing zones of pressure on each side, causing the air to push the ball to one side. He then showed Dan how he could actually know where the ball would go if you knew how fast it was traveling and how rapidly it was spinning.

Fascinated, the boy asked if math could tell him what affect the wind would have on a soccer ball. Rafe nodded, and added that he could even calculate what the temperature might do, and why the ball would carry further if there was a thunderstorm approaching.

And thus a second love was kindled in Dan Vargas, a love of the números. In the unofficially bilingual community, Rafe permitted Spanish only inside the household, reasoning that the more fluent in Americanish the boy was, the better his chances to secure a position, perhaps as a student at one of the great universities of Europe. His own grandfather had told him of the bad old days when speaking Spanish in public could get you imprisoned or even killed, and some parts of the Americas still forbade the use of anything other than "American" for any official communications.

Rafe had to conceal that part of his dream from his son, since during the war it was a crime to send students overseas to study. "Undermining the security and future of the state" sounded like a joke until an acquaintance was tried, convicted, and sentenced to twenty years for smuggling his son out to study at the Sorbonne. And Royal Europe was an ally. Applying to the Great University at Peking would invite the death penalty.

Nobody could know if the people who manned the state cameras ever bothered to scrutinize the antics of a skinny young boy in a remote desert area. If they did, they would have been perplexed. He would kick a ball, and then measure where it landed and start jotting down figures on a notepad.

The boy would come in from the searing heat at dusk, his own inner fire burning bright, and excitedly show his dad the notes he had taken. Those childish scrawls were mostly gibberish, but where there was sense to be made of them, Rafe could often show the boy a clearer way to finding the answer he sought.

It was only a matter of time before the boy started seeing mathematical relationships in things other than futbol.

There was no shortage of math teaching tools around the Vargas household, and Rafe encouraged the inquisitive boy to explore them.

Rafe half expected the fascination with math to wear off, and Dan would go back to being a typical bright kid with a passion for futbol. He was careful not to push. He kept grooming the boy to have a positive attitude toward math. Soon he would be of an age when they began teaching beyond simple arithmetic at school.

The interest in math did not subside, and after he learned how equations worked, his favorite question was "What does this one do?" Dan was lucky in that he had a father who knew; most schools taught math by rote, a method that crushed the interest and value of equations for many of the students who stood to benefit from learning them.

By the time he was ten, Dan had mastered quadratics, and Rafe started demonstrating their applications. The simple and profound equations of Newton and Kepler sang to the boy, and his interest in a naval career gradually shifted from the ocean to space, where fixed math, rather than random winds, set courses.

Rafe wasn't thrilled with the boy's desire for a military career in space. It seemed like there was always a war, and engagements in space, although rare, always proved fatal to those aboard the losing craft. And the longer range weapons made sitting ducks of most craft. Good grades and a degree here could get him a scholarship to one of the great universities of Europe or Anzac, and an advanced degree in math or hard science could ensure a comfortable academic or scientific career.

But the boy was only ten. Time enough for him to think things through.

* * *

Every boy has two secret libraries. The first might be videos, or reading material, cached in an unnoticed directory in storage, and the reasons for the library might be furtive, or they might simply be self-conscious.

The other library was in the heart, and consisted of books the boy loved, but found nobody else to share with.

Dan's ultra-secret library was in the form of an actual book, cover torn and pages frayed and dog-eared. Captain Richard Bolitho, RN was the book, an anthology of three books by Douglas Reeman. The book itself was ancient, printed in 1978, and the era it described – the interval between the first American Revolution and the Napoleonic wars – even more ancient. Dan's great-grandfather and namesake had read it when he was a boy. It was thrilling, it was adventurous, and it described a world long past that offered few securities.

By the time Dan was fourteen, he recognized that the book was romantic nonsense. Not only did the Navy of those days not exist, but it probably never really existed back then. He suspected some passages would have provoked cynical laughter from the middies of the late eighteenth century. He also felt a little uneasy having the book. The central character, Bolitho, was an Englishman from what was then the United Kingdom, and now the Great Britain province of Royal Europe. Worse, his main foe was then the United States, now the Americas. Dan was unable to find electronic versions of it, or any of Reeman's other work, anywhere on the web, which puzzled him. The introduction made it clear the books had been best-sellers in their day.

When he was sixteen, with a stellar academic record in the sciences, he turned to fanfic, and based some of his writing on the Bolitho book. The writing was ironic, and featured a fair bit of slash amongst the crew members, which probably made it a more accurate depiction of the Royal Navy of the late 1700s than Reeman dared portray. Fortunately, even though he specified the ship and Navy as English, nobody flagged the work as potentially subversive. When he showed Rafe some of the milder work, Rafe took his data pad out and carefully laid it on the coffee table, and motioned for Dan to do the same. The two walked out into the early winter evening in the back yard, and strode over to a remote corner.

It was pleasant, warm, but with a light breeze, and the jasmine climbing the trellis in front of the rear adobe wall suffused the area with its rich aroma. The yard featured a koi pond, and frogs and crickets were beginning their evening concert. Passersby often paused at the adobe walls of the Vargas hacienda, struck by the sounds so alien to the desert. Math professors weren't rich in Torreón but lived comfortably. Nobody would think twice about the two stepping out there for a breath of fresh air.

"Censorship never makes any sense," Rafe responded to the inevitable protest. "It isn't the 'friggin' in the riggin'' that will get you noticed; it's that you base your hero on a captain of a foreign nation that is at war with Americas."

He held up a hand. "I know it refers to a country that no longer exists as such, and mentions the source material. The government has better search engines than we do. If someone sees something odd and decides to track it down, they'll flag it as Reeman, and they'll ask just how a sixteen year old boy has access to an obscure work like that."

Dan remembered the unease he had felt about the book. "Are you saying the book is banned?"

Rafe shifted weight to his other foot. "Not banned, exactly. It's not illegal to own it. But if they knew it was there, they would send someone around to ask, as a public service, if you would donate it to the national archives. If they were feeling friendly, they might even offer a stipend. But they would be quite firm about it."

"And if I refused to hand it over, what then?"

"Well, they would start watching you really closely. Everyone breaks several laws a day, usually without even knowing they are doing so. People often don't even know such laws exist. It would only be a matter of time before they saw you breaking one, and you got a summons. The court would decide that possession of material that gave aid and comfort to foreign nations led to your asocial behavior, and recommend, as part of your 'therapy' that it be taken from you."

"But the countries involved don't even exist anymore!"

Rafe nodded. "As I said, censorship doesn't make any sense. I'm sure you've explored porn online."

Only since he was eight, Dan thought, but tactfully settled for nodding. The question, and the veer in direction, confused him.

"Have you seen what's available in hentai?"

That was pornographic manga. The quality ran from fairly good to abysmally bad, and included just about anything the human mind was capable of coming up with.

"I've looked. I didn't see anything I would want to keep."

"Yeah. It's pretty awful. When I was a teenager, I had to remind myself it was only drawings, and the minds that made those drawings were ten thousand kilometers away. But some were censored, right?"

"You mean those silly little red dots?" A full page drawing depicting a violent rape of a child in lurid detail might have such a dot, covering one little strategic spot, but otherwise leaving nothing to the imagination.

"That's the difference in Japan between a legitimate work of art and illegal pornography. It seems incredibly silly, but it's been the law in Japan for over three hundred years.

"Here, it's nearly as silly. The government is concerned with one thing, and one thing only: Disloyalty. It's a result of all the wars. In any event, you're free to do anything you want, so long as you don't appear to side with an enemy of Americas. Unfortunately, that includes just about every other nation in the world at one time or another, and even putting nations that battled the old USA hundreds of years ago in a glamorous light is considered subversive.

"Make sure to remember to change the name of the ship to USS Phalarope instead of HMS Phalarope and you should be fine." Rafe grinned. "Phalarope. Great name for a ship in a slash fiction. I don't remember much else that needed to be changed except home port of call, and put his various wives and mistresses in Boston rather than Cornwall."

"You've read the book?"

"Sure, when I was about twelve. It's been in the family for generations, you know."

"Didn't you want to go to sea after you read it?"

Rafe nodded, grinning. "But as I got older, I realized, as you have, that the world of Richard Bolitho is long gone and never coming back. Now, let's get back inside. It wouldn't do for us to be standing out here too long. Someone might wonder. When you get back in, rewrite it quickly. I'm told they only scan your computer about once every three months or so, but better safe than sorry."

It was only later that Dan realized that despite the lecturing tone, it was his first conversation with his father as an adult. They rarely spoke of childish things again.

* * *

Someone once characterized war as long stretches of boredom punctuated by endless moments of terror. This was even truer of space battles, a trope much beloved of science fiction authors who have space craft zooming around like Spitfires, banking, zooming, and exploding with loud roars. The reality was far less exciting. Two ships locked in a death battle might exchange two shots over ten days and in utter silence. Meanwhile, the combatants raced to develop fusion craft that could overcome orbital dynamics.

Ships had limited amounts of propulsion on board, and limited numbers of missiles. Nearly all the battles occurred in Earth orbit, particularly low Earth orbit, one hundred and fifty to two hundred kilometers above the surface. Maneuverability was accordingly restricted by orbital mechanics.

This left one basic strategy. One ship would get into a favorable position, and fire a missile at the other ship. The other ship would usually not fire back, being in a position where orbital positions gave return fire a disadvantage, but instead would try to avoid the missile. It could accelerate faster than the target ship, but for briefer period of time. So the target ship would hope to outrun the missile, and failing that catch the missile in its 'torch' – the back-blast from the main engine. This would slow the missile, and sometimes disable it.

A captain's nightmare would be to have a ship fire on them, and as they accelerated away, find a second ship ready to launch a missile once they had committed to a particular vector. Usually at that point the target ship was doomed.

For that reason, Americas' ships traveled in pairs in similar orbits about a thousand kilometers apart, watching for unwary Chinese ships.

Satellites were a safer target, but there were thousands of satellites, and both Americas and China had replacements for vital surveillance and communication satellites ready to launch, and often could replace a destroyed satellite within twelve hours. In the meantime, the ship was armed with one less missile (and ships could only carry six). Space navies, for all their undeserved glamor, were not large. The Americas Navy consisted of thirty "warships" with a total complement of seven hundred and fifty members. It was the largest in the world, and a tour of duty – launch to reentry – was at the most three weeks. Neither side could afford to lose any ships, and pot-shotting satellites made ships an easy target.

It usually cost less to just leave the satellites alone.

It was quietly agreed among junior officers that the chief role of a space navy was that of propaganda; civilian populations were convinced that death might come screaming from above at any moment. The reality was that from a tactical standpoint, the space navies made little sense. They cost a lot, and they did little damage other than to one another. But in terms of national chest-beating and inculcation of baseless free-floating anxiety in enemy populations, they were an absolute must. Both sides dutifully reported that the latest space victory saved one major city or another, despite the fact that neither side had the ability to do any damage to said city unless they happened to crash there.

For a junior officer, space battles weren't eventful. Indeed, in circumstances where he was in the attacking ship, he sometimes didn't know they had been in a battle until after it was over, when a captain would get on the intercom to announce that the HC such-and-such had just been destroyed. "HC" was navy-speak for "Heathen Chinese". Or something ruder.

When the *Ticonderoga* was in the inferior position, as happened twice, it was nerve-wracking. Again, there was nothing for any of the ships' crew or off-duty officers to do or see. There would be no overt signs of how the battle was faring, and the only sign of the battle being joined was when the main thrusters suddenly fired without warning. Once, Dan had been in his cubicle reading when the aft bulkhead slapped into him.

Then came the call to battle stations. This consisted of standing next to an assigned corridor hatch, at the ready to slam it shut in the event of explosive decompression. The crew member was literally roped to the hatch, so as to not get drawn away by decompression, and if he happened to be on the wrong side of the hatch, the side that had been holed, well, such are the fortunes of war. In fact, he was the lucky one. A holed craft would be unable to reenter Earth's atmosphere, or would burn up if it tried, and there was no craft capable of taking a crew on board that could reach them in time. Death, either by suffocation or hypothermia, might take two weeks, but it would come.

The first sign that they had survived the encounter would be when thrust was suddenly reduced. Until then, there was nothing to do for up to four hours other than stare at the featureless walls of the corridor, and wonder if death would be noisy or silent.

The odds of surviving such an attack were effectively even. Dan Vargas lived through eight such engagements. When he was promoted to the bridge, he at least had a say, but was just as helpless to determine events once the vectors were deployed.

Daniel Vargas learned how to face personal terror even when helpless.

While on the bridge, he destroyed six enemy ships, a full quarter of the Chinese space navy. He missed eight others. But it gave him the status of being Americas' only 'Space Ace.'

Thus are heroes created.

A few years later, Captain Daniel Vargas of the *RESS Phoenix* would be amused but unsurprised to learn that in evading that second missile, he had expended two hundred times as much propulsive force, and more delta vee, than all ships in the first space war combined.

Chapter 6 This Is Africa

VARGAS STOOD FIRST DUTY and would stand arrival duty on the journey to *nu Phoenicis*. By the time the *Phoenix* reached ten AUs, heading south of the ecliptic at roughly a forty-five degree angle, transmissions from Earth took eighty minutes. It would take another three hundred and six days to reach their target speed of .87c, and the time dilation factor didn't really begin to kick in until about half of light speed. It would take about a hundred and ninety days ship time until Earth was completely cut off.

Except, of course, it seemed to be cut off already. The radio remained stubbornly incoherent.

The war must have gone global. All Vargas could think of to do was pray they hadn't gone to all-out thermonuclear annihilation.

He wondered if his father was OK. Torreón was far enough away from the industrial space plant of Chetumal and the population centers that it was unlikely to be a direct target, even on a third round of strikes. If fallout wasn't a big issue, his father would be alive and well. Vargas had already bade him farewell forever, but it was a death without dying, a grief without grieving. He worried about his father, even as he knew he would never know what became of him.

Vargas felt the weight of his body return, signaling the final acceleration after the ship was pointed in the right direction, and *Phoenix* was finally really on her way.

Now things would assume a more casual air. Vargas would still be "Captain" at all times, and obedience would still be expected, but the four men and two women would dine together and mix in off-duty hours.

Since they were on rotating shifts, each person did four hours a day, more if there were any problems that might require more than one person to solve. One of Spencer's better ideas, Vargas thought, glancing with distaste at the vaguely mauvish corridors. It ensured a structured, but relaxed and adaptable system.

The discipline and order necessary for a fighting craft would actually be a drawback on an unarmed ship that would be facing unknown problems and an assortment of unpredictable dangers. Many of the crew had military backgrounds much like the merchant marine. The colonists were nearly all civilians.

Vargas transitioned from military to civilian captain. He had to walk a tightrope between being Master and Commander, and something. . . more casual.

He remembered a skit he saw at a diplomatic casual dinner on British television which featured Americaner ballet dancers trying to dance and goose step at the same time. He was in uniform at the time, so he didn't dare react too openly. He had the corner of his mouth turned down and was glowering not because he was offended, but because he was struggling so hard not to crack up laughing. His horrified English hosts realized what he was looking at and shut the video down, and Vargas tried his best to assure them he took no offense, but he doubted he succeeded. Americaners were notorious for simmering in passive-aggressive rage.

Doctor Spencer, his chief evaluator at the start of the selection process and now the ship's psychiatrist, had wasted no time laying it out for him in the final days of the selection process nearly two years earlier.

Neither man was comfortable with the other, a situation exacerbated by the oppressive heat of Spencer's office. The room they were in wasn't air conditioned, but merely had a couple of apathetic ceiling fans. The most technologically advanced base on Earth didn't have air conditioning because the locals who built the living quarters and personnel offices didn't see any need for it. Africa, Vargas thought wryly. The place was more a condition than a continent.

"Admiral, the board will meet on Friday to select the Americaner who will captain the *Phoenix*. It will be you. Between your excellent military record and the physical and psychological tests, you are the best candidate for the job."

Vargas regarded the staff evaluator with some bemusement. Spencer, rumored to have already secured a spot on *Phoenix*, was a trim Englishman, about 45 and with the near-requisite pencil-thin mustache common to all RESS medical staff. Even the women, Vargas thought dryly. Black hair, sharp blue eyes, and even when seemingly relaxed, had an air of bird-like inquisitiveness.

"I'm very gratified to hear that, Doctor. . . "

"Shut up."

Vargas blinked in astonishment. Spencer continued. "I think you earned the job fair and square. The only candidate to come close to you was an Englishman, and therefore not eligible for the job. His name is Sheffield. I'm going to push to have him be your top commander."

"I know him." Vargas was puzzled and angry. What had he done to anger the shrink? "Please continue." His frigid tone, coming from a captain, suggested career death for anyone on his ship who provoked his ire. in such a fashion.

Spencer's mouth twitched at the corner. "There's that discipline that you'll need. On this mission, you'll need to be as well-disciplined as your crew."

Vargas realized the words were meant to defray his anger. To his annoyance, it was working. "Thus it always is with command. . . doctor."

"You'll face a number of problems that you haven't been trained for. First, it is a civilian ship. You can neither demand nor expect military discipline. You won't be a military Admiral. You will be the Captain. But you'll be Captain-the-boss, not Captain-the-absolute-authority."

Vargas nodded. This seemed to be belaboring the obvious.

"Second, most of your crew is European. It's likely some of them are covertly hostile to the idea of an Americaner captain." Vargas raised his eyebrows and Spencer shook his head. "I'm not going to guess who. We washed out the ones we judged a potential threat to discipline and eliminated them from the program. Others aren't hostile, but see the fact that the captain must be Americaner as a political appointment, and by extension may view you as unqualified window dressing."

"A few minutes ago, you told me I earned the job. . . how did you put it? 'Fair and square'. Has something changed in the past thirty seconds?

"Nothing has changed. I have your test scores and your academic record in front of me. With your background, you could have been a full professor at any university of your choosing. I also have your career records, and I note that on several occasions, you gave gongs to your crew, commendations and medals, that you could have enjoyed for yourself as Captain. That's why I like you as mission captain.

"But to most of the people on board, you're an Americaner, and a war hero from a war in which Americas did more to alienate her own allies than she did to defeat the enemy."

"Completely out of my hands." Vargas shifted, betraying his irritation. "I had a job to do, and I did it. Ground side politics I left to the ground side politicians."

Spencer smiled for the first time. "That approach probably had a lot to do with you being selected by your government. You are the pure military man, politically neutral, with few friends but no enemies in Parliament.

"Unfortunately, the crew and colonists aren't aware of any of that, and most of them wouldn't care much if they did know. You'll be seen as window dressing—again, as a mere political appointment. It undermines your legitimacy, and that in turn will undermine your authority.

"Finally," Spencer held up a third finger, "you come from a culture that is - excuse me - notorious for oppressive paranoia. People are going to look at you and wonder if you intend to inflict the same kinds of repressive rule on them."

"I was given the impression that the Charter of Human Rights would apply to the ship, rather than the Constitution."

"And you would be correct. But how much authority would the Charter have once we're out past the Oort cloud? We've actually had applicants withdraw because they were afraid any colony led by an Americaner would become an Americas-style dictatorship. Mind you, it's nothing personal; it can't be. Nobody outside this building knows you'll be captain yet."

Vargas repressed a shrug, wondering how the psychiatrist could do his job if he was so oblivious to the power of naval gossip. He had already got The Word. "You know, most Americaners don't live up to that stereotype. We aren't all goose steppers."

"Of course not. But did you know that no less a personage than His Royal Majesty referred to the Americas as just that? 'A nation of goose steppers'?"

"King Edward said that?

"Well, he's a politician, too, you know. So to hell with what he thinks, eh?"

Vargas glanced around, and when his eyes returned to Sheffield, the psychiatrist was smiling again.

"Did you notice your response? When I committed an overt act of disloyalty, your immediate reaction was to scan the room for cameras and listening devices. There aren't any, by the way. Patient confidentiality and all that."

Vargas wasn't inclined to argue the point. "Assume you're being watched" was just part of daily living. People didn't vanish in the middle of the night and live in fear of the knock on the door, but it was well understood that getting out of line could affect your job, your standing in the community, even your credit record.

"Does it follow that I would want to inflict that sort of repressive leadership on others?"

"Sometimes it does. In your case, though, I strongly doubt it. You're not paranoid, and the tests also show you aren't the type to enjoy retribution. That isn't always true of people who have risen to command."

Vargas couldn't figure out what Spencer was getting at, and felt frustrated. "Well. . . I'm feeling like I'm being put in a bit of a box. On one hand, as Captain, I must maintain ship's discipline. But you're telling me the crew will be a bunch of hypersensitive xenophobes who will immediately interpret a directive to perform maintenance as being about the same as a putsch against European freedom. If you're right, then how do you expect me to do my job? For twenty-six years?"

"Well, realistically, one year, and much of that with just five other individuals. Everyone on board will be spending all or nearly all of their time asleep. And the second six months you'll all probably be far too distracted for shipboard politics. And the colonists will pick their leaders. You're certain to be considered, but don't assume you deserve to be colonial leader."

Spencer sighed and rubbed a finger up one temple. "I think I failed to make one very important item clear. I don't expect you to have any serious personnel problems once the ship has launched. I'm worried about the next eighteen months when you'll be training with these people."

"Ah." Vargas felt clouds of confusion parting.

"Once you launch, your political problems are most likely over. It's what you do between now and then that determines that, of course. So. What do you think you can do to smooth this situation out?"

Dan thought furiously. Now that he understood the parameters, he could muster a solid response. "First, as you say, I have to keep in mind at all times that this is not a military operation, and that it's multinational. Don't expect salutes."

"Right."

"Fraternize to a moderate extent."

"How would you define that?"

Vargas considered. There was no longer any doubt in his mind that this was a last-minute test of his suitability for the job. "If invited for a beer after training, say yes. Don't get tipsy, don't get in fights, talk down anyone who looks like they might be going in that direction. Call crew members by their first name, rather than rank or last name, but insist on being called 'captain', even if in familiar tones. Steer clear of talk about politics, especially the China war. Try to learn as much as I can about the people as individuals, but avoid being nosy. Remember I'm getting to know people, and not collecting data on them."

"Good. What else?"

"Cultivate good working relationships with everyone, the crew in particular and the top officers especially. Don't play divide-and-conquer games, respect everyone for the work they do, and be sure to notice work beyond the call of duty. Um, one thing I'm not clear on about the training regimen. I know I'll be training with the crew, but what about the civilians?"

"Colonists, not civilians, and the selection process is ongoing. Some of them you won't meet until the ship has launched."

"So training will be with the crew only?"

"And about twenty-five specialists, people you'll need immediately once you've landed. Exobiologists, the ship epidemiologists, soil specialists, meteorologists, me, and others. However, we just don't know what will be needed the most. Some of them might turn out to be fifth wheels. Others might be as important to the survival of the colony as you, maybe even more. Personally, I'm hoping to be a fifth wheel. I would like to be useful as an alfalfa farmer than as a psychiatrist."

"Eighteen months, with one hundred and seventy five people. I think I can learn to work with them over that time."

"Admiral, have you given any thought to what you want to do after the colony is established? By that, I mean, what sort of rule would you want to have?"

Vargas noted the use of his rank and suspected it was a deliberate ploy to get him thinking in militaristic terms. His dad liked to do the same thing during their too-rare dinner get-together when politics came up.

"Colonial government, you mean? Well, it will depend a lot on what sort of reception the planet gives us. If the landing craft people wake up their first morning on the ground and see twenty-five Tyrannosaurus rexes peering in at them, then politics will just have to wait until we convince the local wildlife to take their interests elsewhere. On the other hand, if we find things going smoothly, well, the reality is I won't have any authority off the ship. People will still follow me out of habit and custom, but the moment we reach the point where we can think about a government, I plan to call for elections for pro tem positions while the colony hammers out what sort of government it wants. If they don't want me for mayor or whatever, then I can probably be of use as a farmer who also teaches math and science. I can even coach football. I was pretty good at it as a kid, you know."

"How about law enforcement?"

"In a town of fifteen hundred people? With everyone carefully selected for personal stability, and work enough for everyone? I don't see crime as a big issue. I guess we'll have a stockade where someone who does get in a fight can cool his heels, but if all goes well, we'll be at least a generation away from needing courts and police and all of that."

"What happens if someone is already there?"

"Native intelligent life, you mean?"

Spencer nodded.

"Keep the colonists in hibernation. Meet with the indigenous personnel, try to determine if they are friendly, see what they have to trade, and what we have to trade to them. If the place isn't crowded, see if we can negotiate a living area. If that isn't feasible, Get ready to move on to another star system."

"Excellent. I think our interview is done. Admiral, I look forward to training with you."

"You can start calling me 'Captain' now."

Spencer chuckled. "As you say. Captain."

Chapter 7 A New Culture

VIRGIL "RED" FARNSWORTH TWIDDLED THE CONTROLS of the remote operations vehicle to bring the craft about by five degrees for a look at stern Camera #26. This was the last of them. Of the first twenty five, eight showed signs of physical damage—dust from the Dry Dock detonation, most likely. The rest appeared intact, so it had to be assumed their electronics were shot. Mounted on the outside of the craft, they weren't hardened against an electro-magnetic pulse. For Red, sitting at a semi-circular console in an otherwise darkened cabin, it was a peaceful and pleasant detail.

Red kept an eye on the monitors for radioactivity, too. As expected, a lot of dust had embedded in the outer skin of the hull, and in quite a few areas it could present problems to anyone who had to go out there. If it was up to Red, they would just leave the dead cameras alone and when they approached the *nu Phoenicis* system, the bridge would just have to live with disappointment. But the Captain might have other ideas.

Most of the material would have a short half-life. In twenty-six years it may no longer be a problem at all.

Red dutifully noted the emissions levels as he moved the remote operation vehicle, a Charlie with air thrusters, from camera to camera. The Charlie would need a good washing down.

For a Manchester yob, this was an amazing place to be. Red might easily have ended up just another footie lout, piling up the ASBOs until he finally committed Grievous Bodily Harm and wound up in the slammer.

But one day, half pissed and wondering what to do with his afternoon, fourteen-year-old Red stumbled into the People's History Museum. He was just looking for a loo, but the museum, with its rich Manchester history of workers' rights and democracy, changed his view on life and gave him something to strive for.

Too intelligent for the life course he was on, he aced his A Levels, got into college and excelled. He enlisted when war broke out with Russia, and six years later was discharged with a pension, a rack full of service medals, and a scholarship for graduate work in Robotics and Imprinting.

What a strange old life it is, he ruminated. Here I am on the first star ship, and all because I was pissed and touching the cloth.

Camera #26 turned out to be the easiest to diagnose. It was gone entirely. Red noted it, checked the emissions, and docked the ROV magnets to one of the ferric straps that ran around most of the external modules. The most important part of the inspection was next, but he was going to take a five minute break before paging the Captain. Vargas had been hovering over his shoulder for the first hour, not interfering but being a bloody brass hat distraction by his mere presence.

This beat Pod inspection duty, a tedious process Red thought he would be heartily sick of by the end of his six-month tour. He hoped the process would be more relaxed on his next tour, twenty five years from now. By then, he reasoned, the sleepers who were going to 'decay' would have, an unfortunate clique that Red hoped not to join.

Helluva note, Red thought. You travel fifty light years, the first human to visit another star, and when you get there you're a hopeless drooler, unable to toilet train, let alone colonize. Red wondered what the Captain was going to do with them. Setting up on a new world was going to be tough enough as it was. Would they space them? Red thought he might if he was a Captain. He wasn't overly sentimental.

Asuka Tsuchishima, the Japanese exobiologist, had shocked him speechless during training by professing ignorance of Manchester football clubs. She had never heard of City, which was bad. But how could anyone not know of Manchester United, especially since the FA Cup was an annual world blowout and had been even during the wars of the past century? Man U and Vostok FC once played a cup match in Japan because Royal Europe and Russia were busily bombing the shit out of one another. The result of that game, Red was convinced, played a major role in Royal Europe winning that war. Didn't Japan have its own teams? He was pretty sure they did. How could they not know about United? When he said this to Asuka, she had given him a smile that was both enigmatic and sardonic, and suggested that perhaps they might each endeavor to learn of the sports teams of each other's countries. Red was pretty sure he got zinged, somehow.

Of course, it was all moot now, water under the bridge. Manchester, like all the great cities of the world, was just an irrelevant name on an irrelevant map. Red hoped to establish footie on the new world. Maybe future generations would look at him at the new world's William McGregor.

Asuka disclosed an unexpected sense of humor. One of her most popular lectures was on what intelligent aliens might look like. Well-trodden ground, to be sure, but Asuka ironically used lurid covers from old SF magazines, pointing out which features might be reasonable and which were absurdities. The next lecture Red was slated to attend, the sample alien was wearing a Man U sweater. He and Asuka became good friends.

Enough wool gathering. Back to work. Red tapped his pad, letting the Captain know he was on his way to the damaged Imprinter module. He unanchored the ROV, and started along the side, about one third the way up the vast craft. Moving in the direction of acceleration was slower, of course, but the sturdy little craft 'walked' up the side of the ship, clamping around the point of contact on the raised strips and pulling itself 'up'. Fortunately, the Charlie didn't mass much.

From his vantage point along the spine of the ship, *Phoenix* looked like a bunch of bananas still on the tree. The central core of the ship, where people lived and slept, was an elongated capsule that ran to the thick ice platform that protected the craft from the engines. Aft of that, the main core was all but invisible because of the modules grouped around it. The modules would end up on the surface of their new home once it was determined the colony would commit to the planet. Some of the modules would become structures, the nucleus of their new capital city.

The damaged area wasn't hard to find. There was a ragged hole along the top of the Imprinter module, which Red estimated to be about three meters long and perhaps a half meter wide at its widest. As his ROV approached, light from inside became visible. At least they got the power restored. That would help.

His Charlie spidered closer to the wound. The high resolution cameras could make out an Exit sign on the inside hatch as his camera arm hovered about a meter from the gap. That was some Exit. Mind the gap.

Red heard a cough from the dimness behind him. "Red, do you have radiation readings?"

"Just preliminary, Captain, but they don't look too bad. Almost all of the dust struck the stern, or the disk. There's radiation, but by the time we get to *nu Phoenicis*, it should be down to fairly safe levels. Reentry should ablate a lot of the dust on the modules, so they might be pretty clean once down."

". . . and module Fourteen?"

That was the Imprinter module. Red nodded at the screen. "It's never going to be certifiable for reentry, but we can make it space worthy again. We can just weld plates inside and out once we have the rough edges sanded. In fact, Captain, if you brought her down empty and in a controlled glide, she might make it down."

"Not with the Imprinter on board."

"No, Ser. Empty. Half-way along the top like that, it's in a spot where the temperatures rarely exceed three hundred. I think we could weld it sturdy enough to survive. . . and here's the final on the gamma emissions."

Both men peered at the screen. Vargas permitted himself a tight smile. "That's not bad. We'll send a Charlie in to see how hot it is inside the module, but it should be safe for men in space suits to work. We may have to do decontamination, but the interior should then be clean enough for people to shirt sleeve it."

"There's a Charlie right over there, Captain" Red pointed. "And I have a counter right here. If you want, we can have him at the airlock in about a half hour."

"Do it." Vargas fished out his data pad. "Let's see. Who's available? Simmons is. Simmons!"

A voice crackled over the data pad. "Ser?"

"Proceed to the Module Fourteen airlock, and wait for the Charlie. You are to suit up and escort him in. Do you have a Charlie talker with you?"

"Yes Ser. I'll suit up now."

Vargas saw no sense in making the man wait in a suit unnecessarily. "Belay that, Tim. The Charlie won't get there for a half an hour."

"What do you want the Charlie to do once he's in there?"

"Get him as close to the hole as you can. We'll have a rad counter strapped to his back, and he's going to tell us how hot it is in there. You'll check his readings as you enter the module. If you feel it's unsafe, I want you out of there immediately, Mr. Simmons."

"Aye, Captain."

The physicist Simmons would know an unsafe radiation level better than anyone else on board. Satisfied, Vargas turned to the Charlie and helped Red make sure it was secure and operating. The robot, shaped somewhat like an eight-legged turtle, had a flat stretch on its back with a set of straps specifically to carry small items from one locale to another. Red took his Charlie talker and told the small robot to go to module Fourteen and await further instructions. The machine trundled out of the communications desk area.

"Red, do you feel up to inspecting the other modules? I know we didn't get holed anywhere else, but I want to be sure that they are all up to reentry."

Red chewed his lip. "Captain, I won't be able to do a good job in one day."

"No, but I would like you to devote an hour to it each day for the next month or however long it takes. If we have any other damaged modules, we need to figure out what's in them and how or where the contents should be moved."

"Ser." What the hell, Red reflected. It was still better than hibernation pod duty.

* * *

Sol was just another star now, and they couldn't even look back to see it. It had been over ten days since electronic anomalies of any sort manifested, to everyone's relief. The Captain had elected to defer on repairing the stern cameras on the premise that it was foolish to expose anyone to radioactivity unnecessarily. The ship was under one gravity acceleration. Anyone unfortunate enough to get cast adrift would still get to the *nu Phoenicis* system. The involuntary explorer would just get there a few thousand years after everyone else, was all, and probably be going too fast to make it worth anyone's while to retrieve the mummified corpse. It was another good reason to hold off on camera repair.

Eighteen days out, they received a garbled transmission directed to them from Earth. The launch facilities in the Gabon desert hadn't been attacked, and promised to maintain contact as long as the time-dilation increase made it practical.

Vargas recognized the voice of the base commander, Gustavo Bécquer, The man usually affected a happy-go-lucky and slightly passive demeanor, and there wasn't an element of the program that he wasn't keenly and intimately knowledgeable about. He often filled in on training sessions, lecturing without notes and explaining complex ship functions with the air of a man who personally designed those functions.

Often, he had.

That was the only time any person on Earth spoke to them directly.

Earth didn't go completely silent, but most of the broadcasts were badly fractured and encrypted. Vargas had the transmissions fed to the main ship's computer for it to chew on. There wasn't much chance of breaking those codes, but it would have twenty-six years in which to try.

Module Fourteen was airtight once again, and to the deep relief of the skeleton crew, the Imprinter was undamaged. Radiation levels were acceptable, and the gash, while large by the standards of most space-faring ships, was small enough in comparison to the volume of the module that decompression had taken about five minutes. The Imprinter's carapace provided effective shielding.

Temperature was another matter. The room was warmed at the rate of ten degrees a day so fragile electronics wouldn't crack, and to reduce the possibility of condensation.

Inspection of the rest of the exterior was going slowly, with Red being painstakingly careful not to miss anything.

Vargas found himself picking up the crew's habit of referring to the hibernators as "the pod people". As a teen, he had seen all four versions of that movie, and approached them with a well-honed sense of teen irony, but here, on a nearly empty ship billions of miles from a home that barely existed, the 1,494 silent white guardians of souls took on a distinctly creepy air. None of the crew liked that duty very much, and each dreaded being the first to discover that a sleeper had entered a spiral into idiocy and madness. Vargas quickly realized crew members should not inspect the pods of friends and loved ones, and had each of the members draw up a list of pod people who fell into that category. It would be a standing order for the rest of the trip.

Julie Steinberg, one of the ship's physicians, was an accomplished pianist who had at some point amassed a large collection of funny, rude songs, and she was more than delighted to have an appreciative audience a couple of nights a week. She was thrilled when she saw the piano, having resigned herself to playing music on lightweight and unsatisfying electronic substitutes. Her infectious delight with this grand toy spread to the Captain and crew.

Vargas eyed her easy smile and sparkling eyes from the lonely heights of the captaincy, and resolved, once on the new world, to see if she could join him and his classical guitar for some *Vamo' Alla* Flamenco.

Vargas noticed that the team members were largely not using the vast library of entertainment. Nearly every novel written since 1700 was there (including all the captain's beloved Bolitho naval sea adventures!), and movies from all over the world covering every conceivable topic. There were comedy routines, and over a million hours of music. Interactive games and board games were popular, with everyone, including himself. Four was just the right number for a game of Monopoly.

Vargas casually queried the five about it. Julie surmised that people preferred to make their own entertainment, a statement not borne out by the past three centuries years of human history. But then, most people on Earth didn't play musical instruments, couldn't sing, tell tales, or paint. They were used, after centuries of mass entertainment, to more passive roles.

Nearly everyone on board showed strong artistic and creative tendencies. Vargas allowed that this group, an intellectual and emotional elite, might evolve a new set of standards.

Vargas was met with vague and deflective opinions on how much the library would be needed for their entertainment. Nobody, it seemed, had really thought about it, nor were they inclined to begin doing so. Until he spoke to Red at shift's end one day.

"Earth's dead to us, Captain. I don't know if they blew their asses all sky high or not, but we all said our goodbyes. Fuck 'em." He studied Vargas' face. "Too direct, Captain?" Red was still angry. Someone on Earth tried to kill him. And it looked like they had all managed to kill one another. Did any of his mates still live? What about his parents?

"No, Red, I think you've got something there. We all said our goodbyes. Earth was a part of our irrevocable past the minute we were selected for this mission."

Vargas let his gaze drift to his data pad, which was softly playing Mozart. Red followed his gaze. "Captain, people aren't throwing away their cultures. They just need time to process the fact that it's all in the past now."

"You've been thinking about this," Vargas said, surprised.

"Well, hell, Captain, I already knew you had asked the other four, and I figured I should have something for you when you got to me." Red wore a knowing grin that could get midshipmen cashiered on some ships.

"Right. Did any of the others have anything new to offer when telling you about it?" Red's answer didn't surprise Vargas. Secrets among a crew this small didn't exist, and everyone paid attention to what the Captain was thinking about. Midshipmen made it their duty to know what the Captain was thinking.

"Not really. Sure glad we have that piano, though. That was not something I expected to see on a space ship."

Vargas laughed. "This ship was originally designed to take four centuries to get to its destination. And the original plans called for four thousand sleepers and a crew of over a thousand to tend to them and the ship. But the new fusion engine left us ridiculously overpowered. . . " Good thing too, Vargas thought, "and we realized we could cut the complement down because the mortality rate was expected to be lower. Four hundred years, they hoped one in four would get there alive. Twenty-eight years, well we don't have as many people who are going to be overhead."

"'Overhead,' Captain?" Julie's eyebrows rested near her hairline.

"That's the term that was used." Vargas decided not to dwell on that. "In any event, it means that a ship meant to store five thousand people for four hundred years now has fifteen hundred people for twenty six years. The sociologists and biologists agreed that was nearly the optimum size for a colony. You have enough people for genetic diversity, and nearly every specialty we might need is covered, but at the same time, it isn't so big that we start out with 'big city' problems like crime and alienation."

Vargas glanced around the room. About the size of his family's living room, it was nearly ideal for up to six people to eat meals and hang out. It had been the bridge mess, and Vargas had decreed that those on active duty—i.e, not hibernating—would be considered honorary members of the bridge. They had tried having a couple of meals in the general mess, and had found the vast hall, designed to seat up to fifteen hundred, intimidating and a bit dispiriting.

"Originally, it was supposed that fifty people would be awake at any given time. But that was when the maintenance demands were much higher, especially the hibernators. Originally, there weren't any Charlies, either, which meant the crew had to do all the cleaning and maintenance in the living areas. In some cultures the taboo against cybertechnology extended to autonomous robots." Vargas was unsurprised to see Red give a dismissive shrug. The man made his living designing and working with machines that could "think" for themselves.

The other two off-duty crew members slipped into the mess, and both men gave them a friendly wave.

"So having refined the mission down to six people being awake at a time, they got around to realizing that those six people would end up feeling like ants on an airport runway, and started thinking in terms of what would be nice to have along, rather than just everything that was essential. I've seen some of the notes on the meetings that came as a result of that. Those engineers had a lot of fun coming up with things they would like to see on the ship. One proposal was for a basketball court."

Julie sputtered. "A basketball court?"

"Yeah. It got turned down when it was realized that the ship would be spending ninety percent of the time in zero gee, and you really can't play basketball in a centrifuge. So we got the gym instead." The gym itself was a marvel. Two rotating wheels revolved around the axis of the ship, the gym and the hamster wheel. The hamster wheel, the lighter but quicker of the two, was for jogging. A person maintaining three km/hour spinwards would experience a full gravity. The larger gym wheel only had a third of a gravity for a person who was stationary, but that was adequate for weights and tension machines. It also contained medical facilities for treating injuries and other conditions that required gravity, along with a small fabrication shop for weight-depended processes. Standing orders were that once the ship was in free flight, crew members had to spend two one hour shifts a day in the exercise area. Because the two wheels adjusted speed against mass to offset one another perfectly, no torque was passed along to the ship.

Red grinned. "I like the gym. I get some of my best thinking done there."

Ian Mann arched an eyebrow at him. "Red, does that mean we all have to settle for your not-best thinking out here?"

Red lifted his chin and declared, "You have to know how to target your audience." Ian howled and chucked an empty drink-bulb at him. Red batted it away without even looking.

They settled into a comfortable silence for a few minutes. Ann Forster broke it by saying, "Do we have a recording of crickets?"

Vargas tilted his head at her. "Crickets? We probably do. We've got everything else in the library."

Ian spoke up. "For that matter, we have fertilized queen crickets in storage. The real thing."

"I doubt the Captain wants crickets flying or hopping or whatever it is they do on the ship. I was thinking about background noises. This is the quietest ship."

Red chuckled. "It's orful quiet out there, ma'am. Too quiet. You'll jinx us."

Vargas shook his head. Manchurians or whatever people from Manchester called themselves shouldn't try to do Americaner accents. The results were like cats singing opera. But Ann was right. *Phoenix*, which had most of its machinery well away from the living areas, was an impossibly silent ship. It was disconcerting. Vargas remembered walking along a corridor and hearing a faint whirring noise. He looked around, finally spotting a Charlie, some fifty meters away mopping the floor. The noise was intermittent, because his breathing would drown it out.

Ian considered. "We've got bird songs recorded too. And I bet we've got stuff like wind going through leaves, and pine branches creaking, and dogs barking. . . "

". . . and these are a few of my favorite things" Red sang, and the group exploded in laughter.

Ann waited for the group to resettle, and said, "Seriously, though. If you had some natural noises in the background, soft, so they don't distract, wouldn't that make this giant mausoleum a little more cheerful. Especially the corridors. I want to kill whoever came up with that color scheme!"

Vargas canvassed the group, using nothing more than his eyebrows. Responses ranged from non-committal to thoughtful nods. "Ann, do you want to make up a mix tape? Birds, crickets, breezes, that sort of thing. We've got a lot of bandwidth on our data pads. That way, everyone gets to decide if they want to have it in the background or not." Nods around the table greeted this.

As if on cue, Ann pulled her data pad out of her shoulder pouch and unfurled it. She set it to hologram mode so the others could see what she was doing. "OK. Four hour loop so it doesn't sound too artificial. Maybe if we save the crickets until the end of the loop. They can be a signal to people that the end of the shift is near. . ."

* * *

As the shift progressed, they found it easier to discuss Earth. Distancing, emotional as well as physical, had set in. By the end of the tour, they weren't even monitoring transmissions. Not that there had been any.

When they launched, there were nearly a billion people on Earth, and they enjoyed most technologically advanced civilization in history. *Phoenix* might be all that remained of that.

Could humanity survive and recover yet again, as it had from endless terrible wars and plagues, the Flare, the Vast Depression, climate change? Dan remembered reading that at one point in the twenty first century, the population was over nine billion.

Red opined that wars were just Mother Nature's way of ensuring population control. It wasn't a theory that was new to anyone at the table. Several major churches spoke of the series of setbacks as proof that God thought there were too many people.

It was Julie who had the most interesting take on it. She felt *Phoenix* was the unwitting impetus for the war. She said, "Flowers disperse their pollen, and promptly shrivel up and die. It may be that we are Earth's seed, and once it was spread to the cosmic winds, it was time for Earth to die."

Vargas nodded, more to himself than to Julie. "Earth as a dying blossom, tossing its seed on the cosmic wind. That notion's been around for a while. We are that seed on the cosmic wind."

When Dan returned to his cabin, he dug into his captain's safe and took out the list of names for the new home planet that the Americas had won the right to use as part of the agreement, along with Vargas' captaincy, in return for funding and use of the Dry Dock. Most of the names were nationalistic: Washington, Reagan, America, Columbus, and Akron. Others reflected the phony values of phony politicians. Faith. Hope. Patriot. World of Heroes.

He took the list and tore it up. The colonists would name their own damn world, thank you very much.

Meanwhile, Red decided to make his own 'nature tape'. Ann was from South Africa and would pick insects and animals Red had never heard except in REB nature documentaries. He decided he wanted the sounds of Platt Field Park, where he spent many a happy college hour reading. And after careful negotiation with an amused Vargas, Ian Mann made up some non-toxic paint and proceeded to rearrange the décor of some of the passageways.

* * *

By the time the shift ended there were two dozen 'nature tapes'. Crew members had a choice of jungle, forest, ocean, suburbs, parkland and riverside from various parts of the world. In the aisles, images of forests and deserts and tundra bloomed. Evocative rather than realistic, many depicted a world was many years past.

The next crew of six, headed by Alan Trapp, the Chief Medical Officer, would make alterations and progressions in this oddly disjointed but viable ship's culture. Early on, they had realized that a lot of the things they left behind them, such as the nature sound tracks, would make little sense, so along with the official ships log and its dreary recital of inspections and shift changes, there was an informal ship's log - a crew's log, if you will - that explained some of the things each shift did to alleviate and improve living conditions, along with ideas that needed to be shared with all the subsequent shifts. Dan looked forward to seeing that log on his next shift, years from now.

It would be a treasure trove for historians one day.

Dan went into the pod with the feeling that everything was going well, and this was going to be a wonderful voyage.

Dan slept.

Dan dreamt.

Chapter 8 Cobwebs In The Night

WHEN HE AWOKE, a technician Vargas didn't recognize was monitoring his vitals. Behind him, an older man with a beard held an overall.

The technician asked Vargas, "What is your name?"

Dan blinked, clearing cobwebs. "Daniel Vargas"

"And where are you?"

"The *RESS Phoenix*. I'm the commanding officer."

"And who am I?"

Dan peered at the technician. "I'm afraid...I don't recall."

The tech sighed. "Red. Red Farnsworth. We served together on first shift."

"Ah. Sorry, Red. I know exactly who you are." Vargas felt puzzled. When first shift ended, Red had about two inches of red beard and hair, creating the faint impression of a leprechaun. His appearance hadn't changed since then. "I guess I'm still waking up. How's the ship?"

The man with the salt-and-pepper beard leaned forward. "The ship is fine, Captain. We're on course, and will arrive in about thirteen years."

Something about that didn't sound right. "Who are you?"

"I'm Doctor Ian Spencer, ship psychiatrist."

"Oh. Of course you are. When did you grow a beard?" Spencer hadn't had a beard before, but he should have recognized him. He felt a rising sense of alarm.

"Captain, let's get you some coffee and food" Spencer glanced at Red inquiringly.

Red gave the readouts a final check, nodded. "He's good to go. Here's your clothing." Red nodded to Spencer, who looked started to see he was holding the coveralls. Suddenly aware he was naked, Vargas gratefully pulled on the clothes.

Vargas might be confused, but he was still the Captain. He was supposed to notice things, and he noticed Spencer make furtive signals to Red. He guessed from the look in his eyes that Red was worried.

"Sers, do you require my further assistance?"

Spencer replied. "I'll take it from here, Mister Farnsworth. Please let Commander Sheffield know that we are done here and the Captain will be available shortly." Red gave a nod and turned away, clearly relieved.

Vargas found himself watching the psychiatrist to see how he propelled himself down the corridor in one twentieth gravity. He was reasonably sure that the Moon was the lightest gravity field he had been in aside from no gravity at all, and at that usually in a cumbersome spacesuit or the tightly enclosed Moon base.

Spencer moved along much like a kangaroo, pushing with both feet, slowly bringing them forward to land and propel on the next 'hop'. Each covered about ten meters as they got up to speed, Vargas trailing awkwardly at first, but regaining the ground as his body learned the new way of getting around. It was surprisingly efficient. Vargas could learn to like it.

As he roo-hopped down the hall with Spencer, Dan realized he wasn't supposed to be awake until the last six months of the journey. Thirteen years, did he say? They were just past the halfway point. Dan felt like a child dragged out of bed by his parents in the small hours of the morning. There were some other people in the corridor, none of whom he recognized, but they seemed to be drifting about calmly, even leisurely. Some greeted him – 'Good day, Captain' – others gave him a nod and a vague smile. It was all very odd. True, he didn't have any insignia on the light cotton casuals, but surely crew members knew what their captain looked like. And why were there so many people out of hibernation?

The main mess had about fifteen people scattered around, lost in the cavernous room. A few nodded, the rest took no notice of the new arrivals. Dan saw one large woman sitting placidly, arms on the table palms up, in a Zen pose. She appeared deep in meditation.

Spencer speared Vargas with a finger point. "Cream, no sweetener, right?"

Vargas peered at the menu on the bulkhead. "Um, right. And oatmeal and toast."

Dan looked around the mess. "Are there supposed to be this many people awake?"

"We've run into a bit of a snag." Spencer spread his fingers, palms down. "Come, eat. We go to the bridge next, and get you filled in."

Dan didn't trust the psychiatrist's calming tone. Something about it reminded him of the tones he himself had used as a boy to convince the family dog that yes, he really did want to go to the vet's for his annual shots.

It also let Dan know that Spencer wasn't going to discuss the problem until the acting captain on the bridge filled him in. Which, Dan reflected wryly, was as it should be. It didn't quell his sense of unease.

"Who's acting captain?"

"Commander Sheffield." Vargas blinked. Spencer had ordered Red to report to Sheffield. How did he forget that?

"So we're at turn around?" In reality the ship could be turned one-eighty degrees at any time during unpowered flight. It was thought good for morale to make the turn at the exact half way mark, a progress marker.

Spencer gave the Captain an odd look and nodded.

"Did they get the Imprinter squared away?"

"I understand they've been making as many spare parts as possible. Some are strapped in corridors, others in cabins."

"Good thinking. Find out who thought of that and tell him he's got a commendation coming."

Vargas then remembered it had been his order in the first place.

The psychiatrist pulled out his data pad, unfurled it so it was facing Vargas. "Captain," he said softly, "can you read this?"

Dan stared at the tablet. "What language is that?"

"It's English. OK, you speak Spanish too, is that correct?" Vargas hesitated, nodded. "OK. Translate this page for me."

"Montréal. . . oranges. . . are regarded as the. . . best in the. . . world." Now frightened, Vargas stared at Spencer. "What does this mean? I have to be able to read well to do my job!"

"We think it's temporary. That you can read and understand Spanish is a very good sign."

"What made you think I couldn't read?"

"A lot of people coming out of hibernation can't, at least at first. When you ordered breakfast, you were looking at the pictures, not the text." He put up a hand to forestall a protest. "Hardly definitive, I know. But I've seen quite a few cases like this lately. I made an informed guess. There are a couple of people who I believe are now fit for duty who couldn't even understand the pictures when they first awoke. Including myself."

"It wears off?"

"Somewhat."

That was less than reassuring.

Dan suddenly remembered how to survive a winter storm in Boston. You parked your car, which for some reason was a beige 1964 Dodge Dart, with the front wheels facing in to the curb. Then you removed the rear wheels. Then you put four by six beams in front of the front wheels. Then you could get on your bike and ride off to the East End with the other kids.

Vargas blinked furiously. He'd never been to Boston in his life, and had only seen pictures of ancient automobiles, and he was pretty sure Boston winter storms weren't all that severe. Not that he had any experience with winter storms, either. In Torreón, a night where it hit ten degrees was considered unbelievably cold, and sometimes you could see a bit of snow on the distant peaks.

Spencer was giving him a quizzical smile. "Judging from the expression on your face, you had what we're calling a 'flash-dream' Everyone is experiencing them. Including me."

"Why are we under thrust? We shouldn't be under thrust." In his own mind, to his shock, he sounded weak and querulous.

"In twenty minutes, you'll be fully informed, Captain. I know this is alarming, but with all due respect, there's nothing that can't wait."

Without asking, Ian stood and fetched the captain another cup of coffee.

He returned to find Vargas staring at one of the Charlies, a floor-cleaner model. "Something wrong, Captain?"

"That Charlie has a face on it."

"Oh." Spencer badly suppressed a grin. "They all do. It was one of those 'entertain-the-crew' projects you instigated with your nature tape. Along about five years ago, someone hit on the idea of printing images of each of the crew from the data log onto sticky back transparencies and putting them on the Charlies. There were one hundred and fifty Charlies and the same number of crew members, so everyone got one."

Vargas stared at the Charlie, which, disconcertingly, stared back. "That looks more like a painting then a printout."

Spencer peered at the floor-cleaner, which ignored him. "It is painted. Crewman Steele's work, I believe. Some people have taken up painting their own Charlies as vanity projects, or painting other crew members' Charlies as favors or gifts. I guess about a quarter of them are painted."

"I see. I think. And would I be correct in assuming that I'll encounter more projects like this around the ship." Vargas' expression was bemused, rather than annoyed.

"You would be correct, Ser. Nothing detrimental to the ship or us. Six people at a time usually provide enough social braking to prevent the more egregious abandonments of perspicacity."

"In English, please?"

"Common sense prevails. Captain, I suggest a quick stop at your cabin. You'll probably feel more on top of things once in uniform." Dan doubted that, but saw no need to argue the point.

* * *

The bridge mess was taking on the role of Captain's post for the occasion. Most of the line officers there, including Sheffield.

Face stolid, he masked the perturbed realization that he didn't recognize more than half the faces.

Sheffield stood up, and the rest followed. Snapping off a salute, Sheffield said, "I stand ready to be relieved, Ser." The rest of the group exchanged glances, and saluted. Sheffield had given him a Royal Europe Army salute; other variants included Americanish, African, and a gesture from Doctor Trapp that was more of a friendly wave than a salute. Vargas tried to remember if saluting was normal protocol here. He was inclined to doubt that it was.

"I relieve you, Commander."

Vargas gestured and people sat. Sheffield remained standing. "Due to temporary confusion we have all experienced as a result of hibernation, I suggest we take turns going around the table and introducing ourselves."

Vargas felt a gust of relief. Several people at the table had their data pads out, recording. Standing order permitted it if the recording was open and with the tacit consent of the commanding officer.

"Commander Sean Sheffield, second-in-command, RESS *Phoenix*, late of His Majesty's Royal Army."

"Doctor Ian Spencer, Chief psychologist."

"Commander Alan Trapp, Chief Medical Officer"

"Commander Apunda Boitumelo, Chief Engineer"

"Commander Madelyne Isaakson"

"Lieutenant Commander Etienne Sorlund, Chief Navigations Officer"

"Chief Petty Officer Nate Harlen, crew chief"

"Commander Gordon Lassiter, Chief Technical Officer"

This brought it around to Dan. "Captain Daniel Vargas, Ship's Master" For some reason Dan thought of a nineteenth century frigate.

Two of the people at the table jumped to their feet, and then looked around, confused. Vargas thought that he had better find the ship's Protocols regarding rank, and soon. These people were so confused they would be saluting Charlies next.

"At ease," Vargas said dryly. "I understand that most of the ship's complement are suffering from cognitive dysfunctions of one sort or another, and realize that some of you simply did not recognize me. I would be less than candid if I didn't say that I needed that round of introductions."

"Commander Boitumelo, I'm pleased to see you've recovered from your injuries."

The tall engineer gave Vargas a perplexed look. "Um, what injuries, Captain?"

In the awkward silence, Trapp spoke. "Commander, I'll fill you in later. Our departure did not go smoothly." He glanced around, saw several puzzled faces. "If you don't know what I'm talking about, come see me after the meeting and I'll bring you up to speed. And don't worry: I didn't remember it when I first woke up, either."

Right, Vargas thought. Somebody fired nukes at us. How odd.

Vargas looked around the table. All of them except Sheffield and Boitumelo had hair on their heads, indicating they had all pulled at least one stint since launch. Hair didn't grow in the pods. It resumed upon wakening and nobody knew why. Presumably it was part of whatever it was that effectively stopped the aging process. It was just another unknown about hibernation that could have done with a bit more investigation.

Sheffield reported first, reading from his pad. "Sixteen people have declined in hibernation and were pulled for their own safety. Another sixteen were shift workers who refused to go back into hibernation, stating they feared further damage to their cognition." He glanced down at the notes on his pad. "And of course the line officers are now awake so we can try and deal with this situation.

"How did you deal with the people who refused to go back in their pods, Commander?"

Sheffield shrugged. "I've only been out of hibernation for about 72 hours. Ask Doctor Spencer."

Vargas gave the psychiatrist an inquiring glance.

"Well, I couldn't just order them back, could I? I listened to them, and told them we were working on solutions."

Vargas nodded, wondering what solutions were available.

Sheffield glowered. "I'll note that at this point, none of the line people other than Doctor Spencer have much experience with the situation. You were all awakened in the past day, so if you don't seem to be quite on top of things, that's why. "

"We'll remedy that, Number One." Vargas looked around the table, projecting a confidence he didn't actually feel. "Doctor Trapp, what was your experience with hibernation problems back on Earth?"

The chief of Medical shifted in his chair uncertainly. "I'm afraid I'm having a little trouble recollecting. . . "

Vargas made a placating motion. "I understand, Doctor. I was trying to recollect what I was told about it, too." He suddenly pounded the table. "Damn! This is like trying to swim in cotton candy!" He glared at Spencer, spread his fingers. "How do we function? How are we supposed to solve this when the tools we need are taken away from us?"

Vargas' glare moved around the table. Sheffield was scowling, Trapp was tight-lipped and projecting his patented avuncular disapproval. Several of the others looked openly appalled. Vargas took a deep breath, realizing the possible damage he had just done to morale. "People, we're the best Earth could find to do this job. We'll work through this." Nobody looked convinced.

"Captain? May I suggest adjourning so everyone can go out and talk to crew members and get a better understanding of the situation?"

Vargas scanned the faces, considering Spencer's suggestion. It was obvious that no one was enthusiastic about discussing the situation. The psychiatrist probably realized most of the complement needed some private time to process the situation. "We'll do that in a few minutes, but there are a couple of things we can address right now. First. The ship is under power. I would like to know why. Doctor Spencer?"

"It was at my order, Ser. Zero gravity was adding to the stress of the insomniacs, and some of them were refusing to use the exercise wheels anyway. I decided a little gravity was far better than none at all."

"And in what direction is the ship accelerating?"

"It's actually decelerating, Ser. We did turn around yesterday. We had been running one twentieth Gee for about three weeks prior, in order to accommodate people, but the physicist. . . " Spencer snapped his fingers, "Doctor Simmons, said that we were approaching 88% speed of light, and some gravitational anomalies were appearing around the ship. I admit I don't understand what he meant by that, but he said we were going too fast for safety."

Vargas spoke to his data pad. "Talk to Simmons. Grav flux?" That might be important. Vargas reminded himself that they were already going over a hundred times faster than any other man-made object and massed more than all other objects man had put into space combined. "Right. So we're engaged in negative acceleration at. . . what, fifty centimeters per second squared? Someone calculate how much time that will add to the journey."

Sorlund, the chief navigator was first. "It will add. . . oh, I see." He looked up, grinning. "We'll stop approaching *nu Phoenicis* about four light years short of the destination."

"OK. Everyone, think about what we can do about that. Obviously a few weeks won't make that much difference. . . no, Mr. Sorlund, I don't need to know how much right now. . . but it's not a tenable situation. The idea is to actually get to the *nu Phoenicis* system."

Boitumelo raised her left arm in a curious gesture, tight-fisted and flat across her throat. Vargas remembered this was a signal to speak in Gabon. Her face was stern. "Yes?"

"Doctor Spencer would not know this, of course, but the stresses involved in starting and stopping the main engine inflict considerable strain on the parts that we would have the most difficulty in replacing. I urge very strongly that we cease this right away and return to the original flight plan. There is a risk we could strand ourselves." Vargas saw Spencer's eyes widen.

"Mister Sorlund, find out exactly what has been done here and get us back on a proper course. Commander Boitumelo, check to make sure the engine is operating well." Scotty was angry. Vargas hoped she wouldn't dismember the psychiatrist over it. The fusion engine was designed to run for years at a time, but not at 5% power. Worse, the "spark" needed to ignite the fusion process involved 16 eight petawatt lasers. Ignition was the most likely moment for major component fail.

"OK. How many here feel they can function on a basic level? I'm not talking command decisions. I mean, how many of you can just get out, talk to people, learn the situation a bit better?"

All seven raised their hands, although several did so with obvious hesitation.

"Does anyone have anything that requires our immediate attention? Anything to report on ship status?"

Sheffield spoke up. "Everything is nominal. Except the crew."

"Let's meet here in twenty four hours, and compare notes."

Chapter 9 Étude In The Mess

VARGAS ELECTED TO GO WITH SPENCER TO THE MESS HALL.

"Doctor, just looking at you, I would say you've been awake for over a year. Would that be correct?

Spencer unconsciously stroked his beard. "One year this time. Two years out of the past seven."

Vargas stumbled slightly in the light gravity, shocked. "You've been awake for two years?"

"I was on shift six. We were in free flight, and things were going smoothly. The previous shift had the first insomniac, and he was making a good recovery. The crew spotted the trouble signals early, and when he was brought out, he was in fairly good shape emotionally and physically, although he reported being troubled by vivid dreams. We were all experiencing flash dreams at that point, but it was easy to dismiss them as the sort of rogue, unbidden thoughts we all have from time to time. I felt fuzzy and disoriented, and knew there were gaps in my memory, but hoped it would abate during the shift. It did, but not by a lot. Everyone else reported similar symptoms. I left an order in ship's log to reawaken me if subsequent shifts had aggravated symptoms."

Vargas eyed Spencer. He knew a CYA directive when he heard one. The psychiatrist had told the crew to do exactly what they were already supposed to do. Still, Spencer would be anxious to show he was doing his duty as best he knew how.

"The second awakening was four years on. That's when crew started feeling disoriented and twingy on awakening, and when they realized they were all feeling that way, they woke me to discuss it. I was a mess, but could see things had gotten worse."

"'Twingy'?"

Spencer smiled mirthlessly. "One of my patients at Bristol Clinical came up with that. He used to dabble in. . . ah, recreational hallucinogens, and that was the term he used to describe his state of mind the next day. He would feel jumpy and jittery, although apparently not in an unpleasant way. He found his thoughts would have little bursts of static, and he would be physically and emotionally jumpy. He claimed to enjoy it, although of course, he knew the symptoms would be gone the next day."

"I see. I think. Never did hallucinogens myself."

"No, you don't seem the sort. I felt like that myself when first awakened. It was about a week before I felt I was being useful to the crew. Of course, by then, most had partially recovered. So I made sure they entered a full description of their experiences in both the ship and crew logs, so the next shift would get fair warning and an explanation, and went back in my pod. Mind you, I barely remember any of this, and most of what I know came from notes I recited at the time." Spencer gave Vargas a rueful grin. "Those notes showed I was seriously faking it, and had lost most of the diagnostic tools that I spent all those years learning. My notes had such profundities as 'Patient is acting a bit weird.'" The grin widened. "I was unfit for duty, but who was going to say so and order me to stand down?"

"They woke me at the start of the next shift, and I felt slightly better, and helped to orientate the new wakers and teach them how to orientate the ones to come after. We discovered that iteration of familiar tasks was helpful, along with playing familiar and well liked songs—fortunately, nearly everyone has those on his data pad, so finding them wasn't hard, even when the crewman couldn't remember for himself what they were. I made sure that nobody became isolated, and basically kicked people out of their cabins to join group activities."

He arched an eyebrow at Vargas. "Most of that I do remember first hand."

"The fourth time I seriously thought about waking you. The symptoms of new wakers were getting more severe, and people were seriously frightened. Many couldn't read, or remember basic facts about their lives. As you've learned, that's a very disquieting sensation.

"I was able to quell some of the alarm by pointing out that I had personally been wakened four times, and that it seemed to be getting easier each time; certainly I wasn't in as bad a shape. Reading my own log, I saw I was troubled that I couldn't remember my Alma Mater, University of Bristol on the second go-around." Spencer gave Vargas a look that feel half way between someone delivering a punch line and someone admitting to his spouse that he had forgotten their anniversary. "Imagine my surprise to learn that I taught there for three years, and would have had tenure except I joined this mission."

"You had to look that up?"

"Yes, but when I woke up the next time, I knew it. And this time, as well. Now I remember stuff that isn't in my CV, such as the names of my best students and who my colleagues were.

"I've been able to keep the situation fairly static, working out a treatment regimen for each new generation of wakers, keeping the insomniacs productive as possible, and training Ann Forster to spell me. I spent most of my time devising games and tools to help people recreate abilities and skills that they had lost. Some of them are pretty . . . elemental, so don't be shocked at what you see. Up until now, we've been able to treat it as a purely medical problem. At the start of shift six months ago, we had twenty five insomniacs, and four refuseniks, including Ann. That was considered optimal. In fact, the only things that we didn't expect were the flash dreams and the twingies. And the disorientation everyone was experiencing."

"Refuseniks?"

"That's what one of the Russian crew members called them, and the name stuck. Apparently it's actually an old slang expression from your country, indicating people who refused to be drafted. Now it means people who refuse to return to the hibernation pods."

"And it never occurred to you during all that time to wake the line officers?"

"Of course it did, Captain. But I knew Sheffield was due to be wakened this shift, and Ann and the other three refuseniks were considering petitioning him to simply end the rotations and let the refuseniks pull a fourteen-year shift for the second half of the journey."

"I don't see how he could have done that unilaterally, even if he was willing."

Spencer shook his head. "Nor do I, Captain, but I know it wasn't a decision I could make. Although I don't believe Commander Sheffield would have been amused at the demand. That also factored in my decision to have you awakened the same day as Commander Sheffield."

"Bloody hell."

"Captain?"

"If this were a military ship. . . well, this is sheer fuckuppery. You should have woken me long before now. You know that, don't you?"

"No, Captain, I don't know that." Spencer's voice became very clipped, and very British. "My actions were in line with my duties as ranking medical officer, and defensible." He wheeled and faced the captain angrily. "Six months ago, we had ten people disabled by hibernation. That is exactly what we expected, and part of my normal duties was to treat them as best I could, and enroll crew members to assist and take over that training. That is what I did.

"In the past six months, we had six more people who had to be pulled from hibernation. And we got six more refuseniks, all in the past two weeks. The entire 25th shift."

Vargas glowered. "You should have woken me or Sheffield."

"I have. Captain. Frankly, now that you are awake, I don't see the situation improving."

Vargas rushed the psychiatrist, lifted him by the front of his tunic at high as his arm could extend and slammed him up against the bulkhead, fist reared back. His fist wavered as Vargas realized that lifting the doctor three feet off the ground, easily done in the partial gravity, left him with few targets he was willing to strike. It would have been an unequal fight; Vargas was trained in hand to hand; the thin civilian psychiatrist was more accustomed to the sorts of dogfights one found in academia.

Spencer looked down at him with a level, calm stare. "Captain, do you really think I've said something to warrant striking me? Think carefully, Captain Daniel Vargas. Is this something you might normally do to a civilian member of your crew?"

Vargas swung his head left, right to see if anyone was witnessing them. Then, with a snarl, he released Spencer and stepped back. The psychiatrist floated leisurely to the ground, making him look more dignified than he probably felt. His fingers twitched, a reflexive impulse to brush the front of his tunic. Realizing his fist was still clenched, Vargas forced himself to step back. Spencer landed slightly awkwardly, since they were still both moving along the corridor when Vargas grabbed him and the laws of inertia kept them going during the brief fight.

"Daniel."

Vargas started, surprised by the use of his first name.

"Daniel," Spencer repeated softly, "we're all affected by this. I apologize. What I said wasn't fair. We're being asked to make decisions and set policy, and the very tools we need to do so have been taken from us. I have a further advantage in that I've had two years to consider matters, whilst you've had a few hours."

"You're right, of course. You know, I think that's the first time I've made a fist in anger at anyone since grade school." Vargas drew his mouth into a thin line. "Is everyone like this?"

"Mostly. We've had to break up some scuffles. Nobody hurt, and we didn't punish anyone, but even without the twingies and flash-dreams, people are frightened and feel that they are in a bad place. It's a situation that lends itself to violent reactions. Fortunately, as you doubtlessly just noticed, low gravity doesn't lend itself to street brawls."

"You don't seem...I don't know. As confused?" Vargas gave Spencer an almost beseeching look.

Spencer had the expression of someone having to repeat himself. "After the second time, I noticed it was getting easier to deal with most of the effects."

Vargas stared at the doctor, his anger forgotten. "It gets easier after the second time? That seems counter-intuitive. Could it be that you've spent less time in hibernation between awakenings?"

Spencer's expression was patient and earnest. "Maybe. For me, the second was the worst, and the next ones were much easier. I think I've got most of my deficits resolved. The second time, I was flying off the handle at people, and as a psychiatrist, that's the very worst thing you can do."

Vargas managed a rueful grin. "It's not a well-regarded trait in captains, either."

Spencer nodded at the implied apology.

As they approached the mess hall, Vargas spotted a mural running along both sides of the corridor. It portrayed the planets of the solar system, four on a side. The orbs were all of a like size, Mercury the same size as Jupiter. Vargas toe-tapped to a stop and regarded the art. "I authorized this, didn't I?"

"I think so. Ian Mann's work. He was on first shift with you, as I recall. There's other art on bulkheads around the ship. For the most part, it's reasonably restrained."

Vargas shook his head admiringly. *Phoenix*, whatever else she might be, was not a standard military vessel.

The two men roo-hopped into the mess hall. The scene was little changed from two hours earlier.

Vargas noticed that several people were reading text on the tables in front of them. Craning his head as he passed, he saw that one was working to solve a Sudoku puzzle, and another, to his shock, was playing a screen version of a preschool training game to match the appropriate 'peg' to a similarly shaped hole. Peering at the game, Vargas felt a rush of intellectual vertigo. He wasn't sure he knew which peg went in the triangular hole.

Keeping his face frozen, hiding his rising sense of panic, Vargas looked around. "I want to talk to these people."

Spencer looked around, leaned closer. "Do you want straight answers, or the sort of answers people give to the Captain?"

Vargas blinked at the psychiatrist, puzzled. "Are you saying they'll lie to me if they know I'm the Captain?"

"Not lie, exactly. But they'll gravitate toward the role of subordinate crew member rather than patient or just acquaintance."

Vargas sucked on his cheeks. "Hmm. I see. I think. If they ask who I am. . . ?"

"By all means, tell them. If they recognize you, they are likely to be less impaired. You need to factor that in, too."

Vargas sighed. "They don't teach about this in Officers Training School." He remembered attending OTS. Vaguely. The pink peg goes in the triangular hole. Right. That was it. He relaxed slightly.

"That's why I'm here. They do teach about it in psych courses. Of course, they are thinking of individual patients and not large groups of people." Spencer lowered his voice to a whisper. "Whether they recognize you or not, keep your voice quiet and calm, use their names as soon as you have them, and if they want to talk, let them."

Vargas nodded,. "Who goes first?"

Spencer peered about, considering. "Her." He pointed to a blond-haired woman, one of the few in a ship's tunic, who was sitting on one of the tables in a lotus position palms upward. As the two men approached, her eyes turned to them, focused, and she gave a tentative smile. "Good morning, doctors."

"Good morning, Susan. How are you feeling this morning?"

"Better, I think. I woke up and remembered a dream I had about a dog I had as a little girl. We named him Happy. He was a retriever. Does that mean I'm improving?"

Spencer gave her a warm smile. "It's as I said, Susan. You'll get a little bit back at a time. Do you remember my name?"

Susan had a slightly condescending look. "You're Ian Spencer. You're the ship shrink."

Spencer chuckled. "That's right." He nodded at her crossed legs. "Are the meditations helping?"

"I think so. Thanks for helping me to remember how to work my data pad. I've been reading my entries. Apparently I meditated a lot before. . . well, before this."

"From what some of the other people here have told me, that bit of info is what we in the shrink trade call a 'trigger memory.' Learning that you used to meditate brings back recollections of how you used to meditate, and why. Is that what you're experiencing?"

Susan's eyes widened, which was answer enough. Spencer nodded reassuringly. "You're improving."

"So Doc, who's your friend? I don't recall seeing his face on any of the Charlies."

Both men tried to avoid looking uncomfortable, failed. "Susan, this is Captain Vargas."

"Oh, shi...golly. Captain, I'm so sorry. . . "

Vargas held up a hand. "It's all right, Ms. Bartlett. Apparently we're all having that problem. I'm glad to hear you're getting better."

As the two men bounced away in the five percent gravity, Spencer glanced at Vargas. "Did you notice you used Lt. Bartlett's last name?"

"I did. Once I had her first name, I knew her. She's in coms. Served with distinction in the Army, I recall."

"That's what gives me optimism. Memories often just need a trigger to restore function. You watch a few minutes of a video, and realize you've seen that show before, even if you didn't remember the plot or any of the actors. But someone says something or does something, and suddenly it all comes back to you."

"I'm still surprised she didn't recognize me." Vargas nodded at the Captain's insignia on his data pad. "What does she think all these stripes are for?"

"That you're auditioning for a toothpaste ad? Captain, my guess is that she was reading the visual cues of our interaction. When we approached, I was slightly ahead of you, clearly leading you. From that, she concluded that you were my subordinate. Maybe even my personal aide. Look, you're still doing it."

Vargas made as if to accelerate his pace, and stopped, stymied. "Well, you are leading me. To the next interviewee."

"I'll point him out to you as we approach." The two men exchanged an amused glance. The situation was both silly and perverse.

"So in the long run, this might not be as bad as it looks?"

"That's what I'm most fervently hoping, Captain." Spencer lowered his voice, even though no one was near. "We're nearly at the point where I would say the mission was compromised. My main concern is the number of insomniacs we're racking up."

Vargas decided not to mention that if the mission was hopelessly compromised, they had little choice but to continue forward, blindly. They couldn't go back, and they couldn't stay put. It wasn't something he wanted to think about himself.

"Was Bartlett one of those?"

"No, she's a refusenik. She woke up not knowing how to operate her com station, and it frightened her badly . She's been awake since the start of last shift, a little over six months. As you might have guessed, she's a lot calmer and more confident now."

"Does the meditation really help?:

Spencer shrugged. "Who's to say? She thinks it does, so it does. It's certainly not doing any harm."

"At the risk of sounding petty, is there really no Charlie with my face on it?"

Spencer considered. "I've haven't seen one, Captain. Of course, I doubt I've seen most of them. A lot of them are in places I have no reason to go."

"I think they get assigned tasks randomly. They aren't normally specialized; a specific unique task is going to require human workers, if you want to stay space-worthy. I'll have to ask the Charliemeister. . . um, as soon as I remember who he is. But let me ask you this: a lot of the disorientation I'm feeling comes from simply not being able to recognize people. Is it safe to say that's true for just about everyone else?"

"Absolutely."

"OK. I'll cut orders for a detail to corral all the Charlies, and on each one, paint the name and rank corresponding to each face."

"Um, what if your detail don't know who the faces belong to?"

"The entire crew is in the public data available on pads. In fact, I bet that's where all the printed faces came from. Crew will just have to match faces to names."

"How closely do people resemble their official images? Most had hair when the pictures were taken."

Vargas ignored the objection, and placed the order into his captain's log.

"Doctor, could I talk to one of the insomniacs?"

Spencer glanced around the room. "Over there. At the piano."

"How'd that piano get here? It was in the bridge mess."

"On my authority. I felt music might help, especially if some of the people could create their own entertainment. I'm afraid to say it hasn't been utilized much."

Vargas started to ask how the piano was secured, since it wasn't an object you wanted flying around during zero-gravity maneuvers. Then he remembered it had been situated there in the first place, and he and four other crew members and grunted and sweated and hauled it to the bridge mess themselves. One-twentieth gravity would have been nice.

The young woman with the short chestnut hair did not greet them as they approached. Only the slightest flicker of her eyes indicated she was even aware of them. Vargas noted that her face might be beautiful if it were animated. Heart-shaped with high cheeks, brown eyes. . .

Spencer leaned down. "Julie? Julie, this is Doctor Spencer. Can you say hello?"

The woman's lips moved, but no sound emerged. "Julie, this is Captain Vargas. Do you remember him?"

No response.

"What's her story, Doctor?"

Spencer frowned slightly at the captain and tapped an ear. *She's right here and she can hear us.* He turned to her.

"Julie, do you mind if I discuss your circumstances with the Captain? He wants to help you."

This time, her eyes darted to Vargas, and then to Spencer. She gave a slow nod.

"Julie was on first shift fourteen years ago."

Startled, Vargas stared at the girl. Julie. He remembered her now. Warm, but a bit reserved, a Londoner. Played the piano beautifully. Oh, shit, Julie. . .

Spencer continued, "About two months ago her readings took a sharp turn for the worse, and she was brought out of hibernation. She appears to be suffering from severe depression, and has been verbally uncommunicative. We have been unable to determine much beyond that, but we're working on that, aren't we, Julie?"

Spencer's eyes didn't reflect the upbeat tone in his voice.

"Julie, do you know where you are?"

No response.

"Julie, can you look at me?"

Her eyelids fluttered slightly.

"Julie, is there anything you would like?"

No response.

Then Vargas knew what she would like.

Vargas thought for a moment, dredging memories up from late childhood, and visualized the opening notes to Beethoven's Fifth. He studied the piano keyboard for a moment, remembering the Morse-Victory sequence he had played a hundred times as a kid. He reached around Julie, and with one finger, played the sequence. He missed the last note by a key, but it was still recognizable.

Julie's eyes darted to the keyboard, and then up to Vargas' face. She looked almost as if she wanted to say something. Then her eyes lost focus, and she settled back into staring at the bulkhead beyond the piano.

Spencer was nodding slowly. "Interesting. Julie, do you play the piano?"

Vargas nodded. "She is an excellent piano player. She was..." Vargas stopped, frustrated. "She said something about the piano once. Damn!"

"It'll come to you. I wonder if anyone around here remembers how to play the piano?"

"I'm pretty sure I used to. We've got lots of piano music in the database. In fact..." Vargas stepped around to the side of the piano. "Ah ha!"

"What?"

"This is a player piano. You see the data connect here? It can access any music you want it to play." He pulled the connect cable from his data pad and plugged it into another port in the piano, and studied the menu. He stopped in frustration. "Doctor, give me a hand here. Follow this path. Music. Piano. Pieces." Spencer leaned in and tapped the appropriate choices. "Oh, I know this one!" Vargas, grateful that his reading impairment didn't seem to apply to proper nouns, picked Gymnopédie No.1 by Erik Satie, and, remembering where the command had to be even if he couldn't understand the word, hit 'play.'

It was a good choice. Somber and slow, measured and quiet. The piano started to play, the keys depressing to match the sequence of notes. Julie stared in fascination. After a moment, she brought her hands up, and her fingers made tentative, ghostly motions, relearning the sequence of the notes.

Spencer leaned down for a better look at her face. Tears were streaming down her cheeks, but she was smiling. He straightened up and asked quietly, "May I use your pad again?" At Vargas' nod, he punched in a complicated series of options. "There." He smiled. "It'll play various piano pieces for the next hour or so. We'll come back in a bit and see how she's doing."

After bidding good day to Julie — who ignored them — they roo-sauntered toward the front of the mess. "You missed your calling, Captain. You should have been a therapist."

Vargas laughed, for the first time since he awoke. "It's a part of my job duties already."

"You were struggling with your data pad, I noticed. Still having trouble reading English?"

"Yeah. I can make out names, though. Spanish isn't a problem. Maybe I should just tell the data pad . . . oh, wait. I don't know how to do that."

"You don't need to. It's got a visually impaired feature. Just cursor over each command and it will tell you what it is, and you can select the one you want. It looks like you can still navigate that thing."

"Of course. Why didn't I think of that? And I've got an ear bud in my cabin."

"It's probably got a translator function, too, but I think it's going to be more productive if you look at the words and hear them sounded out. After all, it's probably how you learned to read the first time around." Spencer gave Vargas his best reassuring grin. "And it will go a lot faster. The knowledge you have isn't destroyed; you just have to re-learn how to access it. This will do that."

Vargas paused at the port and glanced back at Julie. She was staring at the keyboard intently, her hands dancing inches above the ivories. Dimly, he could hear the Moonlight Sonata. "She seems to be picking it up fast. What music pieces did you select?"

"Something called 'Classic Piano pieces, 1742-2218'. It has about forty short pieces. That should engage her. She'll have setbacks, as do all of us—including you, so expect them and don't be dismayed when they happen. But I think your little breakthrough today means we can start to consider taking her off the confined list."

"Confined? She didn't look confined."

"She isn't in here, where people can watch. But I felt she was a possible threat to herself when left alone, so she was spending time confined to a line cabin and watched. Just to be safe, we'll give it a few days. But she smiled, and that's huge."

Vargas grinned like a fool. He wasn't sure why he felt so proud at the praise, but he did.

"A pity you're the only person on board who's awakened more than twice. If we had just two others, that would go a long way toward telling us if what you experienced is typical or not."

"We do have two people who have been awakened three times in the past six months. You're about to meet one of them. Günther Brülow."

"One of the maintenance people?"

"Right. Once we're on ground, he'll be a soil analyst, and then he's signed up to explore the planet."

"And you appealed to the same instincts that make him want to be an explorer."

"More or less. I kept pointing out to him that I had been through five awakenings – six actually, since I spent three days in hibernation on Earth – and that it was getting better for me each time. So he went in, as did Adalena Conti."

"Biologist?"

"Microbiologist. Both crew members, of course. I didn't feel comfortable soliciting volunteers from the insomniacs, although I want to. Both were on their second shift, and both were very unhappy with their status."

"But I'll let Günther tell his story."

Chapter 10 Günther's Tale

GÜNTHER KNEW HE WOULD RECOGNIZE THE CAPTAIN even if he didn't notice the data pad insignia. Identifying people seemed to be getting easier as time went on, and he felt calmer after four awakenings.

He wondered if he should mention the fleeting daytime dreams in front of the Captain. They didn't really affect his duties, which amounted to little more than checking forty pods for four hours a day. But he didn't want the Captain to wonder if Günther was dependable. The middie, blond-haired, blue-eyed, and determined to be the best on board at his job, was annoyed at his ethnic stereotype even as he strove to live up to it.

The Captain. He hibernated, too. He doubtless had flash dreams, too. Günther decided the best thing for it was to be straightforward if asked about it.

He finished checking pod #1034, a colonist named Rebekah Cohen. She was the twenty-ninth pod Günther had checked that day. The readouts were all nominal, and Rebekah would sleep until her next inspection in ten days. He glanced at the readout again. She was due to have a six month shift in about seventeen months. Hopefully the ship wouldn't be flooded with insomniacs, and she wouldn't be one of them.

Heedless of Günther's wordless benediction, Rebekah slept on. Rebekah dreamt.

Günther greeted the two line officers with a friendly nod. His own stint in the European military was in engineering, and salutes and other military clap-trap were reserved for the silly bunts from HQ who strutted through the engineering area and pretended to understand what all the gizmos did. The relative informality of a civilian ship suited him. Typical of his breed, he took his work seriously, the chain of command not so much.

Spencer wasted little time on small talk. "Captain, this is Günther Brülow. Günther, could you please tell the Captain your experiences with multiple awakenings?"

Ye gods, Günther thought. He noticed a look of faint relief on Vargas' face and realized the intro wasn't for his benefit, but the Captain's. Hibernation syndrome, then.

Günther rubbed his nose thoughtfully, hiding his alarm. He didn't want to condescend, but he better not assume the Cap was on the top of his game. He glanced at Vargas, who was eying the white hibernation pods arrayed around them with...distaste? Resentment? Günther could sympathize. Nobody looked at those damn pods the same way anymore.

"It's easier each time after the second time, Cap'n. This is my fourth. I still get those crazy dream images, and my brain feels like there's a sparkler going off in it sometimes. My memory doesn't have any noticeable gaps, and the stuff I need to function is back."

"I find that personally reassuring Mr. Brülow. I'm delighted to hear that you are back on form. But tell me; how did you get Dr. Spencer here to convince you to go back into your pod?"

Günther chuckled. "It took some doin'. We'd been kinda dancing around about it for a couple of weeks, and he was turning himself inside out trying to find a diplomatic way of saying I was well and truly fucked, and might as well try returning to the pod because I didn't have shit-all else to lose." With a disarming grin, he glanced over at Spencer "Come on, doc. You know that's what was really going on."

Spencer maintained a carefully neutral expression.

In any event, Captain, it finally occurred to me that I had been thinking about suicide. I was a mechanic who couldn't remember which way a screw turned to loosen, and a soil analyst who couldn't remember what a pH balance was. I felt useless because I was useless, and here was the doc telling me he used to be useless too."

"You know how to do those things now? Tighten a screw, determine alkalinity?" Vargas' easy smile robbed the words of any possible sting.

Spencer looked slightly startled. Vargas said, "What? I haven't forgotten everything, right?"

Günther nodded. "Captain, one thing I noticed talking to people is that they usually forgot how to do their jobs, but still had a good idea how to do other stuff that wasn't immediately important to them. I could still play the guitar, and knew how to play poker, even though I haven't done either since before I went into training."

"Why is that, do you suppose?"

"Doc, I was hoping you might be able to tell us."

"It's an interesting insight. I'll follow up on it."

"So you decided you had nothing to lose and went back in the pod." Vargas cocked an eyebrow at the middie and nodded. "That took guts."

Spencer shifted uncomfortably. Günther gave him an easy grin.

"Doctor. I know you were trying to help. I just had to put it in terms that would motivate me. It wasn't what you intended, but it worked."

Vargas saw the psychiatrist's eyebrow twitch. Sometimes you took your victories where you could find them. He could sympathize.

* * *

Doctor Alan Trapp stood behind his large mahogany desk, beaming affably. Nodding back in a friendly manner, Vargas let his eyes rove around the Doctor's office. He'd heard that it was the most lavishly appointed cabin on the ship, and he could see why. Designed to resemble the room of a successful physician from the early twentieth century, it featured an old style standing weight scale (pointless in .05 gravity) and an old fashioned Regulator clock whose innards must be electronic since a pendulum clock would also be useless in this gravity. A large globe stood next to the desk, one from the 'The Sun Never Sets' era of Victorian England. The library of books behind Doctor Trapp and the shelves of ointments and other mysteries were almost surely screen images of same, but convincing enough. The air had a faint scent of iodine.

"Libations?" Trapp boomed. Vargas had to marvel; fresh from hibernation and having only a five o'clock shadow where normally there was a full beard and flowing gray locks, Trapp looked serene, confident, and enormously competent.

"Juice, Orange if you have it." Vargas replied.

"Juice for me, too," Spencer seconded.

"Ah. This is a serious meeting, then." Trapp's beam, if anything, widened. He murmured into his data pad, and moments later a small panel opened, and Trapp pulled out three drinking bulbs with orange juice.

There was an awkward silence as each of the three men tried to think of small talk and were stymied. Spencer, the first to realize the problem, spoke up. "Captain, I believe you had something you wanted to ask us?"

Vargas felt a burst of gratitude. "Yes. Doctors. You both have degrees in medical science. Where did you go to college?"

Trapp looked disconcerted and considered, finger tapping his lower lip. Then he focused, an expression of delight on his face. "University of Auckland."

"Royal College of Surgeons, Edinburgh" Spencer answered in a more conventional matter.

"Tell me, did your studies include..."Vargas glanced at his data pad, "'The neurophysiology of cybernetic implants'?"

Trapp looked confused. Spencer retorted, "Of course not! We had plenty to learn without playing around with banned technology."

"It's banned?"

"Yes Captain. Since 2075. I believe it's still a capital crime to employ it on a human being in your country."

"Really?"

"Really. The Flare put an end to that branch of science."

"I was reading in the Library that cyberimplants were used to great effect in patients who had memory and cognitive issues. I know you have your own line of treatment you want to pursue, but should we consider cyberimplants as an alternative treatment?

"Absolutely not, Captain."

Trapp, smile gone, spoke slowly. "I remember now. Everyone with an implant got sick or died. The dead ones were lucky. Madness, intractable pain..."

"That's why it's banned. About 15 million people died outright during the Flare, and the Vast Depression that followed killed over a billion. Economic collapse, hundreds of millions of maimed..." Spencer tailed off, remembering that in old America, they simply euthanized the survivors of the Flare. Few Americaners wanted to talk about that time in their history, and Spencer could understand why.

"I understand that, but we're about three light years from the nearest star right now. Are flares a major concern?

"No. But Captain, *nu Phoenicis* is an F8 star, about 4% more variable than Sol. I should think flares will be a problem there."

Vargas looked frustrated. Trapp was expressionless. Spencer expanded. "I'm not one of these types who think implant technology offended God and so he smote us with the Flare as punishment."

Vargas felt his jaw tighten a bit. Many of his neighbors at home believed exactly that. Spencer added, "It's idiotic to assume that any deity would make knowledge available and then punish people for using it. That's like putting a cap on the sidewalk with a rock under it.

"I don't think it was immoral to use such technology." Spencer continued. "This is the twenty-fourth century. If I thought it could help, I wouldn't hesitate to use it."

"Twenty fifth century," Trapp chimed in unexpectedly. Both the others looked at him, mouths agape. He shrugged. "I looked at my data pad to see what time it was in Auckland this morning. It's 2402 back on Earth."

"Well, Happy New Year," Spencer replied, his accent a bit more clipped than usual. "Anyway, Captain, my main problem with cyberimplant technology is that I don't know the first thing about establishing a cyberimplant in a patient. It's something that wasn't taught at Edinburgh—or anywhere else. Banned technology. Tabu."

Vargas cocked an eyebrow at Trapp who slowly shook his head. From his expression, Vargas assumed he didn't know how to install a cyberlink, either.

"I see. Well, Ian, if your idea doesn't work, will you at least think about mine?"

Spencer wore a very odd expression. "Yes, Captain, if my idea doesn't work."

As they were leaving, Vargas saw Trapp's eyes flicker to his data pad and then back to the Captain. The fixed smile never left his face, but the eye-flick spoke volumes. The Chief Medical Officer of the *Phoenix* had understood perhaps one word in four of what Spencer and he had been discussing.

* * *

The mood around the bridge mess table was somewhat less tentative than it had been the previous morning. Sheffield had everyone introduce themselves again, and Vargas noticed some barely-concealed smiles and pleased nods. Everyone either remembered yesterday's introductions, or had spent some time on the crew log getting to learn about their fellow line officers.

"OK, people." Vargas rubbed his hands. "Let's run down what we have. Number one, what are your findings?"

Sheffield made as if to stand, and settled back in his seat at a gesture from Vargas. Standing was difficult in the light gravity since there was a tendency to overbalance. "I did an inspection and analysis of the ship. For a craft that has been underway for thirteen years and got nuked a couple of times at the beginning, RESS *Phoenix* is in remarkably good shape."

A few chuckles echoed around the table.

"The repairs are all holding up, most particularly those to module Fourteen. Logs show the imprinter has been in use for the past thirteen years fairly constantly and, subject to routine maintenance, has performed flawlessly.

"There were concerns that the damage to the thrusters and external cameras might compromise the ship's ability to maneuver., I'm happy to report such restrictions are very limited, and we won't have any problems with orbital insertions once we reach the *nu Phoenicis* system.

"However, we will not reach the system under the present flight regimen." Sheffield grinned. "No offense to anyone around this table, but navigation really should be left to the navigators. We'll come to a complete halt in about sixteen years, subjective, and still be four light years short of our goal. That's assuming we haven't lost our main engine by then."

Sheffield nodded in the direction of Alan Trapp. "Now, I'm sensitive to the fact that we have a medical issue, and it has mandated that the ship be put under minimum acceleration. And I've sat down with Lieutenant Commander Sorlund. . . " another nod, at the Navigation officer, ". . . and tried to determine if there was an optimal solution that would keep the ship under acceleration and still get us to our destination in a reasonable amount of time. I'm sorry to say there is not."

Trapp gave Spencer a look that said very clearly, "Straighten this out. Sheffield thinks this was my idea."

Spencer lifted a finger and Sheffield nodded at him. "How far can we get before we run out of fuel?"

"That's not really a problem, Doctor, as far as the main engines are concerned. The *Phoenix* has a fusion engine. We use water from within the hull to fuel it, but it will eat mass, any mass, it isn't fussy. The *Phoenix* itself could be cannibalized as fuel, and since the one thing we do not lack is mass, it could probably power those engines for a few hundred thousand years." He gave a tight smile as Spencer pulled his head back in astonishment.

"Then what's the problem? What error did I make?"

Sheffield blinked at the psychiatrist. "The problem is that the engine components undergo considerable stress from the process of being shut down and fired up. We violated a lot of design limits just in the way we fired it up for the first time." Boitumelo gave an emphatic nod of agreement.

"That maiden firing probably cut the life-expectancy of several vital components in half. They are rated for a dozen of each, and yes, we have replacement parts, but some of the most vital ones are limited and cannot be recreated without access to raw materials planet side. We had to unexpectedly replace a couple of vital components after our emergency fire-up at Dry Dock, and we don't have the raw materials to replace them. One of the long range plans for a future colony is to mine the materials needed and get them up to the ship so future exploration to other sun systems is possible. In a worst case scenario, if we are stuck in a system with no inhabitable worlds, we hope to at least be able to mine the materials we need.

"I don't need to tell anyone that should the main engine break down with no way to fix it, we would be doomed. Worse, it would probably take us years to die, without hope.

"We can't come up with a minimum number of firings to slow us down, speed us up, maintaining a pseudo gravity, that doesn't involve adding decades to the journey, or which runs the risk of over stressing the engine components.

"Given the sharp increase in the number of failing hibernators, a major increase in the remaining time is no more optimal than risking failure by the main engine.

"There's another issue, and this is one that will certainly cause serious problems. As I'm sure you've realized, turning the ship one hundred and eighty degrees takes nearly a day and a half—longer now, I imagine, with some of the thrusters knocked out."

Spencer angled his head to the side, conceding the point.

"Well, it doesn't run off main engine power. It runs off conventional fuel. Given the mass of this ship, that means a lot of fuel. And we're running low."

Vargas leaned forward. "How low is 'low'?"

"Well, we were hoping to arrive at *nu Phoenicis* with at least ninety five percent of the fuel. We're presently down to forty percent. Now, if we find a planet there that has water we can extract hydrogen and oxygen from, and carbon-based life, it's not a big problem. We can make more fuel. But if we don't, we might not have enough to travel to another star that might. "

There was dead silence. Spencer looked stricken.

"Accordingly, my recommendation is that we return to a velocity of .87c, and use the engines to bring us down to orbital velocity over the final three hundred and sixteen days, as the original flight plan called for. I'm afraid, doctors, that you'll just have to find a way to get your patients to use the centrifuge facilities."

Sheffield looked down at his hands with the air of a man who wasn't expecting to hear any applause.

Vargas noted the gloomy row of faces. "Comments or questions?"

Alan Trapp spoke up. "Would it be possible to rotate the entire ship?"

"Unfortunately, the ship is designed to accelerate only along its Z axis." Seeing a few blank looks, he added, "If we spun the ship, floors would become walls, walls would be ceilings or floors, and everything would be sideways. We would need climbing equipment to get from here to the bridge."

Trapp looked distressed. "So what it comes down to is we either have to compel our patients to exercise, or let them degrade. That, or stuff them back in hibernation against their will."

Spencer spoke up sharply. "That's not a viable option."

Vargas, looking impatient, replied, "No. However, we do have an infirmary on the large wheel. That's six beds. And we can have the ship's maintenance people cobble together a series of sleeping booths. We could probably set it up so one hundred people could sleep and, well, function there. As for exercising, in fact, I do have the authority to order that." Seeing the looks both doctors gave him, he added, "Unless medically contraindicated, of course," he finished lamely.

Lassiter flicked a finger for attention. "One hundred beds. Three hundred occupants. You could have shifts. If people are under gravity just six or seven hours a day, the effects of zero-gravity are highly mitigated."

"A good suggestion, Mr. Lassiter. Doctors?"

"What happens if we end up with more than three hundred insomniacs?" Trapp asked.

"If we have that many people crippled by hibernation syndrome, then the mission is almost certainly going to fail no matter what we do." Vargas looked to the CTO. "Mr. Lassiter, how many of your people are awake and functional at this time?"

"Two awake, neither fully functional. They can walk and scratch their asses, and with great good luck drive a nail without breaking a thumb, but that's about it." He glanced at Madelyne Isaakson, passing the buck. "Mads, how about your people?"

She shook her head. "I'm depending on the Charlies for most routine stuff. Look, I'll be honest here, and suggest you do the same: we aren't capable of bossing a work crew right now. I can't tell a confused carpenter to build an alcove when I don't have the faintest clue what tools and equipment he might need."

"Talk to Spencer here. He can help you with getting you and your men focused. Pull more from hibernation if you need. I need construction on the wheel to begin soonest."

"Ser."

Sheffield coughed, catching Vargas' eye. "One last thing, Captain. I spoke to Tim Simmons, who as you may or may not know has advanced degrees in physics. I told him of the reports of gravitational variances that started manifesting at .89c, and he went and read the ships log notes on it. He came back disturbed, and I'm honestly not sure if it was something totally unexpected, or if it was part of the general theory he had forgotten. He was very adamant that under no circumstances should the *Phoenix* travel at higher than .89c. He said the intensity of the effects appeared to be logarithmic, and he suggested there was a possibility the ship could literally pull itself apart at any speed above .9c. He thinks the mass of the ship plays a role, but he isn't sure exactly how. Having seen some of the anomalies for myself, I'm minded to take him at his word."

Vargas remembered the note in his data pad to ask about that. "What are these anomalies?"

"Well, you'll be walking along a corridor, and suddenly you weigh ten kilos more than you did a moment ago. But a few steps further, and it's like you're in Lunar gravity, and can Moon hop. I thought it was my imagination, or the engine acting up at first, but nobody else was experiencing the same changes in gravity at the same time."

Silence greeted this bit of information. Vargas reflected that it just showed how far beyond any previous human experience they really were.

Vargas went around the table. The rest of ship's operations had little to report, as he expected. Janice Barney, the officer second-in-charge of the Imprinter, had the very good news that the Imprinter was working flawlessly, with no problems from decompression and no radiation problems. He reminded himself to discuss dismantling the Imprinter and dispersing it amongst other modules once they were in orbit. Finally, he turned to the two doctors.

"Doctors, you have the most important items on the agenda. Which of you would like to address this hibernation and disorientation issue first?"

Spencer replied, "I've been examining patients, most of whom had readout degradation while in hibernation. This phenomenon wasn't unknown to us, and was found to be especially acute among young children, which is why we have nobody under the age of puberty on board. We hoped, based on a population of fifteen hundred people, that we might only see fifty such cases over the course of twenty-eight years. I confess that estimate was based on wishful thinking more than anything else. With only periods of a few weeks tested on Earth, the estimate of fifty was based on what we would like to see, rather than what we could expect. We really didn't know what to expect.

"I ran biometrics, sampling personnel who were awake, and had found the same consistent pattern: a low-level "static" in the alpha wave patterns, punctuated at random intervals with brief, larger bursts that are best described as a form of psychomotor epilepsy. Oddly, it didn't appear in the brain patterns of people in hibernation, although there was elevated activity of the wave patterns associated with deep sleep dreaming, something that hadn't manifested in the Earth tests.

"Aside from that, everyone is in excellent health. No colds or other communicable diseases, and physical discomforts are all clearly secondary to the neurophysical problems. For what it's worth, efforts to decontaminate the crew of communicable maladies appears to have been very successful."

We might all turn into shambling zombies, Vargas thought, but at least we won't have the sniffles.

Nate Harlen was thinking along similar lines. "What if the crew is too disabled to fly the ship? Can we put it on automatic pilot so it will at least go into orbit around, um, the star we're going to?"

Trapp, supposing the question was for him, opened and closed his mouth a couple of times. Vargas came to his rescue. "Perhaps Lieutenant Commander Sorlund can answer that."

"Well, in a way, the ship is on autopilot anyway. We'll enter our estimated position, and where we want to go, and the computer will calculate what is needed to arrive at the . . . " He blinked, shook his head.

"Are you alright, Mister Harlen?"

"Yeah. Just one of those damn dreams. Fish on a ladder, something." He shook his head irritably, dismissing the brief vision. Anyway, we'll arrive at the star system at something below escape velocity. Our job during the main part of the flight is just to oversee and to make sure the computer is functioning properly. Which it is, I'm happy to say.

"But if we are so messed up we can't even figure out how to get there, then we're going to have a fun time of it when we try to navigate in the system. Multi-body orbital mechanics, and I can't even remember the equation to determine gravitational force right now."

Deep silence greeted this. Trapp caught Vargas' eye, who nodded toward Spencer.

"Doctor Spencer, you're of the opinion that the symptoms we're experiencing can be mitigated. Would you elaborate on that?"

Heads snapped up around the table at Vargas' words.

Spencer elected to stand up. "As most of you know, I've been out of hibernation off and on over the past six years, and have been taken out of hibernation a total of six times to deal with the same sorts of personal crises you all are experiencing right now.

"I'm also in better shape than the rest of you. There's no obvious gaps remaining in my memory, my professional abilities seem intact."

He spotted a few scowls and added, "I'm not bragging. But the first two times out of hibernation, I couldn't do any of those things. I was at least as lost and confused as you all feel now. If anything, the second time was even worse. I'm not sure, because I don't remember much of it. But the third time I did better, and a I remembered things. I'm still bothered by what the crew are calling "flash dreams" perhaps once or twice a day, and I still feel vaguely jumpy, although not in an unpleasant way.

"Now, I would like to say that I'm in better shape than you because I'm smarter, or just made of better protoplasm. Really, it would just make my day to say that," Spencer concluded as slowly, chuckles traveled around the table.

"But I can't. The fact is, when I woke up the second time, I had no idea who Sigmund Freud was, or why I should make fun of him." By now the chuckles turned to laughter, except for Vargas and Isaakson, who were both probably trying to recollect who Sigmund Freud was. He paused to let the sense of commonality sink in. Yes, we're all in this together.

"The next time I woke up, it was easier. I recognized more of the people, and the time between those annoying flash-dreams was longer. The first time I was up, they told me I was the ship psychiatrist and that they had a mental crisis and I had better start being a psychiatrist, and I'll tell you, I didn't have a clue what that entailed. So I just kept my mouth shut, reserved judgment, and listened carefully to people. I realized later that that was exactly what the ship's psychiatrist was supposed to do, but really, it was pure luck. The next time is when I figured that out. And that was a breakthrough in a different way. Up until then, I had been doing frantic Wiki searches to find out about the people I was talking to—even their names—and reading theories on how to talk back. Realizing the most basic element of my practice was something that occurred to me on my own, without having to restore it from a computer screen. I can't tell you how proud and relieved I felt."

"Each time I was awakened, it was easier." Spencer knew he was repeating himself, understood the need for reiteration. "This last time, I had no trouble recognizing people. I didn't have to look up interview techniques or theory on how to cope with withdrawal and depression. I could remember ship trivia and who was friends with whom on board and how the social order went. It was all there."

"I persuaded a couple of the crew to voluntarily reenter hibernation for a relatively short period and then come out a few times. Both, on the third awakening, reported the same sort of improvement that I experienced. The Captain was kind enough to accompany me today and interview the two crew members. Captain, could you tell us what you found?"

* * *

Keep it casual and easy, Vargas told himself as he scanned the expectant faces. Spencer had given them hope. Now he had to give them resolve. An eighteenth-century sea captain whispered in the back of his mind. "You know how to do this."

He quickly described what he had learned, trying to penetrate the fog of his listeners. "This means that we have reason to believe that contrary to what we all fear, further hibernation and awakening might make us better, rather than worse. We have three cases including Doctor Spencer where that has been tried, and all three report significant improvement.

"Now, three people isn't much, even if one of them is in a better position to understand the psychological effects than anyone else."

Spencer added, "It's a ray of hope. We're going to need to get volunteers, and if we show that there's consistent improvement, then we might persuade others to return. I intend to return to hibernation in the fairly near future and be awoken a few months later, and then perhaps I can see for myself if there is change."

Sheffield spoke up. "Suppose there isn't an improvement. Suppose the three cases we have turned out to be a fluke, and instead of better, you end up in worse shape."

Vargas studied the alarmed looks around the table. "OK, suppose we continue as we have. Each new shift, we have more people waking up who are more and more disorientated, more are becoming refuseniks, and we're getting an increasing number of insomniacs. Morale is down the tubes, and those who aren't flat-out brain-dead are too disoriented and confused to do even the simplest of tasks, let alone pilot the world's biggest ship to a new planet and settle it." Vargas leaned forward and pressed his elbows on the table, a pugnacious pose. "Does anyone see it playing out any other way?" He had a vision of six crew members working themselves up into a panic and turning the ship around, firing the main engines, and trying to go back to Earth. Crews had mutinied for less. He kept that happy thought to himself.

Nobody spoke.

Sheffield spoke. "Captain, how do you propose to get people to return to hibernation?"

"There's only one way that can work. Persuasion and example. I'm going to start the process myself. We cannot force people to go back into the pods. So we'll have to convince them that returning is the only hope they have of getting their skills and memories back."

Sheffield pursed his lips in disapproval. "All due respect, Captain, but I don't think that is an adequate approach. What happens if the majority of people awakened refuse to go back? Or even a significant percentage? What happens if some people are more damaged rather than less?"

"If need be, the ship can handle a hundred people awake for the amount of time it will take to get to *nu Phoenicis*. I'm hoping, however, that it won't come to that."

Sheffield's scowl deepened. "These people will be damaged. They may be of no use to the mission, and they may even be a detriment."

"Number one, I'll remind you we are currently amongst that number. It's no secret; everyone presently awake knows that we are impaired, too, and if they see us trying to judge their worth to the mission, that will backfire on us."

Sheffield looked aghast. "I'm not suggesting we declare people useless, Captain. I am suggesting we order people to get back in the pods."

"Even if I thought it was a lawful order, how would we enforce it if we ourselves are in the pods? Commander, hibernation aversion may become a serious problem. But let's try persuasion and example first."

Vargas didn't like the openly stymied expression on Sheffield's face. He held the Commander's eye until he looked down.

He paused, looking at each of the eight others around the table in turn. "This can be done. Based on what you know from what we've discussed, how many of you would be willing to return to the pod for a few months, and be awakened for a week, and then return again? Raise your arm." Vargas raised his.

Spencer's shot up. After a beat, so did Trapp's. Then Barney and Sorlund. Harlen shook his head, clearly a "I must be crazy" gesture and raised his.

Vargas looked to his CTO. "Mr. Lassiter? What could I say that might persuade you to at least consider it?

"Captain, I'm more than willing to consider it. But you just gave me explicit orders to renovate the hamster wheel to accommodate the refuseniks. I can't consider it until I've carried those orders out, Ser."

Isaakson's arm went up. "Once my job is squared away, Ser." The maintenance chief considered the orders given to Lassiter to be ones that she would be doing the actual work upon. Correctly.

Looking grumpy, Sheffield raised his arm.

Vargas nodded, hiding the burst of pleasure he felt.

"Some of us have duties to perform right now and can't go in. Most of us, in fact. But we're all willing to at least consider it? All eight of us? Nods around the table. "Then I think we can convince most of the people on the ship to do it."

The bear paused in his fishing as the rainbow quake began. The fish was tasty, but the rainbow quake was very pretty. After a moment, the quake ended, and the bear resumed eating.

Damn.

Vargas clenched his jaw and glanced up just in time to catch a knowing wink from Spencer. He was probably watching all of us to get an idea of how many flash-dreams we are having, he thought. He felt irrationally annoyed, the more so because he knew it was irrational.

"Doctors Trapp and Spencer, I'll work directly with you on the art of persuading refuseniks to return to sleep. We also need to sit down and figure out if we want to solicit volunteers from among the insomniacs. There's some obvious risks, and some ethical questions that we need to address. Obviously, the risk to the insomniacs may be greater than it is for the rest of us. Doctor Trapp, go through your notes and see if there is anything in your experience in the sleep labs that might be of help to us.

"Misters Lassiter and Isaakson, you have the hamster wheel. Use the library to retrain yourselves, and then show your people what needs to be done. You're disoriented; you're not stupid. I have full faith in you."

"Mister Sorlund, get us back on course and on time. We will abandon constant acceleration."

"The rest of you, talk to the crew, and let it be noised about that we think we've found a solution. Don't be specific, because what we have isn't definitive. But let people know that in the next few weeks, the line officers have enough confidence that they are volunteering to try it out.

"Consult with the Doctors. They are going to try to devise some sort of optimum schedule for returning people to hibernation, and waking them up again. Doctor Spencer, what type of schedule did you use with your two guinea pigs?"

Spencer drew a breath, looking a bit whipsawed. Vargas didn't doubt it. In minutes he had gone from the guy who wasted the fuel and nearly destroyed the mission to the guy who might have saved it. He suspected Spencer would have felt an emotional roller coaster even without the twingies. "Twenty days in the pod, ten days awake. Then repeat."

"Any particular reason for that?"

Spencer shrugged. "I have only my own experience, which featured almost random awakenings and hibernation periods. The two-to-one ratio roughly matched the ratio of my own sleep-to-awake.

"It seemed like a good compromise," he finished, looking faintly abashed.

As the officers half-drifted, half-floated out of the mess, Vargas hooked a finger at Spencer for him to stay. Anyone noticing would just assume Vargas wanted to work out the specifics of the hibernation reentry program, and that was true enough. But he had another question.

"Ian, you took time to sit down with my line officers and help them fill in some blanks today, right?"

"I did."

"That included Commander Sheffield?"

"Not yet, Captain."

"Could you happen to tell the Commander that he had a jovial and disarming sense of humor when speaking to a group of people?"

Spencer's face was utterly guileless. "Of course I could tell him something like that. But I wouldn't make someone he was something he was incapable of being." Spencer considered, cheeks sucked in a bit. "I don't see any harm in reminding the Commander of his innate joviality and charm."

"Very good." Vargas gazed into the middle distance, contemplating the possibilities. He decided he liked Ian Spencer at that.

"It probably wouldn't last, Captain. Enjoy it while it does."

Chapter 11 Back To The Future

THE NEXT DAYS WERE BUSY. The Imprinter crew fabricated bunks, walls, and necessary ventilation and power strips to run around the hamster wheel. Fortunately, files to automatically create those items were in the library. The *Phoenix* was brought about to resume its cruising speed of .87c, and the ship's doctors alternated between figuring out a strategy for hibernations and dealing with the emotional and psychological fallout experienced by the forty-two people on board who were awake. The trickiest issue was that of informed consent. Some of the insomniacs were clearly in no condition to give consent, and everyone else was in a more nebulous situation. They finally decided that Joseph Heller's classic "Catch 22" would cover the bases. If a patient was aware enough to be cognizant of, and afraid of the hazards and uncertainties posed by hibernation, then they were competent enough to be asked to face those hazards.

Spencer whistled. "That's some catch, that Catch-22"

"It's the best there is," Doc Trapp agreed with a wide grin.

At the next meeting, they decided on the two to one thirty day scheme devised by Ian Spencer, and Spencer announced he had six volunteers to begin, including two insomniacs.

Vargas interviewed each of the six, ensuring they understood the risks and were acting of their own free will. He assured them that they could back out at any time, and that it would not reflect on them in any way if they did so. He then delayed the process twenty four hours to let them think it over. Trapp and Spencer warned them that the procedure was highly experimental, and might not work, and could even make things worse.

A few days later it got back to Vargas that one of the reentry sleepers had mentioned to the hibernation techs that the Captain was trying to 'cover his ass.' This provoked a roar of laughter from Vargas, who told a smiling Trapp "I am the highest authority for twenty light years in any direction. Just why am I covering my ass?"

It wasn't quite true that Vargas was the Supreme Authority. The captain did answer to a higher authority; the entire complement. He was responsible for them, and to them. Forgetting that fealty was a two way arrangement had caused many failed voyages in the old seafaring days.

All six went into hibernation, and Trapp ordered their readouts to be monitored continuously. To his relief (and some surprise) none of the sleepers showed any signs of distress during the twenty days they were under. All six awoke disoriented and confused, but tests indicated improvement. The two insomniacs did no worse than the four crew members,.

In the week following eight more people volunteered. Vargas accepted the offers, lectured them on the pitfalls, and sent them to Vargas for a second round of what Vargas now sardonically thought of as "CYA sessions."

The first group agreed to a second thirty-day round of the experiment. The second group emerged from their pods, and showed similar levels of slight improvement.

Group one came out the second time showing marked improvement. One who came out early because he showed signs of insomniacs' distress showed improvement. He had not been one of the prior insomniacs.

Three months after the first crisis meeting, it was clear: repeated awake/sleep cycles helped. There were still problems, but people got their memories back. Scans showed the static decreasing. Trapp and Spencer declared themselves mystified but pleased. Vargas and Trapp both went through a cycle while Sheffield, the clear-headed beneficiary of two immersions, kept authority on the bridge.

Julie Steinberg was not one of the volunteers. Trapp was of the opinion that she wasn't competent to volunteer, so she wasn't asked. Spencer had requested that the orderlies put the piano into default player piano mode since it seemed to be stimulating her. Unfortunately, the orders weren't quite specific, and when Vargas found time to visit, he found that it was in jukebox mode, playing what sounded like some twenty second century jazz hip hop fusion, something that didn't involve piano. Julie was staring off in the middle distance, her lips moving to an entirely different song in her head.

He killed the sound track. There were about four other people floating around the mess hall, apparently unconcerned with the lack of gravity, and none seemed to notice the music had suddenly stopped. One of the people, Vargas realized, was Lieutenant Bartlett, one of the refuseniks. She was watching the floaters, presumably to make sure that none developed too much momentum or too little. She glanced his way, and he smiled and nodded, and she gave a friendly wave in return.

It occurred to Vargas to move the piano back to the bridge mess. The ranks of those in the main mess were thinning by the day. The comfortably cozy locale might help Julie, too.

Wishing he could remember any of his piano lessons from his youth, he reached past Julie and struck a note. Something tickled in his memory, and he struck it again. Not quite. . .

He moved his finger an inch to the left. He hit the new note. Yes, that's what he wanted. A Minor. He hit it twice. And he had it. He knew the piece, a twenty-first century Obel composition called "Riverside." He plugged his data pad into the piano and searched. He realized with a start of frustration, that he wouldn't recognize the word "Riverside", so he typed in *"La Orilla del Río."* Obel's face came up, and not recognizing her image, he took a chance and selected.

The music started playing, and with a start of pleasure, he knew he had the right piece.

He strapped himself to the bench next to Julie, tracing the low counterpoint to the melody on the right side of the keyboard. Julie's eyes traveled to watch his hand trace the notes, and Vargas was pleased to see his hand faithfully predicting each pressed key. Now letting memory guide his hand, he watched her face. She shifted her gaze from his counterpoint to the keys depressing the main melody on her side of the keyboard.

After a moment, she raised her left hand and tentatively made ghost motions above the keys.

The song ended, and Vargas decided to look for something that didn't have vocals.

It required a little thought. He couldn't remember how far his own lessons had gotten. Even the titles would be of little use. So he typed "solo piano" and selected what came up, about six songs.

To his delight, he recognized each song. Chopin. Glass. Liszt. Rachmaninoff. Ravel. Tchaikovsky. He could even put faces to some of them.

He looked to Julie. She was scanning the keyboard intently, watching the keys, forming associations, pulling filaments of memory together. She began humming along halfway through the Tchaikovsky. The final note rumbled to an end in a hushed and awestruck hall, and there was a pause of three beats. The Julie threw her arms around Daniels neck and started sobbing into the collar of his tunic. Vargas, surprised, patted at her shoulder, awkwardly aware that crew members were taking this in.

When he got up to leave, a few minutes later, he heard the very faintest of whispers behind him, which could only be Julie's voice.

"Thank you."

* * *

The next time, a year later, went much better. Vargas could recall his childhood in Torreón, his father Rafe, and that he was good at math. Best of all, he could read English again.

He also remembered Julie. The first two times he swung by the mess, she wasn't there. On the third try, she was at the piano, scribbling notes on some sheets. She smiled when she looked up and saw him, and reached to the keyboard and played the first notes of "Riverside." Vargas grinned like a border collie and floated over. Together, they played the song, and Julie sang the lyrics in a slightly quivery voice.

She had returned to hibernation. After three months of increasing piano fluency, the doctors were persuaded that she could be approached and asked to return. Spencer sealed the deal by noting that Captain Vargas was his old self again and asked after her constantly.

She was even more startled at the improvement in Vargas than he was in hers. She admitted that she hadn't really believed returning to hibernation could help, but she was seeing it every two weeks as people emerged for the second or third time, clear-eyed and collected.

Everyone still had flash-dreams. Even as she was speaking, Vargas has an image of skating through deep snow, moving toward the brightly lit rally at the end of the canyon. Julie told the captain that people were recording them into the log, and they were being formed into the first major public works art.

* * *

The sleep/wake cycle needed final fiddling. In the end, at any given point for the first three years, there would be one hundred and fifty people awake, plus about ten or so people to act as guides, to explain to the sleepers why they were awakened, why they couldn't remember things, and how it could be repaired. Trapp and Spencer devised a series of tests to administer to the newly-awakened to determine the extent of their impairment. Some of the questions were subtly couched to glean insight into the emotional state of the awakened.

There was major improvement amongst crew and colonists. Enough so that it was decided to waken those people only one more time before arrival at *nu Phoenicis*. Much later, Vargas wished they hadn't taken that short cut.

Julie Steinberg had discussed her progress with Vargas. What she didn't know was he gave orders to be wakened to coincide with her cycle. He hovered over her as she went into hibernation, and was there when she came out.

Even the unlucky insomniacs showed improvement. Enough that it was hoped a few more rounds might make them functional again.

After ten years, only six insomniacs were left, and they manned the ship for the last four years, "riding her in." They had all shown slow improvement, but remained unwilling to ever hibernate again. The rest of the crew and colonists slept.

And dreamt.

* * *

On the day before he returned to hibernation for the last time prior to arrival at *nu Phoenicis*, a minor mystery was solved for Captain Vargas. All the Charlies had a name and rank to go with the faces, but none had been found that had the Captain's face on it. Vargas was mildly put out, but wasn't about to order that a Captain Charlie be made. It seemed undignified.

He got a signal from Red Farnsworth, the ROV and Charlie wrangler. Like Vargas, he was on what he called "the rinse cycle" of the sleep/wake regimen. "Begging the Captain's Pardon, and could he please visit Module twelve?"

Puzzled by both the formality of the request from the usually insouciant midshipman, and unsure what Module twelve contained, Vargas queried his data pad and then made his way to the Module. Red awaited him with a large grin.

Module Twelve was the ROV and Charlie Maintenance and Repair station. Along with the expected array of work benches and shelved component parts, there was a medium sized imprinter devoted to the creation of Charlies, ROVs, and their spare parts.

There, two meters tall on the metal front of the Mother of all Charlies, was a picture of Captain Daniel Vargas. Mother to all the Charlies. Daniel feigned nonchalance and decided he approved.

$$* * *$$

Notes from Doctor Ian Spencer's personal log, Year 28, Shift 2, Day 14.

Two weeks into my final special shift, and I'm beginning to believe that once this shift ends, I'll next awaken in the nu Phoenicis system.

We were supposed to be there by "now" (I'm not sure what now is, given the time compression thing), but because of the mid-course changes in order to solve the insomniac crisis, we lost two years, subjective. The people on the shifts after me are going to be a bit surprised and disappointed to learn we aren't there yet, I think.

Because we still have the eleven refuseniks, we have only two crew per shift now, since the people who have elected to "ride her in" are more than willing to take over the functions of the regular shift people. Talking to them, I see considerable improvement over the past ten years since I was last awake. Some of that might just be that they are all ten years older, but they all seem calmer and more reflective. They still have flash-dreams and twingies—I think we're pretty much stuck with those for the rest of our lives. But they don't seem to interfere with daily functioning, and I haven't noticed any unusual problems. In most ways, they are the same people I worked with in training, nearly three decades ago. One of the odd things that defies conventional theory about memory is that most people seem to have clear recollections of what they couldn't remember during the first two awakenings. It reaffirms Trapp's belief that portions of the mind weren't destroyed during hibernation, but simply walled off, and the walls came down in subsequent sleeps. I wonder what we are hiding from ourselves?

I traded for this shift because my wife and children are due to be awakened for the third time tomorrow. The first time was awkward; they were badly confused and frightened, and none of them really recognized the old man who resembled their husband and father. That was a mistake on my part. They didn't need to find me suddenly four years older when they were busily trying to figure out who I was and who one another was. I hibernated through their second awakening. And I'm only six months older this time, so our meeting should be less traumatic for them. And they'll be a lot less confused too. Poor Sylvie. She kept going back to her pod, saying she wanted to see Tipsy, our cat. Even if Tipsy survived the war, she would be long dead by now. That was fifty years ago. . .

It's strange that it hit me just now. I'm used to the idea that many of the people we knew on Earth must be dead by now, and there's no possibility I would ever see any of them again. But the notion that some of them could still be alive gave me a sense of. . . I don't know. Continuity? Is that the word I want? Continuity with my old life on Earth. Thinking about poor old Tipsy, and realizing that it is physically impossible for that cat to be alive just gave a body blow to that sense of continuity. Maybe that's what lay behind Sylvie's delusion that Tipsy was on board and needed her attention.

There is cat DNA in the biostorage, although none are going to be resuscitated anytime soon. If the planet has its own ecology, and it would pretty much have to, we don't want cats destroying it before we have a change to study it.

I am noticing changes in people that I think aren't part of Hibernation Syndrome. People seem to be chucking a lot of Earthly conventions. I can't remember the last time I heard someone refer to the day of the week, and in fact have no idea what it might be. NP-4 has a year more than twice as long as Earth's, so I imagine we'll throw out the calendar and devise a new one. I'm not the first to think of that, by the way; Red left a message in the crew's log suggesting that we follow the example of the ancient Romans and name months after our leaders. I'm sure he did that to tweak the Captain's nose. Daniel would be appalled at the notion of a month of "Vargas." I wish I could have seen the expression on his face when he read that! NP 4 has a twenty-four hour day, give or take a minute, so we'll probably keep the same old silly 24 hour, 60 minute method of time keeping. Whose idea was that, anyway? At the back of my mind, I have this notion that it was devised by the old Phoenicians, and if that's true, there would be a certain symmetry to having their work survive on the similarly-named nu Phoenicis, but I'm too lazy to look it up right now. Later.

Speaking of Phoenicians, that is how a large majority of those on the ship now refer to themselves. There's nothing historic about it, of course; it's just the chance similarity in sound between Phoenicia and Phoenicis. There are objections, particularly among crew members who hail from the Fertile Crescent such as bin Laden, who affects being scandalized at being considered a Canaanite. But he does so with a smile, and I predict he'll be using the reference on himself once the colony is established.

People use the library a fair bit. It was the biggest library in the solar system, and if something can be stored as data, it's there. There's even a sizable porn collection. I don't imagine the Americaners or Greenlanders like that! But most of the people, insomniacs and shift people alike, seem more interested in making their own entertainment. A fair bit of it makes it to the crew log, too. We have some very talented people on board. Julie did her shift a year back, and I was very interested to see her playing the eighth Sonata by Prokofiev. Jan never could master it in college, and she was considered a decent piano player. She'll be happy to know there will be someone on the new planet who can teach it to her. Plays and skits are popular with crew members, and the Russian, German and English members have been teaching other people on the crew the fine old art of tavern singing. We'll probably slip into orbit around nu Phoenicis IV with half the crew singing "Three Whores of Tottenham".

In fact, Red Farnsworth was belting it out one time a couple of cycles back. It's been a popular ditty in the northern counties ever since the new Buckingham Palace was erected there. I don't think Red ever figured out why I pulled him out of hibernation during the mid-course crisis. He thinks I needed a Charliemeister. What I really needed was an orderly in case the Captain was too disabled to function. Vargas may have figured it out, but he's not going to say anything at this point.

It's a small sample, but the crew members seem to have lost a certain amount of religiosity they might have had. A lot of them are navy vets of one sort or another, and probably weren't much into god-flogging anyway, but there were a couple who used to sneak deistic references in whenever possible. Ahmed bin Laden used "Allah Akbar" and "If it is the will of Allah" as punctuation, especially in front of the Captain and other Americaner crew members. Between his family name and the constant Islamicisms, I think he was reliving the tensions of the twenty-first century, and that crazy 'war on terror'. If so, the references were wasted on the Captain; his state wasn't even in the Americas then, and the terrorists his ancestors had to deal with were far more immediate and deadly than anything the old United States had to face.

Ahmed has stopped doing the Allah Akbar plosives, and I am watching for an opportunity to sound him out about that.

Not everyone is more relaxed, though. People who were prone to rigid thinking before the ship left Earth are still rigid in most ways. Sheffield is a good example of that. As a military leader, he is almost archetypal, and if Phoenix had been planned as a military mission, I would have recommended him over Vargas, who has a distinctly laissez-faire approach to authority. But it wasn't, and we needed a captain with the sensibilities to persuade rather than command, and Vargas was very nearly the ideal choice. Sheffield handled the dislocation of wakening well by all appearances, but there was one time I was making notes in the ship library, and I heard crying. I floated over to investigate, and spotted Sheffield in a cubicle, weeping uncontrollably. *My professional instincts were to intervene, to give comfort, and to guide him through the moment of crisis, but my gut feeling was that if he knew I had spotted him in such a moment of weakness, I would have found myself with an implacable enemy. Rigid thinking.*

Vargas once told me that he would probably end up as mayor of the colony at some point because people liked continuity, but it was his dream that as soon as the colony was a going concern, he would pack it up and leave, and go exploring. Sheffield would be next in line, all other things being equal. If that day comes, I'll have to talk to Vargas about that. I don't think Sheffield would make a good civilian administrator. In the interests of order, he could bring chaos.

But the changes I am seeing are more interesting, and probably more relevant.

I have to be mindful of the fact that these people a very small and elite sample, and I might be seeing patterns in what is actually just noise—or in this case, lack of noise. In a group of sixteen people, all specifically chosen for even, calm temperaments and high intelligence, should I be surprised if none of them are raving religious nutters?

And I may just be projecting my own feelings onto them. Waking up with most of my memories, and thus my identity, gone out in the middle of a vast nothingness trillions of miles from home, surrounded by frightened and confused people in the same boat as me, left me with the feeling that when we left Earth, we left God, too.

Maybe the Gaists were right, and Earth was God. In which case, will we find a new God at nu Phoenicis IV?

Part Two

Arrival

Chapter 12 Arrival

WHEN CAPTAIN DANIEL VARGAS AWOKE, *Phoenix* was already done with a fly-by survey of *nu Phoenicis* 8 (dubbed "Cueball").

Cueball was a terrestrial planet, furthest of the eight planet system and about 9.4 AUs in distance. Observation suggested an atmosphere and water, but the planet was nearly completely enveloped in water ice, and the average surface temperature to be between minus one hundred and minus one-fifty, significantly colder than Antarctica.

Phoenix moved toward Zhar Ptitsa, the name for the star now universally adopted by the Phoenicians. The designation came from the Russian crew member Nicolai Pushkin, who translated it as "magical glowing bird" or "fire bird".

They passed the orbit of *nu Phoenicis* 5 (Simurgh), a gas giant about six times the size of Jupiter with a swarm of some one hundred and fifty moons. *Phoenix* had slowed to less than one percent of the speed of light. On Earth, it was Christmas morning, and Vargas woke with the same sense of anticipation and joy that he had when he was eight, some eighty-five years before.

Phoenix had to follow a long, Hohmann-type arc from Simurgh to the new world, *nu Phoenicis* 4. With aft cameras still out, the crew whiled away the weeks speculating on what the world would be like, what the captain would call it, and stories about colonization of other planets were in sudden demand from the library. Vargas got word of that and smiled. A favored intellectual stance of the colonists and crew was of disdain for such tales, the imaginings of science fiction writers of whom none had ever left Earth. The complement of the *Phoenix*, who were the real thing, had no time for silly imaginative scribbles. Supposedly.

But with the real landing just weeks away, people sneaked peeks at those stories, perhaps trying to glean some foreknowledge of how to cope with what awaited.

Sheffield lived on the bridge, cursing the damage to the ship's rear sensors and cameras, and cooing with delight over the data they could get. The man's normally dour mien was buried in an avalanche of sheer fascination with their potential new home.

It was amazingly Earth-like. Only the year—nearly eight hundred days—was truly alien, and Vargas wondered if Earth life would be able to cope with seasons over double the length of Earth's. The surface was seventy percent water, with most of the land grouped along the equator. Perhaps seasons wouldn't be that big an issue. Twenty four degree axial tilt, nearly the same as Earth's. Cloud cover suggested similar precipitation levels, wetter at the north and south coasts, which faced vast oceans.

The *Phoenix* backed into orbit about four hundred kilometers over the surface of the planet, and people crowded along the back of the bridge area, or watched the giant display in the main mess, waiting for the planet to slowly rise in the forward cameras.

A blue arc appeared at the top of the screens, and there was a collective gasp. It was beautiful, a deep blue stippled with white. The arc thickened quickly as *Phoenix* approached the dawn terminator, and within minutes, the full day face of the planet was on screen. Vargas heard muffled sobs around the bridge, and found himself misting up.

This was their new home. Vargas was certain. How could a planet so similar to Earth turn up on the very first venture—and possibly the last—from the home planet? On this beautiful sapphire world, the blue was a sharper contrast from the white, and some on the bridge wondered if it meant the oceans were fresh water – or a lot deeper than Earth's. The land lay along a nearly continuous band between thirty degrees north and south, with nothing to block the oceans above and below but the ice caps, the larger one to the north. Vargas queried his God Console about the seasonal tilt. It was winter in the northern hemisphere.

Crew and colonists clustered in front of displays, arguing over the merits of regions. Did they want to be near mountains, with their promised minerals? What about that area that looks like jungle? Might that be a big fresh-water lake? On the bridge, Sheffield and his team plotted landing spots for investigation for possible colonization.

Since *Phoenix* was not a military vessel, Vargas wasn't required by naval tradition to stay on board, but Sheffield had been given the prerogative of leading the first landing team as part of the same deal that had given Vargas the captaincy in the first place. It was an agreement Vargas had no intention of violating, but that didn't ease his sense of frustration at having to watch from several hundred kilometers up. He turned to Sheffield. "So, Sean. Given any thought to what your first words will be?"

"Today, the universe is ours. Humanity has conquered the stars."

That was a bit grandiose for Vargas' taste, but it beat Martin's first words when he stepped onto the Martian surface onto a semi-buried rock and turned his ankle: "Ouch. Dammit." But then, didn't Martin claim years later that he thought that was better than what he had intended to say? Maybe with luck Sheffield would bump his head on the door latch or something.

Sheffield gestured at the screen. "We have a whole new world, Captain. I don't think anybody will ever have the types of opportunities we'll get."

"That's probably true. Or the challenges." Vargas suddenly grinned. "Of course, the challenges might turn out to be the best part."

"Any signs of life yet?"

"Beyond the obvious vegetation? No. And certainly nothing that's broadcasting on any frequency we can receive."

"I honestly can't decide if I want to encounter anything above the level of a cabbage or not. I've read the material about alien contact, and I know about the need to treat indigenous animal life carefully and with respect. I'm prepared to wake up in the craft the morning after we land to find five or six velociraptors staring in at me. I'm even prepared for five or six velociraptors standing around the craft with guns, wanting to know why we desecrated their ancient burial site. I can prepare to face beings that are smarter than us, or deadly antagonistic, or wanting to worship us as gods.

"What I can't decide is if I'm ready to do this tomorrow or not."

Vargas gave Sheffield a somewhat forced sympathetic smile. "Well, remember you aren't seeking First Contact. In fact, if you run into anything above your cabbage, report it in immediately, and if it's showing signs of intelligence, get out of there right away if you can do so without starting a war. You're going to spend two weeks at five different sites, getting soil and plant samples, and recording everything. We're pretty sure there's nothing resembling cities or large towns down there, and we don't see anything that suggests roads or agriculture. You're going to land in fairly open areas, where, if Earth standards apply, predators are going to be very spread out and it might take a few days for one to notice there's something new in the neighborhood. You realize it's probably going to be a month before we send anyone other than surveyors or scientists down. Right now, let's just make sure the planet can sustain human life." Vargas grinned. "And if your velociraptors do show up, jump in the shuttle and get the hell out of there, guns or no guns. You didn't travel forty-nine light years to become dinosaur kibble."

Sheffield gave a thin smile. Vargas had just given him the Cliff's Notes for years of training. "Aye aye, Cap'n. But I still can't decide if I want to be bored to tears or not."

"Opt for bored to tears. Even if the whole place turns out to be no more dangerous as a city park, I'm sure there will be lots of not-boring challenges for us." Vargas looked up at the display. "Damn, but it's a beautiful world. It's got mountains and deserts and big lakes. It's one big national park, and it's ours."

Sheffield shrugged. "If the universe wants it to be ours, then it's ours. I'll just try to be bored and report everything."

Vargas slapped his number one on the shoulder. "That's the best anyone can expect. Bring back heavy sighs and glowing reports."

* * *

Sheffield, a rated shuttle pilot, had the left hand seat. He wore the main video feed camera, so what he saw relayed to over two hundred enthralled people back on board the *Phoenix*. Lieutenant Commander Madelyne Isaakson piloted and, once on the ground, would monitor the drone recorders that allowed the mission to do immediate exploring from inside the craft, and longer-range exploring over the next couple of days. She would edit on the fly and upload highlights to *Phoenix* as they happened. Jim Hartnell, the xenobiologist, and Asuka Tsuchishima, the exobotanist would gather samples of plants and animals. Rebekah Cohen, the horticulturalist, would get soil samples. Finally, Adelena Conti, a microbiologist, would be taking air samples and do probes into the soil and rock to determine mineral content and such things as ambient temperature. Red Farnsworth was along as gopher and ROV wrangler. Normally this was not a glamorous job, but Red couldn't think of anything more exciting in his life.

Sheffield and Isaakson spent several hours with the ship's computer, calculating optimal reentry procedures. Both had done the simulations dozens of times on Earth in everything from three man capsules to experimental shuttle craft nearly fifty meters long. It was a matter of just a couple of degrees between a safe landing, or burning up, or—even worse for a pilot's pride—skipping back out of the atmosphere altogether. The atmosphere was a shade thinner, reflecting the .95g at the surface.

After several hours with the computer simulations, they decided that reentry should be one tenth of a degree steeper than would be used on Earth, and privately crossed their fingers and hoped their calculations were correct. In the meantime, the scientists double-checked all their equipment with excruciating care, and drove Red to distraction making sure that it was all safely stored on the craft and its access immediately available at any time—an absurdity, given there were several hundred items to be stowed in a not-very-large compartment. Red carefully logged the exact position of each unit on his data pad, intent on coming out of this hailed as a mad genius who saved the mission a dozen times through sheer preparedness.

One item puzzled him—a small pine box with Japanese ideograms on it. He surmised correctly that Tsuchishima was responsible, and asked her about it. She blushed slightly, and explained that it was a small, inexpensive calligraphy set, considered a polite gift for a guest to bring to a host.

"What if there is nobody there to accept the gift, Tsuchishima-sama?"

"Then I have a new calligraphy set, and am no poorer."

Red nodded, and went back to his cabin and carefully placed in his suit pocket a family keepsake, an old thrupenny piece with a harp on one side and a hare on the other. A minor coin was considered an auspicious token for new land to be tilled, according to Red's grandfather. And Red liked the idea that something from the Earth itself be placed in the new soil.

* * *

New World Global TV was by far the most popular item on the ship that night. The new world had a moon, one roughly half the size of Luna and about four times further away, but the view of the crescent moon coming up over the crescent planet, evoking images of the Apollo 8 mission, drew gasps of pleasure from nearly everyone who was watching. The camera tech zoomed the image so the moon wouldn't be so disappointingly small. Few poets and lovers would dream below this moon, which resembled a ball bearing held at arms' length.

* * *

Vargas joined most of the people who had gathered to watch on a large screen in the main mess hall, and was reminded again of his mood when he last awoke, the wildly elevated anticipation of a child on Christmas morning. Looking at the number of people floating in the room and reflecting that it had to be nearly all of the people awake, he tapped in instructions to the CPO to form a barricade so the seven shuttle people could get into the shuttle hanger on time in the morning. If the shuttle left at the second it was supposed to, people would have thirty-eight minutes to get to a screen to watch final approach. The crew sounded and looked somewhat like an elementary school classroom on the last day of the school year. Vargas eyed the squeeze bottles that some of the more boisterous crew members held and reflected that Mike Matthews had wasted no time getting his still back in operation. In the DNA library in module 10, if he recalled correctly. He couldn't ask Mike, of course. He wasn't supposed to know about it.

He found himself standing next to Tim Simmons, the physicist-geologist. A mere crewman in the ship, Simmons would be worth his weight in platinum on the planet because of his twin scientific standings.

"Any thoughts on the mineral composition down there, Tim?"

Simmons shrugged. "I've got some theories, Cap'n. I think we may find a lot of radioactives in the ground there. Thorium, uranium, others."

"Why's that, Tim?"

"I've been up in the monitoring area, analyzing some of the scans. We won't know until we get down there, but there may be higher levels of ambient emissions than we see on Earth."

"Problem?"

"I'm not sure. It may be just a few regions, or it could be an artifact. Some of the readings may reflect the fact that we're a bit radioactive ourselves. The ship's hull, that is."

"Oh, right."

"I'm hoping to do more scans, but Commander Lassiter has the crew doing a system survey. He's getting more accurate data on all eight planets, and their moons. I guess he feels he can do a better job up here, outside of the atmosphere."

"That's doubtlessly true." Vargas gave Tim a direct look. "In a fortnight, you'll be down there, and you'll be able to get more accurate tests there, anyway. If you find anything that worries you, report directly to me. The more risks we can avoid. . . "

Simmons nodded. "... the less chance of accident. I'll keep you posted, Cap'n."

* * *

Sheffield deliberately made sure his hands didn't hover over the copilot's controls. There was nothing wrong with Isaakson's piloting; quite the opposite. Both the readouts and Sheffield's seat-of-the-pants experience told him the craft was in perfect control. But he still felt backseat driver syndrome.

He kept sneaking peaks out the windows. The planet was making the transition from space object to landscape, and he was marveling at how much the land resembled Earth.

Behind him there was a quiet jostling. The five passengers, in serious breach of regulations, had unbelted and were peering through the containment mesh that separated the pilots from the freight area. One good bounce from turbulence, and his first act on the new world might be setting broken bones.

But the bounces didn't come. The air aloft was remarkably tranquil and homogeneous. The leading theory was that the cooler climate meant less weather. It was just past the solstice, over two hundred days from the nearest equinox, which might explain the even distribution of air masses.

Or perhaps they just got lucky. Sheffield tried to remember climatology lectures. The icecaps were probably permanent features,

Sheffield turned to glare at the crew members and tell them to get strapped back in, and saw that Red had already realized the danger, and was clipping bungee cords to everyone so they wouldn't accidentally sail into the overhead or the bulkheads. To Sheffield, the notion that a tar would be babysitting all the high-powered talent came as no surprise. He had a deep, but unconscious suspicion that most scientists were people too lazy to make an honest living.

Scanning the readouts, he saw they were ninety seconds from landing on a prime bit of real estate, grasslands surrounded by what looked like old-growth deciduous forest. No roads visible, no structures, and a large stream or river just a few hundred meters from the landing site.

Isaakson looked at the hull pressure and temperature readings, and said tersely, "Deploying wings" and the shuttle made the transition from space craft to aircraft. The ride continued to be almost preternaturally smooth. He could even feel the faint vibration as the vanes locked into place.

One of the scientists whispered, "My god, it looks like Kent!" Sheffield, familiar with the countryside of the English county, had to agree. The land was low rolling hills, very green like Kent was in the late spring (it was more like early winter according to the orbital data, but they were only ten degrees north of the equator). The only thing missing were the fields and farms. From eight kilometers up, it looked green and lush.

Sheffield looked at the display. One minute to go. They flew into a bank of cumulus clouds, and when they emerged, they were only two kilometers up. Isaakson pointed. Their landing site was in view.

The shuttle drifted in, shedding the last of its velocity, flaps and sled-like landing gear deployed. As planned, they did a flyover of the site, doing radar and eyeball scans to make sure the landing would be safe. They did a 360 just above treetop height circling the landing site, watching for possible pit falls. Sheffield didn't know that they were actually trees, but they were close enough for never-mind.

Then they were on final approach. Red had managed to convince everyone to strap in, and Sheffield glanced back. Everyone had their helmets sealed and were living on suit amenities. The suits, perfected during the century of exploration of Mars, were comfortable enough, but in several days everyone would be heartily sick of them. The thrusters gave one last roar, a griffon landing at her nest.

The planed bobbed to a halt with a faint gasp of the hydraulics. Isaakson spoke into her mike. "RESS *Phoenix*, the Kent Survey has landed." She gave Sheffield a grin. "Well, I had to call it something, and this does look like Kent."

For the next ten minutes, scientists waited for the final residual cooling of the hull to finish so they could take accurate measurements. And to watch for velociraptors, of course. The scene outside was mundane. Grass, weaving slightly in a faint breeze, some brush, and toward the river, a strand of trees. William Lombard would have felt at home here.

Jim Hartnell, the xenobiologist, touched Sheffield's sleeve. "We missed a spot. Would it be possible to put mikes on the outside of the craft for the next survey?"

"We've got 'em for when we disembark. They wouldn't survive reentry, so we have to wait until after landing to set them up."

Jim nodded, apparently satisfied. The suit mikes would pick ambient noise as well.

Sheffield glanced at Isaakson, who was watching the radar screen. "Anything?"

"Dead still, Captain. The only motion I see is in the grass, and it's clearly wind-driven. There's no large animal life within three hundred meters."

Hartness spoke up. "Oxygen 22%, Nitrogen 75%. Point nine five oh pressure, ambient temperature eighteen degrees."

A nice day in the park.

"In that case, Ms. Tsuchishima, you're with me." The exobotanist picked up her sample case, and the two moved toward the airlock. They paused before entry to check one another's setting and seals, and then stepped into the lock.

"No flag, Commander?" Tsuchishima cocked an eyebrow.

Sheffield shook his head. "There's no such thing as an 'Earth flag' and nobody could agree on any single flag to plant. And I wasn't about to carry forty of them for each nation involved in this mission. Any locals would think they had been invaded by patriotic clowns."

Tsuchishima chuckled. "I would pay good money to see that."

"Money's no good here. Let's go meet the new world."

The airlock, carefully evacuated, refilled with air from the new world. It had been sterilized aboard the *Phoenix*, and would be again upon return. Sheffield undogged the hatch, and the ladder deployed. He stepped down, with a slightly showy pause before his foot touched the ground, aware that his helmet camera was sending this to two hundred people in orbit above.

"The voyage of discovery is not in seeking new landscapes but in having new eyes," he intoned. On the *Phoenix*, a surprised Vargas looked up, and said, "Oh, I like that one much better!" In the back of the shuttle, Red chuckled to himself. He had suggested the quote to Sheffield, and since Sheffield hadn't asked, he hadn't told him it was Marcel Proust. Red was tickled at the idea that the slightly nationalistic Englishman would be quoting a Frenchman in his Neil Armstrong moment. As for Red himself, his thrupenny was in his tunic pocket, presently inaccessible. He would plant it when the time was right. Erin go Braugh.

The five other scientists scrambled out two at a time, leaving Red and Madelyn. Red gave the pilot a sympathetic glance, and then loaded carefully-planned equipment into the airlock and cycled through.

Tsuchishima was standing next to the airlock, holding a blade of grass between two fingers, eyes narrowed in contemplation. Red heard her mumbling to her recorder. "Graminoid, resembles *Cynodon dactylon*. No, not just resembles—is identical to visual inspection. If this stuff was growing in a field of

Bermuda grass, I wouldn't notice it at all." She looked up to see Red watching her, tongued her recorder off, and shook her head. "Totally Earth-like. I can't believe this."

Red had made a career of not believing things that seemed too good to be true. "Disappointed?"

"No. Just a little perplexed." She tapped at her right ear mike. "I'm glad you spoke. I was starting to wonder if my audio was down."

"Why?"

"Listen."

Red involuntarily cocked his head. His Master's Voice. "I don't hear anything." That wasn't quite true. He could hear his breathing, and a slight ticking from the cooling port nacelle. Otherwise it was dead silent.

"Exactly. In an Earth field like this, you would hear birds, insects would be buzzing, and you might even hear mice or similar creatures scurrying around. This is more like Mars."

Red spent a year on Mars. Tsuchishima was right. "Are there places like this on Earth? Quiet like this, I mean?"

"Well, they say that the Dry Valleys in Antarctica were quiet like this, but if you mean areas that have lots of vegetation, then the answer is no. Wherever there is plant life, there is animal life, and they tend to make noise."

"So there may not be any animal life here?" That might make settling a lot easier, Red thought.

"Can't tell from looking at a few square meters. But on Earth it would be considered a major anomaly."

Red nodded and moved off to help the others set up equipment. He unstrapped a borer from his back and began digging a core into the ground. Since he had to go a meter down, he was relieved to find that the soil was fairly loose, and rock-free. He was done in minutes, instead of the half hour he expected. He dropped a little object, about the size and shape of a hen's egg on a meter-long pole, into the hole. It would measure temperature and hydration, giving them a vague idea of the prevailing climate. Looking around, Red guessed it would turn out to be mild and moist.

That done, he took his own equipment out – a miniature so-lar-powered atmospheric ROV, capable of flying indefinitely as long as there was sunshine. When he wasn't directly controlling it, it would be flying a search pattern around the shuttle, cameras and other recorders sending a steady stream of data on air temperature and hi-resolution video of the vegetation and landscape up to *Phoenix*. When he wasn't gofering for the shuttle people, he would be swooping in for closer looks at anything interesting the craft spotted. In the event of any large animals, he was to drop whatever he was doing and have the ROV fly as close as possible to examine the critter. With an electric motor running on solar power, the small drone was nearly noiseless.

Satisfying himself that the craft was performing properly, he went to help label and store the amazing array of samples the scientists were grabbing. It turned out that according to Tsuchishima *C. dactylon* – or whatever it was – was just one of about a hundred species of grass in that one field. Plus other stuff. By the end of the day, she had over five hundred pieces of vegetation to examine.

The others were nearly as busy, and Red started wishing there were three of him. What was the rush, anyway? They had several days.

Red did finally get a ten minute rest break, and spent it just looking about carefully, trying to see what was different from Earth. There wasn't much, really. The sky was a little bit bluer than it was in Manchester, but then, he was about eight hundred meters above sea level here, too. To his British eyes, the sky seemed relatively free of cloud, though the planet had slightly less cloud cover than Earth. A bit cooler, so less turbulent weather, or so he understood. He wished he could smell the air. No matter how much his eyes assured him this was Earth, his ears assured him it bloody well wasn't, and his nose would be definitive. He might not know what he smelled, but any variation from Earth he would instantly notice.

A glint to the north caught his eye. Sunlight dappling off the river, of course. Red made a quick note to himself work up some ROVs for water exploration. He was surprised nobody had thought of that. That river looked to have good potential to be a trout stream. Red wanted to take up trout fishing one day.

* * *

Evening found the explorers tired and happy. The one exception was Adelena Conti, who had been taking air samples in an increasing spiral around the shuttle all day.

"Wherever we set up the colony," she said, "it can't be here. There must be a lot of pitchblende in the soil, because the radon levels are off the scale."

"Radon?" Sheffield asked. "Radioactive gas?"

"The very same. It occurs naturally just about everywhere on Earth. Clear back in the twentieth century, they realized that in wood structures and places with basements, it could concentrate to levels that could pose a threat to health."

Rebekah Cohen shifted uncomfortably. "My soil samples showed radon and some polonium, thorium, and lead, too. Pitchblende, I assume. Addie's right—this isn't a good locale to settle."

"Radon usually concentrates in buildings, enclosed areas. Are you saying we're getting those types of concentrations out in the open?" Hartnell looked worried. Even without wind, the radon should disperse pretty quickly.

Addie shook her head. "Not the same levels. I wish they were. These levels are hundreds of times higher. On average, about sixty picocuries per liter."

"What's considered safe?"

"Zero. But most countries have an action standard of two or three picocuries per liter. Anything under that, and they figure the odds of you getting killed by it are about one in one hundred thousand."

The jovial mood was evaporated now. Isaakson asked, "Are we in danger?"

"No. We're carrying our own air, and the suits protect us. You can even breathe the air, although I would avoid it. Microorganisms, not radon."

"What sort of symptoms should we watch for?" Sheffield asked.

"None. It's a long-term thing. You can breathe those types of concentrations for years, and be fine. But the thing is, when radon breaks down, it changes to polonium-210, which is a very nasty element that ionizes tissue. At sixty picocuries a liter, that works out to about a hundred and twenty polonium-210 atoms in your lungs every minute. If you figure that one in billion polonium-210 atoms can start a case of lung cancer. . . "

"Lung cancer?"

". . . then on average, you'll have a dose of it in about, oh, sixteen years, again, on average." Addie looked apologetic. "That's really a ballpark number. I can't vouch for the odds, but it's producing a pretty close result to the casualty numbers we saw on Earth. If you stayed here and breathed the air, there are even odds you'll have lung cancer in sixteen years."

Red spoke up. "Lung cancer's treatable, isn't it? I mean, my uncle got it back, oh, fifteen years before we launched, and he got a lung transplant. He did fine."

"We have the knowledge to do that," Sheffield explained. "What we won't have for a while is the technology or the resources. And lung cancer is frequently fatal." He glanced over to Isaakson. "When will we be able to uplink to *Phoenix* again?"

"In about ten minutes. They'll have had time to process our last bit of information. Something you want me to ask?"

"Yeah. Find out how many lung cancer deaths were on Earth for the latest year we have in the library. I have a vague memory of 10,000 people."

"That's a lot."

"Most of it was impoverished regions, of course. And some of it was probably other forms of radiation, such as fallout or residual debris at explosion sites. Even tobacco smoking."

The cabin was silent for a minute. Jim Hartnell broke it. "We can protect against radon. Charcoal activated filters. As long as we don't inhale it, we're fine."

Addie replied, "If it's coming from the water, then we would have to filter that. And it would be in the plants we eat. But let's see if we can find out where it's coming from, and how widespread it is. It may be that the next valley over doesn't have radon at all."

"What's the half-life on it?"

"Radon? Four, five days, something like that. That's why I think there has to be a spot that's pumping out incredible levels of radon. Pitchblende is the main cause on Earth, but there's something else going on here. Radon breaks down very quickly, and the air wouldn't sustain the levels we're seeing out in the open without a lot of replenishment."

Rebekah Cohen added, "It's also the heaviest gas around. So it will hug the ground. It may be we could just build all our structures five meters off the ground and avoid 99% of radon exposure."

Tsuchishima made a dismissive gesture. "There is still the problem of eating plants. The plants can live in these radon levels, but eating them would be a health hazard."

The radio chimed. Isaakson put the headset on and listened. "Pull out your pads," she instructed the crew.

They dutifully did so, and read the response. "Orbital spectroscopy confirms that there is widespread and pervasive high levels of radon toxicity in the lower atmosphere. Concentrations in some regions are registering as high as twelve thousand picocuries per liter. Conclude tests tomorrow and return to *Phoenix* in twenty four hours. Vargas."

Simultaneous tapping filled the cabin as all seven crew members typed responses, objections, demands for more information. Red threw his pad down. "They're writing this place off?" he demanded. "That's insane! Commander, you've got to talk to them."

Sheffield ignored the near-insubordination. "We're all going to be talking to them on our return. I think that's why they want us to return early."

"Did you say twelve thousand picocuries?" Addie Conti frowned at her readout. "I don't think we could live at all in that. Did he say if there were any areas that were safe?"

Sheffield shook his head.

"If we can't settle here, what the hell are we doing to do?"

"Red, we've got options. But one thing at a time." Sheffield looked around at all the sad, still faces. "Let's do our assigned tasks tomorrow, and maybe something will suggest itself." His expression said he had no idea what that might be. "We have several other stars we can visit if worse comes to worst."

* * *

The crew moved as zombies the next day, obviously dispirited at the news that the place was a radioactive hell and apprehensive about the future. Hartnell and Tsuchishima hiked to the river and took samples, observing that aquatic plant life was plentiful, but there was no sign of animal life. Given the respective transpiration systems, they had a sinking feeling that now they knew why. Nothing with lungs would live long on this planet. To nobody's surprise, the radon levels in the water were extraordinarily elevated, a hundred thousand times the already high levels they found at the landing site. The whole crust of the planet must be mildly radioactive.

The shuttle crew wouldn't be returning empty handed. They had thousands of samples, enough that they could start building a framework for the plant kingdom on this planet, and gain valuable knowledge about how the DNA was structured. Some of the plants looked like they might be edible for humans, and so seeds and DNA were particularly noted. In environments that weren't radioactive, they might prove valuable crop plants.

The scientists weren't entirely unhappy. They accumulated more knowledge about alien life in thirty six hours than humanity had learned in the past thirty-six thousand years.

As the sun lowered in the east, Red went about and pulled up remaining probes and made sure the last of the ROVs were stored away. He paused near the nozzles of the engine at the rear of the craft, where he knew there were no cameras. He was alone; everyone else was inside.

He was defying a direct order.

Glancing around furtively, he reached up and undogged his face plate. Lifting it, he sniffed deeply of the air of this unnamed world. It was sweet. So incredibly sweet.

So incredibly bittersweet.

His nose, however, verified what his ears had insisted; this was not Earth.

Red Farnsworth was the only human to breathe the air of this poisoned paradise.

Chapter 13 Disappointment

FOUR HOURS LATER, THE SHUTTLE WAS BACK IN THE BAY, and enlisted personnel were there to help unload and sniff everything with a Geiger counter. Isaakson glanced at the access port to the main part of the ship, which was conspicuously missing a beaming Captain and eager crowds. She leaned over to Sheffield and whispered, "Not exactly the marching band and twenty-one gun salute we were expecting, is it?" Sheffield simply shook his head. The first man to step on an Earth-like planet that could support life, and it had turned out to be a gigantic bust. It dwarfed the moon landing, but in two generations, assuming any of them lived that long, he would just be a dusty footnote on a floppy disk somewhere.

He and Isaakson went to meet with the Captain while the scientists, with somewhat more cheer, hustled their samples off to the labs for further analysis.

Vargas greeted them warmly and shook their hands. Trapp and ABS Tim Simmons were already seated in the bridge mess. Sheffield frowned slightly, puzzled that Simmons would be at a command gathering.

Vargas bid them to sit, and got right to it. "We've determined that due to extraordinarily high levels of radioactives, *nu Phoenicis* 4 is not suitable for long-term human life. Still, we now know that sophisticated and Earth-like life forms can and do exist, and that Earth is not unique in the universe.

"Commander Sheffield, Lieutenant Commander Isaakson, I want you, and everyone who was on the landing party, to understand the magnitude of what you have accomplished. You were the first to step on to a fertile planet. You discovered that other planets can support life that is, at the most basic level, and compatible with our own. You found liquid water, an oxygen atmosphere, and, it seems, soil that doesn't need animal life in order to remain fertile. Anyone one of these feats would have been hailed as the scientific discovery of the century under any other circumstances, and the importance of what we accomplished will not be forgotten.

"So don't beat yourselves up over this not panning out. And I promise we'll find suitable ways of acknowledging what you did over the past few days.

"We have a list of four other star systems that mission planners contemplated visiting should it turn out that *nu Phoenicis* didn't have a habitable planet. But we're not going to discuss them just yet." Vargas paused and took a breath. "We have reason to believe there might be a third oxygen/water world here in this system. We'll go there first before considering a new star system. In any event, there's much to be learned right here, and we're considering a landing team to remain here for a four weeks while we go investigate this third terrestrial planet. We'll be soliciting volunteers from the original team." Vargas, realizing he could no longer be heard over the excited babble, leaned back and gave the group a bland and guileless expression

Sheffield and Isaakson stared at him, stupefied. What on Earth was he talking about? There weren't any other terrestrial planets in the habitable zone. Sheffield glanced at Trapp, who smiled back at him like a stoned Buddha. His eyes traveled to Simmons, and he realized the physicist must have found something.

As if he read Sheffield's mind, Vargas nodded to the physicist. "Doctor Simmons, if you would be so kind. . . "

Simmons stood, assuming a professorial air. Sheffield recalled that he had taught at the University of California Portland. "Thank you, Captain."

He started to turn to a white board behind him that wasn't there, and caught himself with a slight chuckle. He picked up his data pad instead, and nodded to the others to do the same.

"We've been examining the planets in this system in considerable detail, partly for the sake of the knowledge to be gained, and partly because some of them may have elements and compounds useful for storing up on fusion fuel and as raw material for the Imprinter. From orbit and at planetary distances, we learned a lot that we couldn't tell from our own solar system, 49.2 light years away."

"We were examining *nu Phoenicis* 2, a gas giant that we dubbed Hō-ō. It's a super Jovian, about 750,000 kilometers in diameter, and with a distinct ring that, surprisingly, consists mostly of water ice. The ring has a very high albedo. The planet has a rapid rotation, about six hours, and so appears almost like an oval on its side and is predominately red and orange and purple." Simmons paused, looked pained. "Someone said it looked like Santa's belly, and since Hō-ō is the Hawaiian name for a firebird, it got that name. Yes?"

Sheffield had raised his hand. "What's the temperature of Hō-ō?"

"About two-fifty centigrade. Upper atmosphere, of course. It may be hotter further in." Simmons held up a hand to forestall the next question.

"I'll explain, Commander. Hō-ō has an entire flock of moons —about fifty of them. Most are tiny, anywhere from two hundred meters to a thousand kilometers in diameter. But it has one moon that's roughly the size of Earth, and it's the closest in. Our examination of it reveals an oxygen atmosphere, liquid water. . . and possible ice caps."

"How far from Zhar-Ptitsa is it?"

"About one point two AUs. As you doubtlessly know, the habitable zone is one point six AUs on out to about two point two AUs. Nevertheless, it has liquid water, oxygen, and doesn't appear to be all that hot."

Sheffield glared at the physicist, half expecting a joke. Slowly he turned his gaze to Vargas.

Vargas nodded back. "Doctor Simmons has shared his data with the bridge, and we're of the opinion that the evidence is compelling enough to warrant a close-up inspection. At the very worst, if it turns out there's potable water and other minerals there, and it's not radioactive, we can stock up for the next voyage."

"Ice caps? Really?"

"The northern pole matches the albedo of ice. The southern pole is cloud covered. Water clouds. We think it's mostly a water planet with some land, mostly in the northern hemisphere."

Vargas interjected, "And it's cool enough to support an evaporation/condensation cycle. We think the surface temperature is about thirty five on average."

"That's pretty hot. Earth was twenty five, and a good chunk of it is uninhabitable. What's it like at the equator?"

"Hot. We probably wouldn't be able to live there. But if there's a zone capable of supporting water ice, then there's a zone we can work even if it's small." Vargas glanced at the physicist. "Doctor Simmons? Anything to add to your report?"

Simmons nodded. "You can find a more thorough rundown on your data pads under *Nu Phoenicis* 2/1, Hō-ō One. But in summation, there's nothing we can see from here that precludes the possibility of human habitation."

* * *

From the Ship's Log:

Nu *Phoenicis* 2/1

Hō-ō One is the first moon (of about twenty significant moons and thirty lesser moons) of the planet Hō-ō, which is the second planet out from nu Phoenicis, re-dubbed Zhar-Ptitsa (Fire Bird) by some of the crew. The firebird imagery used for the star and its system of planets and moons come from the fact that it was part of the Phoenix constellation, visible in the southern hemisphere of Earth.

Hō-ō is a ringed gas giant. Typical of its class, it has an atmosphere comprised mostly of hydrogen and helium, with no discrete surface. Its mass is a very light $1.52x \ 10^{28}$ kilograms, which may explain why it hasn't achieved fusion. The rings are composed mostly of water ice, floating bergs ranging in size from a half meter to two hundred and fifty kilometers. The rings have a high albedo, which helps explain why they don't simply melt and disperse. There is reason to believe that as they orbit the planet, they do melt during their day, and refreeze at night. Gravitational perturbations, primarily from Hō-ō One, prevent the rings from coalescing at their Trojan points. Or so it is believed.

Zhar-Ptitsa is an F8 star, slightly larger and whiter than Sol, and high in metallics. It is a stable star, with variation of less than one percent, like Sol. It is believed to have a characteristic sunspot cycle of about fourteen Earth years, and coronal mass ejections are believed to be at worst about ten percent more powerful than Earth's. Both this moon and Hō-ō have strong magnetic fields which should provide adequate protection to colonists on the surface.

Hō-ō One is at one point two astronomical units from Zhar-Ptitsa, a distance considered to be too close for human habitation. However, there are mitigating factors that make nearly small portions of the existing land mass potentially suitable for human colonization.

Hō-ō One has an average rotational period of 23.6 hours, and a surface gravity of .77. In orbit just over one point three seven five million kilometers above Hō-ō's center of gravity, it revolves around Hō-ō once every 10.2 days, and has about a thirty degree axial tilt in relation to the mother planet. It orbits in the same plane as the rings, and the large majority of other moons that Hō-ō has.

Hō-ō itself has an axial inclination of nearly thirty degrees, and combined with its orbital period (c. 440 days) suggests that seasons will not only be longer, but more extreme than is found on Earth. During a combined "big solstice" and "little solstice" the Moons angle of inclination will be sixty degrees from the equinoctial mean (Zhar Ptitsa directly over the equator at local noon). That's nearly three times what Earth experiences, and the seasons there can be pretty extreme. The sidereal diurnal period varies by a predictable amount due to orbital precession, including about three hours per ten-day "month" when it is actually moving retrograde to its solar orbit. The amount of inclination overall depends on the axial tilt of Hō-ō during its 440 day orbit, and the result is that in each year of the mother planet, the moon has about 42 "mini years". While the winters might not be too extreme, summer heat in many regions will exceed human tolerance.

Prof. Tim Simmons, 28/127

* * *

The same crew left for *nu Phoenicis* 4 (now universally known as "Disappointment") two days later, with six weeks' provisions and a carefully tuned reverse osmosis/charcoal filter system so the shuttle could avail itself of the outside air. A similar filtration system was devised for a water tank. Finally, small filters were attached to the air tank recharging unit. This made possible a much longer stay on Disappointment. Everyone carried rad counters.

There was a certain amount of bribery involved. In return for giving up on being the first to step out on to Hō-ō One, the seven members of the Disappointment landing crew each got a major land mass named after them. First stop would be on the first large continent they landed on previously, now formally known as "Sheffield." Each member got naming rights for major geographical features in each continent named after them.

It seemed a reasonable payoff for a fairly minor sacrifice. Nobody doubted that humans would find a use for Disappointment, and Hō-ō One didn't seem all that promising. The general consensus on board *Phoenix* was that Hō-ō One would turn out to be one big steamy desert. Vargas had to solicit volunteers for the landing party.

Lung cancer or no, Disappointment was some appealing real estate.

When *Phoenix* backed into the Hō-ō system and was brought about so the bridge could get a look at the planet, the immediate visceral response of everyone on board was a shudder of disgust. The moon was a vivid reddish-purple, a cross between an overripe plum and a black eye. It was ugly. It didn't look habitable.

It took a few moments to realize why it looked that way. They were on the night side of the moon, and Hō-ō was behind them. Hō-ō was nearly full, and reflected a bright red light. "Full moon nights" on Hō-ō One might turn out to be all violets and purples.

Orbit brought them over the terminator in about twenty minutes, and everyone on board heaved a collective sigh of relief. The moon was showing the standard blues and whites of an oxygen-water world. A lot of white, and very pale blue, though.

Spencer stared at the screen thoughtfully. "Where's the land?" he demanded. He had petitioned, with no real expectation of success, to be on the landing crew on the grounds that psychological knowledge might be gained. Vargas, feeling kindly disposed and secretly amused that anyone actually volunteered, had assented.

Vargas replied, "There's not a lot of land on this world. It's about four-fifths ocean. And the possibly usable land is all above eighty degrees north. There's just two land masses; a long thin one that snakes over the north pole – it's at its thickest just south of the pole – and a round island at about seventy five degrees south. There might be land at the south pole, too, but it isn't very big." Vargas pointed to a spot about a thousand kilometers from the pole. "Our first landing will be there. It's smoothly rising terrain, going from sea level up to about nine kilometers. We'll land at about three thousand meters."

"Excuse me, Captain. Did you say nine kilometers? Above sea level?"

"There are some very tall mountains on this moon. Some go as high as twenty kilometers. That's more than double Mons Olympus."

"Wow. Spectacular scenery."

"The really tall mountains are about four hundred kilometers from the landing site. We should be able to see them. It depends on how clear the air is."

"Why that site, Captain?"

"Well, it's at elevation, which means it's cooler. We think the ambient temperature is about forty degrees. It's drier, we think, and it looks to be level and free of trees, ideal for a settlement. In some ways, it's like the Kent site on Disappointment: open country, near a river, and looks uninhabited."

"There have been no signs of life, I take it?"

"Well, vegetation."

"You know what I mean, Captain."

"No BEMs, either."

"Um, Beems?"

"Bug Eyed Monsters. No signs of intelligent life. Or humans." Vargas flapped his data pad closed. with a tight smile. "Final briefing is at 0600 tomorrow. Get a good night's sleep, if you can."

* * *

Vargas dreamed that night. True dreams, rather than the flash-dreams that still irritated everyone several times a day. He dreamt of the jungles of Venus, vast banyan trees acres in size, snakes as big around as a ship module, lovely golden maidens who wanted to know what is this thing called 'love'? Giant orange butterflies drifted under ceaseless clouds, and deep in the jungle, the tom-toms of natives could be heard. Vargas smiled in his sleep and then dreamed of Julie.

* * *

Spencer dreamed. He dreamt of being caught in endless mesh, as incredibly hot fires roared nearby. He didn't feel trapped so much as he felt enveloped. The plains went on forever under a violet night sky, and dawn was announced by flashes of rainbows, prismatic spears across the sky. He didn't smile in his sleep, but neither did he cry out.

Chapter 14 Lassiter's Landing

THE LANDING PARTY LEADER WAS COMMANDER Gordon Lassiter, the CTO. Spencer was second in command. He was pleasantly surprised to learn that the other ranking member of the expedition was Julie Steinberg, herself a doctor and an epidemiologist. He knew about the piano sessions with Captain Vargas, and Spencer wondered if that factored into his request that she come along on the landing. Of course, Spencer didn't have any particular qualifications for a First Landing himself, and he suspected that Vargas was rewarding him for finding the solution to the hibernation syndrome crisis. Michael Matthews, Günther Brülow, Susan Bartlett, and Ian Mann made up the rest of the scientific complement. The gopher was ABS Matthew Bissont, himself a chemical engineer specializing in toxicology, For a second string landing party, Spencer thought, it was a pretty good group. Heavy on botany and farming.

Madelyn Isaakson, nine light minutes away on Disappointment, looked over the specifications for the atmosphere of Hō-ō One, conferred with Sheffield, and sent back recommended angle of entry numbers. Since Lassiter and Mann were the only ones other than Captain Vargas himself rated to fly the shuttles, and her help was deeply appreciated. As Mann assured Spencer with a smile, "Now there's at least a ten percent chance we'll survive the atmospheric entry."

An hour after leaving *Phoenix*, Mann would have regretted that quip if it weren't for the fact he was too busy to remember making it. The atmosphere of Hō-ō One was turbulent, with air pockets tossing the craft around like it was a kite. There was no question of anyone depending on bungee cords to prevent broken bones or death on this landing; everyone was securely strapped in, depending on their data pads to see what the pilots were seeing as they fought to keep breakfast.

The clouds swept in around the craft, and they found themselves flying by instrument, with no GPS or navigation beacons to assist. Lassiter slouched in his seat, watching the radar intently, waiting for Mann to say there was a break in the pea soup. As they dropped below a half a kilometer, the wind abruptly let up, and a small patch of ground became visible. Lassiter slowed the craft as much as he dared, not wanting to risk a stall if the winds should suddenly return, and then they were beneath the clouds. Below them, the landscape stretched, as flat and smooth as a pool table. Mann checked and corrected three degrees. Lassiter scanned instruments. "Outside ambient temperature is fifty degrees. Let's go upslope a couple of thousand meters." Mann nodded, and they flew over the unceasing, seemingly endless green field. Between the flat land and the nimbus clouds, it was a singularly featureless and monotonous landscape. But not dark; the clouds almost shone with an inner white light, and the vegetation below glinted, suggesting recent rain. Mann corrected again and murmured to Lassiter, "Headwind. About sixty knots, I make it, steady from the north."

"What's our altitude?"

"About five and a half klicks."

"And the estimated ground temperature?"

"Twenty eight degrees."

"Good enough. Let's put her down."

"Yes Ser."

The landing, after the rough ride, was uneventful. The craft slid to a stop, and because there was still a fair bit of wind, Mann deployed the 'anchors' so the craft wouldn't get flipped by a stray sideways gust. They suited up, and Lassiter reached to his pilot's side console and drew out a slip of paper. He caught Spencer's eye, held it up, and nodded. Spencer, still looking a bit green from the wild entry, nodded back.

He and Spencer entered the airlock together, but due to rank, Lassiter stepped onto the land first. Opening the piece of paper carefully, he intoned, "It seems to be a law inflexible and inexorable that he who will not risk cannot win." He gave Spencer a grin. "Did I get that right?"

"Sure did. Back in Cornwall, Douglas Reeman's nose is itching." And that will make the Captain happy, Spencer thought. They had discussed Vargas' childhood reading habits before.

Lassiter blinked. He liked the psychiatrist, but he said some strange things sometimes. He had acceded to a request from Spencer that these be the first words uttered on this world, and since he was utterly stuck for a good phrase of his own, it looked like it would work. He had no idea who Richard Bolitho was, or why Douglas Reeman would have an itchy nose. But he liked the "no risk, no win" sentiment. It sounded like something his boyhood hero, John Paul Jones, might have said.

"Looks like the North Slope," Lassiter remarked. He took a long, searching look around, and shouldered his rifle. He gave Spencer a thumbs up.

"Yeah. Only flatter and less interesting. Let's hope this planet isn't going to be a bust, too." Spencer walked to the front of the shuttle and waved. It's OK to come out, folks.

Two by two they left the shuttle, blinking at this strange new world.

Bartlett bent down and picked a blade of what Spencer had taken for grass and peered at it. Some moisture dripped from it, and she brought it up to her faceplate to sniff at it, and stopped, embarrassed. Spencer quickly diverted his attention so as to not disconcert her from his noticing the faux pas. Now curious, he bent down and examined the turf. Rather than blades, they were thin tubes, vivid green, and ranging from a millimeter to about a half meter in height. He picked a tall one, and it broke off readily. The moisture, he saw, was in the hollow middle of the tube. The outside appeared slightly waxy, not unlike some desert plants he'd seen. He eyed the lowering clouds. This sure didn't look like a desert climate. He sniffed, and caught himself, laughing at his foolishness. Hadn't he just spotted Susan making the same mistake?

He realized he was blinking a lot, and his eyes were starting to itch. He turned to Lassiter. "Gord, I think there's something wrong with my air recycler. My eyes are itching." Gord turned to examine him, and Spencer realized his eyes were blinking and watery, too. Lassiter suddenly looked around. "Everyone! Polarize your face plates now! Right now!" He lifted his arm and adjusted his. Abruptly his face darkened.

Feeling slightly puzzled, Spencer turned his down. The landscape dimmed. He hadn't realized just how bright. . . ah.

Gordon looked at the rest to make sure everyone had obeyed. "We're under an F8 star, and here it's about thirty percent brighter than the sun we're used to. We're getting snow blindness."

Günther spoke up. "But it's cloudy, and there's no snow."

"Doesn't matter. UV gets through the clouds just fine. Keep your faceplate polarized at all times during daylight hours. That's an order."

Julie peered up into the clouds. "If we settle here, we're going to have to worry about sun exposure. Not just our eyes, but our skin. I don't think we could be out in this long without the protection from our suits. It's not as big a problem as radon, but. . ."

Gordon nodded. Obviously that had already occurred to him. He rubbed his gloves briskly. "Right, people. Let's get our gear set up and start finding out what sort of place this is."

* * *

By the time they returned to the shuttle, Zhar-Ptitsa was low in the west. Days were nearly a half an hour shorter here, and Spencer wondered how that would affect human biorhythms. Basically, they would be moving their clocks ahead 24 minutes a day. Some people had trouble adjusting to the annual Daylight Saving Time, and that was only once a year. Not every second day. There was a fair bit of material in the library about human maladaptation to the Martian Sol.

Once out of their suits, eaten, and freshened up, they gathered to put together a concise report for *Phoenix*. There had been a steady stream of data sent up during her five passes overhead, but it was raw data, uncollated and uninterpreted. Gordon pulled out a keyboard and typed furiously for a couple of minutes. "Here," he announced, and hit send. Spencer read his data pad.

"This moon has an atmosphere of 26% oxygen and 73% nitrogen, with trace amounts of other inert gases. The elevated oxygen levels (Earth is 19.5%) do not present any immediate health problems for humans, but there is a clear and obvious danger with fire. Concentrations of carbon dioxide, methane, carbon monoxide, sulfur dioxide and radon are negligible. It is unknown what, if any effect the elevated oxygen concentration (about 205 millibars partial pressure) will have on horticulture.

CO2 levels are roughly 150 parts per million, and Earth plant life may need some sort of artificial augmentation."

Bissont said, "Commander, we're going to have to make sure our clothing is utterly nonflammable."

"Good." Lassiter typed. "Anything else?"

Julie was staring out the front window. "Speaking of fire, I think we have one to the east."

The crew looked, and crowded to the windshield for a better look. A red glow was visible along the eastern horizon, and was visibly spreading as they looked. Lassiter beckoned Mann. "Let's get the shuttle ready for a quick take off if needed. If that is a fire, it's coming this way."

There was a thin whine as the engines started. The pilots started doing a rundown for atmosphere-only flight.

Gordon heard Günther exclaim "Scheiße!!" Similar gasps came from the rest of the crew as they realized what they were looking at. Günther shook his head. "Just how big is that verdammt thing?"

The entire eastern horizon was a deep red, swollen above the horizon, slowly forming an arc.

Mann looked up. "Fuck me. Is that Hō-ō?"

In minutes there was enough of the mother planet in the sky that there could no longer be any mistaking it. Because of the thin clouds, it was a featureless outline orb, but still awe-inspiring. "It's huge!" Julie gasped. It must be ten times the size of the Moon."

Bissont tapped keys on his data pad. "It should subtend about. . . keerist. . . forty degrees of arc. About eighty times the diameter of our old Moon, I would say." Lassiter, feeling a bit silly, shut down the shuttle's engine.

The top of the planet vanished behind a thicker layer of cloud, which promptly turned a sort of luminescent beet red. Spencer thought to himself that something that big rising in the sky ought to have a soundtrack. If not Wagner, at least a deep, loud rumble.

"I hope this cloud cover breaks," Matthews said. "I would truly love to see that thing when it's angry."

"It looked like the cloud cover was starting to break up when we came in," Gordon replied. He pointed. Look there." About ten degrees above the horizon, some of Hō-ō shone through the cloud. As he watched, a shooting star streaked across the gap. The sky was now nearly all beet red, and the green foliage outside was now a deep purple. Eerie, Gordon thought. This will take some getting used to.

When *Phoenix* was next overhead, Gordon had more to report.

"On a non-scientific note, the sight of Hō-ō at night when it is in opposition is breathtaking. The rings extend across the sky as a thin white line, somewhat iridescent. Not all our members appreciated the beauty, and some found it mildly oppressive. The deep red light is actually a bit spooky.

"So: back to this moon. The primary area investigated is a grassy plain, roughly triangular, with an apex where a glacial-fed river branches, forming two sides of the delta to the sea. Roughly three hundred kilometers from apex to base, it covers an area of about thirty thousand square kilometers. The most distinctive feature is that the entire region appears to be given over to just one type of tubule. Our botanist, Doctor Susan Bartlett, is of the opinion that while the plant, which averages about fifteen centimeters in height, is not suitable for human consumption, but appears to have the fiber and nutrients that Earthly ruminants, such as cattle, horses or deer, might be able to utilize.

"The method of propagation for this plant is unknown. It may be that it flowers or bears fruit, and is simply out of season. Also unknown is why is so completely dominates this locale, but is not in evidence at all on the other side of the river.

"That other side is densely populated with many types of trees, which are presumed to be deciduous. Similar to Earth-evolved trees, they appear to have a woody trunk that will prove valuable in construction, and the leaves tend to be thick, waxy broad leaf, or needles. These are configurations associated with extreme climates on Earth, but may mean something else entirely here. However, the river, which is very fast and about fifty meters wide, is impassible, and we will have to relocate the shuttle in order to get a closer examination of the biota. Consider this a request to relocate tomorrow morning.

It's the feeling of the crew that we have, for now, exhausted the possibilities of discovery in this location."

Spencer had an unbidden memory of a paper he read at college, of the amazing variety of life to be found in the flat and seemingly featureless lawn of an English county estate. He wondered what secrets the army of little green tubes hid.

* * *

Notes from Doctor Ian Spencer's personal log, Year 28, Day 137.

Our first night on this strange new world, and it was a somewhat troubled one. We retired at 2200 hours, shortly after Phoenix's last flyover. The cloud cover that had obscured our view of the nearly-full Hō-ō broke about an hour before, and the planet really is a tremendous sight. It's mostly reds and yellows, with other colors mixed in a complex pattern of bands and swirls. There's a thin white line across it that I'm told is the planetary ring, and the shadow of the ring falls on the planet, about ten times as wide and to the south. Doctor Brülow tells me that the shadow can tell you at a glance what the planetary season is, since it's a sort of orbital sundial. If the shadow is south, then it is summer in the northern hemisphere. According to Ring Shadow, we're just coming up on the summer solstice. Everyone has the calendar and a clock on their data pads, and both are perfectly useless since they are calibrated to Earth orbital motions. So until someone figures out a new clock and calendar and programs the data pads, the seasonal shadow may be of some limited use.

There's a lot of shooting stars. All you have to do is look at the night sky and you'll probably see one. Some are bright enough that even with Hō-ō behind them, you can spot them easily.

I had just drifted off to sleep when shrieks tore through the cabin. It was Michael Matthews, who was wakened from a terrible nightmare. He wasn't able to give the specifics, beyond a feeling of being pressed upon, and a deep feeling of dread. He apologized (unnecessarily) and went back to his cot, and went back to sleep instantly.

Less than an hour later Gordon Lassiter had a bad dream, and Julie Steinberg not long after that. Julie's was of particular concern to me because she had been an insomniac (in the hibernation-adverse sense of the word) for several years on the ship, and struggled back from significant personal impairment. At times I had harbored doubts that she would be fully functional again, but she is. But I worry that she might be more vulnerable to this emotional dislocation than the others.

I realized that the moving 'moonbeams' from Hō-ō were fully on each of them at the time of the nightmares, and suggested, as an experiment, that we fully opaque the windows (ports) of the landing craft and see if that helped.

Apparently it did because nobody else had any dreams. At least, nobody woke up screaming. I'm tentatively postulating that the light from Hō-ō is of a hue that people unconsciously find disturbing. Or even consciously—I know I find it a bit oppressive when I'm awake.

I woke up myself about an hour before sunrise...excuse me, Zharrise, and realizing I was unlikely to fall asleep despite feeling fairly tired, I made myself a cup of coffee and grabbed a breakfast bar and slid into the copilot's chair to watch the Zharrise. Even though Hō-ō was behind the craft, setting in the west, I was careful to draw the curtains behind me before deopaquing the windows.

With the sun well below the horizon and Hō-ō very nearly set, I had a good view of the night sky. At first glance it resembles the night sky on Earth, and on second glance, it is at least somewhat familiar. The Milky Way is still there, of course, and I could recognize several constellations, although some of them were a bit different. It sort of puts the vastness of the galaxy in perspective. We traveled fifty light years over twenty eight years and if the galaxy could be viewed as a big city, we traveled less than a single block. And the galaxy is only one of trillions. . .

One important difference here in the night sky. The angle of the Zhar system is different, with the orbital disk on its side compared to the solar system. So here, the Milky Way rises in the east and sets in the west each night. We're at the time of year when the center of the Milky Way passes overhead about midnight. In two hundred and twenty days, Günther tells me, the night sky will be darker and less interesting. And slowly return in the spring.

I happened to glance at the outside temperature sensing unit, and got a mild surprise. It was only thirteen above out there. It had been thirty seven the previous afternoon, so that's quite a temperature swing. And it had been mostly cloudy during the day. If it's that cold on a partly cloudy summer night, what are the winters like?

Oh. It is "little winter" here. We're at a point in our orbit around Hō-ō that the northern hemisphere is away from the sun. This overlay of seasons is going to be confusing.

We can survive twenty-five degree daily swings in temperatures, but can our plants? Maybe Susan will have an answer to that.

I decided to go outside, and watch the Zharrise. First human to see it. Pure narcissism on my part, of course. Moving quietly, I was able to don my suit and retrieve a gun from stores. I wasn't particularly anxious to carry a weapon, but Lassiter decreed that everyone be armed until we're certain there's nothing out there that might be a threat to us. Sheffield told me of one flash-dream he had in which he woke up on nu Phoenicis 4 in the shuttle to find dinosaurs peering in at him hungrily. As I stepped out, I looked carefully for dinosaurs. I'm happy to report there were none.

I was sorely tempted to remove my face mask and breathe the air, but we're under orders. We don't know what kinds of microorganisms are in the air here, or if they can invade our systems and perhaps cause harm or disease. Similarly, the scientists want as much time as possible to study this place before we infect it with our own microorganisms. One human turd could contaminate the entire planet.

I thought they were joking but then Trapp reminded me of the "Life on Mars" furor in the late twenty-first century. They found microorganisms on the Martian surface during the first manned landing, and excitedly announced there was life on Mars. But then it was discovered that they were Earthly organisms that apparently rode in on the Viking spacecraft, which landed nearly a century earlier and a quarter of a planet away.

They found more organisms on the Martian coin, too. For anyone who doesn't know about that, they visited the roving site of a robotic Americaner. . . no, it was American back then,

American robot probe, and were greatly perplexed to find several dozen meters away from the inert corpse of Curiosity a minor American coin known as a "penny". Even more perplexing, the coin was dated 1909, over a century before the probe was launched.

Assiduous research determined that the technicians building the craft did attach the penny to the cowling of the craft, apparently with the knowledge and consent of the authorities. Why they did this is unknown, at least to me. But they found Earth microorganisms on the coin and around it in the dust. Seventy five years after the coin got there.

Nobody knows how the coin ended up so far from the craft. Wind storms, perhaps?

But if human germs can survive on Mars, they can certainly survive here. . .

Here's the sunrise. The first thing on this moon that I can unreservedly call beautiful.

[Break]

It's five hours later. Julie and I have been taking samples all morning. Our suits do a good job of shielding us from the glare and heat, but it's still sweaty, tiring work. We lifted off about two hours after sunrise, leaving Brülow and Matthews to determine how to get soil samples. Apparently there's a thick mat of roots under the tubular grass, and they've been having trouble penetrating it. The rest of us crossed over the river into a clearing. We can actually see poor Brülow and Matthews from here, and I gather they're going to try to burn through the roots with phosphorous next. Poor Matthews has been all but screaming in rage and frustration at the nearly impenetrable mat under his feet.

My mood, and to a lesser degree the mood of the group, is somewhat contaminated this morning. I had an odd confrontation with Lassiter shortly after sunrise.

He came out of the shuttle, and just from his body language I could tell he was upset. He approached me, and demanded to know what I was doing outside. I explained that just wanted to get more of a feel for this place, and, under the impression that he was upset that I had taken an unnecessary chance, showed him that I brought a weapon, and had been carefully scanning to make certain nothing was approaching me. He asked how long I had been out there, and I told him it had been forty-five minutes, well after first light. (Dusks and dawns are elongated this far north).

He then demanded to know if I had been in contact with the Captain. I said that I had not, and that the Captain wasn't even due to assume normal duty for another hour and a half. He asked if I had been in contact with anyone aboard Phoenix today, and I said I had not. He glared at me and said, "I can check that, you know." I smiled and acknowledged that he certainly could, and asked him why my speaking to anyone on board would be of concern. He refused to answer, instead telling me that I would have to do without breakfast since I had been "lallygagging" out here. I refrained from mentioning that I had already eaten breakfast, and asked him if he was really going to deny me breakfast for disobeying an order that hadn't been given. In retrospect, I was perhaps a bit too confrontational. Not very professional of me, I admit. He snapped that I was violating a standing order not to be outside alone, and I did have to concede that I hadn't been thinking, smiled and apologized.

He looked openly angry, and told me the others would be out in a minute, there was a lot of work to be done, and he didn't have time to indulge some prima donna psychiatrist who had no business on board in the first place. He then stalked away in a towering passive-aggressive snit, leaving me dumbfounded. His whole tone toward me had changed just like that. We had, I thought, been on cordial terms.

I speculate that he is embarrassed that he woke up screaming in the night like a child the evening before, and the hostility is just his way of processing that.

Later, when we got here and he assigned teams to do certain jobs, he teamed me with Julie and made the snide comment that the fact we were in ground suits meant he wouldn't need to send a chaperon along. Julie wasn't in earshot, or I would have filed a formal complaint against him on the spot, and I may yet when we return to the ship. That was entirely inappropriate. I was perplexed.

Now I'm angry.

What's going on?

Chapter 15 Dereliction of Duty

IAN MANN LOOKED UP from locking the copilot's console and realized the shit was about to really and truly hit the fan. Vargas was glaring at the shuttle, and Mann couldn't recall seeing such an expression of cold fury on the Cap's face. He didn't even want to be in the same time zone as that expression. Carefully avoiding eye contact with Commander Lassiter, with whom he had argued all the way back to *Phoenix*, he went back and waited for the airlock to cycle open. He was the first out, with the four other crew members right behind him, Lassiter taking up the rear. Vargas shook his head slightly at the crewmen, signaling them to get the hell out of his way, and strode up to Lassiter.

"Commander, I do not see Doctors Spencer or Steinberg in your party. May I ask why that is the case?"

"Sir, there were instances of gross dereliction of duty and insubordination. It was my judgment that they presented a danger to the crew and to myself, and there was no safe way to restrain them for a trip up to the ship."

"And so you marooned two of our top physicians on an unknown alien world?"

"That's correct, sir."

"And did you leave them extra air? Food? Water?"

Lassiter's silence was an answer.

"Weapons? Shelter?"

Lassiter shook his head.

Vargas gave him an icy stare. "Commander, you are relieved of duty and may consider yourself confined to quarters. And so help me, if you disobey, I'll have you shot. Dismissed." Lassiter started to say something, and the Captain roared, "DISMISSED!" Tight lipped, Lassiter strode to the decontamination bay.

171

Vargas focused his attention on Mann. In a milder tone he asked, "Lieutenant, do you feel up to returning to the landing site and retrieving the Doctors?"

"Um, yes Ser, but I'm not rated for the right hand chair."

"No matter. I'll be flying it."

"Ser?"

"Do you see any other rated pilots around? My two lead pilots are on Disappointment, the rest are all still in cold storage, and the Commander has apparently lost his. . . is indisposed. I hope. That leaves me and thee, and we have two people down there that I don't fancy leaving after night fall." He turned to one of the shuttle mechanics. "When will this be ready to return to the landing site?"

"Um, not until tomorrow, Ser? It needs to be. . . "

"Any others in the ready queue?"

"Ser, yes Ser. In module Three. You can probably have her out the port in twenty minutes."

"Good man. Lieutenant, let's go."

* * *

Once targeted for reentry, there was nothing for the two men to do for the next eighteen minutes except bounce around in the turbulence. They ran down a belated flight check, and Captain Vargas pulled out his data pad and turned it off. He gave Mann a direct look, which Mann understood. He turned his off. Time for private-speak.

"Ian, I'll be giving you a formal debriefing once we get Spencer and Steinberg back. What you tell me now will go a long way to determining your role in any proceedings we need to take as far as discipline goes. Am I clear?"

"Perfectly, Captain. Ask away."

"What did you see?"

"There had been some friction between Commander Lassiter and Lt. Commander Spencer earlier in the day. I'm afraid I don't know what the exact nature of it, except the commander complained to us that Spencer was undisciplined and a bit of a prima donna. I thought it was odd to hear that."

Vargas' tone was dry. "It's not something they teach you to do in Officer's Training School. What happened after that?"

"Well, we were taking samples in a field on the north side of the river, and were finishing up for the day. The two doctors were still getting their equipment together, and they were probably a bit slow about it because it wasn't really anything they trained for." There was an instant of silence as Mann realized he was dangerously close to making a reproach on the Captain's decision to send them down in the first place. But Vargas seemed content to merely listen. "Commander Lassiter saw the rest of us were ready, and said that we would go and get Brülow and Matthews, who were at the first landing site, still working on getting soil samples. He stated we could then return to get the doctors."

"Did that strike you as odd?"

"A bit, but I knew the doctors were armed, and nothing had presented itself as any kind of a threat."

"Did Commander Lassiter seem to be conscious of a timetable?"

"Yes Ser. Although I'm not sure why. By the time we retrieved Brülow and Matthews, and then went back and got Spencer and Steinberg, we would have missed the takeoff window and had to wait another ninety-five minutes. It would have saved time to just wait for the doctors to finish up."

"So you picked up Brülow and Matthews. What happened next?"

"That's when Lassiter informed us that Spencer had made threats against himself and us, and Spencer was vowing to cause the shuttle to crash because we were going to recommend colonization to begin and Spencer said...the Commander said he said that this world was not suitable for human habitation and he would oppose us by force."

"Did you believe him?"

"Ser, he was my commanding officer."

Vargas searched Mann's face. "Very well," he said after a moment. "You mentioned some friction earlier."

"Yes Ser. I don't know the exact nature of it," Mann repeated nervously.

"Right. You were leaving two lightly-armed medical personnel on an unknown planet. Even if there were no obvious dangers, there are a million possible threats. Did you, or anyone, object?"

"Captain, we all objected, and I believe everyone uploaded a formal protest to the ship's log. A couple of us even considered the possibility of taking control of the shuttle and returning."

"And you decided not to do this because. . . ?"

"Part of it is my training. I also considered a brawl on a shuttle in flight to be a bad idea."

"I'm quite sure it would have been. For any number of reasons." A bump rattled the craft. "Right. What's our angle of descent?"

* * *

The shuttle swept around the perimeter of the field with a roar. Zhar-Ptitsa had set nearly an hour earlier, but the long northern dusk gave them some visibility. The ground itself was darkened, and Vargas just had to hope when they put down, the doctors would be able to move out of the way. Then Mann spotted the physicians, standing near the center of the field and waving their penlights. He shook his head but remained silent. The two civilians were right where he planned to put down. Just lucky he spotted them.

He straightened the shuttle out and brought it to a stop about fifty meters from the two. Tapping the console, he sent a message to the data pads of the two castaways to keep their distance. They came in "hot" and there was a risk of fire. The doctors obediently scrambled back a couple of hundred meters and waited patiently. Spencer, Mann saw, was holding a weapon and glancing around the meadow.

* * *

Captain Vargas sealed his suit and recycled the lock. As he waited in the privacy of the airlock for the air to evacuate and be replaced by outside air, he allowed himself the liberty of a grin. The doctors were unharmed, easing the sense of crisis.

If it weren't for the fact they he would probably have to bust the man down to Charlie for what he did, he would kiss Lassiter for giving him an excuse to come down to the surface. Ever since Disappointment came into view on the forward vids several weeks ago, he had been constantly fighting an urge to disregard his responsibility as Captain and go exploring. It was immensely frustrating reading the second hand reports, looking up at the displays of the new worlds, and know that it might be months before he would get a chance to go down there. Indeed, he could be among the last of the crew to do so. He knew he would be in all the history books, but his inner child didn't want history tomes; it wanted comic book adventures.

He suddenly remembered how, during training, he mentioned to Trapp the frustration he felt at having to stay in orbit as a twenty-four century Michael Collins. Both men were off duty and having a drink, and the affable doctor had slapped Vargas on the shoulder and boomed, "Just think of the colonists who face years in hibernation before they get to come down. Years!"

All fine and good, Vargas had answered. But they were totally unaware. They didn't have to look up on their screens and see the promised land, day after day. Trapp merely shook his head at him. Self-pity wasn't productive.

Vargas bounced up on the balls of his feet, savoring the unfamiliar gravity, three quarters that of Earth's. It was a nice change after the orbital micro-gravity on the ship.

The lock cycled, and after a quick check with Mann to be sure everything looked OK, he opened the port. Descending the steps, he waved the two figures to approach.

Unbidden, he thought of his father. Rafe always spoke of the need to find new worlds to explore. Surely dead by now, he lived to see just how literally that would apply to his only son. Daniel took a deep breath, and realized, with a faint feeling of foolishness, that it was just suit's air he was breathing. He looked forward to sniffing the breeze.

Neither doctor looked surprised to see Vargas. Of course, *Phoenix* doubtlessly told them rescue was coming, and wouldn't miss mentioning just who was rescuing them.

After a brief greeting, Vargas helped load equipment in the dock, and signaled Steinberg to climb in first. The lock sealed, and while they were waiting for it to cycle through, Vargas turned to Spencer. "Ian, as soon as we board, you and Julie will be on Captain's detention pending board review. Mister Lassiter is already under quarters detention. Are you pressing criminal charges against him?"

* * *

Spencer felt uncomfortable. Whether it was the nature of the question or the fact that the Captain was clearly in a state he couldn't say.

"I think he reacted to the environment down here—in particular, the nighttime light from the primary. It has an extremely disturbing affect. I don't think it seized control of our minds or anything fantastical like that. But I think it is oppressive and perhaps a little frightening, and we all have a bit of the twingies from ... before. I don't know if it explains what happened here in any way, but several members of the crew had apparently vicious nightmares while sleeping in that light, and Commander Lassiter was one of them."

So was Julie, Spencer thought, and remembered she was in hysterics when they realized the shuttle was returning to orbit without them. He had felt apprehensive, but didn't doubt rescue would come within a couple of hours, hopefully before Zharset, and definitely before Hō-ō rose. He glanced to the east. There was a faint reddish glow on the horizon.

"Thank you for getting us so fast, Captain. I didn't fancy spending a night out in the open here."

"In this man's navy, we always took care of our own. It's a custom too valuable to discard."

Spencer, for once the one whose feeling were being massaged, felt a burst of relief and gratitude.

Chapter 16 A Hearing In Space

EXPLORATION OF THE MOON WAS SUSPENDED. After a conference with Trapp and Nate Harlen, the crew chief, they picked a list of twenty-five sleepers to awaken. All had cycled at least three times through the sleep-wake therapy Spencer had devised, and were, it was hoped, functional.

The unexpected challenges from both Hō-ō One and personnel left Vargas wondering if it had been a mistake to leave Sheffield and his team at the more pleasant, if toxic Disappointment.

He spent most of the day with Trapp simply reading reports relating to the incident. There were the personnel reports, complaints and debriefing reports from all of the crew members, both on the state of Hō-ō One and the events leading to Lassiter leaving the two doctors stranded.

The reports from the Sheffield team had some unexpectedly good news. The planet was rich in minerals, and they had found gold just sitting in large lumps along one stream bed. Sheffield and his people had been running impromptu brain trust sessions each evening, and had come up with an impressive list of reasons why Disappointment could still prove to be an extremely valuable find. Sheffield clearly was thinking of having the planet as an industrial colony planet. With little effort, they had found aluminum, bauxite, uranium, iron and silver. They had even identified a tar pit, strong evidence of copious amounts of oil.

Trapp and Vargas turned their attention to the reports from Hō-ō One. Brülow and Matthews had encountered surprising difficulties in getting standard soil samples. Everywhere they tried to sink a probe, they found an impenetrable mat of root material, so solid and pervasive that Brülow expressed the opinion that the "lawn" on that forty thousand kilometer triangle of land might actually be one huge super organism, a single plant.

Dryly noting that they hadn't come equipped to drill through impenetrable objects, they quickly abandoned the soil probes and tried a variety of ways of getting through the mat. Even phosphorus failed to burn its way through.

Matthews finally hit on trying his sidearm, a standard 300-burst laser weapon. He finally did get through the root mat, completely discharging the weapon in the process. Once holed, they found they could sink a probe without further trouble for about thirty centimeters, and then encountered another mat.

They wound up with one sample from between the two mats, the total they could get after six strenuous hours of effort. The core sample was in quarantine, awaiting examination by a ship's lab.

Brülow was of the opinion that it contained micro-organisms, and preliminary tests suggested that there were nutrients available that could make farming Earth crops feasible. He also suggested that a high-power laser be brought down from the ship and used to test cutting the root mass. He noted that most automatic cutting equipment would be likely to foul quickly in the tangled mass of filaments. Vargas clipped that part of the report and sent it, with a few annotations regarding design suggestions, to Isaacson.

Whatever the personal conflicts might have been the other team had done better on sampling, coming back with a couple of dozen samples, along with a fairly wide variety of vegetation samples. The crew had even found what they first took to be animal life, but realized was a mobile type of plant that slowly moved about, consuming fallen debris from the other vegetation. It took a day to move one meter, but was very thorough. Mann suggested it filled the ecological niche of the ant.

The preliminary climatological survey showed that, as feared, over half the land area on the planet was too extreme for human habitation. The equatorial regions reached into the seventies and eighties, and one spot clocked one-ten, well above boiling.

One area in the tube grass triangle, on the other side of a small ridge that divided the triangle roughly in half, had a temperature anomaly. While the area of first landing had between swings between considerable warmth during the day to coolness at night, This region seemed to have milder conditions. In fact. . .

Vargas zoomed in. There was one area about a thousand meters lower that clocked a high of twenty and a low of ten. Vargas circled it, and sent it to the ship's meteorologist, André Morley, with a question mark.

He signed, leaned back, and looked at Trapp. "Not the most appealing choices, are they?"

"I was just thinking that. We have a paradise that will kill most of us in ten years, or a place that doesn't appear poisonous, but has a climate like Arabia on steroids. Did you notice the tides? Seventy meters, and as high as a hundred meters in some spots!"

"Oh, of course. That bloody big primary. You know, by all rights this moon should be tidally locked, the way Earth's Moon is, one side always facing Hō-ō."

"I can't figure out why it's as cool as it is."

"You call a hundred and ten degrees cool?"

"Yeah, when you consider that it should be closer to three or four hundred degrees. This place should be another Venus."

"Another mystery." Vargas jotted down a note on his data pad.

"Too bad we can't just swap the location of the two worlds."

Vargas smiled. "That would solve a lot of problems."

* * *

When a notification popped up on his data pad from Lassiter requesting permission to address the Captain, Vargas was first tempted to ignore it. Still angry over the stranding of the two physicians, he wasn't inclined to listen to whatever excuses or rationalizations the man might have to make.

But he couldn't just leave him in his cabin.

It was time for a Captain's Post. Trapp and Harlen had already read the formal complaints filed by the two doctors and read the accounts and protests from the crew members involved in the mission. After conferring with them, Vargas opted to ignore the request for a personal meeting, and instead sent a message to Lassiter informing him that Captain's Post would be held in forty five minutes, at 1600 ships' time, and his presence was cordially requested.

Vargas had to smile at the RE military phrasing. In the Americaner military, the order to appear would be just that; a direct order. In RE law, the accused actually had the option of not appearing, although that was considered a prima facie admission of guilt. Vargas found himself half-hoping Lassiter would sit the Post out, although he knew that wasn't going to happen.

The main reason for his reluctance to handle the situation stemmed from the fact that they didn't really have many options in the way of punishment. The ship didn't have a formal brig, and he couldn't exactly strand the man on the planet for the crime of stranding someone on the planet.

And a small voice at the back of his head kept demanding to know why the normally level-headed Lassiter had behaved as he had. Vargas wasn't sure which was worse: a criminally negligent line officer who couldn't be incarcerated, or a man not wholly responsible for his actions, and Vargas had a sinking feeling it might prove to be the latter. That would make a just solution even more difficult.

Captain's Post – the space navy equivalent of a court-martial – was to be held in the Bridge Mess. The somewhat cramped quarters made for an almost friendly session and after looking over the seating, Trapp elected to have the crew members standing by in the nearby chapel room to testify if needed, with only the three line officers, the two doctors, and the accused to begin with.

The proceedings would be recorded in entered into the non-public section of the ship's log, although Vargas himself couldn't have told anyone just whose benefit it was being recorded for. If Lassiter didn't like the results, would he be filing an appeal to the Admiralty? The Admiralty was fifty light years away, and probably a still-cooling radioactive memory.

Still, the unwinking glass eyes would sit in stoic judgment, and would ensure that everyone would strive for a fair result. So it wasn't ridiculous, exactly.

At 1555, Vargas dispatched a crew member to accompany the Commander. It was another empty formality; the "prisoner" was in a cell that didn't lock, and big as it was, the *Phoenix* would still offer few options to an escaped prisoner.

Lassiter came in, wearing a dress uniform and, Vargas noted with grudging approval, with head up and shoulders back. Whatever had happened with the man on the ground, this was the Line Officer Vargas had trained with for over eighteen months.

"Mister Lassiter, please be seated." Lassiter hesitated for a beat, obviously relishing the advantages of remaining standing, and then slid into the chair facing Vargas.

"Commander, you are accused of marooning two officers of the ship on an unknown world, putting their lives at risk. You are also accused of making improper remarks against the two officers, and against crew men who protested what they perceived as illegal orders. These are the most serious of the charges lodged against you, and in the interest of expediting this, I would ask if you are willing to make a plea on those two charges at this time."

"I am, Captain. Guilty on both charges."

Well, Vargas thought to himself sardonically, that certainly simplifies matters. "Commander, the charges are quite serious, and any decision this board makes could have long-lasting and adverse ramifications for you. Are you quite certain this is how you plead?" Vargas wasn't sure if his offer was even remotely required in RE military justice proceedings, but wanted to be sure the man understood what he was getting into. He wished Spencer was there as consulting, rather than as accuser. He could have used some of his expertise on evaluating Lassiter's response.

"Captain, will I have leave to discuss what happened down there before you determine my punishment?"

"We were hoping that you would, Commander. If you're prepared to speak now, we're prepared to listen."

Lassiter nodded. "First, a personal matter." He turned to the physicians. "Doctor Spencer, Doctor Steinberg, I want to apologize for my behavior. It was negligent, unfair, and irrational."

He turned to face Vargas. "Further, I want the record to show that Doctors Spencer and Steinberg at no time behaved in any way other than as exemplary members of the team. Doctor Steinberg disobeyed no orders, and omitted no duties. Doctor Spencer did disregard a standing order, but in retrospect I realize that it was an oversight and not a willful infraction, and could have been remedied by simply referencing the order in question. Captain, I wish to retract the charges I filed against these two. The report is, in its entirety, a fabrication."

Vargas nodded. That, too, made life easier. He was beginning to see a way to resolve this.

Trapp leaned forward, fingers intertwined, chin resting on them. "Commander, why don't you tell us what happened to you down there? I think this panel knows you well enough to know that you weren't yourself. Just tell us why you did it."

Lassiter gave Trapp a level, and to Vargas' eyes, guileless stare. Lassiter had to know the options for punishment were limited, and Trapp would be asking out of professional curiosity, rather than a desire to get Lassiter to self-implicate. More than once, Vargas had heard Trapp tell tales of various disciplinary panels he had been on, and the vapid lust some board members had to get the accused parties to spin rope just so they could hang themselves. Trapp hated the breed.

Lassiter had sat in on the same bull sessions, so his cooperation was no surprise. With slight bemusement, Vargas reflected that the ship had no lawyers on board. That bode well for their future.

"I just felt extremely anxious and unsure of myself. I was thinking paranoid thoughts, convinced that the doctors and others were acting in union against me. Looking back, I know there isn't any rational basis for those feelings. There was no conflict amongst the crew, other than what I was creating myself."

Trapp nodded as if the answer were no surprise to him. "Did you feel that way when you were leaving the *Phoenix* on this mission?"

"No, Commander. I was feeling buoyant, if the truth be told. I was going to be the first man to step on a new world. Who wouldn't be excited?"

"And there was no conflict with the doctors at that time?"

"None. In fact, I was sort of stuck for famous first words, and Doctor Spencer was kind enough to give me a suggestion." He glanced at Spencer apologetically. "I'm afraid I was a bit excited and left the author's name off." Spencer shook his head, dismissing the implied apology, smiling. Lassiter took a piece of paper from his tunic and pushed it carefully across the table.

Vargas opened it up and read it aloud. "It seems to be a law inflexible and inexorable that he who will not risk cannot win." His jaw dropped open and he glanced at Spencer, and added, "Alexander Kent." No wonder the quote had seemed familiar. It was from his favorite book as a youth.

"You read the reports of our first day ground side. I certainly wouldn't call them routine, but everyone, myself included, were carrying out our duties in a calm and professional manner. That was especially true when we tested the air and found it was suitable for humans. I did remind everyone to keep their masks in place, since we didn't know what microorganisms Hō-ō One might have.

"We encountered problems with getting some samples, as the reports detail, but everyone on the crew was performing their tasks competently and with no friction.

"Then the day ended. We gathered up everything we didn't want to risk losing to unknown dangers overnight, got back in the shuttle, and had dinner. Then Zhar-Ptitsa set.

"The reports from the Sheffield expedition on Disappointment had actually prepared us for some of the strangeness of this new world. The silence, for example. We discovered no large animal life in the areas we were in, just like the Sheffield team, and so we were kind of prepared for the silence.

"We adjusted to the gravity pretty quickly. But nothing prepared us for Hō-ō. First, there's the sheer size of the damn planet. Hō-ō in opposition is a deep blood red color, and it's a shade that just jangles the nerve ends. The landscape that was green is now the color of an eggplant, and it just puts your teeth on edge."

From the side of the table, both Spencer and Steinberg nodded agreement.

"We turned up the inside lighting in the cabin, and that made the atmosphere a lot more tolerable. Of course, we turned the lights back down when we turned in, but we figured, hell, we would be asleep, our eyes would be closed, and the light wouldn't be a problem.

"But it was. First Matthews woke up screaming, and then I did. No, I don't remember what the dream was, just that I was scared out of my wits. Then Dr. Steinberg had one." Vargas glanced over at Julie, who looked openly startled and glanced at Spencer, who nodded affirmation. Interesting, Vargas thought. She doesn't even remember having the dream.

"Someone hit on the idea of opaquing the windows, and then we all slept through until Zharrise."

"Star Rise?" Trapp inquired.

Lassiter smiled, "That's what the crew called morning on Hō-ō One. From Zhar-Ptitsa, you understand. Zharrise."

"I see." Vargas tried not to smile, failed. "Do go on."

"All of us except the doctor."

"Doctor Spencer, you mean?"

"Right. He got up early, and went out right at Zharrise."

Vargas looked to Spencer. "Will you confirm that, Doctor?"

"I did. I should have waited and gotten permission from the Commander. We had standing orders to only work outside in groups of twos or threes, and I neglected that."

"Commander Lassiter, what was your reaction when you saw that Doctor Spencer had left the craft alone?"

"I would have to say it was disproportionate. I should have sent a message to his pad reminding him of the standing order and to get back inside the craft, and if I felt his response was reluctant in any way, given him a private lecture later. Instead, I went out and yelled at him, and. . ." Lassiter bit his lip and looked down. ". . . and I told him that because he went out, he wasn't getting any breakfast."

"May I say something?" Spencer asked.

"No!" chorused all three line officers as one. There was a flurry of quick glances amongst them, and Vargas explained. "You'll have your chance to testify, Doctor. But for now, it's Commander Lassiter's floor."

Lassiter was looking at Spencer intently. He turned back to the panel. "May I have permission to ask Doctor Spencer a direct question? It pertains to my testimony."

The three exchanged glances again. None of them had ever sat on a courts-martial like this before. Finally Vargas nodded. "Ask away."

"Doctor, what was your emotional reaction to my behavior?"

Vargas leaned forward. "I would remind you, Doctor, that your respective roles here are adversarial in nature, and he may be trying to get you to impeach your own testimony."

"I understand, Captain, and appreciate the advisement. I think I know why he's asking me that." Spencer took a breath. "I spent the rest of the day in a passive-aggressive rage. I was stomping around in a quiet fury. I found myself imagining various revenge scenarios, not the least of which was that of sneaking into his cabin once aboard *Phoenix* and short-sheeting his bed."

Trapp drawled into the pained silence that followed that remark, "As head of the ship's medical staff, I would sincerely ask you to reconsider that course of action."

There were chuckles around the table, and everyone visibly relaxed.

"Captain, I think. . . " Spencer stopped as the Captain raised his hand.

"In time, Doctor. Please let the Commander finish."

"I didn't get a chance to talk to Matthews, who spent the day at the first landing site trying to secure soil samples. From the language he was using over the coms, he wasn't having an easy time of it. In retrospect, it was odd. I've worked with Matthews for years, and he's level-headed to the point of being stoic. Usually he handles frustration well."

Vargas glanced at Spencer, who was wearing his Significant Look. Clearly he found the description of Matthew's bad day at work relevant, too.

Lassiter obviously spotted the exchange of looks. "Exactly. All three of us were behaving in extremely volatile and tense moods, and reacting to minor challenges disproportionate to their actual import. I was furious because the doctor disobeyed an order, and while it was an important order, his disobedience was without consequence. He, in turn, spent what should have been the most memorable day of his life pouting at me. Excuse me, Doctor, but that certainly sounds like what you were doing." Spencer grimaced slightly, nodded. Lassiter now wore a wry smile as he continued, "And Matthews was turning the air around him blue because he was having trouble with his weeding."

Trapp spoke up. "Are you attributing this to the light from Hō-ō? Hadn't it set by then?"

"It did, Commander, but I think these were aftereffects, not unlike the effects we all had during the first few rounds of hibernation.

"I know that I'm essentially saying that we were all driven mad by the baleful rays of Hō-ō, and it sounds like every really bad Sci-Fi show we ever saw. But I'll remind the panel of how much all of us loathe and despise the corridors in this ship, which got painted that gawdawful purple."

It took real effort for Vargas not to glance at Spencer. Let the psychiatrist suffer alone. Unbidden, he thought of H.P. Lovecraft, the nineteenth century author. He wrote a story that scared the piss out of Daniel as a child. "The Colour Out of Space" it was called. Yes, color could really influence mood. But it didn't drive people to nearly psychotic behavior. Unless you were in a Lovecraft novel, of course.

As if hearing the thoughts Vargas had, Lassiter continued, "I'm not saying we all just went nuts. I was still me, and I didn't think Doctor Spencer was a hostile alien or an ax murderer or anything crazy like that. It was like I was really short on sleep, had too much bad coffee, and just hated the whole world." Lassiter paused for a beat. "Well, this world, anyway."

Harlen leaned back, hand on chin. "You sound like you had a change of heart. When did that happen, and do you know why you had a change of heart?"

"I was already questioning my actions by the time I got back to *Phoenix*. The reaction I got from the Captain made it clear that I had committed a grievous error. I would have to say that by the time I reached my cabin, I fully understood the seriousness of my actions, and the Captain's reaction to them."

Trapp cocked his head. "Commander, you've pointed at Hō-ō for this. You've suggested that Hibernation Syndrome may have played a role." He frowned, portentously. "Do you think perhaps you are trying to evade responsibility?"

"No, Commander. I think those items have contributed in some way, the way metal-on-metal scraping might antagonize someone who is already on edge. But in the end, I was the one who acted."

The panel considered this for a minute. Vargas looked to each side. "Do either of the panel officers have any further questions for the defendant?" Both shook their heads. "Very well, Doctor Spencer. Would you be kind enough to tell us your version of events?

There was little in Spencer's testimony that wasn't already in his report. He acknowledged that he had failed to adhere to protocol, and reiterated that he, too, had been emotionally strained, and attributed it to the sheer alienness of the moon.

Trapp asked, "When you saw that shuttle was leaving, how did you feel?"

"It was all I could do not to panic on the spot. I saw it take off, and I thought, oh, good, they got Matthews and Brülow and they'll get us and we can get the hell out of here."

"Was it really that bad down there?"

* * *

Spencer paused to consider the question. The day had elements of a day at the beach combined with a horror movie. "No, Mister Harlen, it really wasn't. During the day it got hot and sticky, but otherwise actually rather pleasant. There was a steady breeze. The sun was a bit smaller and brighter than we're used to, and the gravity is a bit strange, but otherwise it was almost like a city park in Bristol. But I had been feeling dread and rage all day.

"So I felt relief when I saw the shuttle lift off, but then it kept climbing and climbing, in in a few minutes it was obvious that it was on a trajectory to go back to the ship. I very nearly lost it. I wanted to scream and cry. I was scared." Spencer remembered, but elected not to tell the board, that he had even considered taking his firearm and shooting at the departing shuttle. He had the mad notion that if he shot at it, it would jar

Lassiter back to his senses and they would come back and pick him up.

"Surely you knew someone would come and get you."

"I was frightened because I didn't want to be out in the open on the ground after Hō-ō rose."

"Did you do any of the things you felt like doing? Screaming, crying, anything like that?"

"No, Doctor Trapp. I was able to maintain some composure."

"And how do you feel you were able to manage that? I mean, we have testimony from both of you about how you were barely in control of yourselves down there. What allowed you to regain control of yourself at that moment?"

"I saw that Doctor Steinberg was having considerable difficulty processing what had just happened." Spencer saw a flicker of a smile cross Trapp's face and knew the Commander had penetrated the fog of shrink-speak. In point of fact, Steinberg was screaming curses, tears rolling down her cheeks, and Spencer's training kicked in. Steinberg was a patient in crisis, and he could help. He had to be a psychiatrist first. "I distracted myself by assisting her."

"Very well. Doctor Steinberg. Do you have anything you wish to append or amend to your report?"

* * *

Julie's testimony mirrored Spencer's. Feelings of unease and fear, paranoia, even a slight sense of doom.

They were dismissed, and the panel conducted interviews with the crewman involved in the case. They all reaffirmed what was in their reports, and were sent back to duty.

Vargas glanced at his data pad and sighed. 1830, and they still had Sheffield's reports from Disappointment to go through.

"Doctor Trapp, I would like to hear your opinion."

"I believe that something happened to those men down there that affected their judgment. I think that's the most important thing this hearing has determined. Before we send anyone down, we need to have a mechanism in place so the crew leader doesn't start executing people for looking at him funny." Harlen chuckled. "Mister Harlen," Trapp said, slightly defensively, "I think there's a very real possibility that these conditions could result in something that extreme."

"As for guilt or innocence, I vote to dismiss the charges. Clearly both men were acting while the balance of their minds was impaired, and both genuinely regret their actions. This isn't a fort on the edge of the abandoned territories, and we don't need to have lockstep discipline. The vast majority on board are civilians."

"Thank you. Your finding, CPO Harlen?"

"Well, the more serious charges against Doctors Spencer and Steinberg brought by Commander Lassiter were dropped at his own request, so we don't need to worry about those. I vote to find Commander Lassiter guilty of the charges that remain, but recommend discretionary mercy."

"Thank you. Looks like I'm the tiebreaker." Vargas lowered his head in thought for a minute. "OK, here's what I propose..."

* * *

Twenty minutes later, Lassiter and Spencer were ushered back in to learn their fates.

"Lieutenant Commander Spencer, you have been found guilty of willfully ignoring a standing directive, potentially putting yourself at needless peril. The panel has determined that you will receive a letter of reprimand to be placed in your permanent file, and that you be fined five thousand pounds, portions of which will be removed from your future paychecks."

Spencer blinked. Permanent records and money had all been left behind on planet Earth. The punishment was meaningless. Spencer saluted and declared, "I accept my punishment, Sers."

"Commander Lassiter, you have been found guilty of perhaps the most heinous crime a commanding officer can commit. You willfully abandoned personnel in your command to potential risk to their lives and well-being. You abused your authority as commanding officer, and you acted in a manner unbecoming an officer. Therefore, this panel recommends that you be stripped of rank and dismissed from the service with dishonorable distinction, and be no longer eligible for a pension. This panel elects to remand you to review by the Royal Military Courts of King Edward the Ninth, with the acknowledgement that His Majesty may impose further punishment of between fifteen years prison and execution. Mr. Lassiter, if England and Edward the Ninth still exist, I heartily recommend that you avoid that place."

Lassiter gulped and stared at the Captain in disbelief. Slowly, the implications trickled in. He was being given a punishment commensurate with what he had done, but, as with Spencer's punishment, it was, in the main, meaningless. *Phoenix* would not be returning to England for him to face the Crown's wrath, and indeed, it was unlikely that King Edward, or for that matter Royal Europe, still existed. But the being cashiered. . .

"Captain, may I request a clarification? Part of your decree isn't clear to me."

"Proceed."

"Am I to now be considered one of the colonists?"

"Given that you are here, I should assume so. I note that once we do colonize, we both will be fully reverting to civilian status anyway. In the meantime, it effectively means you won't have command of any more exploratory expeditions, at least not as a formal commander. If your fellow colonists want you to assume leadership positions, I certainly won't interfere in any way. In fact, I won't be able to."

"I see. I think. I accept my punishment, Sers."

Vargas lifted his chin at Lassiter. "I have a request, if you would be so kind."

Lassiter's astonishment was plain. "A request, Captain?"

"Yes. I want you to work with Commander Trapp and Lieutenant Commander Spencer to work up a system of safeguards in order to prevent anything like this from occurring on any future expeditions. Do you feel you can function in his manner?"

"I believe so, Captain."

"Doctors? Any objections?"

Trapp spoke. "None. I think his first-hand knowledge of what went wrong will be far too valuable to ignore." Spencer nodded.

"In which case, this tribunal is adjourned." Vargas clicked his data pad, shutting down the recording devices. "Lassiter, if we were on Earth, I would kick your ass around the block six times for the stunt you pulled. But we aren't, and as Alan mentioned, you're far too valuable to just toss away. But soon we'll be a frontier society, and when that happens, if you do anything like that again, you might face worse than being stripped of a rank that will soon be meaningless anyway. Spencer?"

"Sir?"

"Can you work with Lassiter? I want both of you to brain bust on this. If there's something down there that caused this time of behavior, I want you two to cooperate on countermeasures. Can you do it or not?"

"I can do it, Ser. Gordon and I have always had a good, cordial working relationship." Spencer turned and faced Lassiter directly. "I want to work with you on this, Gordon, and get it fixed."

"So do I . . . Ian." Lassiter looked back to the Captain. "I won't let you down, Ser."

"See that you don't. Now both of you, chow down, get some rest. We have a twenty-five people fresh out of hibernation, and I want both of you to brief them on what they face down there. Spencer, that's an order. Mr. Lassiter, that's a request." Vargas was greatly relieved to see Lassiter grin and reach toward Spencer to shake his hand.

Chapter 17 Paperwork, Paperwork

VARGAS WALKED WITH THE TWO PANEL MEMBERS back to the bridge. They faced at least three more hours of work, evaluating the flow of reports from both worlds. Complementary reports from ship specialists interpreting the on-the-ground findings would be starting to trickle in, and be a flood pretty soon.

As he downloaded reports from his God Console, Vargas became aware that every eye on the bridge was on him. He posted the findings of the Captain's Post, and heard a few gasps and murmurs from the crew. That, he hoped, would reduce the intensity of the gossip some. Speaking into his unit, Vargas informed the ship that because of evidence uncovered in the testimony, further exploration of Hō-ō One would be suspended until a new system of fail safes could be implemented to ensure the safety of the crews. He added that it was his hope that such explorations could begin again in a few days.

Retiring to the Captain's alcove, they set up a holoscreen so that the three could view and discuss the same information. The reports from Disappointment came first. They began with a video of a grinning Sheffield hefting a softball sized rock, apparently gold. That he had to strain a bit to catch it with both hands suggested that it weighed lot.

As if reading their thoughts, Sheffield nodded. "Yes, it's gold. Surprisingly pure, and boy, is it heavy." He crouched down, setting the gold down on the grass. "I found it in the bed of that stream over there. . . " the camera swung around to reveal a creek, about three meters wide. ". . . right on the edge of the bed under the water, plain as day." Sheffield shook his head, marveling. "If I had found that on Earth, my comfortable retirement would have been assured. There's over twenty kilos of gold there. We'll bring it back to the *Phoenix*, of course. Captain, do you mind if I claim it as a souvenir after testing? I know it's not worth that much here, but it is pretty. Oh, and everyone else has found chunks along the stream bed. The whole ground party is feeling pretty giddy about now."

"It's not fair," Harlen chuckled. "They go to the krapnatz planet with the poison air, and they're happy as mice in a cheese plant. We go to the place with the light gravity and pure air, and end up at each other's throats. And they get the gold!" Trapp and Vargas both laughed.

Sheffield got down to business. Disappointment was mineral-rich. At least, the two sites they had investigated over the past two days showed an incredible wealth of useful materials. Fly-over analysis confirmed what the orbital survey had suggested, and there were widespread deposits of bauxite, aluminum, iron, gold, and pitchblende. The levels of radon were not much different from areas that didn't have pitchblende.

"But here's the oddity. In the areas we've been, there's a radioactive powder. It's only a couple of millimeters deep, and seems to be in a very fine granular form, not much bigger than two or three molecules per grain. We haven't even actually seen it, since we didn't pack an electron microscope. Our instruments just tell us it's there, and it's nearly everywhere we go. I don't remember ever seeing deposits like those on Earth. We've taken about a dozen samples, going down as a far as four meters, and we just don't seen any more of this powder below about three centimeters."

"As it happens, Midshipman Farnsworth minored in geology in college. He says that he doesn't see how such a distribution is possible. He does say that it would explain how there could be so much radon without the entire planet being so radioactively hot that we couldn't even orbit it safely. I'm not sure why, but when we put together this party, we didn't think to include a geologist, so Red's been a most fortunate addition.

"What we're seeing from the air pretty much backs up the orbital survey. The climate at the equator is mostly temperate, and the vegetation that we're seeing suggests that it doesn't get extremely hot or extremely cold. We took some seedling plants and put them in the portable cooler and in a solar oven that Jim Hartnell cobbled together, along with a couple of control plants just out in the sun. The plants that were in below zero or above forty temperatures promptly up and died."

Suddenly Sheffield paused, blinked and shook his head slightly. Flash-dream. The crew were already taking a Japanese approach and simply not noticing when it happened.

"Erm. It's a pretty limited sample, and it doesn't mean that temperatures don't get that hot or cold, but it is suggestive. Um, you should find the images of that under 'biota.' Harlen tapped a key, and the images of the plants appeared. Vargas thought they wouldn't have looked particularly out of place in his father's flowerbed.

"Asuka is pretty sure there are micro-organisms in the soil, and her gas spectrometer suggests that at least some of them transpire like animal micro-organisms on Earth. She's picking up a fair bit of oxygen, and some CO_2. The CO_2, of course, would be what the animal micro-organisms are exhaling. We're also picking up methane, another solid indication of life since there doesn't seem to be any volcanic activity in these parts.

"So far, that's the closest to animal life we've found. If confirmed, though, it's huge, because we haven't found any other indication of non-plant life. Tsuchishima, Adelena, Rebekah and Jim have been driving themselves nuts figuring out how the soil aerates without nematodes, or how plants pollinate—or even if they do.

"The weather has been nice. Granted, we're staying pretty close to the equator, and Jim says that from what he remembers of college meteorology, this is a stagnant zone. Storms begin to form here and get swept out by Coriolis effect into the tropical bands. He speculates that radon levels might be a bit lower outside the equatorial zone. Subtropical starts roughly at the tropics, and arctic at sixty degrees north or south. It's a lot cooler than Earth. About twelve to fifteen degrees cooler. However, nearly all the land is within twenty degrees of the equator. Vast Pacific-sized oceans to the north and south. If it was hotter, the weather here might be a lot more challenging than what we're used to.

"Since you went gallivanting off to explore strange new worlds, we don't have our orbital survey, so the weather is a bit of a mystery to us beyond what we see eyeballing the sky. It's mostly cloudless here, with just a bit of high cirrus, and temperatures have been running about twenty above, plus or minus seven degrees. Comfortable. This area's a bit hillier than Kent, so we named it Devon. Spencer should like that—he's from Bristol, as I recall.

"We'll stay here at least one more day, and unless we find something really interesting, we'll pull out and relocate in some even hillier country at about twenty degrees north. I've dubbed that Northumberland.

"Captain, you have the detailed data in the attached packets, and various on-site reports that we sent during the day. I realize that it's probably going to be about 1830 ship's time when you get this, and I imagine Hō-ō One is keeping you very busy, but if you could spare a few minutes, we're all dying of curiosity down here! What's your world like?

"Sheffield at Devon base, signing out. I'll monitor starting in about a half hour in case you have a reply. Remember in three hours you'll be below our horizon. Best of luck with Hō-ō One!"

Vargas leaned back and glanced at Trapp and Harlen. Discuss Hō-ō One. Hooo, boy. He could see it now. "Well, we sent a team down and it was lovely, with fresh air and breezes and waving grass, only there was a demonic light that drove the crew mad and they tried to kill each other, and now we're figuring out what to do about that."

He glanced at his two fellow panelists, and was greeted with a pair of "I'm glad you're the Captain" looks. No help there.

"Good evening, Commander Sheffield. We received your reports and summation of same, and everyone here is very excited, as you might imagine." If you imagined real hard, Vargas thought.

"I'll get these reports to the appropriate people by morning. I don't know if we mentioned it in last night's message, but we awakened about thirty members amongst the colonists and crew today, in preparation for processing the reports from your team and people on Hō-ō One. I'll check to see if there's a couple of geologists who might have some thoughts on your pitchblende and mystery powder. Tell Red how much we appreciate him. I don't know how we forgot to send a geologist along with you, and I'm glad he's there to fill that gap." Vargas hit pause and sat back and queried Trapp and Harlen. "Do either of you have any questions or suggestions?"

Trapp said, "Could you politely remind them to maintain strict quarantine with microorganisms? Does anyone there have any medical training?"

Harlen added, "There's also a mini inflatable greenhouse in the survival gear. It's only about three cubic meters, but they might be able to use it for experiments."

Vargas clicked the mike. "Doctor Trapp urges you to be extra careful with the microorganisms since they are unknown. And Red will probably know where it is exactly, but CPO Harlen says there's a greenhouse in survival stores that you might find useful for botanical samples.

"As for Hō-ō One, we retrieved the first landing team yesterday. Several of the members had problems with the alien nature of the place; it's a lot less like Earth than Disappointment is, especially at night when Hō-ō is full and high in the sky. I've been told by several members of the team that it's absolutely overwhelming, and there's nothing in their experience to compare with it. Several of the members encountered personal difficulty in adapting to it, to the point where we are holding off on further exploration for several days until we find ways to mitigate the situation. If that sounds a bit mysterious, I apologize, but it's hard to describe. If any of the landing crew have a free moment, I'll get them to post a recording of their experiences. Now that they are back on *Phoenix*, they seem to have made a good recovery.

"Now the good news. There are temperate zones on Hō-ō One that can support human life. They don't cover a broad expanse, but they exist. The atmosphere is an oxygen-nitrogen mix, suitable for humans, and apparently non-toxic. There is vegetation, but no sign of animal life. There may be velociraptors hiding in the bushes and secretly learning our language so they can steal our technology, but we haven't spotted them. Or any other form of animal life." Vargas paused, wondering just where the 'velociraptors on alien planets' meme came from. It was shorthand for dangerous indigenous life forms, but it sure didn't make any sense on the face of it.

"You'll be amazed to learn that we've spotted immense glaciers to the north of our landing site, and in fact the river that divides and sweeps by to the north and south of the site is from glacial melt. That suggests a constant supply of cold, fresh, tasty water.

"The geography of the place is very strange. Bigger than Earth, but with only three quarters gravity, so it's a lot less dense than Earth. More ocean area, and the oceans are deep. They think there's an area about one thousand kilometers east of the landing site that might be ninety thousand meters deep. There's a lot of water here. We didn't find much in the way of minerals, but so far all we have are a couple of random probes at two sites less than a kilometer apart.

"Most of the moon is too hot for human habitation, but there are, as mentioned, temperate areas. We're hoping that the soil is suitable for cultivation. The first landing site was full of something the party dubbed tube grass, which has a nearly impenetrable mat of roots underneath. A second site in wooded territory featured more conventional vegetation, almost Earth like. We haven't named any of our sites yet. I was born in the Americas sector state of Coahuila, which is mostly mountain and desert, so I'll have plenty of opportunity to name parts of Hō-ō One's main continent after my home state. One of the landing team was born in the northern part of the Americas, in a town called Sackville, and I'm devoutly hoping he'll pick a name based on his state or county, and not his home town. . .

"Even though we are suspending landings on the moon for a couple of days, we'll have a ton of stuff coming in from orbital telemetry, and we'll be happy to send it along. Remember, though, that what you're doing there is just as important.

"Vargas, signing off."

He included a packet of data Harlen and Trapp had assembled while he was speaking, and sent it. With a laugh, he said, "In about eighteen minutes, Commander Sheffield is going to be watching that and saying, 'what the fuck?'"

Trapp nodded. At the age of fifty seven, he was one of the oldest members of the crew, and the slight jowliness and salt-and-pepper mutton chop sideburns suggested a man who didn't laugh much. The impression, while professionally cultivated, was incorrect. Trapp laughed frequently, and this was one of those times. "I'm not sure which of us ended up with the booby prize."

* * *

By 2300 hours, Daniel was more than ready to call it a day. He had put in four hours reading scientific analyses of the two worlds, densely and sometimes impenetrably packed with scientific jargon. He could only hope the people writing these reports understood what they were saying better than he did. Discovering new worlds should be more exciting than this. The late hour combined with the events of the day to change his twingies into what he thought of as janglies.

He clicked on his cabin screen and scrolled through the New World Global TV feeds. A camera had been left on Hō-ō One, and it had been busily recording wind blowing though tube grass all day. Now it was still recording wind blowing through tube grass, only it was dark, Hō-ō hadn't risen yet. Likewise the two feeds from Disappointment were on the far side of that planet.

Just as well. Even the explorers of his youth in their books rested at night. And that was with wild animals and possibly hostile natives at hand. The greatest personal risk he faced on this expedition was razor rash. He remembered fantasizing about the stories that would be written about the exploits of *RESS Phoenix* on various worlds old and new, and how his name would live forever as the stalwart captain.

They sure wouldn't put much effort into that writing if they knew what a bloody bore most of this was, and how paperwork had reduced the expedition leader to the position of mid-level bureaucrat, rubber stamping documents he didn't fully understand.

Speaking of which, what was he supposed to name this ruddy, odd-shaped world? Plum? Eggplant? Bruise?

Daniel, still seated at his desk, began to doze. At the back of his mind, his hind brain chuckled at the fact that he had just managed to bore himself to sleep.

His door chimed, and he started. Lifting his head from his chest, he looked at the old-fashioned dial chronometer above the desk. 2315. He must have just started dozing.

"Come in" he called as he waved the door open, puzzled and a little concerned. Few people knocked on his cabin at this hour unless there was a problem that needed his immediate attention.

Julie Steinberg was standing there, holding what looked like a tea tray.

"Lieutenant Commander, good evening. How can I help you?"

"I thought the Captain might like a cup of herbal tea before retiring?"

"Thank you. Please come in." Vargas was struggling to cover his confusion. In all the time he had been Captain, he had never had anyone deliver food or drink to his cabin. On the military vessels, with a crew of twelve, cramped quarters made such luxuries as pursers unknown, even if the captain had a cabin of his own. That was a prerogative of rank Vargas hadn't enjoyed, even though he technically commanded a crew of one hundred and fifty on what was technically a passenger ship, rarely were more than six of them on duty at any given time during this strangest of voyages. Even now, with many crew members awake, demanding room service struck him as an abuse of his authority. True, an old-time sea captain was free to order as many tankards of rum as he wanted from the cabin boy, but he was also expected to bully his crew because he could, and do his country's service whilst intoxicated. Times had changed.

Julie looked around, at a loss where to place the tea tray. Vargas smiled and motioned for her to step back. He tapped a selection on his desk display, and a table and chair set smoothly unfolded from the bulkhead on his left.

Julie giggled. "Most impressive. But with all the space this ship has, why not just give you a bigger cabin and a regular dinette set?"

"This way it's one less thing that needs securing when the ship is under acceleration. And I'm sure the contractor didn't mind the extra money involved." He watched as Julie poured. His nose caught the aroma. "Ginger?"

"Ginger lemon."

"My favorite."

"Well, I suborned one of the line officers to learn what your choice in tea was." Vargas cocked an inquiring eyebrow. "Doctor Trapp wasn't going to tell me. He really wasn't." She mimed a pout. "I had to promise if I got a puppy, I would name it after him."

Daniel laughed, a little uncertainly. Flirting didn't seem to be the style for either of them.

Julie smirked. "I told him it would be the biggest, ugliest junkyard dog I could find, and her name would be 'Shut Yer Yap, Trapp.' Then he saw reason."

Daniel whistled. "I'm glad you weren't after any military secrets. Not that we have any out here." His fatigue seemed to have vanished, and he found himself delighted with the visit. He blew steam from the surface and sipped. "Um. This is good tea."

"Thanks. It's from my personal stash. I bought up about thirty pounds and had it vacuum sealed. I was worried the quarantine procedures might ruin it, but it came out fine."

"You can thank the Navy for that. There would have been a revolt if policy tampered with Navy coffee. So they made sure to modify decontamination so the taste wouldn't be affected."

"OK. Thank you Navy." Her eyes lit on Daniel's display screen, which had a picture of Disappointment as a screen saver. "It's so beautiful." She inclined her head at the image. "Disappointment, I mean. I wish we could live there."

Daniel nodded in agreement. "Sheffield and his people seem to think the radon isn't a game ender. They were sending inquiries about chelation procedures and plant life earlier. None of them said why, but the implication is there."

"Interesting. Plants themselves can be used to chelate soil."

"When I had them put in a fortnight there, I had in mind a kind of post postmortem. Confirm that the planet wasn't suitable for human life, that sort of thing. I told Sheffield that if they did find some kind of work-around, I would name one of Disappointment's moons after him."

"It has moons?"

"Two of them, very small. The larger of them is about as big as Venus seen from Earth."

"It still has to be an improvement over Hō-ō as a sky ornament."

"Can I ask about that? Was the light really that disturbing?"

"It was and it wasn't. Hō-ō itself is incredibly beautiful, hanging there in the sky like a giant luminescent apple. It almost reminded me of some of the old style paper Japanese lanterns. Having it overhead is a bit overwhelming, but I think you would get used to that in time. It's the effect of the reflected light that puts your teeth on edge. The grass is purple, and the rest of the sky looks a nasty sort of greenish-black when you look at Hō-ō and then at another part of the sky."

Afterimage, complementary color. On a black background. Daniel could see where that would be unappealing. But it's easy to drown out the relatively weak reflective light, he thought. Maybe some blue-green or yellow lighting?

"That's what I was so afraid of when I realized we were stranded. That the sun would go down, Hō-ō would come up, and we would be all alone in that giant dark bruise of land and sky.

"I wasn't afraid of dying. I mean, I was, on some level, even though I thought there was nothing there that could physically harm me. What I was really afraid of was that the light would tear away at my mind, and leave me where I was when I first woke up and barely knew my own name. I think there's some sort of link between hibernation distress and our reaction to Hō-ō.

"I mean, Ian was there, and he was being a good psychiatrist. He really helped me get through the initial panic."

Daniel smiled. "You helped him get through it too, did you know?" Julie shook her head, puzzled. "It was in his formal report. He said he was scared, but he could see you needed help, and his training and instincts as a therapist kicked in. That kept him centered and focused, and stopped him from losing it. I could relate. I don't know if you remember, but when we both first woke up, I was trying to help you regain some of what you lost by playing the piano with you. You do remember that?" At Julie's emphatic nod, he continued, "I wasn't sure. But that helped me. What I was trying to do for you I wound up doing for myself, too.

"You seem to have that effect on people—helping them to help themselves. It's valuable."

"That brings me to the reason I came to see you tonight, Daniel. I do remember playing the piano with you, and I remember the feelings of relief and joy when I realized it was helping, and I was finding myself again.

"And more than being stranded, or Hō-ō, or Commander Lassiter's strange behavior, that's what frightened me the most." Her eyes searched his face, and she suddenly smiled, a Zharrise. "I was frightened I wouldn't be able to thank you." Standing swiftly, she swept around that table, and pressed both hands to Daniel's cheeks, and kissed him deeply on the mouth.

After an instant's hesitation, Daniel began kissing back.

He had planned to tell her that he had set up a piano keyboard console on his desk so they could practice together.

But that could wait until after breakfast.

With a happy sigh, Daniel fell into Julie.

Chapter 18 Back In The Saddle

"I'M NOT SURE I UNDERSTAND. Why is the climate so different in the north side of the triangle?" Mann looked at the orbital shots that encompassed the first landing site on Hō-ō One.

"There's a ridge running almost exactly down the middle. It's not much of a ridge, a gentle rise of about one hundred meters, but it's just enough to funnel the katabatic winds off the glacier. To the south of the ridge, the winds are warmer and wetter, and also a lot more variable. But the wind that blows on the north side is a pretty constant temperature."

Lieutenant André Morley turned to his audience and tapped forefingers together. "Of course, that's based on one hour's study of thirty-six hours' worth of data, so don't hold me to that."

A few chuckles and understanding nods greeted this news. The officers seated around the bridge mess table understood that Hō-ō One had some very strange features, not least of which was the climate. Between the significantly hotter surface temperatures and the broader expanse of ocean, the weather was likely to be wilder and more changeable than anything they had seen on Earth.

"I'm told that there's only one type of vegetation in this triangle, and that's this stuff you call 'tube grass.' If I had to guess, this monoculture means that it's an invasive species of plant that simply crowds out all competition. It hasn't taken over the whole planet, so it has limits. Normally for a plant like this, the things that can impose such limits are waterways, climate, altitude, soil type, existing vegetation, and drainage.

"It obviously stops at the rivers. For whatever reason, it can't cross the streams and invade on the other side. Now, maybe the plant life on the other side can fight it off somehow, but I'm guessing it can't cross the water. It doesn't cover the whole triangle either, so other factors can stop it.

"Now, the triangle converges on this glacier, the foot of which is at about nine thousand meters." Morley shook his head in disbelief. The bottom of that glacier was higher up than

Mount Everest. "The katabatic wind starts at about twelve thousand meters. . . is that correct? twelve thousand? Is there even air that high up? The wind is at about minus fifty centigrade, and moving at a fair clip, about a hundred and twenty kilometers an hour. It sweeps down the glacier, warming from compression, and hits that small ridge here at about twenty below freezing. Most of it goes this way, and the rest goes that way. The south side shows that it's warmer, because the tube-grass starts growing at about eight kilometers. On this side. . . " tap, tap, "it starts growing at six point five kilometers. The air's colder there. It goes below minus ten fairly often, and your grass doesn't like it that cold. It starts to die off.

"The reason I think it's steadier is that on the south side, you can see little areas of other types of vegetation and patches of tube grass here and there. My best guess is that the temperatures control the tube-grass, but only intermittently. Still, it's enough that other things can take root. They can handle cold better than the tube-grass, but not constant cold.

"The wind sweeps down the north side, and keeps the temperatures the tube-grass likes down nearly to the beach front. It looks like it finally stops at about half a klick inland. On the south side, it stops at about twenty-five hundred meters, and the infrared suggests temperatures on that side get to about fifty or sixty degrees, at least twenty degrees warmer than on the north side at the same altitude.

"It's also less likely to get storms, and from what I've seen from the orbital survey, this moon has far wilder weather than anything we've ever seen on Earth. Katabatics tend to be very dry because they start out very cold and have little opportunity to pick up moisture. I bet the ridge gets some pretty good thunderstorms."

"West facing mountain slopes on the other side of this peninsula got over three meters of rain yesterday. In one day. I think it's safe to say we don't want to set up a colony there.

"So I would recommend that a preliminary colony be set up about here. . . " He clicked, and an X appeared on the north side of the triangle at about four kilometers altitude. It was about seventy-five kilometers from the landing site.

"You think the climate will be suitable for humans there?" Vargas asked.

"Captain, I don't know. I don't have a data set. But the tube-grass is happy there, and where it's happy, I think we'll be happy. And the vegetation on the other side of the river seems to be evenly dispersed and roughly the same color, which suggests a stable climate. It doesn't get to fifty above there, and I don't see it going below zero."

"Thank you, Lieutenant. I understand that we put you on the spot, and we appreciate you trying to make sense of this world as far as you have."

"All due respect, Captain, but I can't make sense of it at all. Why is it so cool? It should be far hotter." Morley glared at the screen as if it were at fault.

"It's a question we're all asking, and you'll have about fifty other scientists puzzling over it alongside you."

"Doctor Trapp, you're up. Do you have anything to report regarding the emotional dislocations some of the crew experienced?"

"We have some EEG monitors that can be worn comfortably in the suit that should give us insight into the neurophysical reactions the team experience. I plan to have the suits rigged for tomorrow's landing, and we can use that as a control."

"A control?"

"Right. Hō-ō won't be the presence it was the day before yesterday, Captain."

"Just four days past full?"

Tim Simmons, who had been silent during the session, cleared his throat. Vargas looked at him expectantly. "Ho-o One is in an orbit around its primary that takes just over ten days to complete. A bit over a third the amount of time the Moon needs to go through its phases. It precesses about thirty-five degrees a day. In other words, each Hō-ō rise is about two and a half hours later than the day before. So by tomorrow, Hō-ō will be one day short of, well, 'new moon'."

Vargas blinked and chuckled. "You know, I actually thought the phases would be slower due to its immense size. No, I know that has nothing to do with it. It's the orbital period, I understand. And we're the ones doing the orbiting, at that. Still, the images suggest a certain ponderosity."

The chuckles spread around the table.

Trapp continued. "Aside from the personal testimonies of the individuals who were on Hō-ō One on that first expedition, we have precious little to go on. I've been in consultation with Doctor Spencer, who was one of the individuals who went down there and experienced the emotional dislocations that caused problems. He feels it might be the light from Hō-ō that triggered the reactions that led to impaired judgment and overly emotional responses."

"I understand it might be the effect the light has on the appearance of the landscape and the immediate surrounding sky that could be the real problem."

Trapp looked surprised. "Nobody indicated that to me, Captain. This was one of the seven who went down?"

"Yes. I . . . it was Lieutenant Steinberg."

Trapp nodded. "I'll sound her out about that. It could be an important distinction.

"The other mitigating factor is that we're going to request that all members on the subsequent crew maintain live feeds. It's an imposition on privacy, and I want to be sensitive to that, not that there's a lot of privacy on the shuttles. But if we're monitoring discussions, we might spot a problem before it becomes trouble and defuse it. Captain, is it in your power to order the crew to do that?"

"It is, but I prefer to begin on a voluntary basis. Most of the crew on the last trip had the monitoring active whenever they were outside the shuttle, but unfortunately there was little in the broadcast dialogue to alert us to signs of trouble. Everyone will be briefed on the problems the first crew ran into, and encouraged to report any unusual behavior in others, or if they have reactions that involve anger or fear. "

"That reminds me. Captain, have you selected members for the team?"

"That's the next order of business, as it happens. I have about one hundred volunteers, and elected to choose based on what we learned from the first trip. So it probably won't be any surprise that most of the crew are those who went down once before. Brülow, Buchanan, and Forster. Harlen. André Morley will be in command. Pilots will be Mann and Lassiter."

Thunderstruck looks flashed around the table. "Lassiter, Captain?" Trapp peered at Vargas.

"He won't be in command. Morley has that. He'll be pilot, in a civilian capacity. And he has as much expertise as any member of this mission. Yes, he was convicted, and I cashiered him. The rules on that are simple: there are no mitigating circumstances. But as a civilian, he is still an important member of this mission. Does anyone object? I'll listen to anything anyone wants to say on it. I should mention at this point that both Mann and Brülow both expressed comfort with Lassiter being along as the pilot."

Trapp had one more question. "Is Comm. . . is Mister Lassiter aware that you've selected him?"

"Of course. It's a volunteer mission. He's raring at the bit to go back down. I would describe him as highly motivated to do an exemplary job."

Vargas looked around at the group. Some looked thoughtful, and some openly skeptical. Lassiter had strenuously argued for the chance to redeem himself, and Vargas, hoping to put the entire matter behind them, had assented. Don't let me down, Gordon, he thought. "People, we're all in this together, and if help exists at all, it's about forty-seven light years away. We aren't in a position where we can afford to throw people away for mistakes, even if we had a way to throw them away.

"Finally, remember that it could have been anyone who reacted that way. We don't understand what happened, but he has a first-hand experience that none of the rest of us have. He might be the one who prevents others from blowing up."

Vargas searched faces. "If anyone thinks he shouldn't be on this mission, now is the time to speak up. Anyone?"

Nobody looked particularly happy. But nobody objected, either.

* * *

"Hold your fucking horses, Buchanan. This damn thing weighs three hundred kilograms, even in this gravity." Rudy Harlen stepped back from the laser cutter/drill and took a few deep breaths, grateful for the rich oxygen mix in his suit. The native air was supposed to have an even higher concentration of oxygen, but there was concern that screaming white lung death awaited anyone who dared sniff the local air.

Buchanan resisted pointing out that the reason the bulky equipment was there was because Harlen insisted on bringing it along. Briefly, Buchanan wondered if the outburst would cause concern on *Phoenix*, now thirty thousand kilometers above in stationary orbit. He had a hunch it wouldn't; Harlen had a reputation as an asshole.

Morley and Forster also stepped back, welcoming the break. Once deployed, the cutter/drill had four fat rubber tires, rolled readily and had a small motor to propel while cutting. But Your Tax Dollars At Work: in order to get it from Stores to Planet side, policy required it be crated, negating the presence of the tires. They had about five meters to go, now on level ground, so one more set of heave-hos would do it. Buchanan eyed the distance covered, up the ramp and into the rear storage of the shuttle. That's when he belatedly saw the power dolly secured against the forward bulkhead. It had been hidden by the crate in the beginning. They could have just lifted it onto the dolly and rolled it down the ramp. He sighed. Americaners had an expression for this sort of operation: fifteen monkeys fucking a football.

He looked around at the scenery. There wasn't any. The horizon was flat, the landscape featureless in three directions. All he could see was this weird grass that reminded him unpleasantly of human fingers poking out of the ground. Behind him was a nondescript river, the far bank of which was a wall of jungle growth. That might be mildly interesting except that it was utterly silent. No monkeys screeching (they were all busy moving this goddamn drill), no vivid parrots flittering through the trees, no lazy crocks waiting for unwary swimmers. Even Manitoba had religious lunatics to liven it up. Not this place. And that sun was hot. He had been carefully instructed to polarize his helmet before disembarking, with the warning that symptoms of snow blindness could begin in just minutes under Zhar-Ptitsa.

Harlen gathered them up by eye, and, gasping and panting, they trundled with their burden the last few meters, and they more or less dropped it onto the springy tube-grass.

"I vote if it works, we just leave it here for the next shuttle to deal with", a winded Forster complained. "We can put a sign saying 'Do not steal this' for the Hōvians."

"The who, now?"

"The Hōvians. They're three meter tall bright green chipmunks with radar dishes for ears, and they live in a giant mountain at the north pole. They love to steal laser drills."

"I can think of a few people on board ship you wouldn't want to say that in front of," Buchanan offered.

"Especially Doctor Spencer," Morley laughed. "Besides, there really is a giant mountain at the north pole. You don't want to start rumors."

Buchanan spoke up. "Um, guys? The big fire bird in the sky is listening to every word you say, and Morley here has orders to bubble wrap us and strap us down if we start acting twitchy." Morley grinned and waggled his eyebrows at Buchanan.

The conversation resumed on a more sober note. They unpacked the crate and rolled the drill a few more meters. Nobody was really thrilled at the constant monitoring, but lurid details, some of which were even true, had circulated around the ship in the days following the inglorious return of the first mission. That the figure central to the rumors was working not fifty meters away tended to reduce the levity. The crew didn't know if Lassiter was actually in disgrace or not, and if he was, did this mean the fact that he was on this expedition indicate that the Captain saw it as a shit detail?

Forster pointed east. "Look. It that a rainbow?"

The other three peered. After a pause, Morley spoke. "No. That's Hō-ō."

The giant planet, in final crescent stage before the 'new moon' the following day, had formed a pale purple arc stretching over a wide swath of the eastern horizon. Color aside, it was easy to see why Forster had first thought it a rainbow; it was a delicate object of beauty, undefined against the pale blue of Hō-ō One's sky.

"It doesn't look very scary," Harlen scoffed. Still, something about the position tickled at the back of his mind. He wondered if you could see the shadow of Hō-ō One on it when it was full.

Everyone paused to stare. Even as a thin crescent against the bright day lit sky, it was an impressive sight.

Morley, the team leader, looked over at Harlen. "Rudy, it's your show. Why don't you fire this thing up and show us what you had in mind?"

"Right. Just a mo." Harlen opened his data pad, and tapped some commands and sent them to the drill. It lit up with surprising silence, and after a few moments a bright gold glow shone from under the carapace. Harlen gave Buchanan an inquiring glance. The heavy equipment operator flipped open his own data pad, summoned the commands from the drill, and looked them over conscientiously. He gave a nod, and Harlen pressed the execute button.

Soundlessly, the drill moved forward slowly an exact meter. Then it clumsily executed a ninety degree turn and rolled another meter. Twice more, and it had performed a perfect square. It rolled more quickly to a spot about two meters away and shut down with a self-satisfied sigh.

Harlen walked around the perimeter, and nodded approval. "Right. Ann, you grab on here. You two, take a corner, and we'll worry it up."

They reached down, pushing their gloves through the cut in the root structure and getting a grip in among the tangled fibers. Lifting and shaking, they slowly pulled up the square meter of root mass, exposing a square of clean black earth below.

"Heavy" Morley commented, now holding the roots himself. He shook it clumsily. "It's got a bunch of dirt in it. I'm going to take it to the river and wash it out and we can see what this stuff is like when we get back to *Phoenix*."

"Watch for crocodiles," Forster said.

The three set up probes to get soil samples for up to five meters deep while Morley dragged the heavy mass to the river, some twenty-five meters away. At the bank, he noted that the tube grass grew right to the water's edge and no further. That was different. Every stream in his experience had varying rates of flow, so he expected to see some flooded out areas on the bank, and submerged land vegetation. It was a clean break. The heavier and more varied foliage on the far side appeared to stop in an equally clean break between land and water. No flood or drought zones. He recited this to his data pad, aware that the hidden listeners on *Phoenix* would be picking it up, too.

The current was so smooth as to be invisible, and he broke off a finger of tube-grass and tossed it in to gauge the strength of the flow. Satisfied that he wouldn't get swept away, he stepped into the water, about a half meter deep at the edge, and dipped the mat of root in, watching to see what would happen.

A muddy cloud of topsoil spilled out of the root mass, and was quickly swept away by the current. Dividing his attention between his task at hand and keeping a close eye for any signs of life in the water, he kneaded and sloshed it, washerwoman style, until the water ran clear. Then he lifted the sodden mass and examined it. Even with water still running out in rivulets, it was noticeably lighter than the mass he had dragged to the river.

Cleansed, it was a startlingly bright white. When he was a teen, he and his brothers and father had refurbished an old rural home where he spent his high school years, and they had torn out a bunch of old pink fiberglass insulation. This stuff felt much like it. He couldn't really get a feel for the texture through the gloves, but his eyes told him it was more fibrous. He peered closer. There was a solid mat on top, about five centimeters thick, and a similar mat at the bottom, about two centimeters thick. Between was looser and more fibrous. He tried breaking a strand, about the width of a human hair, and couldn't. He pulled out a pocket knife and tried again. It couldn't cut the strand. His eyebrows shot up. Tough stuff. He wondered if there might be a use for that stuff, and typed a note on his pad to requisition an item from the Imprinter. Call it a wild hair idea. He held the mass, now drained of water and quite light, up between his head and the sun. Brighter than Sol, Zhar-Ptitsa only managed a feeble glow through the mat. He cautiously unfiltered his face place and looked again. It blocked nearly all the light. Not bad for plant mass only thirty centimeters in thickness. He wished he didn't have his suit gloves on. He got the impression all the water drained around the edges of the bottom mat, and not through the mat itself. Certainly, the underside looked dry.

Slinging the object over his shoulder, he walked back to where the other three were still coring. With the root mass out of the way, the work was proceeding easily. He crouched down and rubbed some of the top soil tailings between his fingers and thumb. Alluvial, and it looked like something was putting nutrients in it and aerating it. He was going to be curious to see what the soil people had to say about it, but to his semi-knowledgeable eye, it looked like good rich loam.

The first day passed without incident. As did, to everyone's relief, the first night. Lassiter insisted the windows be set to full opaque, even though Hō-ō wasn't in evidence.

* * *

The following morning, the crew spent the first few hours establishing semi-permanent recording devices; meteorological, soil hydration, seismic activity (so far little had been detected, which astonished the geologists, given the tidal stresses Hō-ō One experienced) and even listening devices just in case something did come out of the woods and swim across to investigate all the odd activity in the field.

There was a clearing a half kilometer north of the river, and the crew began packing up the equipment into the shuttle that they might need at the other site. There had been showers the night before, and Morley had made them re-crate the drill, but permitted them to let it stay behind for now.

He was emerging to get some of the remaining probe samples, and realized it was getting dim out there. He adjusted his face-mask, and discovered that it was at the setting it had been all morning. Puzzled, he looked up to see if it was clouding over. The light wasn't just dimmer—it was redder. Smoke?

Zhar-Ptitsa looked like it was balanced on the rim of a very long bow. A brilliant red curved line extended from each side of the star. It took him a moment to make sense of what he was seeing.

"Everyone, get everything in that you can. We're losing our light." Glancing around he saw all the other members gaping up at the sky. "Move, folks. We've only got a few minutes before it gets dark."

A voice cut in, Commander Trapp from high orbit. "It's one hour past dawn there. What do you mean you're losing your light?"

"Check your orbital image, Commander. We have a new terminator."

There was a pause longer than the thirty five thousand kilometer distance would justify. Trapp swore softly. "You're being eclipsed."

Moving quickly, Morley stowed the samples, and scurried back out, clutching the ultra-high resolution recorder. He set up the device rapidly, and started a stream of images to *Phoenix*. They would be seeing it with the same resolution his eyeballs were.

The sight was extraordinary. Hō-ō was a rosy ring floating in the sky, brighter on the side Zhar-Ptitsa had just moved behind, with a dark center. Around the ring, stars were coming out. He heard gasps and exclamations from the others. The sight was beautiful.

Glancing over, he saw Gordon Lassiter tapping into his data pad. Mildly curious, he moved over to see what the older man was up to.

"I'm just getting a rough calculation of how long this will last. Let's see . . . oh, fuck me."

"OK, how long?"

"About twenty three hours. A little over."

"Hours."

"Yeah. Nearly a full day. And I just realized, Lieutenant. This moon is in the same orbit as the rings, stable over the equator of Hō-ō. I think it may actually be a part of the rings, just bigger than most. So it's not like Earth's Moon, which kinda wobbles all over the sky, sometimes being eclipsed and sometimes not. This is going to happen every ten days. It's even longer when Hō-ō is at its equinoxes."

"Mister Lassiter, are you telling me that it's just going to stay dark until tomorrow?"

"That's what I'm telling you. And it's going to happen every ten days. In fact. . . " Lassiter tapped keys. ". . . in fact, there will be times where it'll be dark for much of two days. Up to thirty hours at a time."

On the bridge, Vargas showed up on Trapp's console. "Commander, I just happened to look up at my orbital display here at my desk, and Hō-ō One seems to have vanished from under us. Could you explain that, please?"

Grinning despite himself, Trapp replied, "They're having a solar eclipse."

"Really? The whole moon?"

"The whole thing. It turns out that solar eclipses are on a bigger scale here. You might consider a request to come to the bridge. I think we have part of our answer as to why the place is cooler than it ought to be."

Down on the surface, Morley dithered. Standing orders were for everyone to stay in the shuttle at night. The horizon was no longer visible, which was his definition of full dark. Just that big rosy ring in the sky. Peering, he could make out, very dimly, the patterns and swirls of Hō-ō's perpetual cloud cover. Suddenly a concentric series of expanding bands of rosy light spread across the planet's face from the side Zhar-Ptitsa was on. He had no idea what he was looking at, but it was extraordinarily beautiful.

Everyone else was still transfixed at the sight. Switching to a private frequency, he asked Trapp if the crew readouts were OK. Trapp replied that he saw nothing unusual. "What are they doing, Lieutenant?"

"Commander, they're all staring up at the Hō-ō like turkeys in a thunderstorm."

"I can tell you the bridge is doing pretty much the same at the main screen. That's quite a remarkable sight. Still. Why don't you go around and talk to people, make sure they're OK. Watch their expressions. I can get voice tones and content from here."

Morley made the rounds, chatting up each of the crew members. As far as he could tell, everyone was simply enjoying the show. He made sure they all understood they would have to return to the shuttle soon, and everyone was reacting the way he expected. Still, he was glad that Spencer and Trapp were double checking him on this. His training didn't include impromptu shrinkage.

Ann Forster was squinting at Hō-ō when he approached her. "Lieutenant, am I going crazy, or is Hō-ō sparkling?

Morley looked at the giant mass. Sure enough, there were pinpoints of light flickering all around the face of the planet. It took him an instant to realize what he was looking at.

"That's lightning. Damn big flashes for us to see them from here. Pretty, though. At least, from way up here."

"Up here?"

"We're the moon. It's the primary."

Ann conceded the point with a nod. "They look like fireflies."

"You spotted them, you have naming rights. But can I make a suggestion? Hōvian Fireflies. How's that?"

Her face lit up. "Perfect!"

When he came to Lassiter, he asked, "Is this anything like what you saw on the first trip down here?"

Lassiter shook his head. "No. That was a baleful light, an angry light. It was ugly. This is lovely, and actually kind of soothing."

Soothing sounded good. Beside him, the pale rosy ring floated, a god's eye peering down at the new aliens.

Chapter 19 What Elephant On The Bridge?

"HERE'S WHAT I DON'T UNDERSTAND, and I'm not trying to blame anyone. But we have some of the finest scientific minds around, including people trained in celestial mechanics. How is it that nobody—including myself—saw this coming? Vargas looked around the bridge mess table, perplexity on his face. "How did we all miss predicting these eclipse periods?"

Tim Simmons felt obliged to defend the physics community. "It's not really something we experienced on a day-to-day basis in our own solar system. Um. We all knew it happened with the large primaries, but. . . " He trailed off with a vague gesture.

"There's gas giants in the solar system. Doesn't this phenomenon happen with them?"

"Certainly. But it wasn't relevant to us."

"Say what?"

"From Earth, we only saw a portion of the night side of Jupiter or Saturn. We would see moons wink out as they moved behind the planet, and our computer models showed it was a regular occurrence. We knew it happened, but it was never important to our daily lives. Nobody put two and two together here."

"Please understand, Dr. Simmons." As captain, Vargas was entitled to call Simmons 'mister', but used his title to placate. "I'm not casting aspersions. I took two years of orbital mechanics at the academy, and majored in math at university. I should have realized it, too. I'm just amazed that none of us thought of it."

Sorlund said, "We've all been dazzled by these new worlds. Nobody in navigations noticed it, although if our arrival had been timed for arrival during an occlusion, we would have spotted it instantly."

"Well, now that we do know about it, what does it mean? Do we write this moon off as uninhabitable?"

Harlen looked through his screens. "There's a report here from Mann. . . Here. He says that they'll need to test, but he think Earth plants will be able to grow there. He's got a little garden started in his greenhouse, and he's planted a green bean, a kernel of corn, a stalk of wheat, a tomato, and a pea plant. Oh, and a blackberry."

"That's a mistake. Blackberries will overrun the whole planet no matter what."

Vargas waited for the laughter to subside. "So does Mann think we can live there? Even with this . . . extended night?"

"He thinks we can adapt. He isn't sure about the plants, but he says that artificial lighting can overcome that if needed. He's more worried about the small cycles, the change in axial tilt in relation to the sun as we orbit Hō-ō. Plants might adapt to a 440 day year, but not a ten day year. He thinks that might be a problem. A lot of Earth plants cue their flowering and dropping leaves on the angle of the sun."

Trapp spoke up. "As far as colonists go, I'm also more worried about the rotational period of the moon. This eclipse phenomenon might actually help here. Let me explain. I'm one of those people who has jet lag. A strange affliction for an air force officer, I admit, but it was never debilitating. Just annoying. I fly three times zones east, and I feel rotten, out of sorts for three days.

"Let me ask: how many of you come from countries that change the clocks back and forth every fall and spring for daylight savings time?" Most of the people raised their hands.

"And how many of you find yourselves a little fatigued when you move the clocks forward in the spring?" Most of the hands stayed up.

"OK, because of the rotational period, which is about a half an hour faster than Earth's, it means that every two days, we will be moving our inner clocks ahead by an hour in order to keep pace with sunrise and sunset. Or Zharrise and Zharset, if you prefer."

There was silence while everyone digested that. Then Trapp continued, "I think this period of darkness will give us a chance to get caught up. Some of us won't need it, some won't be able to function without it. It'll be a good chance for everyone to sleep, or socialize, or pursue hobbies, and just take a break from the routines of a small agricultural community. And if it turns out that it really is a bad idea for people to be out running around under Hō-ō when it's full, then this will be a good chance to get out on a warm summer evening and enjoy life."

"What other oddities have we discovered? People?"

Aaron Kessler, one of the newly awakened, raised a hand. "Yes, Mister Kessler?"

"I've been looking over the orbital radar findings. The tides on this place are incredible. I see the reports mention the ocean tides, but did you know the land has tides, too? At the equator, the altitude varies by up to three meters! And someone who weighs a hundred kilograms would weigh just ninety-eight kilograms when Hō-ō is overhead. But here's the thing: the seismographs show activity that's pretty clearly consequential to tidal fluxing, but I'm not seeing anything that suggests tectonic activity. Does this planet have a liquid core? And if it doesn't, where does the magnetic field come from?"

"More mysteries. Does anyone have any theories? Nobody? OK, what else?"

Simmons spoke up. "The oceans are a lot cooler than they ought to be. The area of land that's on the equator is showing temperatures as high as a hundred and ten degrees. The ocean should be literally boiling at the equator. Instead, we're seeing surface temperatures of about sixty degrees. Still hideously hot by our standards, but at least twenty degrees less than I would expect to see in the best case scenario."

"Any idea why?"

"I factored in the eclipse element. It's still cooler than I would expect. We know the oceans are very deep. Up to a hundred kilometers deep in some areas. There may be bodacious convections there. On Earth, you don't have to go very far down before you find temperatures near freezing. It may be the same here, where you go down a kilometer, and the water temperature is two above."

Aaron Kessler interjected. "It may be that there's a lot of ice down there. The water is less salty, according to this report, about one third as salty as Earth Oceans. So there could be a big strata of ice."

Simmons looked over. "Wouldn't the tidal stresses cause it all to melt from friction?

"Hm. Maybe not if it's fractured. Or if it's mixed with something that reduces friction."

"Like what?"

"Um. Let me get back to you on that, Ted."

Vargas sighed. "Another mystery?"

"Another mystery."

"OK. We'll shelve that for now. Jim Hartnell, you're acting climatologist with André planet side right now. How's the weather down there?"

"Tranquil where the team is, but this planet has some wild weather. There's a hyper cyclonic storm about fifteen hundred kilometers to the west of them and moving their way."

"Should we be concerned?"

"No. There's a twelve thousand meter mountain range. Even a storm like that isn't going to get over those. I don't even want to think about how much rain is falling. . . " He faltered as Vargas suddenly waved him to silence.

"Excuse me. I'm getting a priority." Vargas tapped his data pad and blinked at what he read. Hooking an ear-piece in for privacy, he said, "Put it on."

Sheffield's face came up on his pad. "*Phoenix*, we are requesting that you break orbit and come and assist us as soon as possible. We have suffered a contamination breach, and while nobody is in immediate danger, we are unable to leave our suits due to high levels of radioactivity. The shuttle is severely contaminated, and we have high rates of alpha particle emissions. Request entry to *Phoenix* via contamination module so we can undergo decontamination process." Vargas paused the message and called up André Morley.

"Lieutenant, gather your people and break off immediately whatever you're doing. Return to *Phoenix* immediately. The ship will be leaving for Disappointment as soon as you're aboard."

Everyone around the table looked thunderstruck. Aaron Kessler leaned over to Ted Simmons and whispered, "Didn't I make it clear the storm wasn't a threat to the ground crew?"

Ted shook his head. "Whatever it is, that's not it. You heard him. Disappointment. That's at least six days round trip, more if there's real trouble."

A moment passed without a response, and everyone around the table could see Vargas was visibly beginning to cloud up.

Lieutenant Commander Etienne Sorlund waved for Vargas' attention. "Captain, I just ran the figures. We'll be at optimal orbital departure point in ten minutes, with an ETA of two days, sixteen hours. If we wait for the ground team, we won't be able to arrive until well into the third day."

"Fuck. André, where the hell are you?"

"Sorry, Captain. I just had to confer with the team. It'll take about three hours to get everything bundled and stored."

"Belay that. Stand by for further instructions."

Vargas looked over at Trapp. "How long are they tasked to remain down there?"

"Five days. Five and a half. We wanted them to go through a full Hō-ō orbital cycle."

"Lieutenant Commander, what's our optimal time to get to Disappointment and back?"

Sorlund poked at his screen. "Should I assume the shuttle has made orbit already, sir?"

"Um. Yes."

"Assuming good reinsertion point and conjunction with the shuttle, not more than six and a half days, Ser."

"How much time before we have to launch?"

"Eight minutes, Ser."

"Chief, are you on the bridge?"

Harlen's voice came back. "Yes, Captain."

"Have you been monitoring Commander Sheffield's transmission?"

"Yes Ser."

"Can he make orbit? Did he say?"

"Yes Ser. He says the shuttle is contaminated with a radioactive substance, but with filters at hand can breathe cabin air safely. The shuttle itself is apparently undamaged."

The suits had several liters of water and probably could be safely replenished by the water tank on the shuttle. So they were probably in decent shape for air and water. Food and personal relief. . . Vargas winced. Those suits were meant to be on for ten hours, not several days.

"Lieutenant Morley, give me as concise a report as possible on the status of your mission."

"Everything's good, Captain. No problems to report."

There were a few chuckles around the table. That was concise. Vargas decided it would do. "Lieutenant, the Disappointment party has encountered problems and will need our assistance as quickly as possible. If we leave right now, we can be back in six days. I don't need to tell you that Hō-ō will go through a full phase before then. If we wait and pick you up, it delays our arrival by over a day, and Sheffield's people are stuck in their suits. Do you understand?"

"Yes Captain. That's why the delay in answering. I told the crew that we might be on our own for a while."

Vargas kept his expression stolid. One of the people down there he had just cashiered for doing the same thing he was proposing to do now.

"Captain, rescue the Disappointment people. I don't have any problems with supplies and provisions, and everyone here strongly affirms that we can stay. Um one moment, Ser."

There was a pause, and Gordon Lassiter came on. "Captain, go get Sheffield and his people. If we have problems here while you're gone, we'll make orbit and wait for you there."

"Thank you, Mister Lassiter, Lieutenant Morley. We will maintain hourly contact."

"Over"

"Lieutenant Commander, get out on the bridge and set course. I want acceleration in about six minutes?"

"Aye, Captain." Vargas hit a display window, and general quarters and acceleration warnings flashed around the ship.

In the artificial night of the great eclipse, the ground crew saw the spark of the main engine ignite, and begin to move, scale reducing it to a crawl, across the face of Hō-ō. Gordon Lassiter was not a man given to a deep sense of the ironic, and so did not feel sardonic as he watched *Phoenix* leave. Instead, he resolved to bring everyone safely through the night of full Hō-ō, five days hence.

It was his chance to exonerate himself.

Chapter 20 Is We Smart Like We Uset To Be?

THE SECOND DAY *EN ROUTE* TO DISAPPOINTMENT, Vargas set up an appointment as a client to see Doctor Spencer. It had been Trapp's idea after the Captain expressed some misgivings to him. "Spencer's your man. Not only is he the authority on this, but you've worked with him before. Go see him. All I can do is give you a pep talk."

When he arrived at Spencer's office, the psychiatrist promptly produced a data pad of forms for the Captain to sign. Vargas looked them over. One was the standard confidentiality agreement. This, however, was tempered by a second form which gave his acknowledgement of psychiatric conditions under which Spencer could relieve him of command. He looked up at Spencer. "You know these have no legal relevance out here," he commented.

"Nor does your captaincy, if it comes to that. Lacking higher authority, we have to see to our own discipline and policies." He tapped the data pad. "These have served us well."

Vargas grunted and signed them. He looked up at Spencer as he did so. "I'm not here for psychotherapy. Mostly I just need to discuss things that must not be repeated."

"I'm perfectly happy to just talk, Daniel."

For a few minutes the two men discussed the plight of the crew on Disappointment. The radioactive contamination was polonium, apparently from something like tube-grass.

"There's tube-grass there? That's odd, isn't it?"

"Well, he said something like tube-grass. Even Earth has something like that. 'Ice plant', it's called. It just about took over southern California back in the twentieth century."

"Polonium, eh? Nasty stuff. Where the hell did that come from, do you think?"

"Well, when radon breaks down, that's what it breaks down into. So it's not entirely surprising they ran into it. But they must have somehow let a couple of grams lose in the cabin somehow. Alpha emitter readings are sky high."

"Will we be able to handle that when they board?"

"Certainly. If there's one thing we gave long and hard thought to back on Earth, it was the possibility of contamination. Any kind of contamination."

Spencer stayed silent, sensing Vargas was about to segue.

"Well, almost any kind. Nobody foresaw the types of problems we had coming out of hibernation. We saw the possibility of in-pod degradation, but not what happened to all of us." He paused.

Spencer waited.

"Ian, did we all lose some of our intelligence because of that? Are we all a bit dumb now?"

Spencer didn't have to pretend to consider the questions. It was something he had asked of himself. After a moment, he said, "What leads you to suppose that's the case?"

"It most recently occurred to me the other day, when Hō-ō eclipsed the moon. There wasn't a single one of us who wasn't taken by surprise."

"Isn't it the sort of thing that's easy to miss?"

"Humph. You were on the selection committee for this mission. What kind of mind were they looking for?"

"Um. OK, I see what you're getting at. We were looking for the sort of mind that could have visualized this before it happened. One that adapts readily to new and alien phenomena."

"Right. People who can, to some extent, foresee such things. I'm wondering if we we've lost that ability."

Vargas tapped his thumb against his lower lip, a tell in poker that he was trying to decide something. "OK, not lost, exactly, but we aren't doing it as well as we could. For example, when the eclipse started, I was pestering Morley's people for images of the eclipse. It took me a couple of minutes to realize that we were in orbit directly over them, and merely had to turn our own cameras on Hō-ō, and get even more vivid pictures."

"OK, so you're like any tourist who got excited by the local wildlife and forgot his camera. It happens."

"Well, I felt more like the old uncle who's looking for his lenses, and ends up realizing he's wearing them."

"Help me to understand. There will be eclipses every ten days. We should be back from Disappointment in time for the next one."

"Actually, we have images. Simmons was observing the planet. It seems Hō-ō's night side has quite the light show. Immense electrical storms. Lightning bolts as long as the Earth is wide, trillions of volts. So he got the whole thing on ultra-res video. Even he was taken by surprise by the eclipse, though."

"You should put that on New Earth Global TV. You have all those people milling around *Phoenix* without much of anything to do for the next few days."

"Good idea. I'll do that. Ian, I find myself questioning my own judgment. For example, what on Earth was I thinking when I left a team on Disappointment? Now, instead of a methodical and straightforward exploration of a new planet, I find myself leaving one team in potential peril so I can rush off to save the other team. It didn't take much imagination to visualize that the Sheffield team could get into some sort of trouble and need rescue. And we were at least three days away."

"Shackleton. Or Perry. I forget which."

"Huh?"

"Twentieth century explorers of the Antarctic. Large polar expeditions would drop off small teams and then sail away so as to not get trapped in the ice, and come back to see if any of them survived ten months later. Mostly, they did survive. But not always. It's the nature of exploration. You have small groups of people, sometimes even individuals, who go off on their own to take unknown risks, with no safety net. For that matter, the early space programs were like that. You would have large teams of people who tried to guess every risk and avoid it, but in the end, you still had three men in a tin can several days away from any possibility of rescue.

"Daniel, I doubt there's a single person on either team who resents that you had two teams going at once. It's the nature of exploration.

"Alan Trapp was telling me this morning that each of the two teams is utterly fascinated by what the other is finding. Sheffield's team may not be in immediate peril, but they are in considerable discomfort. However, the first thing they wanted to know about was the eclipse phenomenon. They were dying to see pictures. They asked about that before they even asked about the rescue operation."

"OK, they're keeping one another entertained. There's that. But why did I divide them up like that? It's not like there's a rush. It took fifty two years to get here. A few extra months doesn't matter."

"We both know there's over a thousand people in cold storage, and even though they don't know we're here yet, you feel the pressure to find a place to decant them."

"That doesn't make sense. Why should I feel pressured by sleepers?"

"Because your main duty was to get those sleepers to a new world."

"And nobody expected we would have to choose between two of them. OK, I get that. But I still feel like I've lost a step off my pace, like all of us have."

Spencer eyed the Captain. The change in topic was a ploy, designed to gauge how concerned the Captain was about what Spencer thought of as 'the judgment issue.' Clearly, Vargas was deeply concerned.

"Daniel, it's no secret that we're all a bit more prone to more emotional responses than we might have been before. There are these damn flash-dreams, which affect our moods. There's the twingies, which leave all of us feeling we've had one cup of coffee too many. There's one element of physical evidence that will amuse you, by the way. Coffee consumption per capita on the ship is less than one half what it was among the same people during training."

"Ye gods. You psychometric types actually tracked how much coffee we drank?"

"We tracked how often you went to the bathroom and how long you were in there. Disqualified some people over that, too."

"Why . . . no, never mind. We can have that conversation another time. Let me ask you a question, and try not to answer with another question, Doctor. Did you personally expect things to get as . . . random . . . as they have on this expedition?"

"Actually, it's going better than most of our scenarios projected. We had dozens of possibilities on things that could go wrong, up to and including mutiny, rival gangs and eventually cannibalism on board *Phoenix*."

"Really? You considered that?"

"Really. While you studied hundreds of possible setbacks like engine failure or hostile aliens, we tried to think of everything that could go wrong, based on human nature. For instance, we played with the idea of enforced calming music played 24/7. The most likely result of that was that *Phoenix* would arrive with a small pack of naked, shivering cannibals who no longer understood they were on a star ship. Just as Robert Heinlein forecast three. . . no, four hundred years ago."

"Is our grip on reality that poor? Do you really have that grim a view of human nature?"

"May I remind you we left Earth in the throes of a nuclear war?"

"Point. So tell me; do you have any hope for humanity?"

"One. I have children. Two. I brought them along on this journey. Of course I have hope for humanity.

"Daniel, on any endeavor of this scope, with this many individuals and unknowns involved, anything short of utter chaos should be considered an accomplishment. I'm sure you know that the expedition was only given a one-in-ten chance of establishing a self-sustaining colony. It wasn't based on the likelihood of finding a suitable planet, or at least not that alone. Mission planners actually considered that a likelihood. It was the sheer buggery of human nature they were worried about. Sheffield, Trapp and I all have orders in the event that you are incapacitated, as I'm sure you know. . . "

Daniel nodded. He had even helped draw up the orders.

". . . including various 'Captain Ahab' scenarios. We had to consider what to do if you were mentally incapacitated. Which you were, the first two times out of hibernation. We spent a fair bit of time considering how you would react to various challenges, including a few that came close to the problems hibernation produced. The very best scenario we could come up with was that you would approach me or Trapp and ask, 'Is this affecting my ability to Captain this vessel?' And voilà. Here you are. This is what we were hoping for.

"Does that give your misgivings a little perspective?"

Daniel thought back to his first awakening, when he had lost the power to read English and was struggling to find music on his data pad the piano could play for Julie. That had worked out rather well, hadn't it?

He could do this. "Actually, Ian, it does. So you think I'm still fit for command?"

"You're still fit for command. And doing a good job of it, too. As for whether peoples' judgments have been affected, so far we haven't seen anything alarming."

As he headed for the door, it crossed Daniel's mind to wonder how Spencer and Trapp had evaluated his handling of the Lassiter situation. He nearly asked.

But that would cross lines beyond the doctor-patient relationship. Maybe when they were both old and happily retired, he could ask about it.

* * *

Ian spent a few moments gazing at the door the Captain had just left by, frowning slightly. Normally he had a duty to discuss concerns about the welfare of the crew he had with his superiors, including the Captain of the ship. And he had discussed it with Trapp.

For over a week, he and Trapp had grappled with the idea of testing the crew to find out what deficits they had taken from hibernation, and if possible, just what the nature of those deficits were.

That they all had deficits was beyond doubt. Everyone had shorter attention spans, tended toward irritability, and seemed to have more lapses in judgment. They all considered the flash-dreams and twingies to be minor plagues, but Ian wasn't convinced they were all that minor. The experiences of the first team to land on Hō-ō One, including himself, had sharpened that concern.

Trapp and Ian hadn't figured out a way to test people without it being evident that they were doing just that. People were mildly impaired; they weren't shambling morons. They would spot it in nothing flat.

And what was now a free-floating anxiety shared by everyone could rise up and could become a morale crusher. Once a colony was established on one world or the other and there was a bit more room for human emotional frailty, they could test, and share their suspicions with the colonists.

A crew that could still function, if not as well, with vague doubts was better than a crew that had just learned it was damaged irreparably.

Chapter 21 Tubular Knells

DESPITE THE FALSE GRAVITY OF CONSTANT ACCELERA-TION, the crew had done a remarkable job of converting the loading bay to a decontamination chamber. The final touches were done just in time for the operator to evacuate the air and open the winged doors. Sheffield's shuttle drifted in slowly, and without a bump, came to a halt millimeters above the bay floor. Clamps reached out and secured the shuttle.

Cheers went up on the bridge, where the rescue operation was being monitored, but the riskiest part of the recovery still lay ahead. The rendezvous was a marvel of timing, with the shuttle meeting *Phoenix* moments after it cut engine having dropping into orbit, and the shuttle was secured when, slightly less than a half orbit later, the engine fire for the return trip to Hō-ō One.

Following instructions from the hanger chief, Sheffield and his crew, still in their ground suits, exited the shuttle, and, since the suits weren't really rated for hard vacuum, wasted no time floating to the air-lock-cum-steam-shower near the shuttle's landing spot.

The crew rotated under scalding hot jets of water, arms raised above their heads, for several minutes. Long enough that the people inside the suits, parched and with skins already crawling from three days of being sealed up in the suits without adequate personal relief features, could remove the suits without inhaling lethal amounts of polonium dust or absorbing dangerous amounts of radiation. Monitors carefully tracked the vicious mineral. The water was simply flushed away into space. It was from the hull reservoir, and they had plenty to spare. The crew, now feeling overheated as well as vile from the least refreshing shower they had ever experienced, waited with mounting impatience as Waldos placed the detection instruments around them, sniffing carefully.

The all-clear was given, and with an immense sense of relief, the crew members stripped off the suits, noses wrinkling at their pong. Waldos promptly pulled them away for processing to see if they were salvageable.

Captain Vargas' voice came over the intercom. "Take your showers, people. Consider the hot water unlimited, and take as long as you want. And remember, the hot meals we promised you await."

The radiation detectors took one last sniff at the now-naked crew, most of whom involuntarily cringed back from the snake-like sensors. No radiation was found. The seven slid through into another chamber, this one resembling a conventional set of crew showers. In fact, an entire section had been disassembled and moved to the hanger bay for this very purpose. With carte-blanc from the bridge, the orderlies had put in the best toiletries the *Phoenix* had to offer, and with huge grins, Sheffield and his people proceeded to expunge the foulness of three days trapped in those suits.

A half hour later, wrapped in towels, the seven underwent a final inspection by the radiation sensors and, proclaimed completely free of any radioactive contamination, walked through a final port and into the disembarking chamber of the *Phoenix*.

There, Charlies waited with ship's tunics for the seven. They pulled the lightweight garments on, and for the first time in days, felt reasonably human, if ravenous. The suits carried one day worth of unappealing field paste, plus water, and they had made the water last three days, at least.

Intent on keeping morale up, the Captain had asked the individuals to list the foods they most wanted to eat, and promised them a banquet.

The entire main mess was theirs for the eating, and they set to. They had entered the docking bay in near silence, not joining in when the bridge cheered. The decontamination and cleaning procedures hadn't encouraged talk, and all seven responded in monosyllables if they had to say anything at all.

But now, freshly showered, and with hot favorite dishes arrayed before them, the crew began chatting among themselves. They probably weren't expecting the meal to be served from the Captain's formal tableware, featuring pure silver and cut crystal. Red Farnsworth, never one to stand on ceremony, had requested a toad-in-the-hole false pork pie and a pint of ale. He looked openly stunned as the unassuming Irish fare was served from a tray of silver, the dark Guinness in a crystal flagon. Tsuchishima had asked for a chizburger and sake, and was similarly amazed. The beer and rice wine weren't even supposed to be on the ship, but Nate Harlen knew of many things on board that officially didn't exist. Less well known was that Vargas had contributed the Guinness from his private stock. Trapp and Vargas, listening from the bridge, smiled at one another.

This had all been carefully choreographed during the trip to Disappointment by Vargas and the doctors, and Sheffield and his crew had gone along with it, if a bit perplexedly.

"We've had two expeditions that ended in near disaster. The first trip to Disappointment resulted in news that nearly crushed the spirits of everyone on board. The second trip to Hō-ō One blew up in our faces and has everyone a little afraid of the place. Sean, do you really want people seeing your expedition as 'strike three'?" At Sheffield's perplexed look, Vargas amplified, "If we let it, this mission could also be seen as a failure. And at that point we would have a severe morale problem."

Sheffield had replied, a bit sharply, "But the mission wasn't a failure. We've got an entire hold full of new discoveries!"

"So we're going to make sure that people hear that."

Vargas had heard the rumors about 'demon light' that were making the rounds. He was devoutly hoping that Morley and his people would be able to demonstrate that Hō-ō didn't drive men mad.

"This one has the potential to be a farce. A team utterly paralyzed and in need of rescue from what we thought was a harmless plant. What can we do?"

Both doctors chorused, "Give them a heroes' welcome!" looked at one another and burst out laughing. Miserable in his suit, sitting in an overcrowded shuttle with a group of people just as unhappy as he was, Sheffield could only shake his head.

Vargas waited patiently, and asked, "How does that help?"

"Old vaudeville trick," Trapp said. Noting the blank look, he added, "Live shows, often performed extemporaneously in front of an audience. If a performer dropped the ball or flubbed a line, make it look like it was intentional, part of the act. Even if the audience knew better, they would usually go along, and the fact that the flub occurred would be quickly forgotten."

"We aren't lying," Spencer added. "Sheffield and his crew are heroes, and even if there's elements of the ridiculous to this —I don't see them, by the way—then it's all the more important to remind people that they were facing unknown dangers, and on a new world, nothing could be taken for granted. Despite their best efforts, they wound up in a hazardous situation."

Vargas considered for a minute. "Sheffield and his crew do deserve it, don't they?" At their nods, he continued, "Let's give them a heroes' welcome, then. Make it fancy."

As *Phoenix* neared Disappointment, and the light-speed lag dropped to a few seconds, Vargas had personally debriefed the crew. Sheffield had stared blankly, and then looked around the cabin of the shuttle, silently canvassing the crew. He got nods of agreement, some eager.

As soon as they finished eating, the rest of the *Phoenix* crew were allowed to crowd in and shout questions and listen to the informal story. The Captain and the Chief Medical Officer led the crowd in, and were the first to walk up to the table, still covered in the Captain's finest linen, and shake their hands.

The line officers smiled approval and happily joined in when a coached April Anderson, one of the chefs, called for three cheers. Inevitably, there were calls for a speech after, and, smiling, Sean Sheffield rose to his feet.

"First, I want to thank everyone for the warm welcome. We're sorry we had to cut the exploration of Disappointment short, but as most of you know, we were exposed to a radioactive substance. I understand that our suits were the true heroes, giving their all so that we might live."

There was a burst of laughter, and Vargas reflected that those suits would probably end up getting spaced. No matter. *Phoenix* had lots of spares. He was worried about the shuttle, though. They only had eight of those, and needed every one of them.

"Even after the contamination, we were able to continue exploring. Disappointment may not be suitable for colonization, it is still of immense value to us. It has an untold bounty of minerals, and we found everything humans might need to build a civilization, a lot of it just lying on the ground.

"There's a little something I brought back from Disappointment that I want to share with the ship's complement." He glanced at the line officers. He hefted an object about the size of a baseball on to the table, letting it drop the last ten centimeters. It landed with an audible thud in the acceleration gravity. "Captain, if you would be so kind. . . "

Vargas walked up to the table, wondering what Sheffield had. It was smaller than the lump of gold Sheffield had played with in his report, and rounder. He lifted it, surprised at the weight, and saw that it wasn't a perfect sphere. There was engraving on it. He looked closer, and grinned.

Turning to the audience, he held it up. "It's a globe, a map of Disappointment, and it's made from pure gold. It reads, 'Handcrafted by the crew of Disappointment One, 28/274, and inscribed this day by Asuka Tsuchishima and Red Farnsworth. May Disappointment never live down to its name. Followed by all their names."

A volley of cheers rippled through the crowd. Spencer noticed that some of the audience were gawping at the golden orb with almost hypnotized awe, and reflected that the explorers had managed to ensure that no matter what, humans would be returning to that place. Gold fever still existed, even when gold had no value beyond some fabrication and just looking pretty. But then, that's all gold ever was, he reflected.

Vargas shook the hands of each of the crew and, still smiling, returned to his seat, globe carefully nestled. Despite himself, Spencer leaned in for a closer look and Vargas glanced and said, "Would you like to hold it?"

Gingerly, Spencer took the object—worth enough on Earth to ensure he would never have to work again—and enjoyed the sensually soft weight of it. He handed it back with a twinge of reluctance, and a keener appreciation of gold fever.

"The storage area of our shuttle is loaded up with metals and minerals that we found just walking around in various areas. Along with pitchblende, we found lithium, bauxite, copper, gallium, iron, lead, silver and zinc, just lying around. We found other minerals that we think might be wolframite, scheelite, coltran and some rare Earths. We need to get a full analysis lab set up on that planet pronto.

"And have the lab boys take a closer look at those lead samples. Red thinks a couple of them are actually molybdenum. We also found carbon and tungsten.

"Plus gold, of course. We didn't see diamonds, but maybe next time.

"I recommend that we set up mining operations on this planet. Unless your moon is as mineral rich, and from what I'm hearing, it isn't. . . "

"Lots of nickel and iron" Vargas interjected.

"OK. That's good. We need to sit down with Lieutenant Commander Jeanine Barney. She's got a full list of items needed for the Imprinter. But we found some that are worth ten times their weight in gold on Earth because they're so rare."

"How much did you collect?"

"About eight tons." Sheffield chuckled at the captain's expression. "Really. It was that easy to find. We also have about two hundred and fifty different types of plants, including, unfortunately, this world's equivalent of tube-grass. And about seventy-five soil samples.

"The mission was a huge success."

Sheffield added, "And we did most of it after we put in the call for an early pickup. Now, I'm going to set myself down, and let Adelena Conti tell the tale of our radioactive grass. Captain, crew, thank you very much for your warm and wonderful welcome back!"

Conti nodded and stood up. "First, I'm so very, very glad to be back on *Phoenix*, and I want to tell you how glad I am for your support and your love.

"It was our seventh day on Disappointment, and things were going well. We had surveyed about a dozen sites, including the mountain pass where we found the rare earths. The drawback was the radon levels were generally high, and there seems to be a shallow layer of radioactive topsoil—usually only a couple of millimeters—everywhere. I have no explanation for this. It's like someone came along and sprayed the planet with a coat of radioactive gunk. You don't have to go far to find good clean soil.

"We set down next to a field of what looked like a type of tall succulent grass. It was separated from us by a stream about five meters wide and about a meter deep—too deep to risk crossing on foot. So when we got done surveying the spot, we decided to hop the shuttle over to that side. We were paying closer attention to that area because the radon levels were sharply lower. About ten picocuries/liter. We had been noticing that wherever the tube-grass grew the radon levels dropped. We wanted to know why this spot was different. We had also been reading the reports from the Hō-ō One team about tube-grass, and the remarkable properties. We wanted to see if this was the same plant, and if so, why it was so much taller—over a meter tall—in this one area. And yes, it was tube-grass.

"So we hoped across, and Red and Madelyne jumped out and started getting samples. We have some in a sealed box.

"Now, a little perspective is in order. The suits have radiation alarms, but because of the generally high radon levels, we had been getting a lot of false alarms. We eventually turned them off. The shuttle also has radiation detection equipment, but unfortunately, it's in the top of the craft.

"We only spent a few minutes getting samples of the tube-grass and stowing it in the back storage area. Then we hopped back in and flew back to where the rest of the crew were. We were just landing when the first radiation alarm went off.

"We lost time looking in all the wrong places. We thought we had landed on a hot spot upon our return, and looked there. The others, outside the craft, found no undue levels of any radiation beyond the radon levels. We checked the airlock and found it heavily contaminated. Finally, we realized that it was a fine powder on the outside of our suits. But by then, we had walked around the entire cabin area, and it was hopelessly contaminated, as well.

"We conferred, and realized there was nothing to be done for it. We weren't sure what the material was, or where exactly it came from. We were stuck in the suits until *Phoenix* could come and get us.

"We finally figured out that the radioactive material was Polonium 210, at least ten grams of the stuff. We knew we were reasonably safe as long as we stayed in our suits, and thus couldn't inhale or ingest any of it.

"We've since discovered that the tube-grass itself is loaded with the stuff. One strand might have a tenth of a gram, which is ferociously toxic, when you consider a couple of nanograms can kill.

"I see a couple of worried expressions out there, and I can tell you that the Captain assured us on the way here that they did some fact test the Hō-ō One samples and found no unusual levels of any radioactive material.

"Here's the important part about all this. This plant can apparently capture radon, and store it and accommodate its half-life decay into Polonium. It can handle incredible amounts, as well.

"It also neutralizes the radioactives in the soil. How it does it, and in what manner, is an absolute mystery. We think there is some sort of chelation process in between the layers of tube-grass root mat. Maybe.

"The area east of the river had clear evidence that tube-grass had grown there and then died off, allowing other species of plant to come in. We found some of the root mat characteristic of tube-grass growth in shreds in the ground. Apparently the stuff does eventually break down. But the ground itself was free of radioactives, which is why the radon level was so low.

"When the plant dies, the polonium is released as an extremely fine powder. Polonium 210 has a half-life of about 138 days, and it breaks down into lead. We surmise that it's eventually blown or washed away to sea.

"If we're right, then this plant could be key to making Disappointment a habitable world for humans, possibly within a generation or two."

Conti abruptly sat down. Sheffield stood. "Thank you, Miss Conti. Folks, we aren't going to take any more questions, partly because what you've heard pretty much covers what we know, and second, we would all like to get some rest. It's been a trying three days. I promise we'll have all the details in the ship's library tomorrow, and include some ideas we had to make Disappointment work for us. Thank you!"

Sheffield gathered his crew up by eye, and they sidled out the rear entrance of the mess hall. The audience reformed into small groups of excited chatter, and Vargas was unsurprised to see the physicist, Simmons, in vigorous debate with a couple of geneticists.

And tube-grass had seemed such an unassuming little plant, he mused.

He wandered around the gathering, pausing to listen at each group, smiling, greeting people, and offering no opinions of his own.

If it was the same plant, what was it doing on two planets that were further apart than Earth and Mars? What sort of ecological niche did it fill? Vargas asked himself that as they began drifting away from the victory celebration. Listening to the chatter of various crew groups around the mess hall as he circulated, he learned that most of his people had identified that as the single more relevant data point toward solving the mystery of this strange planetary system.

* * *

The lurch occurred moments after turnaround, when *Phoenix* was forty hours from Disappointment, half-way back. The main engine engaged, acceleration swiftly grew to a gravity, and then suddenly, the engines cut out. Gravity quickly vanished for three seconds, an eternity to the wide-eyed members of the bridge. Then acceleration resumed, just as suddenly.

Vargas, at the God Console, contacted Engineering. "What just happened?"

"We're still trying to figure that out, Captain," a voice Vargas tentatively identified as Günther Brülow's said. "Scotty's on her way here now."

"What are the readings showing?"

"Uh." Günther peered frantically over the vast, complex console that covered nearly aspect of the engine's well-being. Even as Günther searched for an answer, Scotty's accented voice came over the Captain's data pad.

"It is possible that the main scanning computer had an unscheduled check," Lieutenant Apunda "Scotty" Boitumelo said. "Midshipman Brülow, would you please give me the readouts for the ignition configuration? I shall be there in about ninety seconds."

That meant she was flying full speed down the long corridors of the ship. Vargas pitied anyone who got between Apunda Boitumelo and her beloved engine. She stood one eighty and weighed close to a hundred kilograms, making her somewhat larger than the captain. She was probably employing a full load of velocity.

Vargas clicked to private mode. "Scotty, are we in trouble?"

"I do not think so, Captain. But we must recheck everything before we restart the engine again. I fear that was our only warning." She sounded a bit out of breath.

"Give me a report as soon as you can."

Barney poked her head in. "Permission to go to the engine room, Captain?"

Vargas nodded assent. Next to Boitumelo, nobody knew the engine better than the Imprint Officer. If a spare part was needed, she would have it. If it was something hard to refashion, and vital, then the ship would have to be shut down on arrival until a second spare could be made. And with the schematics for every part of the ship right down to the mess cutlery in Imprinter memory, all she would need would be the raw materials.

Some of which might be a little scarce forty-seven light years from Earth.

Vargas looked around and realized everyone on looked concerned. Lurching was rarely a good thing. He clicked his data pad to address the ship.

"This is the Captain. Most of you felt that lurch. We don't know exactly what it was, but Engineering assures me that it was in the ancillary components, and not a failure in the engine itself. Our estimated time of arrival at Hō-ō One remains the same. It probably does mean we'll have to make some repairs once in orbit around the moon, so those of you who were thinking of prospecting for gold will just have to be a little patient."

Chuckles sounded around the bridge. A rumor had already made the rounds that Sheffield had made a life-size solid gold statue of himself. The rumor was untrue, but Sheffield's report had made it clear that there was more than enough gold just lying around that he could have if he wanted to.

As Hō-ō One filled the screens, they determined what component was planning to fail, and ensured there was a replacement at hand. That done, Jeanine Barney was tasked with determining what raw materials would be needed for a new replacement, since ships regs declared it vital enough for mandated triple redundancy. The ship shouldn't fly without at least two spares at hand. And Scotty had replaced it once, following the multiple turnarounds at the half-way point.

Vargas knew a sensible rule when he saw one. Without backups, the ship could end up without the ability to start the engines up, or shut them down. And the estimated failure rate on this component was about one in ten uses.

Morley's team, still enjoying a reasonably uneventful survey on Hō-ō One, planned to return to the original landing site on the morrow. They had spent the night on the north facing slope of one of the vast ring of mountains below the pole, with a full Hō-ō just a red crescent on the horizon. Temperatures were well below freezing at fifteen kilometers, but they had discovered large amounts of thorium, the component most needed to keep the shuttles fueled.

Armed with that news, Vargas ordered *Phoenix* into a high synchronous orbit on the same longitude as the original landing site. The ship would be on the southern horizon, about twenty-five degrees above the horizon, and able to maintain constant contact.

Acceleration cut out three seconds early. The people on the bridge barely had time to exchange puzzled glances before Boitumelo reported. "That is it for that component, Captain. It just failed."

Vargas acknowledged and turned to Etienne Sorlund. "Steve, I make it we're coming in at thirty meters a second hot. Can we still get parked in synchronous orbit?"

The CNO tapped his screen. "We can come in on an elliptical and use the thrusters to get us positioned in synchronous orbit. Um, it'll be a high eclipse. We're near escape velocity."

"How long?"

"I can get you in sync in about five days. Our first pass over the site should be in about twenty-six hours."

"Do it." Vargas settled back, reflecting. They had the spare component, but only the one spare. They would need raw materials for a new one—and Hō-ō One seemed mineral-poor.

Phoenix could be fired up in an effort to get back to Disappointment if needed; but there was a one in ten change the replacement component would fail each time the engine engaged. The result would be an out-of-control ship, either unable to start the engine, or unable to stop it. The latter was even worse than the former.

He didn't bemoan the lack of planning or poor engineering. *Phoenix* was a bird with over seven billion moving parts, the most complex device ever made by humans. It had gotten them to Hō-ō One, and that was nothing less than a miracle, an incredible accomplishment.

But until they found minerals, *Phoenix* hadn't just gotten them to Hō-ō One.

It had gotten them to their new home.

Like it or not, they were committed to this torrid, strange new planet.

Part 3

Settlement

Chapter 22 Settlement

HE WASN'T AWARE OF IT FOR SEVERAL WEEKS, but Red Farnsworth had the distinction of being the first human to have stepped foot on four different planets—five, if you counted Earth. He had been to the Moon, Mars, Disappointment, and now Hō-ō One. When a grinning Lassiter pointed it out to him, he vowed, once the colony was established, to start selling 'I been to' patches for those eligible. The vast majority of people on board would only qualify for two patches; he would be one of two dozen who qualified for four. And now that Sheffield had stepped out on to Hō-ō One, he was one of two men to qualify for all five. Unofficially, Red was the only man to breathe the atmospheres of Earth, Disappointment and Hō-ō One, but officially of course, he had obeyed all directives.

Not bad for a yob from Manchester. Or a yob and a toff from Manchester. Briefly, he wondered if any of the folks back home would have guessed at their feat, and then realized that even if home still existed, nobody knew about there being two Earth-like planets here, and for all of that, they would be, at best, names in the history books. "Home" was 48.6 light years away and in the irretrievable past.

Red shook his head with some impatience. Between flash-dreams and the twingies, he sometimes found it hard to focus.

Ian Mann, playing with a surveyor's laser nearby, spoke up. "Something wrong, Red?"

"Nuh. Just woolgathering." Red found the featureless terrain actually interfered with his concentration, and wondered at that. There were no sights or sounds to distract. Red pondered the quandary as he used the laser to drill for a soil sample.

To his surprise, there was no underlying soil, but just bare rock. They were several hundred meters away from the edge of the field of tube-grass, on the southern side, where in an irregular but sharp line it gave way to just bare rock. They had been dispatched to try and determine why it stopped growing there.

Red marked the location on his data pad. He stretched and yawned loudly. Smacking his lips in satisfaction, he glanced at Ian, who was looking at him with mild disapproval.

"They're not watching us, you know." He nodded toward the sky, where *Phoenix* lay invisible behind the pale blue.

Ian pursed his lips and nodded, clearly skeptical of Red's assertion. Red gave his fellow middie a slightly vexed look. "You think the Captain is watching what we do and say this very moment? Come on! I know he's an Americaner, but it isn't like..." Red suddenly trailed off, realizing he had stuck his foot in it. Ian was from the Americas.

Red faced, he continued, "Look, I didn't mean to imply..."

Grinning, Ian raised a palm. He said, "No, I was acting to type. 'Assume you're being watched.' It's the informal motto for the Americas. I saw the Captain's orders about ground parties."

"Didn't you believe them?"

Ian grinned. "I do now that I stop to actually think about them." The surveillance of ground parties had been lifted during daylight hours within days, and then on nights when Hō-ō wasn't full. In the settlement area, where night lights defused the tone of Hō-ō's temper, surveillance had ceased even then.

Red said, "I have to admit when I first heard about the surveillance orders, I thought for a moment, 'oh, here we go', but the Cap really doesn't think that way, does he?"

"Like an Americaner, you mean?"

"No! Well, I mean, yes, but you know the sort. You're not like that. Nor is he."

"No, and if I had to guess, it's for the same reasons. First, we were watched, rather than the watchers. That's always less pleasant."

Red chortled. "I can imagine."

"Second," Ian held up two fingers. "We're both from regions that got involuntarily assimilated, and we never really got into the whole Americaner thing. The Cap's from Torreón, where a bunch of people got put to death for speaking Spanish the century before, and I came from Churchill, not far from where people were put to death for speaking French. And yeah, that was in the past, but we never really

forgot. There were a lot of separatists up my way, and I bet there were down in old Mexico, too. The rest of us never really considered ourselves to be full Americaners, but maybe a bit better. And people in our position hated the surveillance."

Red stared at Mann, startled. "Really? I never knew you felt like that. How did you get selected to be part of the Americaner crew?"

"You think we talked about it back home? At all? With video and audio capture everywhere? It was just something we all knew. The only places we ever talked about it was places like this, far from anyone else, and in places where even Washington wouldn't stick cameras or mikes."

Red glanced at the small jewelry pin in Ian's right earlobe. The devices, which immediately identified Americaners, were tiny GPS receivers that allowed the government to ping and locate any citizen at any time. Removing or disabling it was a capital crime. There was a rumor they could transmit conversations, one that was dispelled before *Phoenix* reached Jupiter. Vargas, in an inspired move, had ordered that the devices be disabled or removed from any former Americaner who so wished. Every Americaner given the option had opted to disable the devices. Most had elected to continue wearing the now-harmless decoration, including the Captain himself.

Red shook his head, half admiringly. "I had no idea. How did you get past the Selection boards, though? Don't they give lie-detector tests, all that shit?"

"Beating the tests is easy if you learn to do it from the age you can walk. After that, it's just a matter of honking the right patriotic noises. And we're taught those from the moment we start watching video." Ian smirked, looking into the middle distance. "I sometimes think the selection boards were looking for people who were disaffected. I know in my case, there were times where I thought, 'OK, they must know I hate being watched', but they never seemed to twig. Maybe Washington saw this project as a way of dumping several hundred potential troublemakers."

"Or maybe they thought people like you would make better explorers," Red suggested. "I asked Spencer if they had some set criteria for picking candidates, and he said they were looking for what he called 'settler types' and 'explorer types.' He mentioned that both were the type who got into mild sorts of trouble when they were young, and later proved themselves to be capable at what they chose to do. They actually looked for people who were at least mildly dissatisfied with life as it was."

Ian considered. "Would people who were satisfied with their lives have applied in the first place?"

"Ha. Good point! I don't know. I do know this, though; none of the Americaners...not you, not the Captain, none of the ones I trained with, acted according to the paranoid stereotype. That's why I asked Spencer about it, although I didn't tell him why."

Ian pursed his lips and nodded. "During the interview, Spencer made some anti-government noises. I now think he was testing my 'surveillance response.' At the time I assumed it was a loyalty test, and it wasn't until later that I remembered he was RE, and not likely to care what I thought of Washington."

"Wheels within wheels." Red shook his head in mock admiration. "Who are we mere middies to divine the sacrosanct thoughts emanating from the brows of our noble leaders?"

"Well, since we can't be overheard, what's going on with the Cap?"

"What do you mean?"

"Well, he's leader of the expedition, but he's staying up on the ship. I would have thought he would be down here, helping to set up the colony, being the leader."

Red looked down at the tube-grass, and plucked at his tunic. "I think the Cap's pretty much decided this isn't a good place to colonize. I overheard him telling the XO that he wasn't going to wake most of the colonists until a full local year had passed. Told him it would be that long to determine if humans could really live here or not."

Ian gave Red a shrewd look. "From your tone, you don't agree."

"It's a big world, and the photos show a lot of variety. Over those mountains," Red nodded northward, "there's dense jungle. Thousands of different plants, none of which grow here. There might be animal life there. The deserts look barren, but we won't know for sure until we put feet on the ground and look. There might be life forms that are perfectly happy at 200 degrees. Hell, we don't even know if there's an island at the south pole or not. If there is, what's there? Plus the oceans..." Red trailed off, aware that Ian had stopped listening and was looking over Red's shoulder at something in the distance.

"Weather coming, Red."

Red looked in the direction. There was a tall wall of cloud, pink-tinged by the light from Hō-ō, off to the east. It appeared to be boiling in slow motion.

"Red, I'm from Manitoba. Flat land, like this. And when we saw something like that approaching, we took cover. I've going to page Sheffield."

Thunderstorms weren't unknown in northern England—and they were standing in a field flatter and more even than any part of Manchester. Lightning would be very dangerous.

As Ian called in, Red gathered up his pad, and closed the lid to his soil analysis field kit. Ian telescoped his laser and folded it under his arm, and the two men trotted toward the safety of the shuttle. By the time they covered the hundred meters, the clouds were foaming overhead, and the air was taking on a sticky, hot feel that Red didn't like at all.

Their data pads flashed a warning as they entered the airlock. Sheffield, some twenty kilometers to the south, had maybe twenty minutes to get everyone to shelter. He was wasting no time.

It was mid-morning, but the thermometer on the craft assured them it was thirty-five degrees out. Red was still getting used to the astonishing swings in the length of day that Hō-ō One experienced every ten days. He was spending a lot of time feeling seriously whipsawed by sidereal tables that could have days of midnight sun, followed within five days by a day of continual night. That the whole cycle precessed by five hours each cycle, further confusing his inner clock, didn't help.

The shuttle was cool and dry, a welcome relief from the sticky heat outside. Normally the air at the as-yet unnamed landing site was fresh enough, a comfortable twenty degrees, but this air had a sort of a scorched scent to it. It reminded Red vaguely of the morning after Bonfire Night, when the air carried the scents of gunpowder and burned wood. There were usually thunderstorms on those days, too, he thought.

Ian pointed out the windshield to the north. Red looked, and gaped. A solid wall of water approached, rain falling so hard it appeared blue. Acting on instinct, he reached toward the controls, casting an expectant look at Ian.

Ian shook his head. "We're better off staying on the ground," he said. "And in case you're wondering, then yes, this shuttle can float. For a while, anyway."

It was almost a religious tenet among inhabitants of tornado alley that they never admit they could be impressed by anyone else's thunderstorms. Manitoba and Saskatchewan had the biggest and nastiest thunderstorms in the world, local lore had it, and the best Siberia or Antarctica could come up with were just spring showers in comparison. And they had the steel-door storm shelters to prove it. But Ian felt a sense of awe at the rapidly approaching waterfall. He reached out and turned on the outside microphones, then hurriedly reduced gain. No rain he had ever heard produced a gurgling roar like that.

The light had an irregular blinking quality that both men realized would be blue-white strobes if it were night. The lightning was nearly continuous and the unending volleys of thunder were drowned out – literally – by the approaching squall line.

The shuttle actually rocked when the rain reached them, and then all outside references vanished in a wall of foaming, swirling water on the ports. Ian went to turn down the microphones again, and stared, astonished, at the gain, which was at zero. The sound was inside, the hammering of the water on the hull.

Both men sat still in their pilots' seats, scarcely daring to breathe. The shuttles were tough, durable craft, tested in three hundred-plus years of refinement in Earth orbit, but they had never encountered anything like this.

Any display can pale if it doesn't change much, and after ten minutes, Red pulled out his data pad and set up a game of checkers. Picking black, he had just finished annihilating the last of Ian's pieces when the roar of the water suddenly let up. Started, the men peered outside. And blinked in disbelief.

Outside, the only evidence rain had fallen at all were the drops still sliding down the front of the windshield. The tube grass sat, erect and seemingly undisturbed. Overhead, the clouds were rapidly breaking up, revealing the milky blue sky of Hō-ō.

"Shouldn't there be runoff?" Red inquired.

"I thought we would be bobbing helplessly in whitewater rapids. I don't understand. Where did the water go?"

"Let's call in, and then we can go look. Commander Sheffield?"

"Sheffield here. That you, Red?"

"It is, Ser. We had extraordinary rain here, lightning, and thunder. But no flooding. In fact, you can barely tell it rained."

"It's just beginning here. . . oh, holy shit!"

The two men grinned at each other. Clearly the storm hadn't lost much of its potency in the twenty kilometer trip north.

"The modules can take it. I hope that stream doesn't wash them out."

"Let's get back there, Ian." He glanced at the chronometer. "We're due back now, anyway."

"In a minute. I want to poke my nose out."

The two men stepped out, cautiously. The tube grass took no sign of the pounding it had just taken, and didn't so much as squelch as they stepped on it. The air was fresh, and much cooler. It was pleasant, in fact.

"Damnedest thing," Red muttered. Stretching, he peered around. The storm was off to the nouth east now, and the west side was back-lit by Zhar-Ptitsa, a brilliant golden color.

Ian pointed, mouth agape. Clearly visible at the back corner of the storm, a tornado bobbed and weaved.

Red looked around anxiously. "Any more of those?"

"I don't think so," Ian replied. They're usually at the tail of storms like those."

"You've seen storms like that before."

"Well. . . " Local pride struggled with scientific honesty. "No. I've never seen anything like that."

"Where is that twister going?"

"Oh, shit!" Ian picked out his data pad, and sent a red alert to the camp. The modules could take the rain. A tornado, on the other hand. . . Moments later, Sheffield flashed an acknowledgement. "Sorry. Had to make sure we were battened down. What a storm!"

"You've got a tornado coming your way, Commander. Pretty big one, I think."

"Wonderful." Sheffield's English accent thickened. "Let me know if it starts snowing next. Listen, just stay where you are until you hear from me. That will be when the storm is done here."

The two men waited. Zhar Ptitsa came back out, still rising in the southeast.

Ian walked a slow circle around the craft, occasionally stamping the ground, unable to believe that all that water had simply vanished. He scanned the horizon, and Red had no trouble understanding that he was visualizing various drainage scenarios. Red, not exactly illiterate in the dynamics of hydrology, was similarly stumped.

Finally they got an all-clear from Sheffield, and fired up the shuttle and swept home.

The camp, which consisted of fourteen modules that had been sent down from *Phoenix* over the past fifteen days, looked little the worse for wear. A couple of the crew were gingerly resurrecting a tent that had been pounded flat, but aside from that, there was no evidence of damage. Ian craned his neck, trying ineffectually to get a glimpse of the river.

The Command module, a capsule roughly fifty meters long by ten high, was also home to the telemetry and broadcast gear. Sheffield's shouts could be heard from outside. Exchanging a glance, the two men silently entered.

Sheffield was still shouting. "Look, I don't care if the guy was a trained meteorologist or not! If a big mass of clouds are approaching us, that means we have fucking weather coming! Even a chimpanzee can figure that out! And why is there only two goddamn met men awake, anyway? Didn't it penetrate anyone's head that this place has wild weather?"

The voice coming back was muted, but Red was pretty sure it was the Captain. Sheffield listened, fingers tapping. "Look, it was a twister! It missed us by less than a hundred meters! It could have destroyed the whole camp! The only warning we got was a couple of people doing soil analysis north of here. They just happened to spot it. That gave us fifteen minutes' warning. Fifteen minutes!"

Pause. "Lieutenant Morley did warn us about this! He did! We were both at that meeting!"

Pause. "OK, never mind that. Ser, please get some qualified people on constant observation!" The words were a plea, the tone an order. Red tapped Ian's sleeve, nodded at the door. Let's get the fuck out of here.

Too late. Sheffield swiveled around and saw them. His eyes flicked back to the com console, and he glowered at the two middies. The glower became a level stare, unmistakable Naval Command Speak for What You Saw Didn't Happen. Red, who knew how to react, snapped to attention. A beat later, so did Mann.

"At ease." Sheffield swiveled back to the console. "Ser, my two middies are here. By your leave, Ser?"

Pause. "Ser. Thank you, Ser."

Sheffield turned to the two. "I'm damned glad you two were out there in the field and paying attention. I had people right where the tornado came through. If you hadn't called it in, they might have been killed. Thank you for being on the ball."

"Ser, were there any casualties?"

"No, Red. We dodged a bullet. How did you two manage out there?"

Interrupting each other, the two eagerly told the Commander their tale. Sheffield listened carefully, making the standard appreciative noises.

"That matches what we observed here. The stream didn't even rise. Any thoughts on where that water went?

"Ser, we know there's a thick mat of root material under this grass. Could it be acting as a giant sponge?"

"Hm. I don't think so. We got over a half a meter of rain in twenty minutes here. If that root material were full of water, we would notice. But I think it has something to do with it."

"What would we find if we went to the low end of this area of tube grass?"

"An interesting question, Mr. Mann. Why don't you and Mr. Farnsworth take the light craft down there and take a look?"

Red opened his mouth, but Mann was faster. "Yes Ser. We'll report back as soon as we return."

The two trotted out toward where the camp's three light propeller craft were parked. Mann grabbed Red's arm and steered him toward the shuttle. He whispered, "It's a hell of a lot faster, and we can just say we misheard him when we get back."

"What the hell did you volunteer us for, anyway? We've been on duty since 8 pm, and in case you haven't noticed, that was fifteen hours ago. It's eleven in the morning."

"It's ten minutes by shuttle, and I'm the one doing the flying, remember. We'll get this dog detail done in a half an hour, and then we can get some shut eye."

"Yeah, but what the fuck? Why are we brown nosing Sheffield?"

Mann gave Red a sardonic look. "We overheard him reaming the Captain, and he knows we overheard. I figure we do this little favor, and maybe he forgets that we saw him being insubordinate."

"What do you think he would be worried about us for? What are we going to do? Report him to Vargas for being rude to Vargas?"

"No. But there's the old saying about how it is unwise to know a king's secrets. It can lead to unfortunate accidents. Sheffield doesn't strike me as the sort who it would be healthy to know secrets about."

"Oh, come on. Sheffield's a hard case, but he's not going to ream us over for something like that."

Mann pushed the control to open the airlock to the shuttle, and didn't answer.

Twelve minutes later the two men circled a cataclysmic flood in the brightening light of the ambiguous dusk. Below them, a vast white torrent of water roared, dozens of kilometers wide and moving at a good hundred kilometers an hour, audible in the well-insulated craft.

"Keerist," Mann said. "I guess we know where the water went. You getting this?"

Red nodded and flicked a forefinger at the hires camera. "In color, three dee, and sound. You ever seen anything like this before?"

"Never. I've seen images of when the Pine Island ice dam burst in 2074, and I think this is a bigger flood. This might even be bigger than when Ice Summit Lake in Greenland broke out in 2130." The tsunami from that destroyed much of the western Ireland coast and eventually was why Red was born in Manchester instead of Ireland.

Mann brought the shuttle about and dropped to about two hundred meters, as close to the raging fury of the waters as he cared to approach. The cameras gave soft, satisfied purrs, unheard over the thunder of the incredible water flow. Hands ready to counter any air turbulence caused by the roiling water, he moved upstream, to where the water erupted from the ground just meters from where the vast field of tube-grass ended. Once above the emission point, he dropped to a few meters and flew carefully along the lead perimeter of the flood, depending on the cameras to catch anything that might help explain this phenomenon.

"How far is it to the ocean from here?"

"Um, about two hundred and fifty kilometers, I think."

"Let's have a shufti, eh?"

"I thought you wanted to sleep."

"Not any more. I mean, fuck! This is a once in a lifetime thing!"

"Do you really think so? I get the feeling the tube-grass plain gets storms like that fairly often. In fact, Simmons and the rest were all wondering why there wasn't any top soil for hundreds of kilometers from here to the ocean. Just bare rock and streams of mud. Well, now I can tell them why."

"Call it scientific interest, then. Besides, maybe we'll find a place we can take samples."

"Samples of what? The rain water?"

"Yeah. I'm curious to see what it's carrying away. There has to be some sort of logic to this. We've been trying to figure out the ecological role of tube-grass. Maybe this will tell us."

Mann considered. They might both be just middies on board the ship, but both held double doctorates, and this phenomenon came within both their areas of interest. "Oh, what the hell. Sleep is for sissies."

They cruised above the foaming rapids, drawing to one side of the roughly triangular region that was home to tube-grass. As the area broadened, the breadth of the rapids widened, to the point where it stopped being a rapids and became a swift, immensely wide stream. At that point Mann felt safe in dropping to within a few meters of the water and Red leaned out the air-lock with a glorious disregard for flight safety and dipped a bucket in the water. He retrieved it, poured it into a plastic bag which he carefully labeled with the shuttles positioning system coordinates, and they moved a few kilometers toward the ocean, and repeated the process.

At the ocean, the runoff was a river thirty times wider than the mouth of the Amazon, but then moved into a vast fan of silt which channeled it into dozens of daughter rivers. Where they emerged from the silt bank, they pushed the breakers of the ocean back several hundred meters from where they would normally break on the shore. Mann raised the shuttle so cameras could catch the extent of the silt laden fresh water. It was clear that a vast alluvial plain was slowly forming.

Red flopped into the copilot seat and wiped his brow. "Whew! It's getting nasty out there."

Mann glanced at his console and laughed. "I should think so! Fifty five degrees, and the wet bulb says forty three degrees!"

He glanced in the direction of Zhar-Ptitsa. "Hot sun, hot planet."

"Simmons was saying that the cloud cover and ambient water vapor give the place a higher albedo than Earth."

"What did he base that on?"

"What, the albedo? Upon reflection, of course." Red's face held no sign of guile.

"Gawd. I walked right into that. Eat shit and die in a fire, Farnsworth."

Both men guffawed, and Mann sent the shuttle in a wide arc back toward camp. Cool air and comfortable cots awaited them.

Chapter 23 Urban Planning On A New World

THE LAST MODULE TO SEPARATE FROM *PHOENIX* and dive into the atmosphere of Hō-ō One was Module Fourteen, the one damaged in the nuclear attack. All the inner workings of the Imprinter had been carefully disassembled, labeled, and placed into spare areas in all of the other modules. Only the casing had been left, and it was presently stuffed with supplies and material swapped from other modules in order to make room for the Imprinter parts. Nearly all of it fell under the category of 'just nice to have around' and included makings for a still and marijuana seeds and various luxuries. One last item jammed in struck a bemused Vargas as passing strange. What, he wondered, would someone down there need with a spinning wheel? Sheffield had OKed the requisition, and Vargas saw no reason to object.

On the bridge, Vargas watched Sorlund's display from the God Console. As the remote craft came through the ionization stage and reestablished contact and control, he shook his head. He honestly didn't think it would make it without burning up.

At the camp, a loud cheer erupted as it came into view, trailing condensation. Nearly all the modules had gotten roughed up coming through Hō-ō One's turbulent atmosphere, a journey that everyone had come to loathe, especially the area between fifty kilometers and fifteen kilometers, known to all as "the vomit zone".

Under Sorlund's now-expert hands on the *Phoenix* bridge, the capsule swept a wide arc around the camp site, losing the last of its velocity and shedding some of the residual heat. It came to its appointed spot, and with a final loud roar, settled onto its struts, never to move again. It had done its job, and to everyone's immense relief, the tricky job of getting all the supplies and material needed by the colony was now complete.

Ever since the modules started dropping, and the camp took the first steps toward becoming a colony, Sheffield sensed that the tone of the place was shifting away from that of a ship's operation to that of a settlement. The dual identities of the crew as both military and colonial persons, sustainable aboard *Phoenix*, were breaking down rapidly. Nobody had ever been required to salute in any case, but now there were a lot of dropped 'Sers' and unmistakable signs of fraternization.

Worse, the Captain seemed to be encouraging this. The mission plan called for this, butSheffield thought it was a mistake to implement it too rapidly. Most of the colonists were still in hibernation, and the crew was split evenly between *Phoenix* and ground side.

It was still more of a camp site than a colony. Not only had no permanent structures been built, they were debating what the structures should be. The realization that violent weather, including tornadoes could sweep through on a regular basis had permanently shelved plans for lightweight, open structures. Mosquitoes and temperature extremes were not a problem, but tornadoes were. It was a challenge.

Vargas had promised to get a few architects and engineers down there within a few days, and in the meantime the crew were living in tents and keeping as much material as possible in the reasonably tornado-proof modules. It was an awkward and often frustrating arrangement.

Sheffield stewed. It also showed how little they knew about this place. Sheffield knew more about Disappointment than everyone knew about Hō-ō One. Krissakes, the place didn't even have a proper name yet! Another thing the Captain was lagging on.

Sheffield was a professional, and genuinely felt no resentment when Daniel Vargas was named Captain as a result of the deal that brought the Americaners on board. Without the Americaner support, the ship would still be sitting in Dry Dock (or, more likely, be radioactive debris in a million degrading low Earth orbits). Sheffield firmly believed the mission came before his own ego.

And Vargas had been admirable as ship's Captain, facing problems that no Captain had faced since Ulysses. Part of Sheffield's method of dealing with flash-dreams and twingies had been to think of them as sirens, trying to lure him, or at least distract him to his doom.

But as the mission eased from space flight to settlement, Sheffield felt his administrative abilities were stronger than Vargas', and had already decided he would challenge for colony leader.

But that was later. For now, Vargas was still the Captain, and Sheffield was still his first officer.

Only he wasn't being much of a Captain any more. He'd even heard Mann refer to him as "Daniel" once, which got the middie a rebuke.

With the Imprinter in place for parts fabrication, Sheffield was making construction of a bridge over the River Styx his first priority. Given that they were living in tents and had no agricultural projects going yet, it seemed a strange priority, but Sheffield was convinced settling in the tube-grass was a mistake, and that the clearable land and wood resources they needed were all on that other side.

Then, inexplicably, the Captain had ordered Sheffield to put the bridge project on hold. He noted that there was now plenty of fuel for the shuttles, and they could be used to transfer personnel and wood and the like for the time being.

The Captain noted that the discovery that animal life, microbe-sized but animal nonetheless, begged the question of larger animal life on the jungle side. He felt being in a zone believed to be free of possibly dangerous life forms outweighed the inconvenience of the occasional tornado.

It was Ian Mann, with his experience from Earth with tornadoes, who finally persuaded Sheffield that it was wiser to stay on this side of the river.

"It isn't the winds that do the damage, by and large. It's the debris the winds pick up and throw. Tornadoes pick up tons of material and spin it around wildly at hundreds of kilometers an hour, and that's the stuff that kills people and destroys buildings. Without the debris, a tornado can pass a dozen meters from you, and you'll get your hair mussed. Well, OK," Mann grinned. "You'll probably get knocked down. Just so long as you don't get sucked in, you'll be OK. Tornadoes can't pull up the tube-grass, and there isn't anything else for them to throw about, so they're a lot less dangerous here than they are on the wooded side."

And the shuttles were more efficient at bringing lumber back to camp than any ground vehicle, especially given the lack of roads.

Grudgingly, Sheffield put the idea of a bridge on the back burner.

When some colonists went to examine the meter-square excavation the first landing party had made, they were dismayed to discover that the tube-grass had completely overgrown the spot. Only a slight square indentation was there to show it existed at all.

This was a more serious problem than tornadoes. The tube-grass was the perfect invasive species, crowding out all other forms of plant life with its impermeable mat of fibrous root. They wouldn't be able to grow anything in it.

Attention focused on the field, which had top soil, and tests indicated that with treatment with Earth creatures and nutrients, it would support a fairly good number of crops. But it was on the other side of the river, visible from camp and about a half-klick to the north. Adelena Conti was already busy over there, seeding the ground with microbial life from Earth.

"Why does tube-grass grow on this side, but not that side? Ann Forster, the botanist, demanded. "For that matter, why aren't there bands of this stuff over most of this continent?"

Michael Matthews, head of the agricultural team, nodded toward the stream. "The water blocks it."

"How?"

"It's vampire grass. It can't cross running water."

"I think that's werewolves."

"The weather over there is basically the same as here. There's a lot of diversity in a small area. It's not as flat; there's a hill north of that field that we think acts as a kind of rain shadow."

"It's just a hundred meters. How could it affect the weather?"

"Deflects the lower winds, which sweep the rain around. Unfortunately, some of it sweeps toward where the camp is."

"OK. But tube-grass isn't anywhere else on that side."

"Well, that's the question then, isn't it? Why isn't there any?"

"Like I said, running water. I think tube-grass is essentially one big plant, and the unifying element is that root. It's never more than about fifty centimeters deep. So if you have running water that's consistently more than, say, a meter deep, it can't get past it. And that's how it spreads; we don't have anything to suggest it pollinates or seeds anything at all. In fact, I can't figure out how it got started in the first place."

"I don't even want to think about the evolution of this place. The present botany is weird enough. How do we test your water theory?"

"Simple. We dig another sample. Only this time we dig a canal from the river, and have water at least two hundred cm deep flowing around it at all times."

"How sure are you of this notion? It seems like an awful lot of work."

"I don't know. But if we don't try it, we'll never know. If it works, we can farm on this side of the Styx."

"Good luck getting Sheffield's OK on that."

But to their surprise, Sheffield was more than happy to lend them the laser and excavation equipment needed. He was unhappy about being separated from the fields by the river, even though there were no known predators or pests. The colonists weren't even sure weeds would be a problem. Nonetheless, Sheffield's family lore was to always guard the crops.

Because the slope of the tube-grass area was very gentle, they had to go two hundred meters upstream in order to have enough inclination to ensure water flow. They burned and dug a trench about twenty centimeters wide and a meter deep, carefully rolling up the turf for retrieval by Morley, who for some reason was collecting the stuff, backed by orders from Vargas. What the meteorologist wanted with sod was anyone's guess, and he wasn't saying. He would be returning from *Phoenix* in a few days now that other climatological people were coming out of hibernation.

In two days they had the trench dug to the site of the new garden, and by now it was a full meter deep, aiding the natural incline. They could have done it in one day, but the days were getting short again.

This time they dug a pattern of sixteen one meter-square sites, four by four and separated by ground-level pathways with meter deep water trenches on each side.

On the third day they dug an exit trench back to the stream, and pronounced themselves satisfied with the results.

Then they refilled the crossways trenches because they weren't getting any water flow, and wound up with four parallel strips of land, one meter by four meters long.

They waited five days, and when no evidence of tube-grass incursion showed, they got seeds from stores for beans, peas, corn and alfalfa, and planted them under the gimlet eye of Rebekah Cohen.

By now most of the camp was taking an interest in the project, and whenever off-duty hours and daylight coincided, people found excuses to wander down to take a look at the little patches of Earth.

No, Michael Matthews reflected. It wasn't the little patches of earth they were so fascinated by. It was the little patches of Earth. This was a little corner of a home impossibly far away. People looked at the brave little shoots of green as the emerged from the dark, treated soil, and got a little misty eyed.

Matthews had cameras recording the growth and carefully measuring the rates. One of the big questions were how plants that depended on Earth-style sunlight for photosynthesis would manage the brighter and far more variable light of Hō-ō One. That they even germinated was a victory.

Before leaves began unfurling from the stalks, André Morley arrived on a shuttle and requisitioned a tractor to gather up the bales of tube-grass root that dotted the channel to the garden. If it wasn't clear to Sheffield what this had to do with gathering vital climatological data, Vargas, with an irritating grin, asked Sheffield to indulge the meteorologist. "I know we don't understand the weather down there, Sean," Vargas said in reply to Sheffield's protest, "but André is working on a theory that could have much larger implications for the colony than even the weather." He proceeded to fill Sheffield in.

"Hm. Captain, I have to see it before I'll believe it."

"That's fair enough."

"What's the status on weather monitoring?"

"We've got five qualified people, and you have one monitoring at all times. You won't get taken by surprise. Having said that, I've got one for you. The polonium plant on Disappointment and the tube-grass here are the same plant. Exact DNA match. Our tube-grass is fairly rich in heavy metals in some spots, which would have been a surprise under other circumstances. The flesh of the stalks, not the sap. The botany people are kicking around the idea that the plant is a natural chelation process."

"Is that possible?"

"Not just possible, but known on Earth. The other plant samples you've sent up have sparked a furious debate, since none of them seem related to tube-grass.

"It gets worse." Vargas grinned.

"They are finding stretches of DNA that are matches for DNA found in plant life on Earth. As a result, it's set off a big debate over whether they could be related, or if it's just congruent evolution, the way dolphins and sharks have similar shapes. Discovering that tube-grass is the same plant on two worlds and not related to anything found on this one has just added to the confusion."

"What do you make of it?"

"I'm a mathematician, not a botanist. I don't understand the biological science, but I can calculate the raw odds. It is several quintillion to one, which means it's effectively impossible. The congruent DNA, I mean. I can't calculate the odds of panspermia."

Sheffield nodded. The notion that microbial life could migrate from one planet to another was, in his mind, settled by the infection of Mars. But that just showed one way it could happen. Man did it. He had no idea what kind of naturally-occurring mechanism could do the same thing.

"OK, next question, Captain. Have your architects come up with a feasible design for housing yet? The reason I ask is that one of my colonists down here, a fellow named Cyril Voss, is an architect, and he's come to me with several ideas I'd like to try out."

"They're working on it. They had plans for every type of climate known on Earth. We could have survived on the high peaks of Antarctica, or the middle of the Kansas desert. But the mix Hō-ō One gives us has them flummoxed. Especially since the weather is variable in ways we didn't expect. But by all means, have your man Voss—I met him in training, he's a good man—work out some ideas. If you can benefit from on-site ideas, I strongly encourage it."

"I'll let Voss know he's got a green light. Did I mention, Captain, that we actually range about twenty-five degrees. From about five to around thirty. It's the two-day nights and midnight sun that cause it. Fortunately, it's reasonably humid, which moderates the temperatures.

"Despite that, Steinberg is treating a lot of dry throats and chapped lips. She thinks it's a combination of the thin atmosphere and the higher oxygen content. She thinks we need to be wary of chronic bronchitis and possible lung inflammations. She would like to see people wear masks for a while longer because she's concerned that we don't know what might be in the dust in the air. Super anthrax, all kinds of nasty possibilities."

"Sean, are you telling me that some people aren't wearing masks?"

"I think some folks are taking them off when nobody's looking. In the humid heat, they are pretty miserable to wear."

Vargas blew out his cheeks. "Tell Steinberg to put the word out that if the masks are really that difficult for some people, they should return to *Phoenix*. Certainly there's plenty of work for them up here. And we're awakening another hundred people this week."

"It's going to be crowded down here."

"A lot of them will stay up here. Top priority is going to be building homes, though."

"What do your people have at this point?"

"Well, we started out with the idea of Polynesian huts. We wouldn't even need screens or mosquito netting. Just enough walls to give people a little privacy, and not much else. But then that tornado came through. Then we realized that we needed to block the daytime glare, and the light from Hō-ō at night. Now we find out that it gets both hotter and colder than conditions led us to believe that first few days we were here. And most of the metals we have need to go to plumbing and electricity. So we're working on wood-frame houses that can withstand super-torrential rain and near misses by tornadoes." Vargas shook his head ruefully. "We've even played with the idea of going underground, like on Mars or the Moon."

Sheffield shook his head. "I've lived in both. I don't recommend it. Especially since the ground here is damp. Keep in mind we might have some unique materials to work with down here. Did you see the reports on the growth the crew are calling steelwood?"

"I did. It tests out about as strong as aluminum, and as light."

"You can mold it, too. It reshapes in slightly acidic water. Doesn't become brittle."

"I'll pass that along. I think the hydrological readings should make it evident that underground living just won't work there, but sometimes when it's a row of numbers, the obvious can get missed. How's the garden coming along?

The segue was pretty obvious. "They all germinated, but the corn is dying. We think the Zharlight has too much UV. We're looking into possible sunscreen that would be feasible on a large scale."

Vargas nodded. "We were expecting something like that, and we're working on it."

"Back to the mask problem. Um, we're still having problems with sunburn and snow blindness. People get overheated and take their face masks off. And with no offense intended, some of the people I suspect of doing this are people who I believe are more valuable down here."

Vargas snapped his fingers. "Actually, now that I think about it, there's an easy solution to that. Have your Imprinter look up part number. . . " Vargas tapped his data pad "X-04-ACPH-62545. Any raw materials he doesn't have at hand, we'll send down. We've got it covered."

Sheffield typed the number in and grinned. "Personal solar-powered air conditioning units! That's beautiful! Why didn't anyone think of that before?"

Vargas shrugged. "I trained in Mississippi. Sixty degrees and humid. Those ACPHs kept us sane. They have hydration, too. That might address Doctor Steinberg's concerns about dry throats. I don't think it got mentioned in mission training, because everyone figured we would either end up at a dry and coolish world like Disappointment, or an arctic wasteland like Cue Ball."

"That reminds me. . . permission to speak freely?"

"Granted."

"You need to give this place a name. If you don't, you're going to find that public consensus will do it for you. Some of the people are already starting to refer to themselves as Hōvians. I don't want to live on a planet called Hōvel or something equally dismal."

Vargas scratched his head, a standard tell that he was feeling pressured. "I'm on it. Give me a day or two."

Vargas, in fact, knew about the tell, and knew when to fake it. He had a name picked out. He also knew Sheffield wouldn't like it. But Vargas didn't like that Sheffield referred to Julie by her last name only, without even the dignity of rank or title. So he didn't much care if Sheffield liked it or not.

Chapter 24 Taking Time To Do It Right

TIM SIMMONS MADE A STUDY OF TIME HIS CAREER. Time might be the one thing no human could ignore, but physics was no closer to determining the true nature of time in the twenty-third century than it had been in the sixteenth century. He was used to considering time as a matter of quanta, a progression of irrational states that the Higgs boson used to create mass. Like most physicists, he believed mass/energy and space/time were interrelated, perhaps even controvertible, but nobody had come up with an $E=mc^2$ moment to explain exactly how that worked.

And even though the Higgs boson explained why mass had, well, mass, it didn't explain gravity. Nobody knew if gravity traveled at a set speed, since the only way to tell would be by creating mass from nothing, a trick nobody had mastered yet.

It meant that he was more apprehensive and more excited about the gravitational anomalies that *Phoenix* exhibited at . 89C then anyone else on board. He desperately wanted more data on that, but couldn't think of a way of doing so that didn't risk destroying the ship. That would be an unfortunate outcome. He had needed time to weigh his options on that one.

It did not, however, mean he was an expert on resetting the clocks. As he grumbled to Davis McDonald, the computer expert who got roped in on the clock project, "Damn it, I'm a physicist, not a teleologist!" McDonald needed a moment to think about it before guffawing. Thereafter, the two men referred to the project foisted on them by Captain Vargas as "The Watchmaker Project."

The problem was this: Hō-ō One had a rotational period that was just a bit faster than Earth's. A full "day", local noon to local noon, was 23 hours and 36 minutes. The result was that each daily shift began 24 minutes each day. Vargas and the brass were taking the hopeful stance that humans could adjust to the shorter day, but the clocks were adding a psychological burden to that adjustment.

Setting the clocks in the computer's core was easy. A second was 9,192,631,770 transition cycles of energy levels in a cesium-133 atom. To adjust the length of a second, all that was required would be to work out the exact multiple to get the reduced amount. In this case, 153,210,529.5 less cycles. That would allow everyone to keep the accustomed 24:60:60 format, and the time specifications in all the ship library and computer data only needed to be reduced by that one and two-thirds percent.

Unfortunately, the brass couldn't decide what they wanted to do. They all agreed that the time should be the same every 23 hours and 36 minutes, but they couldn't address the method. Sheffield wanted to make the hour between 2300 and midnight 36 minutes long. His argument was that the different sized time units could mess everything up, from orbital mechanics to cooking recipes. Vargas wanted to simply shorten the time units. Trapp, the radical, advocated a decimal time: ten hours a day, one hundred minutes an hour, one hundred seconds a minute. Simmons liked it, but recognized that people would have a lot of trouble adapting. He remembered reading of French Revolution efforts to create a more sensible calendar. He suspected the digital time would be a similar fiasco.

They wanted him and McDonald to work up approaches to all three of the suggested options. From a digital standpoint, both Trapp's and Vargas' ideas were easy to implement. Sheffield's was a nightmare, and even though it might be the easiest for people to adapt to, it was a nightmare convincing the computer that the complex coding needed to simply make twenty-four minutes unhappen—McDonald called it the "anti-leap hour"--could work well with all the diurnal processes computers did.

Over coffee, Asuka Tsuchishima had come up with the most original suggestion. "Eliminate clocks on the planet," she said with a smile. "We're simple people, returning to the land. Let's live by the sun and the moon, the way our ancestors did."

Unsure if she was joking, Tim had noted that the periods of the sun and "moon" on this planet were quite mad, and anyone who tried living by them would be a gibbering idiot in the space of fifteen days.

Asuka had grinned, and noted that she had seen what reasoned intelligence had accomplished on Earth, and maybe gibbering idiocy should have its own innings. Tim decided she really was joking. He hoped.

Tim and Davis were putting in eighteen hours a day on the project, since the brass wanted to implement a solution soonest.

The clock was literally ticking.

* * *

Lassiter, Farnsworth and Morley sequestered themselves in one of the modules for several days with the bales of root mass and the mystifying equipment they had gotten from the Imprinter. The night following was the night before little summer, when darkness fell for only a couple of hours, squeezed between long twilights. They flew out to the logging area Lassiter had been overseeing, known informally as Lassiter's Landing. Over the course of the next ten hours, people at camp heard the shuttle take off several times, and then after a brief, variable period of time, settle back to Earth.

A little fall night settled, and the three returned on one of the skipper craft, leaving the shuttle untended at the landing. Sheffield grumped about that, since standing orders were to have the shuttles in a state of readiness should an emergency evacuation be needed, but the weather forecast was cool, damp and cloudless, and by now everyone had concluded that there were no immediate threats in the environment.

"Ser, we'll lose six hours of work if we bring the shuttle back."

"And if things go pear-shaped, Mister Farnsworth? What then? Are you willing to risk the colony to indulge your little project?"

At which point Lassiter stepped in and requested a word in private with Sheffield.

Lassiter grinned at him once they were alone and asked if he thought the tube-grass was planning to attack. Sheffield gave him a cold glare and replied, "You, of all people, should know this place has some mysterious dangers. Didn't you have some problems on your second day here?"

"Sean, we both know there are no supernatural properties to Hō-ō. Our problems, and yes, that includes my problems, we

brought along. Shakespeare figured it out seven centuries earlier: 'The fault, dear Brutus, is not in our stars, but in ourselves.' Hō-ō didn't twist my mind; I fucked up. And Sean,
you're headed down the same path. I think the stuff that happened to us in hibernation has a lot to do with it."

Sheffield shifted irritably. "Look, my duty is to keep the
camp secure."

"Nobody questions that. But we've got a hundred and
twenty-five people on the ground right now. In the event of a
sudden need to evacuate, how many could the shuttles carry?"

There were presently four shuttles at camp, including the
one at the landing. Sheffield paused. "About one hundred of
them."

"And that's if you're not fussy about casualties. I wouldn't
want to go through this world's turbulence zone without being
strapped in and I certainly wouldn't want to be in the cargo
hold.

"The only real physical danger we know about is the
weather. I've looked at the met report from *Phoenix*; there's
nothing in the offing between now and morning. And everyone
can get to shelter in the modules. The fact is four shuttles has
absolutely no effect on camp security that three can't provide."

Seeing that Sheffield still wasn't swayed, Lassiter added one
more thing. "I've been working with Morley on this, and what
we thought might be a reasonably useful resource might just
make this area the most valuable patch of land on the planet.
No, I'm not going to tell you why; I plan to be here to see your
reaction when the shuttle returns tomorrow. If what Morley and
Red have cooked up doesn't knock your socks off, I'll accept a
recommendation that I be returned to *Phoenix* until you see fit
to let me come back."

"Lassiter, I don't want to do that."

"Well, you're not going to punish André and Red over this.
I'll raise a stink."

"May I remind you that you got cashiered?" Sheffield's tru-
culent glare pierced the gloom of the module. Lassiter met his
glare calmly.

"And yet here I am, working with the crew and the Captain's authorization. Where would you have me be?"

"In the brig, if we had one." Sheffield paused to consider. "For a week or so, anyway."

"We don't have a brig, and Captain Vargas made his decision. And you just said you didn't want to send me back up to *Phoenix*. Obviously you consider me of some value."

Sheffield didn't take the bait. "If he was going to slap your wrist, he could have just invoked the recordings and waited for you to tell him it was poisoned fruit."

Lassiter, despite himself, nodded. The same question had occurred to him. In theory, under Royal European law, no recording was admissible in court unless it had been secured under warrant, or with the express permission of the person being recorded. It was blow-back from the surveillance scandals of the twenty-first century.

Even though he knew he was being recorded, Lassiter could have said he didn't give permission, and the Captain could have simply declared a miscarriage of justice. Instead, he had avoided that and handed down a punishment that, while it sounded horrific, amounted, out here, to nothing more than a slap on the wrist.

"Sheffield, if you really have that big a problem with this, I suggest you call the Captain."

Sheffield's glare wavered. "You really, truly believe this is that important?"

"I do." Suddenly, Lassiter wore a wide grin. "Prepare to be wowed."

Sheffield glared, but in the high beam of Lassiter's infectious smile, found the corner of one lip curving up. "Wowed, eh? I'm holding you to that, Mister Lassiter."

* * *

How strange it was, Vargas reflected, that *Phoenix* felt like it was emptying out. There were actually more people up and moving about than at any point during the ship's journey, and the absent modules and shuttles weren't apparent from within the ship's main hull.

In fact, *Phoenix* had more activity now than at any point since construction—including the panicked dash from Dry Dock. Various work groups worked on a wide range of projects including planning a viable architectural model for the village-to-be to figuring out new clocks and calendars for Hō-ō One to running tests on plant life to see what could be adapted to the elevated ultraviolet from Zhar-Ptitsa. Vargas had been monitoring that last work group with mounting concern. The Earth-born plants didn't like the UV, and early indications were they would like the wildly swinging day lengths even less. Mature plants grown in hydroponics were sickening and dying when exposed to the type of regimen Hō-ō One had to offer. The rainstorm gave rise to yet another concern; few crop plants could withstand the type of torrential downpour that had struck the camp a few days earlier. If worst came to worst, the colony could grow their food hydroponically, but that was an awfully limiting choice, not just in the fare, but in how many people it could support. It would do if the colony didn't intend to grow, and a colony that couldn't grow was doomed.

Orbital survey groups scanned Hō-ō One for potential mineral deposits. The southern continent, in the south sixties, was permanently shrouded in cloud, and radar reported heavy constant rain and indications of lush jungle-like bioregions. It was also extremely hot, fifty-five or sixty, at the upper limit of what unprotected humans could survive for short periods.

On their own land mass, the polar highlands, known as the Boitumelos, offered hope of mineral wealth. Unfortunately, conditions ranged from arctic to near-space, and mining would be a significant challenge for the colonists. Conditions at nine kilometers were at least as bad as those to be found in the Himalayas on Earth, with an entirely different set of challenges.

That left a bit of the continent they were on, a sinuous strip of land bisected by the Boitumelos and swooping away in a vast 'S' shape on each side. It showed some promise, although prospecting from orbit had severe limits. The colony would have to just get out and explore when it could. Until then, no trips to mineral-rich Disappointment were likely.

'Do it all, do it now' was the unofficial working motto, and yet Vargas had the indefinable feeling that *Phoenix* was already a part of the past for those who were now building a colony.

Those people tended to look at her with an air of "oh, are you still here?" More and more, Vargas found the enthusiasm of the colony builders disturbing. This place didn't feel like home.

The ship would be the mother and lifeline for the colony for years to come. The library was still on board, and she was the remaining option if the colony didn't work out. Even after Vargas journeyed down to become a colonist himself, nearly a hundred people would be on board at any given time, doing orbital surveys, plumbing the library, tending the hydroponics so no matter what, the colony would be fed. Indeed, hydroponics were going to triple in size over the next hundred days or so.

Vargas shrugged it off. It was silly to think of *Phoenix* as a relic, when it was about to begin its most vital and productive stage.

Perhaps it wasn't the ship that was the relic; perhaps it was the Captain. Sheffield, in one of their increasingly testy exchanges, had hinted that the Captain felt his authority slipping away. Vargas had ignored the jibe, easily enough since once the success of the mission was assured, and he wanted nothing more than to put down his authority.

Vargas chuckled to himself and moved into the mess, where a giant 3D imagining studio had been set up. Lassiter had promised him a magic show, and nearly everyone still on board who was awake had crowded in to see what miracles might unfold.

Chapter 25 Hanging By A Thread

WITH A SLIGHTLY LABORED ROAR, the shuttle rose above the tree line into a cloudless pastel sky, shadows in sharp relief from the Zharlight to the east. Lifting slowly, it continued up as the colonists watched from the tube-grass side of the river. As it rose, it turned slowly, bringing its nose about in the direction of the watchers. Sheffield peered intently, puzzling over the curious bobbing motion of pitch and yaw that suggested the craft was lifting a massive load. Yet there were no signs of the cables it would normally employ for such a purpose.

It continued upward vertically, and under it a second object rose above the tree tops. The shuttle began moving forward very slowly, thrusters working to dampen the motions from its load.

But there didn't appear to be anything connecting the object —a large tree trunk, it was evident—to the shuttle.

Engines roaring, the shuttle came across the river, and Sheffield saw that most of the main thrusters were devoted to maintaining altitude, and thrusters were being used, not just for damping the motion of the suspended log, but for the craft's forward motion.

It hovered briefly over the expanse of tube-grass near the river, and then carefully descended. The log settled onto the tube-grass, and the four sets of grapples on the underside of the shuttle opened, dropping what looked for all the world like strips of toilet paper. It crossed Sheffield's mind to grumble about having a shuttle operating so close to the settlement structures, but the shuttle was a good hundred meters up. Not that tube-grass minded either way: the green shoots would crisp away under the flame, and grow back within days. The root mat seemed utterly unfazed by the superheated exhaust.

Relieved of their burden, the engines fell to a normal level of exertion, and the shuttle settled on the tube-grass a short distance from the log and away from structures.

The engines cut out, and even as the cooling shuttle lay ticking away the heat, Morley appeared at the airlock and with a wide grin, beckoned Sheffield and the rest of the audience to come forward.

Forming a half circle around the craft and its burden, the crowd murmured in puzzlement. As magic shows went, it seemed a bit short on drama.

Sheffield strolled over to the log and examined it. It was a local deciduous the colonists had dubbed steelwood, an immensely dense wood that, while hard to cut, was strong and considered a prime candidate for construction. The only drawback was that a mature tree might have two thousand rings, suggesting a very slow rate of growth. Samples had been sent up to *Phoenix* for closer analysis after Sorlund had noted a disquieting variation in the growth rates, suggesting a wide variability in climate.

Morley wore a wide grin as Sheffield picked up one of the strings that had attached the log to the grappling mechanism under the shuttle. The shuttle, rated for up to one hundred tons, had two centimeter cable or eight millimeter monofilament. This was no thicker than fishing line. Sheffield glanced up the length of the log. "How many of these did you use to support that log?" he asked.

"Eight."

"Eight. I see. And how much does that log weigh?"

"We estimate it's about eighty tons. Might be more; the shuttle had to strain a bit to carry it over here."

Sheffield had already realized that. From his experience with shuttle craft, this one sounded like it was trying to lift over a hundred tons. Which meant in Earth gravity it might well have been 130 tons. Steelwood was heavy.

At the very least, these threads were carrying a load of at least ten tons each. He snapped one between two gloved hands, testing it.

"You won't be able to break it, Commander. If that log couldn't, then you certainly won't. You won't be able to cut it, either."

"Say that again?"

"You won't be able to cut it with that knife of yours."

Sheffield carried a knife on his hip at all times. The blade was one hundred and fifty millimeter with a double edge, and he liked to proudly show how he could drop a piece of paper on it and the edge would slice the paper.

Sheffield, to Morley's hidden delight, glowered. Nobody was going to insult his knife by claiming it couldn't cut fishing line. He pulled it out.

A few minutes of sawing in utter futility finally convinced him. Sorlund strode over and begged him to stop, citing damage to the knife's edge. Already convinced he wasn't going to cut it anyway, Sheffield nodded and put the knife away. He glanced over to one of the cameras. "Captain Vargas, are you catching all this?"

"Loud and clear, Commander."

Shifting his gaze to Sorley, Vargas demanded, "Lieutenant Commander, what exactly is that stuff?"

"It's tube-grass root, Ser. We used a cutting laser set to eighteen femtoseconds at ten kilowatts using a magnesium blue light. We separated the bottom and top mats from the overall mass, and wove the strands into rope. The mat was cut into support strips to prevent the thread from sawing through the steelwood."

Vargas blinked in disbelief. "You really thought it would saw through that log?"

"Ser. We weren't sure how much lateral motion there would be due to pendulum effect, and we didn't want to have it suddenly partition and fall from under us."

"You wove it, you said." Sheffield was holding the thread closer, peering.

"Yes Ser. We used that spinning wheel and a braider to do it. We set it out with the mats and some of Comm. . . Mister Lassiter's men felled the log right on to it. Pretty good work for guys who never felled a tree until three weeks ago."

Sheffield remembered as a teen, helping his dad fell a Wellington whose roots were threatening the foundation of their house. It twisted as it fell, coming down about twenty degrees from where they wanted to put it. Fortunately, it was twenty degrees away from the house, so they weren't left homeless and widowed. But it totally destroyed the backyard tool shed.

Vargas spoke up. "Exactly how much tension can that line support?"

Lassiter, having checked to ensure the shuttle no longer had any of the lines attached, replied. "We don't know, Captain. The equipment we had could only test to thirty tons per strand."

Even with the lapel mike, Vargas had to raise his voice to be heard over the excited hubbub that was rising in the mess hall. "So you haven't done any fail tests?"

"We still need to devise some, Captain."

Vargas blew out his cheeks in disbelief. A fail test meant to test the line to the extent where on half the occasions, it would break or separate. "You can't break it?"

"We haven't yet. We were scared to go beyond thirty tons. We can cut it with the laser, but that's about it."

"Does it have any other vulnerabilities?"

"We haven't found any yet. Of course, we don't know how long it lasts before it breaks down or decomposes or whatever it's going to do. We don't know what sunlight. . . or in this case, Zharlight, which is even worse—will do to it. It may be it falls apart when it gets wet. We want to know what can stiffen it, and what might cause the strands to separate."

"I'm ordering you to bring as much of that up to *Phoenix* as you can carry for a full range of tests here. Commander Sheffield, have your people work up some environment-specific tests you can run down there. Let's make sure this isn't fools' gold."

"Yes Ser."

"With pleasure, Captain." Sorlund raised a finger. "There's more, Ser."

"What's that?"

"The mat material can absorb some water, but as it does, it expands, and becomes watertight. The triggering mechanism seems to be the water pressure, rather than the mere presence of water. Oh, and we need a loom."

Vargas blinked at the non sequitur. "A loon?"

"A loom. We can weave this stuff into sheets. We want to find out what those sheets can do."

"Can't the Imprinter do that?"

"Yes. We need wood material and thread. . . oh, shit. Never mind, Captain. We've got all the wood and thread we need right here."

Vargas chuckled. "Very good. Carry on."

* * *

Ted Simmons was not happy. It wasn't over the decision of the Bridge over how the clocks should be set; he had expected they would decide to cut the baby in half, and that's exactly what they did. The *Phoenix* would remain on Earth time, and *Phoenix* would pro-rate the time periods to fit the rate of rotation.

Ted knew that would become a clusterfuck in short order. He understood the need for the ship to remain on a constant time; reprogramming all of the thousands of computer routines the ship relied upon for day-to-day function would be a huge task. Of course, it put the ship increasingly out of sync with the ground. Would shuttle computers base orbital mechanics on ship seconds or Hō-ō One seconds? That sounded like a recipe for disaster, and he could just picture an unmanned shuttle pancaking into the side of *Phoenix* because someone forgot to convert. In part of the Americas, they used something called "The English System", a nightmare of duodecimal based measurements, eighteen inches to the pound or something like that, and in an incredible lapse, they once used the system for plotting some of an unmanned lander to Mars, and forgot to convert, which caused the lander to land on the planet at thirty thousand kilometers per hour, a less-than-optimal outcome.

But there was another, more serious problem.

The first week in orbit, they had put a transponder at the first landing site, and used it to calibrate the moon's rotational period. A Hō-ō One "second" was 9,039,421,240.5 cesium-133 cycles.

At least, it was twelve days earlier. Yesterday's measurement showed it was 9,039,420,800.3 cycles.

The difference was infinitesimal, 440 cycles out of over nine billion, but it was enough to make Simmons frowned and did another careful diurnal measurement. It showed a further loss of 38 cycles.

It was a change that a normal person wouldn't notice over the course of a life time. In seventy five years, it made a difference of perhaps a hundred seconds in the length of the day.

For purposes of accurate time keeping, and the delicate physics and engineering that depended on consistent units of time, it was an utter disaster. In fields were it was routine to go to the twentieth decimal place in order to have falsifiable accuracy, it meant that the time units proposed for Hō-ō One would be inaccurate within an hour of being implemented.

Thanking his lucky stars that most of the line officers were trained in math and/or science, Simmons appeared before a hastily convened session.

"The problem is that the rotation of the moon is slowing, and it's slowing quite rapidly. I estimate it will be tidally locked to Hō-ō within fifty thousand Earth years."

"At which point the average day will be about 242, 243 Earth hours, right?"

"Captain, that's assuming the moon's revolution around Hō-ō remains constant. Between the clutter of other moons, and the gravitational anomalies of the planet itself, I wouldn't want to guarantee that. In fact, I wouldn't even guarantee that Hō-ō One would even still exist."

The line officers exchanged glances. Trapp opened his mouth, as if to say something, and settled back. As an aching silence stretched, Simmons wondered if there was anything he should add. The expressions on the faces across the table from him suggested he didn't need to.

Finally Vargas broke the silence. "Well then," he said, tapping a finger distractedly on the table, "we need to consider this moon to be just a way station, and devote our efforts to getting *Phoenix* ready for deep space. I don't think this star system has anything humans can use permanently."

Trapp spoke. "Mister Simmons, I don't intend to dispute your findings, but three samples over a fortnight seems a bit light. You're using thirteen days as a baseline for something that will take sixty thousand years. Shouldn't we investigate a bit further before making any dramatic decisions?"

"Commander, I agree that further study is warranted. But I think that it is incontrovertible that the rotation of Hō-ō One is slowing, and that we cannot, must not base our time system on the rotational period. I really didn't intend this to be a discussion on whether we should even settle here. I'm just focusing on the fact that nobody really knows what time it is. Therefore, I'm recommending the option that I previously opposed due to implementation problems: keep the standard units, and simply have the final hour of the day, 2300 to 2400, be thirty-six minutes in length. I further recommend that *Phoenix* adopt the same time system for personnel use, so everyone is on the same time, and let the ship's automated systems remain on Earth-standard time."

Vargas actually groaned. Trapp blew out his cheeks. Boitumelo had a distant look on her face, clearly considering the implementation problems. With no sense of envy, Simmons realized he had just dumped much of that on her shoulders. He liked Scotty, and resolved to be of what help he could in setting up if the line officers collectively had just enough sense. . .

Vargas glanced to each side. "I propose we tell Commander Sheffield to implement the so-called 'anti-leap hour' for the camp, and the ship will remain on Earth time until we can determine how best to implement the needs of humans vs. the needs of their mechanical masters."

Chuckles, some rueful, echoed around the table, and Simmons knew that he had won.

He drew little solace from that. It wasn't the type of news that anyone could have said to have 'won'.

Vargas adjourned the meeting and everyone went through end of meeting motions, standing up, shutting down data pads, getting coffee. Vargas tapped the table with his knuckles, getting everyone's attention.

"I hate keeping secrets as much as anyone," the Americaner captain grated. "But I am requesting that we not discuss Mister Simmons', um, forecast for this moon just yet. It may be years before we can ready the ship for another interstellar journey, and I don't want people thinking their efforts are completely in vain. Can we agree to downplay that? It's not something we have to do something about today."

Slowly, nods spread among the group. Simmons nodded too, reserving to himself the thought that the brighter crew members and colonists would figure it out in due course. Even before the clocks gave the game away, someone was bound to look at the seventy meter sea tides and wonder what sort of tidal drag the moon was experiencing—and how long those forces had been in effect. The answer raised many more questions.

* * *

The following day, the brave little gardens all exploded.

André Morley contacted Sheffield said, "You've got a system coming in from the southeast. We think it's the same track as the last super cell that hit you. I make it arriving late tomorrow afternoon."

Sheffield, pleased that he got some warning, passed word along to Ann Forster, who had helped design an adjustable canopy that could be lowered nearly to ground level against inclement weather but otherwise served as a Zharscreen.

The storm swept in, and, like the one before, dumped an impossible amount of rain on the camp while the colonists cowered in the modules and the shuttles, protected from the crushing rainfall and the omnipresent lightning strikes. At least there were no signs of tornado.

From start to finish, the storm lasted about fifteen minutes. The rain, a thunderous roar moments earlier, was now just a light drizzle, and blue sky was spreading rapidly from the north.

It was then the geysers erupted. Where the gardens had been, water jetted fifteen meters or more into the air, fire-hose streams of water barely affected by the stiff breeze. It returned to Earth with barely a splash, sinking rapidly into the tube-grass. The canopy was found, intact, about two kilometers away several little years later.

When the colonists ventured out for a look, no trace of the gardens remained; just the squares showing naked lower mats of root mass, with all the top soil completely blown out by the force of the water coursing through under the top mat of the root mass. Red reminded people of the vast surge of water that he had seen storming out from the bottom edge of the tube-grass in the last storm, and speculated that an incredibly pressurized stream of water, a nearly horizontal Niagara Falls, coursed under their feet every time a storm passed through. Red was dryly amused to see several people glancing nervously down at their feet.

Red was mystified as to how the how the water jetting out of the garden squares was getting back in to the high pressure stream. It violated every law of fluid dynamics he knew. Actions operating to cause the water to sink were roughly eight hundred millibars of atmospheric pressure, and .77gs. Acting against it was pressure high enough to send sixteen square meters of water jetting fifteen meters into the air. He tried to work the numbers in his head, but between the twingies and the jet lag of Hō-ō One's berserk day/night cycle, found himself unable to do so. But it was not much pressure at all effortlessly overcoming a hell of a lot of pressure, and that just didn't make any sense at all.

The more he learned about tube-grass, the more mysterious the stuff seemed.

* * *

The next morning found Sean Sheffield in a surly mood. Even though it was becoming apparent the plants were dying because of the UV radiation, which hit a peak in "Little Summer" two days before, the destruction of the gardens the day before had been an emotional body blow to the colony. This wasn't Jamestown; nobody was going to starve. But as pro tem mayor of the colony, he wanted it to be as self-sufficient as possible as soon as possible. A permanent colony wouldn't be feasible if it was dependent on the star ship for all its food.

Then there was the matter of the clocks. The decision by Vargas was utterly inexplicable. Two time systems. The ship was to remain on Earth time, meaning they would get more and more out of sync. It had to be the stupidest decision Sheffield could imagine.

A lot of colonists were unhappy about it, too. Their data pads were synchronized by the ship's clock, still on Earth time. There was an override in the pads themselves, but Sheffield was buggered if he knew how to tell the clocks to adapt to an anti-leap-hour.

Now Sorlund and Morley were pestering him to come and look at bed sheets. Bed sheets? Kee-rist. What he wanted to do was ram a thruster up Vargas' smug Americaner ass, and he had to deal with bed sheets?

Another source of annoyance stemmed from the fact that everyone's tent got flattened in the downpour. Most of the tents actually did survive, and there were spares at hand for the ones that didn't, but it showed that living in tents and sheltering in the modules wasn't tenable for the long run, or even the remainder of Big Summer. Nobody knew what kind of weather Big Winter would bring, some two hundred days from now. The colony needed housing that would protect people. People hadn't seen real kitchens or air conditioners or had any real privacy since leaving Earth, and the continued durance vile in the tents was beginning to wear. Sorlund swore up and down that they wouldn't need to worry about snow and ice, but fierce tropical storms were possible and even likely, and the near constant dark would fray on people's nerves. Sheffield had been hoping for a harvest of some sort before winter dark settled in, with only the poisonous light of Hō-ō to play on the minds of the jangled colonists.

Bed sheets. Fuck me rigid, Sheffield thought.

When he came to the work area near Lassiter's Landing, he had a surprise. A white sheet of cloth was suspended tautly between two steelwood trees. Sorlund was standing next to it, holding a shotgun.

"Commander, would you be kind enough to shoot the sheet?"

Sheffield took the shotgun, hefted it, and broke it to check the loads. Before flipping the safety off, he walked over to the sheet—which appeared to be a standard white linen bed sheet—and peered around it to make sure nobody was there.

He walked back five meters and took a stance. He gave Sorlund a quizzical glance, and Sorlund nodded eagerly, with a wide grin.

Sheffield braced himself somewhat awkwardly. He hadn't shot one of these things since he was a teenager. The gun fired with a roar, and Sheffield found he had been unconsciously waiting for the sound of frightened birds taking flight.

He lowered the weapon and stared in disbelief. The sheet was intact. "Was that a live round?"

"It was. Buckshot, and at that range, you should have torn it to ribbons." The two men walked over and Sorlund plucked some shot out of the grass. "I don't know if this was yours or one of mine. I've shot that sheet a dozen times from as close as half a meter. You did hit it, by the way—I saw it flutter. It stops bullets."

"I'm impressed. There's bound to be a use for bulletproof bed sheets."

"It might have some uses," Sorlund replied, undismayed by Sheffield's ironic tone. "But come over here. Buckshot isn't the only thing it stops."

The two walked over to where Lassiter and Morley were shuffling read outs. Sorlund pointed to the display. "It blocks nine tenths of UV light, A and B. It's water resistant. And it's very light weight." With that, he reached through the display and picked up another sheet, folded to about a half meter square. "Here."

Sheffield took it, and his eyebrows shot up. "Is this the same as the sheet between the trees?"

"The very same size and weave."

Sheffield rubbed it between thumb and finger. He had to admit it was surprisingly soft, and would make good bedding.

"What you've got there, Commander, is four meters square, and it weighs about forty grams."

"A ten grams per square meter? That's all?"

"That's all."

"I assume this is tube-grass root."

"The really thin stuff in the middle between the mats, yes. Turns out it weaves just fine once it's spun. I think we've found some clothing material so people can be comfortable under Zhar-Ptitsa."

"How is it needles can go through it when bullets won't?"

"We need to get it up to the ship for testing, but the favorite theory is that it's pressure reactive; the greater the impact, the stronger the resistance. A very thin needle will go through if you push it through very slowly. The Imprinter has schematics for a laser sewer, and coherent light can cut it quite readily."

Red poked his head around from behind the sheet they had been shooting at. "Are you guys done fucking around with this thing? Rebekah wants to suspend it over the garden, see if it blocks UV well enough for the plants to grow." Belatedly spotting Sheffield, he added a breezy, "Sorry, Commander."

Lassiter grinned. "That's a helluva good idea!" He turned to Morley and Sheffield. "If it's suspended securely enough, it would protect the plants from the downpours. Ann's canopy was weighted down. We can cement this in! Between Zharlight and the storm, we lost everything on this side, too."

Red turned to Sheffield with an annoying grin. "By the way, boss, André and I have been messing around with the bottom matting from the root mass. We may have come up with a solution for your housing problem."

"What would that be, Mister Farnsworth?"

Red's eyebrow twitched, but he visibly decided not to notice the Commander's tone. "Well, the stuff is sorta rigid to begin with, and does a pretty good job of dampening sound and light. It's light weight, and like this stuff," Red tapped the sheet he was pulling down, "extremely resistant to pressure. But it breathes if the air is moving slowly. And it's flame resistant. In Earth atmosphere we would call it fireproof."

Sheffield considered. A lot of potential materials had been rejected for housing because of the elevated risk of fire in the oxygen-rich atmosphere.

"Is that sheet flame resistant, too?"

"I'll have an answer to that in an hour. But if it does burn, you have to promise Rebekah a new one. She wants a garden."

"So do we all, Mister Farnsworth. So do we all. Well." Sheffield slapped his hands and looked around. Despite the good news, he still felt annoyed.

* * *

Instead of contacting *Phoenix*, Sheffield went to the module where Cyril Voss was working on a town plan. Voss, a civilian, had experience building tracts and urban neighborhoods on Earth in a wide variety of climates and cultures. Sheffield himself had some experience in the layout of water, sewage and electrical for such tracts. Before the *nu Phoenicis* project starved all other space projects, he had helped design cities for Mars.

The town layout wasn't particularly impressive. A concentric series of circles, centered halfway across the river, making it (and the bridge Sheffield still wanted) the focus of the design. The circles had roads at the ordinal points, and each of the four sectors bisected by a secondary road. For now, only the tube-grass side would be implemented. The first circle was set aside for public structures, and included the modules. Each successive circle would be fifty meters further out, allowing lots of room for private structures. Sheffield hoped to build a thousand of those by the end of the next summer.

To that end, he needed a design that was light, simple, and completely interchangeable. At the same time, it had to be able to withstand cloud bursts of up to ten centimeters a minute, and the occasional tornado.

Worse, the utilities had to be above ground. Water and sewage. That, or each residence could have copies of the dozens of small "comfort recyclers" that were scattered all around *Phoenix*. Each unit would be self-contained as far as power and the modest demands for heat or cooling.

The ship's library had dozens of plans that might cover anything from torrid heat to the type of cold found only in the mountains of Antarctica on Earth. It had never occurred to the designers that in addition to protection from wild weather, the homes would need to be opaqued against UV, and that it might have to be opaqued against visible light, as well. And certainly there was nothing to cover tube-grass.

On the other side of the river, a two meter bank on that side subsided gradually away from the Styx for several hundred meters to a chasm, obviously the result of erosion, which turned into a white water nightmare when the rains came.

The question was why the small river next to the colony never seemed to flood. Even when the amount of water falling in place was enough to raise the level by a meter, and never mind runoff.

When he got time, Sheffield wanted a closer look at the banks of the Styx. Morlin had brought to his attention the fact that none of the water coursing under the tube-grass and between the mats was gushing into the river. Why not?

Fortunately, Vargas was going slow on bringing people out of hibernation. About one in six were awake now, most on the ground, and the logistics were becoming problematic. Nonetheless, Sheffield knew Vargas was under increasing pressure to get the rest out and on the ground. Another project where Vargas seemed to be dragging his heels. Where possible, they had brought out unmarried colonists, so the problem wasn't that of broken families; in fact Spencer seemed to be the only one with a spouse in hibernation, and was one of seventy five or so who had grown children along, also still in hibernation. But there was increasing demand for specialists as the needs and potentialities of the people on the ground grew.

Vargas and the mineralogists wanted to grab a shuttle and go exploring in the polar mountains. Sheffield understood the need to get a local source of raw materials for the Imprinter—just a large cache of plain old iron would address a lot of issues. But Sheffield felt letting a shuttle go might endanger lives at the camp. It bothered him that Vargas seemed to treat Hō-ō One like a way station.

Of course, on board ship, Vargas was Captain, god of all he surveyed. The Captain was as close to an absolute ruler as humanity could come. When the ship was underway, none could question his orders and demands. It was an intoxicating brew of power and might. He clearly didn't want to lose that power and might, and so wanted to turn the mission into a perpetual search for a suitable world.

Sheffield found it easy to imagine Vargas deeming each new world as unsuitable, for ever more ludicrous reasons. And keep the mission going for the rest of his life.

Sheffield resolved not to let Vargas get away with that.

Chapter 26 Trampoline

GRINNING MADLY, REBEKAH SAILED A FULL TEN METERS above the ground, marveling at the extra time she had to descend and prepare for her next bounce. It was a good ten years since the last time she was on a trampoline, and that was in Earth's gravity. Still, it was like riding a bicycle. It only took a few minutes for all those years to vanish, and she was handling the leaps like the high school champion she had been.

Easing her way up, she performed a simple somersault, a barandi, a one and three, a two and three, and finally a full full —a double somersault with a full 360 twist on each one. It was a difficult move on Earth, nearly effortless in Hō-ō One's three-quarter gravity and with this extra springy outsized trampoline.

Enjoying the oohs and ahs from the audience, she tried something she had never done on Earth: a triple full. She missed on the first one, launching back into the air in an undignified tangle of arms and legs. She eased her way back up to trying a second one, letting her body remember the overcorrection, and pegged it to appreciative yowls and whistles from the two dozen spectators.

She landed on the grass, and hurriedly pulled her ground suit back on. Even low in the sky, Zhar-Ptitsa could give a nasty sunburn, and Rebekah had very pale skin.

Grinning at Red, she said, "I think you've just invented a sport for this world. It's your invention; why don't you give it a try."

Grinning back, Red shook his head. "Not me, Becky. I'm strictly the four on the floor type. I'd break my fool neck if I tried what you did."

"Well, if you want lessons in how to bounce, call me. They called me Bouncing Becky in high school, and with good reason."

Ouch. Not too subtle, that. Still, she could see that Red was considering alternate possibilities for that nickname and was secretly pleased. She'd wanted to jump Red's bones since training camp, and it looked like he was finally beginning to notice her.

The trampoline was twenty-five meters square, framed with steel-wood and with about twenty square meters of tube-grass root matting as the bouncy surface. Getting the requisition for the springs hadn't been easy, and came only with the stipulation that they agreed to recycle them should the need for the steel crop up for purposes of keeping the colony going. Red and Rebekah had their hopes that in a few months that stipulation would be quietly forgotten.

Beneath the trampoline, plants grew. Corn, peas, beans and carrots. Some were nearly ten centimeters high now, and showing no signs of sunburn. Better still, they had survived two cloudbursts, with only harmless drips of water seeping through at the start and finish. Supplemented by grow lights, the light that came through the mat was enough to keep the crops happy.

When they had first come up with the idea for the canopy, Red had taken one look and said, "Why not mount springs so people can trampoline on it?"

It was a big trampoline, with the mat a full three meters off the ground. The main part of the mass was the steelwood and the metal brackets and springs, which brought the mass up to over twelve hundred kilograms. At that, it was pegged into the ground at all corners, since it was light enough in relation to the sail area of the mat that a wind gust could tip it over. Red estimated that without the springs, it would weigh about three hundred kilograms less. Most of the mass of the frame was there simply to handle the tension of the mat.

It made agriculture feasible. Not all plants, but enough for a colony to sustain itself. They might even be able to raise livestock under these UV-blocking canopies. On Earth, animal meat was for the very rich. Everyone else ate insects and vegetables. The British Isles were an exception. They ate animals. Red didn't mind insect fare, but he missed the taste of lamb.

Red wasn't wearing a ground suit. He was wearing light garments made from the same material as the trampoline mat, only considerably thinner. Even though it covered him like a burqa, it was lightweight, wicked away moisture, and was comfortable after a few washes. Instead of the hot, sweaty face plate, the garment had a veil over the face, which did an adequate job of protecting the eyes and preventing sunburn. It would be foolish to look directly at Zhar-Ptitsa through it, but then, when was it ever not foolish to look at the sun?

There were several others in the crowd in the same garb, and Red reckoned the unpopular ground-suits would soon be a thing of the past. Some of the crew, the women especially, didn't like that it covered them so completely, but unless someone figured out a way to turn down Zhar-Ptitsa so it was a nice sedate G7 or G6, it was just going to be a way of life for the foreseeable future on Hō-ō One.

Sheffield was unimpressed with the trampoline, but pleased with the crop reports. He also realized that Red's assembly could be converted to prefab sections for housing; the tough wood and incredibly tough matting were flame-resistant, water-resistant, cut out UV rays, and were in copious supply and light weight. Sheffield was certain he had found the holy grail of his housing project, and was chatting happily about having several hundred homes built by the end of Hō-ō One's autumnal season.

* * *

For the first since Earth, Doctors Trapp and Spencer could just relax and spend time recreating, thinking about nothing at all important, napping, whatever suited them.

After three months on the surface of Hō-ō One, it was clear that there weren't any pathogens with a taste for humans. Neither doctor was foolish enough to believe that was a permanent state of affairs; in the ever mutating world of bacteria and viruses, it would only take on switch in one strand of DNA to make humans a good host. And if the history of epidemiology on Earth followed the same rules here, the first few waves of a pandemic would be extremely acute, with sudden, scary symptoms and a high death rate. All the doctors could do was ensure that there were lots of broad-spectrum antibiotics close at hand.

After three months, Steinberg was still the only doctor on the ground. And she had a lot of time on her hands, enough that she had requisitioned a piano from the Imprinter. Jeanine Barney, imprinter maestro, was more than happy to accommodate

Julie's request. Aside from the fact that she dabbled in the piano herself, there was the problem that nearly all of the items being stamped out by the Imprinter were assembly-line parts for Sheffield's housing project. Absolutely necessary, and Jeanine was looking forward to trading her own tent in for a proper home, but it was work that could be done by a chimpanzee.

Chimpanzees. Jeanine missed animals. As far as anyone knew, humans were the only animals on the face of this moon. She missed cats and dogs and horses and sheep. She missed the noises and the smells and wondered when, if ever, humans would unbottle their companions.

For Steinberg, the piano was also a welcome diversion from the fact that as camp physician, she had very little to do. There were about two hundred people in the camp and another fifty at Lassiter's Landing, and they were all young and healthy. There were no poisonous plants or stinging insects, no communicable diseases, and surprisingly few opportunities to even fall down and hurt yourself. It was impossible on the tube-grass, and infrequent in the more Earth-like wilderness around Lassiter's Landing.

She joked to Vargas that if it weren't for the trampoline, she wouldn't have anything to do at all. Sheffield had wisely ordered netting placed around the perimeter of the mat so jumpers going off course wouldn't fly head-first into the supports, or break their backs on the cross struts. But with people achieving heights of twelve meters, some sprains and strains were inevitable.

Julie missed Vargas, and looked forward to the day he could just stop being Captain and move down here. She would see him after the next little spring for the formal Naming Ceremony. Hō-ō One was finally getting a name. Everyone had jumped to the conclusion that as the Captain's consort, she was privy to the secret knowledge of that name. She was, of course, but was sworn to secrecy. She had fun relaying some of the wilder guesses and rumors making their way around camp. One colonist, Winston Sanders, was campaigning for the name of "Akron."

It was her desire to see Daniel that informed her decision to remind him that if he didn't get off the stick and give the moon a name, along with the camp, the colonists would do so through unspoken consensus. Nearly from the start, they had been referring to themselves as Hōvians and suggested, half-jokingly, that he devise a name that fitted around that in some way. "You could even refer to the camp as ' Hōvel' until Sheffield gets his Levittown built."

"'Levittown?'"

"The very first pre-fabricated suburb. The old United States, twentieth or twenty-first century."

"Hmm. Levittown," Dan repeated the word, tasting it. "Better than Hōvel, I'll give you that. Think we might be violating someone's trademark?"

"Out here?"

"Point. OK, I'll take that under consideration."

Vargas flew a shuttle down himself. As a pilot, he savored the challenges of the turbulence zone. Julie was waiting with a tube-root outfit tailored for the Captain just the day before.

She climbed in and helped him change into the oddly comfortable garb. She held up a mirror so he could inspect himself.

"I look like a Japanese beekeeper," he complained.

"Maybe, but you will be a very comfortable and cool Japanese beekeeper."

A flash of pale blue caught Daniel's eye, and he turned to three-quarter profile to the mirror for a better look. There were four stripes on the sleeve, the top one with an upwards loop in it. He smiled. "I see. But that's the RESS insignia. I was in the Americaner forces."

"You're captain of an RESS ship, aren't you?"

"Um. . . huh. OK, that makes sense. I wouldn't want to try wearing this into the Admiralty, though. Why blue?"

"That was Rebekah Cohen's idea. She thought it would show up better against the white over the gold."

"I see." Daniel dryly reflected that he thought he left emotional baggage like national pride and flags behind him. "A new tradition. Tell Becky it has my blessing."

Both felt relieved and a bit odd at the same time. Transmissions between them were usually duty oriented. Ship's business left little opportunity for pillow talk. Mostly Daniel wanted to know if anyone as having post-hibernation problems. Everyone was a little bit twitchy, and when tired, perhaps got a bit more scattered then they might have before. And several times a day she would see people pause, blink, and sometimes mutter something under their breath. She knew the symptoms of a flash-dream well, since she still experienced one or two a day. Everyone did. Most coped well enough.

The other point of psychological concern had been Hō-ō's ocher light. It was agreed that the light was unpleasant and should be avoided, but outdoor lighting was all that was needed to rid the crimson night of the worst of its spooky aspects. It seemed the shade of the vegetation under the raw light bothered people, rather than the light itself. Julie had been right.

Morale benefited from the enforced rest periods during the eclipses. People generally stayed in and got caught up on sleep, watched videos, made love, or just did personal chores. Nearly everyone reported a decrease in the frequency of flash-dreams in the days following the "Gentle Night" of the eclipse. Still it wasn't unusual to find a group of a dozen people or more seated with beverages, watching the light show of the vast lightning flashes on the darkened side of Hō-ō and committing acts of pareidolia, finding patterns in the constant and ever shifting patterns of light. Given that most of the objects in the star system owed their names to patterns of otherwise unassociated stars that, seen from Earth, vaguely resembled a mythical bird, it seemed a very apropos sort of thing for people to do. Even Hō-ō's little moonlet, a hundred and twenty kilometers wide and only ten thousand kilometers up, got named for a bird as it raced across the sky, in honor of the native state bird of Vargas' home state, Coahuila—Roadrunner.

The naming ceremony had a dual purpose, and nobody had guessed at the second one; in addition to naming the moon Hoyl, Daniel and Julie were announcing their marriage.

* * *

Spencer was restless. With the crises of hibernation and Hō-ō mostly resolved, there wasn't much demand for his services amongst a group of people who had been selected for intelligence and emotional stability to begin with. Further, he had a wife and two children, and he was uneasily aware of the fact that where they had only aged a few months on the trip, he was nearly three years older than when they left Dry Dock. He was afraid he would become a complete stranger to his family, a gray-bearded mature man whose interests and appetites had changed, if subtly, from those of the younger man who boarded *Phoenix* a half century earlier. He often wondered how old he should think of himself as being. By one metric, he was forty three, by another, eighty nine. And the effects of hibernation had changed all of them. He wanted to reclaim his family before it was too late.

Alan Trapp was perfectly willing to leave him do that. To his surprise, it was Daniel Vargas who dug his heels in.

"I want to send you down there, but I want to do it in your formal capacity as ship psychologist. I'm sensing some irritability in the people I'm talking to. Now, it may be stress from trying to establish a town, but I want to be sure there aren't other undercurrents in that."

"What sort of undercurrents do you mean?"

"You're the psychologist. I'm hoping you'll be able to tell me."

"Captain, that sounds pretty vague."

"I realize that, Ian. And I don't expect you to open an office and start psychoanalyzing or run tests or anything formal. I just want you to get around the camp and talk to people, and get a sense of whether they're happy or not."

Spencer saw his opportunity for a little quid pro quo. "And this precludes having my family along in what way?"

"It doesn't. But what are they going to do? Your wife. . . Maureen, is it?"

"Maureen, yes."

"She will be an animal doctor on a world that has no animals. And there's no school for your kids, nothing to keep them really engaged. Oh, they could all pitch in on the home construction project, although they would probably find that pretty boring. As for agriculture, we already have about three people watching every plant grow as it is. It seems labor-intensive enough already."

"I thought about that, Captain, and I have a suggestion. Red Farnsworth's ROVER project starts in the next little spring, right? Both the kids are keen on ROVER guidance, and you yourself speculated that there might be animal life on the transpolar side of this continent. So Maureen needs to be at hand to interpret anything like that should it be found. Now, I've spoken to Red—no, don't look at me that way Captain. This is his project, and he was soliciting for volunteers, so I didn't overstep your authority. In any case, Red is more than happy to take the four of us into the project. He knows the kids from training, and knows they are demon wranglers. And I pointed out to him that I could give assessments on how people will react to whatever the ROVERs find over there."

Vargas leaned back and pretended to think about it. He remembered the kids, video enthusiasts, and had little doubt they would make good copilots for the job.

The ROVERs—Remote Operating Vehicles, Extended Range —were an adaptation by Red Farnsworth and Madelyne Isaakson. One happy discovery was that Zhar-Ptitsa made for hyper efficient solar cells, and in the lighter gravity, a craft weighing up to a ton would be capable of extended flight. It would have to put down during the irregular dark periods, during which time it could record ambient noises and collect samples from the local soil, vegetarian, and watch any animal life it might find. With nearly all the resources of the colony directed toward establishment, it was a compromise on the compelling need to explore. After ninety days, they still only knew one percent of the continent they were on, nothing of the second continent below the equator, and they still weren't sure there wasn't at least a large island at the south pole. Vargas had to admit that as explorers, they were real slouches.

"Are the kids responsible enough? You're their father, and I'm your Captain, so I appreciate the most honest answer possible."

"You're really pulling rank on me? Never mind, I see that you are. OK. Honest, you say?

"I think Jim is ready. He's sixteen, and stable and level headed. I saw him on first emergence from hibernation, and he handled the disorientation and deficits better than most of the crew members.

"Sylvie will need closer supervision, at first, anyway. She's thirteen, no, fourteen, and still a bit. . . adolescent. You'll remember that we weren't going to have any colonists under the age of eighteen because we didn't think they could handle the various stresses of this mission. But those kids scored so spectacularly well on all tests. . . "

"That, and you made it clear you wouldn't come along without them, and Trapp considered you indispensable."

"Thank you. But there were other psychologists available. The kids really did earn their wings. And blazed a trail: there's about a dozen other teens in hibernation."

"And there will be work for Maureen. Rebekah Cohen tells me they're going to uncork some sheep and goats and raise them under canopy over in Scafeld."

Vargas looked up, eyebrows lifted. "Really? Why haven't I been told about this."

Damn. Spencer didn't mean to undercut Rebekah like that. "Er. Well, she did say that she was going to approach you this afternoon. She seemed to believe your acquiescence was a given."

Vargas glowered, and then grunted assent. "Humph. Well, it probably is. We've been discussing this for some time. She got the requisition for fencing off a square kilometer just south of the Landing."

"The Landing? Not Scafeld?"

Vargas noted that like everyone, he pronounced it "skah-feld" almost like "scaffold". Some Englishman he turned out to be! It was actually named for a place in northern England, which meant "Field by the River Sheaf" It referred to the semi-circle of farms that radiated out from the same central point on the circle that the housing project of Hoyl referenced. Sheffield really wanted that bridge and laid out everything in anticipation of it being built.

"Is there a problem?

"I'm just surprised."

"We wanted it away from the population. Goats don't smell very good."

"Flies? No, wait. . . "

"No, but we probably are going to have to introduce insect life soon enough. Ants for the animal waste, bees for pollination. . . " Vargas shook his head sadly. "There goes paradise."

Spencer shook his head and grinned. "Earthside thinking, I'm afraid. I just thought of Maureen walking a kilometer each way and immediately thought of dangerous wildlife and criminal elements. Neither of which we have here."

"Not yet. Give us time." Vargas shrugged, a mock surrender. "OK, your family deserves to see this place before we mess it up too badly. Let the Hibernation people know to queue them up for retrieval tomorrow. And Ian—remember, you have to keep those kids out of trouble."

"I'm sure that won't be a problem, Captain. And thank you."

Chapter 27 Apikoros and the Hoyl Goyl

"SO YOU'RE SAYING A HOYL IS A KIND OF PHOENIX?" Red was getting tired of stretching out fencing—four kilometers worth—and was looking for a chance to goof off.

Rebekah nodded. "There's a Jewish fable about a creature called the hoyl.

"The hoyl was a bird that was around when Eve ate the fruit of forbidden knowledge, which was the reason Jehovah threw them out of the garden of Eden and made them mortal. When Eve decided to share the fruit with all the other animals, she ensured they would all die, too. How she got a cat to eat a piece of fruit would be a story in itself. They all ate, and so that's why they all die."

"Harsh."

"Well, Jehovah was a hard case. Anyway, this one bird, the hoyl, wouldn't eat the fruit, so it now lives forever.

"But it's not the sweet deal you might think. It lives forever, but there are no other hoyls, so it's a kind of lonely existence. Further, it can be killed, and is, in all kinds of unpleasant ways, and when it is, a hoyl egg magically appears and it is reborn to go through the whole thing again."

"So if Eve hadn't had the munchies, would the human race consist of one person, living and dying endlessly?"

"Hm. Good question, Red. You'll have to ask a Biblical scholar about that."

"They seem to be in short supply. But that reminds me. You know that one of the public-use structures in Avalerion is meant to be a church, temple, meeting place, whatever?"

"Sure. We've been having sing-alongs each little summer there."

"Bin Laden was showing me the schedule of events."

"Hoo, boy. OK, I'll bite. Why did he show you that?"

"He was perplexed. The place gets lots of use, but there wasn't a single religious-themed event on the schedule for a full four little years."

"Well, all he has to do is apply. I know there's only about two dozen Muslims in the colony, but nobody will begrudge them the use of the place."

"He wasn't looking to set up any events. He was just puzzled. There are no religious-themed events on the schedule at all. No Muslim, no Christian, no Jewish, nothing."

"That does seem a bit odd. Raving fundies got weeded out of the program early on, but I would say at least half the colonists have some sort of religious orientation. None of them wanted to set up services?"

"I guess not."

"Who's in charge of the list?"

"David McDonald. He also designed the meeting place, and did it with various services in mind. It's even got a nave."

"Yeah, I remember he held non-denominational services back in training. He wore a dog collar."

Rebekah grinned. "Dog collar? You mean that white thing."

"Yeah. That's what we call 'em in England."

"Well, he was Church of England."

"Really? Mac was Anglican?

"Yeah. And why do you say 'was'?"

"Um. I don't know. He doesn't wear that collar. . . "

"How would you know under the Zharsuit?"

"Well, he never talks about religion."

"He wasn't much of one for that before. If he was, he wouldn't have been picked for this mission."

"What about bin Laden? How did he get past the screens? The guy never misses a chance to praise Allah."

"Didn't you notice he only did it with the Captain and some of the other Americaner officers? He knew his name had some connotations, and was no fan of the Americas after the massacres in the middle east in the twenty-first century. That's just his little way of taking a poke at them. He's no more religious than we are."

"So why was he looking for religious events on the sked?"

Rebekah's grinned widened. "We were talking, and I asked him if anyone had figured out when the Sabbath began, and whether the daily call to prayers should follow Earth's rotation or Hoyl's. He laughed and said the only thing he was reasonably sure about was what direction Mecca is in to one millionth of a second of arc. Nobody's sure what day it is on Earth within three days because of the messing around they did with the ship's vectors during the Hibernation crisis. Sheffield thinks we got here about six weeks behind schedule.

"Anyway, Binny looked at the schedule to see who might care when Friday sunset at Jerusalem or first crescent moon over Mecca would be locally. Had they come up with anything? That's when he noticed the lack. So he asked around, and got a bunch of shrugs." Rebekah was clearly enjoying her narrative. "His pose as Intifada Man kind of whipped around and bit him on the ass. He found himself spending more time explaining that he, personally, didn't give a rat's ass about the Sabbath, but was just looking to see if anyone did. I don't think many people believed him."

"Well, that'll show him. I'm not trying to pretend the Americas didn't have a pretty bad track record in the twenty-first century, but that doesn't mean the Americaners who are descended from those madmen should be hassled. It would be like yelling 'Sieg Heil' whenever Günther came in the room."

"I think Binny was starting to figure that out. Still, in his defense, I think he had to put up with a lot of flak over his family name. Imagine if Günther's last name was Hitler."

Red considered, nodded. He remembered the first time he met a kid whose last name was Cromwell, resolved to never call bin Laden 'Osama'. "I'm glad to see he's seeing that he was being annoying. But that's interesting that there's no worship services. I remember this same group of people used to have services of various kinds back in training. What changed?"

Rebekah paused, gave Red a direct look. "I can only speak for myself. . . " at Red's nod she continued, ". . . but to me God was always the God of the Desert, very much a figure bound to

Earth. When I had lessons as a girl, we didn't think in terms of a Covenant on Mars, or a burning bush in Andromeda. God's home, like ours, was the Sinai. When I left Earth, I left the things of Earth."

Red felt like something had clicked and his own feelings suddenly took a solid form. "I understand. I think part of it is that this world really isn't meant for humans. We're very much visitors. How can God be a part of a world that isn't a part of us?"

"You really don't think humans are supposed to be here?"

Red shook his head. "I always feel like I'm trespassing. It's weird, because I didn't feel that way on Mars or the Moon, and they're a lot more alien than this place."

Rebeca's eyes traveled to the pentagon of five planetary patches Red had over his heart. The only other person with all five that she had seen was Sheffield. Red was in a very exclusive club.

"Were you religious on Earth?"

"Not really. You?"

"When I was a girl, yes. But after my Bat Mitzvah, I . . . well, I just moved away from all that. I think part of it was that I signed up for this mission, and spent five years waiting to learn if I would even qualify for the first round of rejections. I had to wait through the war, and I asked God for a sign every night when I went to bed. Five years, and it was finally an army corporal who let me know that I had been selected to participate in the first round of tests."

"What would his rating have to been for you to keep your faith?"

"That had nothing to do with . . . oh, fuck you, Red!" She waited for the irritating man to stop chortling. "OK, that he was just an NCO did kind of tweak my sense of the ludicrous. An event of that import, you expect at least a Major if not an arch angel."

"Is that really when you became a nonbeliever?"

"No, that started a couple of years before, and kept happening. I didn't sit up one morning and go, 'Oh, I'm Apikoros!'"

"Ah pee core us?" Red repeated carefully.

"Non-believer. There's a joke among rabbis that you need to study the Talmud for five years before you can become Apikoros. I managed it by considering farming in space.

"I don't know if it was the letdown of Disappointment, or that this place is so strange, but it was definitely after we left Earth. That's when I went from Apikoros to atheist."

"Do you remember your therapeutic awakenings? The hibernation syndrome ones?"

"Eh? Well, not the first one, not really. I just remember being confused. The second and third I remember OK. Why do you ask?"

"Something Spencer said. He told me he noticed, during the height of the hibernation crisis, that nobody seemed to be using religious tools to deal with the deeply personal challenges everyone was experiencing. So I'm thinking it may have started before we even got here."

"That would destroy our theory that this place is causing it."

Red nodded. "Spencer and his family are coming down this little late autumn."

"I know. The kids were going to be working with you on the ROVERs."

"Yeah. I've met 'em before. They seem like a good pair of kids. You'll be working with the Missus on getting some livestock going, won't you?"

At Rebekah's nod he concluded, "OK. Whichever one of us sees the Doc first asks him about this plague of hibernation secularism."

Rebekah grinned. "That might be the perfect name for it if you're right. I was thinking of myself as a Hoyl Goyim."

Red stopped, struck by a thought. "You know, the Captain had a Zharsuit made especially for him."

"Yeah, I know."

"Well, whoever did it got his insignia wrong. He was an Americaner officer, not Royal Europe. And off the ship, he's an Admiral, not a Captain."

"Oh. Has he complained?"

"Not that I know of. But the insignia is a baby blue."

"Um, what of it?"

"Well, you designed it, right? And you're from. . . "

"Red." She reached up, put a finger on his veil where his lips would be. "I just like that color combination, OK?"

"Did you suggest 'Hoyl' as a name for this planet?"

"No, I can honestly say I didn't."

Chapter 28 Date Confusion and the R.O.V.E.R

IAN SPENCER TOOK A DEEP APPRECIATIVE SNIFF of Hoyl's oxygen-rich air, and turned to Lassiter. "OK, Gordon, you said when we got here, you would demystify the Hoyl calendar."

"Oh, damn. I did, didn't I?" Lassiter was shaking his head but grinning. "Fair warning, hey—it don't demystify."

Spencer felt relieved. He wanted to make sure the events of the disastrous first landing that occurred between the two of them were resolved, and Lassiter's easy and friendly manner made it evident he felt the same way.

"OK. A Hoyl week is ten days, but every five weeks we have a leap day, which is eleven days. It's based on the fact that Hoyl rotates around Hō-ō every ten point two days." Spencer nodded. "As it does so, Hō-ō goes through phases, and because Hoyl has a thirty-degree tilt of its own, we have, well, call them sub-seasons that are a bit over two and a half days each. With me so far?

"The week begins at the end of each eclipse, where Hō-ō blocks Zhar-Ptitsa. That day is Little Early Spring. The next day is Little Late Spring. Then you have Little Summer Waxing, Little Summer, Little Summer Waning, Little Early Autumn, Little Late Autumn, Little Winder Waxing, Little Winter, and Little Winter Waning. Every five weeks you have Little Leap Spring."

Spencer shook his head, perplexed.

"Most people drop the 'Little'," Gordon offered helpfully. "But here's where it gets really goofy. Hō-ō rotates around Zhar Ptitsa every 440 days, and thank the fucking universe that it's more or less in sync with 440 Hoyl days exactly. It's only a few seconds off per year. No leap day nonsense there. So they've come up with twenty months of twenty-two days each." Lassiter waved his arms in the air and laughed. "Why twenty? Fuck if I know. They're still trying to hammer out names. All I know for sure is the Captain has promised to keelhaul anyone who names any of the months after him."

"Matt Bissont tells me Hoyl's revolution period is growing. Won't that affect the number of days per year."

"Yeah, but hopefully we'll be gone from this place before that becomes a serious issue."

"OK, it's goofy, but it's only twenty months. People can remember twenty-six letters in the alphabet, they can remember twenty month names."

"If the names are sensible. Ann Forster is pushing to have them all named for Earth flowers. Tulip, Hyacinth, Chrysanthemum, on like that. Scotty wants at least a couple of African names, and the ones she wants involve that inhaled click they use in Africa. Vargas just wants them to be numbers, One through Twenty, and points out that the calendar we have on Earth worked that way."

"How's that?"

"September, October, November, December. Sept is seven, Octo is eight, Nove is nine, Dec is ten."

"I never thought of that. But wait. Those are months nine through twelve, not seven through ten. How did that happen?"

"The Romans named a couple of new months after Julius and Augustus Caesar. They thought it would be undignified to tack them on the end of the year, so they just kind of inserted them." Lassiter paused, remembering. "Oh maybe it was because March 1st was New Year's in the Roman calendar." He gave a slightly irritated shrug. "Next time I see a Roman, I'll ask him."

Spencer winced. "I hope we can do better than that. Something more coherent, at least."

"We won't."

"What makes you so sure of that?"

Lassiter stared at the ground and shook his head mournfully. "Think about the names of the days. The week starts with Little Early Spring, right?"

"Right. . . "

"Only in two hundred and twenty days, ten months from now, when Hoyl comes out from behind Hō-ō, what time of year will it be here? The little year, I mean?"

Lassiter watched, amused, as Spencer extended both his forefingers pointing straight up and moved his hands around each other in a circular motion, clearly trying to track the orbital mechanics. From his own experience, he knew Spencer would need a third hand. "It means. . . No! Are you serious!?"

Lassiter nodded, pleased. "It means that the Little Early Spring will actually be the first day of Autumn. And the other two seasons at the big equinoxes."

Spencer stared at the wall of the ROVER building, clearly at a loss. Lassiter crossed his arms and watched the psychologist think. "There's got to be a better way. This is ridiculous."

"If you come up with anything, let the Captain know. I have it on best authority he's tearing his hair out over this."

Gordon didn't seem overly distressed by that, Spencer noted.

* * *

"Wakey wakey, master Jim! It's Red Rover time!"

Jim fumbled for his data pad, looking to slap Red Farnsworth's annoying voice out of existence. He slapped at the pad, missed, and knocked a cup of water to the floor. Now he would have to get up.

"M'wake," he mumbled into his data pad, and shuffled off to get the mop. At the door he hit the light switch, and blinked against the sudden light. He looked at his pad. 0700. Why was it still dark out?

"Red?"

"Yes, my boy?"

"First, I'm not your boy. Second, what time is it?"

"All time is relative, my boy. But in your relative existence, it is 7 O'clock in the morning."

"Why is it dark?"

"You want a digression on orbital mechanics?"

Jim returned to his bed side and started swishing the mop around. "Just the Daylight-for-Dummies version."

"It's dark because the sun has not come out. It will do so in about an hour and a half. This is little winter. Hō-ō—that's the big red thing covering a quarter of the sky—is between us and Zhar Ptitsa."

"Why can't sunrise and sunset make sense on this world? Uh, never mind." The fog was beginning to lift. "Did you say the GPS was up?"

"Yeah. Captain Vargas just gave us the green light fifteen minutes ago. Your sister's already on her way."

"Hey, that really is good news. Now I don't have to kick your ass for calling me a boy."

"Oh, and I was so looking forward to it. But enough flirting. Get your ass in here. I'm ramping up the ROVER now. And we only have three hours of light until Zharset, so let's move it."

Jim pulled on his Zharsuit and, stuffing a breakfast bar in his face, started jogging toward the ROVER building, about a half a kilometer away. Sheffield had finished paving the walkways and all the stand-alone streetlights were in place, so his surroundings had only a slight pinkish tint instead of the ugly eggplant hues from the light of the full Hō-ō. Those colors gave him the creeps.

Three hours would be just enough to send the ROVER out about fifty kilometers, make a circle around Avalerion, and return. It was capable of night flight, but for now training for him and Sylvie was daylight hours only. When and if they occurred.

They had been waiting on the global positioning satellites which Morley and Brülow had been deploying. One in polar orbit, and two more in synchronous orbit, and they would serve as communication, GPS and observational satellites.

Until the GPS was on line, testing with the ROVER was line-of-sight only, since if they cleared a hilltop and got turned around, they might not be able to guide it back. That would be embarrassing, and Red didn't fancy trying to explain it to Vargas. Fortunately, the level terrain offered plenty in the way of line-of-sight. Later, they would bounce signals off *Phoenix*, accepting a half second latency in return for being able to pilot the craft to 80 north, at which point the ship would drop below the horizon.

When he got there, Red and Sylvie were giving the solar wings a check. Without being asked, Jim punched his data pad to get his coordinates: 60.15.8658 north, 0.00.2450 east. Prime meridian was only a few dozen meters west of them. Jim remembered the tourists who used to show up back home and visit and straddle the prime meridian at Greenwich so they could say they had been in the eastern and western hemispheres at once. He wondered if anyone would do that here. Thinking back to his confusion when he was first woken up a half hour ago, he wryly thought that the International Date Line would be a lot more confusing here than on Earth.

He called up the coordinates on the ROVER, and found them nearly the same. At four significant digits, just standing a meter to the side meant slightly different readings. It was exactly where it thought it was. He then asked his data pad where the ROVER thought it was, and got the same numbers. He asked it how to get it from there to where he was, and was told to move it sixty-eight centimeters to the south west. He politely turned down the offer to have it comply, reasoning that at seventy kilograms, it wouldn't squash him but it wouldn't be comfortable.

Sylvie, under Red's careful gaze, plugged her own data pad into the joystick control used to steer the ROVER. There were going to be times when manual override would be easier.

"OK, boys and girls, let's see if this turkey will fly." Red flicked a switch, bringing up small running lights and a whole list of menu commands on their respective data pads. After a moment of electronic dithering, the ROVER slowly spread its wings. It now looked like nothing so much as a giant six-winged dragonfly, a meter and a half long and with wings at least its own body length extending from the sides. The first two set of wings mimicked a dragonfly's motions, allowing it to hover, reverse, lift vertically or horizontally, and even slip sideways and upside down. The rear two, nearly as flexible, were the solar panels, programmed to seek and fixate on Zhar-Ptitsa no matter what the angle and inclination of the craft.

Red spoke to the device. "Rise." The forward wings blurred into near invisibility, and with a slight rocking motion, the craft lifted under Sylvie's still-inexpert guidance.

"It lives!" shouted Jim.

"For Science!" exalted Sylvie.

Red grew a wide grin, delighted with the craft and the enthusiasm of his trainees. Nonetheless his eyes maintained a constant flicker between the craft and his readout, excluding all else.

The ROVER reached an altitude of about twenty meters. Red checked his readout. 19.7 meters. "OK, Syl, take her on a tour around Avalerion, will you? Have her fly along the streets in a zig zag, and let's see what there is to see."

As Sylvie concentrated on following the route, her tongue poking out in concentration, Red and Jim watched the video from the flyer. It bobbed along the streets, over the heads of mostly unaware pedestrians. A handful, however, spotted it, did a double-take, and then pointed and laughed. Some even waved. Red wished he could wave back. Well, maybe the next model.

"OK, let's tour Scafeld, and then head out to Lassiter's to see what they're up to."

The dragonfly whirred past the ever-popular trampoline, passing a jumper at eye level and startling him so badly that he returned to the mat in a wild jumble of flailing arms and legs. Feeling slightly rueful, Sylvie backed the ROVER away, hoping the man hadn't hurt himself.

Banking around with a soft whir, the flyer flew toward the logging camp. Red noted with approval that they were being more selective in their cutting. The realization that trees that took two thousand years to mature – Hoyl years, at that—had caused them to rethink the philosophy of cutting down everything in sight.

"Looking good, Sylvie. Are you comfortable with the controls?"

Sylvie nodded, concentrating. "It's a bit like flying an ultralight, only you can't use your inner ear."

"OK." Red glanced at the readout on his pad. Plenty of time. "Let's do the autonomous flight."

With a slight glance of regret, Sylvie set the autopilot to five hundred meters above terrain and switched over. "Jim, your innings."

Jim uploaded the flight pattern he had programmed, and they watched on screen to see what would happen. Red kept his hand near the override, but he had vetted the programming. He wasn't expecting any serious problems.

The ROVER flew out over the featureless plain, following the Styx downstream. At fifty kilometers, it banked to the right and the autopilot began following the circle. Red craned his neck unconsciously as he peered after it. It was no longer visible to the naked eye. If the GPS and autopilot both failed, they might get it back with a little bit of luck.

The device was sending back a steady stream of data. Temperature, wind speed and direction, humidity, and an ongoing mapping of the uneventful topography. There was even a slightly jittery line that depicted the height of the vegetation they were passing over. Being tube-grass, it wasn't a very dramatic line.

After an hour and ten minutes, as the GPS passed the two hundred kilometer mark, the Styx appeared in front of the ROVER. The three pilots leaned forward. This would be new and more varied terrain.

"Big stand of steel-wood there," Jim commented. "Some of those trees must be over a hundred meters tall."

Red felt an irrational pang of regret. All the data, including the visuals, was being transmitted both to *Phoenix* and to Sheffield, and Red felt he had just doomed that stand to the logger's lasers.

They were over foliage that Red tentatively labeled deciduous. He didn't know that they actually dropped their leaves in the fall, of course. Perhaps in a few months they would find time to land the ROVER in a clearing and have it explore on the ground. It couldn't handle rough terrain, but fairly level unobstructed ground wasn't a daunting. . .

He nearly dropped his data pad when it suddenly began flashing red, and sounding a klaxon. He turned to the kids, who looked stunned. "Did one of you do something?"

"No!" Jim said. We were just monitoring. Everything was nominal."

The readout stopped flashing and red bold text appeared. "It's an order to general stations. The *Phoenix* is in trouble!"

The text scrolled.

"INCOMING OBJECT SPOTTED. THIS IS A LARGE OBJECT, CAPABLE OF SIGNIFICANT DAMAGE TO ENVIRONMENT. ESTIMATED IMPACT 0945, LOCATION 30 E 55 N. TAKE SHELTER IMMEDIATELY. GET TO MODULES AND TAKE SHELTER. CONSEQUENCES UNKNOWN, MAY BE SEVERE. POTENTIALLY DANGEROUS SHOCKWAVE FROM ENTRY EXPECTED 0948.

TAKE SHELTER IMMEDIATELY."

Red checked the time. They had twenty-two minutes. They could bring the ROVER back, or they could run to the modules over on the Avalerion side of the Styx, but not both.

He sent an acknowledgement so the flashing and alarms would stop, and had Jim and Sylvie do the same. He didn't like the location of the impact—in the water, and several thousand kilometers away, but nothing between the edge of the tube-grass field and the point of impact but open ocean.

"OK, let's find a place to put her down."

"It's only fifty klicks away. We can get it back. . . "

"And put it where? The shed may or may not survive whatever is coming, and we can't put it in the modules—it's going to be awfully crowded as it is. Look, there's a clearing. Aim for it."

Sylvie glared, and did as he asked, overriding the program. It glided over the field, rotating 360 degrees as it did so, and Red pointed. "There."

There was a small space between two steel-wood trees. The durable and ancient trees, which had survived who knew what for two thousand years, might provide adequate cover for the flimsy craft.

It sailed in, rotated face out, and landed. Sylvie rotated the head camera to watch carefully as the wings folded into the 'carapace'. They were the most fragile elements of the craft, and if they survived whatever was coming, then they might be able to retrieve it. Assuming, of course, they survived it. She felt her legs shaking, sternly told them to stop. It didn't help.

"Let's go, guys." Red latched the door to the shed, wishing it had been reinforced with tube-grass mat like most of the structures in Avalerion were. They started on a dog trot toward the bank of the Styx, where shuttles were ferrying people across.

The shuttles weren't even extending landing gear, just hovering long enough for everyone to jump out and sailing across for more. Red watched as one left in the direction of the Landing.

They jumped out as the shuttle hovered, careful to stay clear of the nacelles. Red looked around. "There's your Dad." He saw Spencer scanning the group anxiously, and waved. Spencer urgently beckoned them over. He hugged both his children. "Your mom's already in the module. Red, do you have specific duty anywhere?"

Red checked his data pad quickly. "No orders."

"Then come with us. There's room."

As they moved toward the module, Red asked, "What is going to hit us?"

"I couldn't get hold of Vargas. Doctor Trapp thinks it's a comet."

"Preposterous. How could a comet sneak up on us?"

"He's a doctor, dammit, not an astrophysicist."

"OK, OK." Red stopped, tapped a message to Tim Simmons. "?"

Nothing in response. Of course not. Who did he know on board who wasn't on the crew and thus at station? He thought. Hard to do with the easy hubbub of voices around him. Man couldn't think in this chaos. Impatiently he shouldered his way to the hatch and jumped out to the ground.

Sheffield was there. "Just where do you think you're going, Farnsworth?"

"Nowhere, sir. I just want to try to raise a civilian on the ship, try and find out what is coming our way."

"I just happen to have that information, mister. It's a big chunk of ice, about five hundred meters wide, and it's going to impact us in thirty-eight seconds. Now get your ass in there so we can dog the hatch."

"Ser." The two men turned to the hatch. There was a blinding light, and reflexively, both men turned to see what it was.

A gigantic meteor tore across the sky, incandescent and trailing a huge plume of smoke and fire. Whatever it was, it clearly wasn't just ice. They both watched for an instant, stunned by the sight. They turned back to the hatch, to find it crammed with people who wanted to see what happened. "Get back! Get back!" Sheffield shouted. Make room so we can get in and close the hatch. Get back!"

Red glanced over his shoulder. There was a ripple on the horizon. It took him an instant to recognize what it had to be.

"Cover your ears!" He screamed. "Cover your ears! Shock wave! Cover your ears!" Putting action to words, he covered his own, and took a deep breath and held it, knowing a sharp pressure difference was coming. He saw Sheffield knocked down by someone pushed through the hatch by the pressure of the crowd. He grabbed the Commander by the arm to pull him up and pantomimed opening his mouth and covering his ears. He pushed Sheffield's arms into place, and then slapped his hands over his own ears.

It was the loudest sound Red had ever heard. He had been in thunderstorms, stood near cannon fire, went to a few Nihilsüng concerts as a teen. This was louder than them all—combined.

Lancing pain shot from both ears, but he didn't have time to investigate. A panicked mob of people were trying to shoulder past one another to move away from the hatch, and he and Sheffield were on the floor and in their path. He pulled the dazed Sheffield to his feet—the commander was bleeding from his ears—and scrambled away.

"Move back!" He knew he was screaming, but his voice sounded dull, distant, almost like he was underwater. Somewhere an alarm was ringing. "Move back! More shock waves coming!" One of the colonists said something to him—cursing him, maybe. He grabbed the man by his front and rudely spun him back toward the module. "Get BACK!" he screamed.

He glanced toward the hatch, and saw Spencer standing there, shouting, waving both arms. His message was clear. "Get back in!"

There were several people who had actually swarmed back out onto the tube-grass. They were staring around, taking stock of their surroundings.

Red swiveled around. The village looked serene, untouched. There was an angry reddish scar across the sky, and a flickering glow to the south east. Outraged sky, quiet village. It was an image that would last the rest of his life.

He could see little pulse-puffs moving from the sides of the aerial scar. They had moments to get inside before more shock waves hit.

Chapter 29 Ice Fall

"GET IN! GET IN!" With what seemed agonizing slowness, the colonists turned and stepped back through the hatch. Red glanced up at the main hatch, three meters above the ground. It was meant to be the one used, based on the possibility of animal life that might be smart enough to crouch in wait outside their little mouse hole, but not be smart enough to climb ladders. Once it became clear nothing at ground-level presented a threat, they switched to the more convenient secondary hatch. Lucky, that.

Pushing from behind, Sheffield and Red got the last of the colonists through the hatch, and stepped through, with Sheffield slamming and dogging the hatch. The slight overpressure caused them lancing pain in both ears.

Red saw everyone stop dead at stare upward, and took that to mean another shock wave had ripped past them, one big enough to be heard inside the module. Anyone still outside would be dead, probably.

He glanced over and saw that Spencer was herding people up the coiled staircase to the second and third levels of the module. Once spread out, it wouldn't seem so crowded.

Red wondered what kind of provisions they had. He knew that each of the eight modules designated as emergency shelters were supposed to have food and shelter for fifty people for ten days, a little year. He had no idea how many where in this module. It seemed like more, but in the chaos and confusion there was no way of telling.

Sheffield was peering intently at his data pad, and glanced up to see Red looking at him. He waved him closer and turned his data pad so Red could see. Red peered, feeling a bit surprised. The dour commander had always treated the Middie as furniture, and anything on his data pad was not going to be shared with a mere rating. Evidently Red's efforts to save his ass a few minutes ago hadn't gone unnoticed.

The image was an external camera shot, presumably from the top of the module they were in. It showed some squat Avalerion buildings, and beyond them, the plain of tube-grass stretching to the far horizon. The horizon appeared to be wriggling.

Red, his damaged ears forgotten, peered closer. The wriggling was clouds. Even as he watched, a wall of cloud grew above the horizon boiling, foaming, thrashing. Sheffield mouthed something, and Red shook his head. He never could lip read. Sheffield tapped out on the data pad. "Storm front".

Moving deliberately, he reached out with his left arm and grasped a wall rung designated an anchor when the module was in micro-gravity and nodded at Red. Red got it and grasped an adjoining rung. He saw Sheffield lean his head back and shout something, presumably a warning to everyone to grab something and hold on.

To his horror, the massive module actually rocked back and forth several times as the storm front hit it. Looking around wildly, he saw a dozen people, all with their mouths open, screaming, shouting. The module continued to rock from side to side, gradually subsiding, resembling an Earthquake. After a few minutes the motion subsided to an occasional tremor, something that in itself would have been unthinkable minutes earlier.

Red glanced at Sheffield's data pad. He had changed the display to show four camera shots. Two were dead, snow crash static. The other two showed nothing but uniform dark gray, and Red wondered if the cameras had died, and realized that he was seeing what they saw; impenetrable walls of water. They were visibly darkening as he watched. The module shuddered, and one of the cameras winked out. Red realized, with some awe, that this was one of the cameras that had served as *Phoenix*'s external cameras, and had survived a nuclear explosion and twenty six years of hard vacuum and extreme temperatures, only to die in a rain squall.

People were still staring upward, shouting. Red assumed the inhuman rain striking the module was probably kicking up a holy racket.

Sheffield's data pad was showing it nearly full dark, and Red glanced at the time. To his surprise, there was still a half hour until Zharset. Just two and a half hours ago they had been launching the ROVER under cloudless skies.

A hand grasped his upper arm, and Red turned to see Julie Steinberg. She had grabbed Sheffield's arm with her other hand, and now was towing the two of them to the end of the module like an angry teacher towing two recalcitrant students. He and Sheffield glanced at each other and exchanged rueful grins. Red didn't think he had ever seen Sheffield smile before. The effect was spoiled by the dried blood below his ears.

She sat them down, and signaled Red to slip a mask over his face. As he did so, she grabbed an otoscope and peered into each of Red's ears. She then moved in front of him and shook her head, but he could see from her expression, a slight smile, that it was an exasperated head-shake, not a despairing one. He felt relief. She clearly thought the damage wasn't permanent. She pressed a hand on his shoulder, pushing him back until he was semi-reclined. Then she reached over to a small console and pressed a button. Red felt a slight overpressure in his face mask, and moments later was sound asleep.

When he woke, his ears felt numb, and the blood had been washed from his neck and shoulders. Glancing down, he saw he was wearing a new top, one that didn't have his prized planetary insignia. He hoped it would be kept; if the blood didn't wash out, he at least wanted those patches back.

In the adjoining medchair, Sheffield was asleep. Doctor Steinberg was still working on his ear away from Red. He caught her eye and lifted an eyebrow inquiringly. She held up a hand with two fingers extended, and with a sigh, Red settled back to let her finish.

Red reached for his data pad, and with some dismay, found it was gone. Was he holding it when the shock wave hit? He thought it was. It was replaceable, of course, but he would lose all the data from that morning's ROVER flight. Damn. He wondered if the module had any spares.

It took five minutes rather than two for Steinberg to finish work on the Commander's eardrum. She then moved back to Red, typing as she did so. After a moment she held her data pad up for him to read.

"You sustained compression and overpressure damage to both eardrums. I was able to repair the damage. I want you to say a sentence. Anything.

"Um, my name is Red Farnsworth, and I'm a United supporter."

Steinberg typed. "Can you hear your own voice?"

"Dimly. It sounds like it's under water."

Tap tap tap. "That's normal. Both ear drums were punctured, but they will repair themselves. I've glued the tears back together and it should heal in a matter of days. Your nerves were shocked by the sound blast, but apparently still function. Are your ears ringing?"

"Yeah, sort of. It's more of a growl."

"I think that will go away."

"You -think-?"

"We'll probably know in about three to five days. My own ears are ringing, and I was upstairs, well away from exposure. Everyone's are. But you and the Commander and two dozen others were right by the hatch, I understand. You caught the full blast."

Red moved his head in an ambivalent manner, and immediately regretted it. His gyros spun. "If we had caught the full blast, we'd be dead now."

"Do you feel any pain anywhere else, or nausea? Dizziness?"

Red nodded. "Dizziness. Just now, when I nodded."

"OK. You'll live. Check with me once an hour today and twice a day after and we'll see how you're coming along. If you don't improve after five days, we'll get you up to *Phoenix*. They can grow you new eardrums if needed" She hastily added, "But I don't expect you'll need that."

"Why once an hour today?"

Tap tap tap. "It's a precaution. People caught in blasts like you were sometimes suffer internal injuries."

Red nodded, but he felt a sudden stab of doubt. All four shuttles were racing to low orbit almost immediately after he and the kids stepped out. How long before the blast was it? Did they make it to orbit?

"How are Spencer's kids?"

"Are they in this module?

"Um, no, number four." That was the adjacent module. At some point in the confusion, they went to separate modules.

"They should be OK. We're out of contact right now."

Steinberg moved back to check Sheffield's vitals. He glanced over. Sheffield's data pad lay on the stand between the two recliners. Viewing it could get him court-martialed, though he noticed that Captain's post hadn't done Lassiter any real damage. He just didn't have to 'Ser' Vargas any more.

He noted it was still set to the external cameras, the remaining one showing outside climate, which was a close up of Niagara Falls. Clicking, he checked the status on the shuttles. One was in low orbit, the other three were climbing toward *Phoenix* and requesting maintenance docking on arrival which told Red they had all sustained damage of some sort. Still, they were out of harm's way, and none were broadcasting emergency requests.

He ran through the menu, so much longer than his own. Vargas was at the God console, and he saw that his videos were showing a vast concentric target of clouds that covered over a quarter of the moon's surface—including them. Shaking his head, he reset the data pad back to the camera view and carefully placed it back. Steinberg didn't notice, and Sheffield was still out. He had gotten away with it.

Night fell shortly after, and people started getting information on what had happened. Red found a generic data pad in stores, and read the analysis from the *Phoenix* with interest. The blast overpressure was estimated at about a hundred and fifty kilopascals; he was lucky he had his mouth closed when it hit, or he might have taken severe damage to his lungs. For that matter, he was lucky he had any eardrums left at all.

Winds four hundred kilometers an hour. He wondered if any of the village was still standing. He doubted his shed survived. Or the ROVER. He felt a pang.

It took nearly two hours for Simmons and the rest to determine what had happened. Hoyl rotated Hō-ō as the innermost moon, on the outside edge of Hō-ō's ring. The ring consisted of water—fluid on the sun side, frozen quickly in the shadow. The result was ever-changing icebergs that jostled and bumped one another as they rotated, sharing the same vast orbit. The innermost moved a bit faster than the outermost, and that's where collisions would be most likely to occur.

One new iceberg happened to get knocked out to Hoyl's orbit. That wasn't unusual, indeed happened several times a day. But this time, Hoyl happened to be right there.

By cosmic standards, the collision wasn't high velocity—in fact the iceberg got nearly all of its momentum from Hoyl's gravitational well. But it was still traveling a thousand kilometers an hour when it hit. Enough to make a gawdawful racket and splash.

Red perused the report with mounting unease, reflecting on the nearly constant shooting stars that populated Hoyl's night sky. He had a sudden suspicion he knew where Hoyl's fantastically deep, wide oceans, nearly completely fresh water, came from. This place had seen many ice falls in its time. And would see many more. The goddamn place was a cosmic shooting gallery.

Later that night, the rain eased up, and turned to snow.

Snow, on this strange, hot world.

Chapter 30 Modular Snowfall

NOTES FROM DOCTOR IAN SPENCER'S PERSONAL LOG, Year 30, Day 186.

And this brings us to day four in this damn module.

Excuse me. I want to try and keep this dispassionate, but I've been listening to complaints from my fellow inmates all morning. "It's hot" "It's crowded" "It's too dim." "Are we going to get out of here?" Some of it rubbed off.

Physician, heal thyself. Recognize that it is a bit stressful telling people that their concerns, while valid, are not productive, and they should try and focus on more proactive approaches.

Easy advice to give, not so easy when you feel exactly the same way the patient does, and just want to join in a chorus of "Get me the fuck out of here!"

There was a little bit of a subdued panic this morning. The snow buried our one and only outside camera the afternoon of day three, and we tried to open the hatch. It opens outward, of course, and guess what? We're snowed in.

So a crowd of us went upstairs to the upper level hatch. Most of the people have never seen snow in their lives. It wouldn't open and we started getting a rising hubbub from people who were convinced the snow had covered the module to the top. Someone pointed out that if that was the case, we wouldn't be able to communicate with any of the other modules, or even the Phoenix. I think that was wishful thinking, but still. . .

Finally one of the colonists, from Sweden, I believe, said the door was probably just iced shut, and all we had to do was apply heat around the perimeter.

Easier said than done. The modules, after all, are insulated against the extremes of space and reentry. Not that they didn't spend the better part of an hour trying while everyone milled.

Fortunately, claustrophobia was one of the psychological conditions that got screened out at the outset. Finally Harlen hit on the idea of removing the inner access hatch on the hatch itself, forcing the manual override to disengage the bolts, and then placed a jackhammer butt first against the outer skin of the hatch. The insulation blocks heat, and to a degree, radiation. It does not block vibration. After a few minutes the ice holding the hatch in place broke loose and fell away, and the hatch swung open.

It was still snowing, but we could see mounds where the buildings were. That's promising. Mounds suggest they're still standing. If so, it's an amazing tribute to the architectural design of Cyril Voss and Sean Sheffield. Counting the steps on the access ladder, we determined the snow was two and a half meters deep.

This led to the next problem. Nobody thought to bring snowshoes or skis along. And our Swedish guy advised against stepping out onto three meters of fresh-fallen snow. "Very fast, you die" is how he put it. He tossed a container of liquid soap out to illustrate, and it vanished into the snow with barely a puff.

So we decided someone would have to climb down the ladder and start digging. Third problem. Digger lasers are utterly ineffective against snow, and in Module Six of the RESS Phoenix, the crowning pinnacle of man's technological achievements, nobody had a shovel. A jackhammer, yes. But no shovel.

The good news is we aren't as trapped as we thought we were. The bad news is that we are trapped, nonetheless.

Reggie Spaulding died this morning. He was one of the ones outside at the time the shock wave hit, and was unlucky enough to have his mouth wide open. The overpressure probably ruptured half the alveoli in his lungs, and they filled with fluid and he drowned. He died hard, taking four days to do so. Red kept looking over at Reggie, especially in the final day. I'm sure he knows how lucky he was he just got far enough inside when the shock wave hit.

Julie and I have been checking everyone who was directly exposed to the shock wave at least once an hour for the past ninety four hours, and some of the people inside who we felt might be symptomatic. Compression injuries to internal organs are common when people are exposed to blast waves, and happily, there seems to be little evidence that anyone still alive took significant damage. My own pet theory is the size and distance of the blast gave the blast wave a long period in relation to its amplitude, cushioning the impact just a bit.

So we have four known dead among the eight modules, all from overpressure trauma, and three missing, who simply didn't show up at any of the modules. I will be very surprised if any of them are alive. We have thirty injured, but all the injured are expected to recover at this point.

Julie had me go around with a clicker today, checking the hearing of the hearing cases. About half of them have at least enough hearing back I would declare them fit for duty. Julie told me she isn't too concerned about the ear cases, which includes Commander Sheffield. She expected it might take up to a week in the cases where one or both ear drums were actually punctured, and most of those could at least hear something from the clicker.

Provisions are good for at least another ten days. I thought Sheffield was engaging in a little overkill when he mandated that each module be able to fit the needs of fifty people for up to ten days. And perhaps he was. After all, the worst danger we thought we faced where the super cells and tornadoes—and we haven't seen a tornado since that first one ripped through in the first days of the colony. It may be that tornadoes are as common here as they are in Manitoba, but folks in Manitoba can go their entire lives without seeing one, if they're lucky.

In any case, Sheffield was right. I should be grateful, but I feel slightly annoyed. I'll need to contemplate that. It seems a peculiar thing to resent. Perhaps I actually just resent being cooped up in here. But honesty compels me to admit that I find Sheffield annoying.

Vargas realized that boredom was the biggest problem we faced, and shut down some of the ship's self-monitoring operations in order to have the bandwidth available so everyone could access the ship's library all at once if need be. Oddly enough we can't access the one only one hundred meters away. One of the most popular items has been the high resolution video shot from a shuttle in low orbit in the immediate aftermath of the impact. It was entering orbit in the opposite direction of the meteorite's angle of attack, and they bypassed one another, fortunately missing one another by about fifteen hundred kilometers. Even at the upper edge of the atmosphere, the shock wave was enough that the pilot had to seize control to bring the ship back to trim. His orbit brought him over the impact site in some seventy-five minutes, and it looked like a nuclear explosion—a high anvil cloud reaching into the uppermost part of the atmosphere, surrounded by a boiling sea of low-level clouds. There's a small archipelago of crater islands about fifteen hundred km from the impact, and shuttle cameras happened to be pointed there when the tsunami hit. The water hit with a slow-motion explosion, a geyser of spume that totally obliterated the islands. If there was anything living on them the moment the water hit, it's gone now.

It's strange being able to view a global catastrophe that you are a part of. Images from the shuttle, the Phoenix and the satellites show that tsunamis up to a kilometer high swept the coastlines of all the continents. We now know from the wave patterns that there is land of some sort, at least one hundred kilometers across, at the South Pole. Waves washed right across the low-lying desert areas to the south of us, crossing up to a hundred and seventy kilometers of land. The southern continent, which we believe to be jungle-like, took massive coastal damage, with flotsam and jetsam visible from orbit. Naked-eye visible, that is; the debris discolors the water for some distance around.

It puts our inconveniences in perspective. A little snow. Phtt! Nothing!

I wonder if Vargas had that response in mind. The waters run deep in that one.

We're under a vast cyclonic mass of cloud that covers nearly half the northern hemisphere. It had a distinct eye in the first days, which we're told is where the impact occurred. Winds must have been fifteen hundred kilometers an hour there. There's nothing built by humans that could withstand that type of wind. Even the pyramids would be sandblasted away to nubs.

We're under it, fortunately near the edges where the winds aren't nearly as daunting. We've had steady seventy kilometer an hour here, but it's dying down.

The eye of the storm has collapsed on itself, which Morley says means it's losing steam rapidly. He promises we'll see some Zharshine in the next twenty-four hours.

But there's an awful lot of snow out there. How long do we have to wait for it to melt?

There's about forty people in here and not much in the way of sanitary facilities. I miss the fresh air.

* * *

On day six of the incarceration in the modules, Sheffield's data pad started flashing yellow. That meant it was important, but not a dangerous situation. Sheffield automatically noted the time, even though his breakfast made it pretty self-evident. 0600. Little full summer, so Zhar-Ptitsa was already high in the sky. He clicked in.

The text read, "Attn all residents of modules. Ensure hatches are firmly closed, and do not attempt to exit until 0900 while snow clearing operations take place."

What the hell? Snow clearing operations? What was that?

Looking around, he saw everyone else was looking at their data pads in varying degrees of puzzlement. Spotting two crewmen, he sent them orders to check the hatches, and asked for confirmation from the other modules that the check had been completed. Vargas wouldn't have yellow-flashed that without cause.

The two crewmen flashed acknowledgement that the hatches were secure. He signaled Vargas and told him "All hatches secure. Do whatever it is you intend to do."

About five minutes passed, and Sheffield heard what, back in Manchester, would have been the most mundane of sounds. It was a buzzing roar that rose and fell, exactly like someone running a vacuum over a carpet in the next room. Then there would be a steady roar for a few minutes, followed by the rising-and-falling pattern. Only the modules were damn near sound proof; they had, after all, protected the hearing of everyone who was safely inside when the Ice Fall occurred. Whatever was going on out there was *loud*.

The environmental readouts over the main hatch suddenly flashed red, and Sheffield called up his God console to see what had the idiot program upset. It was reporting temperatures outside above eighteen hundred C. "Unsafe for unprotected access". Yeah, that summed it up pretty well. Rather nasty mix of hot hydrocarbons, too. Sheffield started getting an idea what was going on.

He tried to raise Vargas, and discovered he was in red-screen only mode, and to refer routine inquiries to the bridge.

That's when it struck him: his hearing was back! It had been there, but dim for the past thirty six hours or so. He realized the conversations going on around him were at normal volume. His irritation that he couldn't readily raise Vargas vanished. His hearing was back. That was far more important.

The buzz and hum outside receded, became a very distant sound. Sheffield guessed that his module had been the first for snow removal "treatment", which mollified him a bit.

After an hour, the readouts at the hatch turned green, and the God Console told him it was thirty five and the air quality was good. He checked his time. 0650. One hundred and thirty minutes to go.

His data pad flashed a message from Vargas. "Sean, I don't know if you can hear me, so am texting. I monitored your module readouts just now. Safe for your module to open up. Wait on the others; we're still working."

Sean signaled acknowledgement, and walked over to the hatch and pressed the open button. The temperature outside was still dropping, now down to a reasonably comfortable thirty. The hatch swung open, and Sean had to raise a hand and squint against the glare. Belatedly he dropped his tube-grass root veil.

And stepped out. Around the hatch were a few patches of half-melted snow. There was a path leading from the hatch to a central point, and huge banks of snow on each side. The roar was loud, but bearable.

Sheffield took a deep breath, savoring the first fresh air in six days.

Except it wasn't that good. It smelled of ozone and ketones. He double checked the readouts, confirming it was reasonably safe for human consumption.

His data pad flashed. Farnsworth spoke. "Commander, please come up to the upper hatch. You have got to see this!"

"On my way, Red."

He had to shoulder his way through a small muttering crowd. Red saw him and scrambled up the ladder to make room for him, and pointed.

Once securely planted, Sheffield looked where Red had pointed.

One of the shuttles was moving slowly over the field, nose elevated to about a forty five degree angle over the tail, with both fore and aft thrusters firing.

Sheffield knew you could hover in the Shuttles, although he certainly wouldn't try it just ten meters off the ground. For one thing, the blast would burn the hell out of ... ah.

"Snow removal. Gods." It was like brushing your teeth with a grindstone. Certainly, it would do the job, but. . . Sheffield realized the piloting skill needed. Not only did the pilot have to hover at an odd angle, just ten meters up, but he had to have the craft move forward very slowly, taking care not to damage any flammable objects in Hoyl's oxygen-rich atmosphere as he did so. This was one impressive performance, Sheffield had to admit.

"Who's the hot dog flying this thing? Does Vargas know he's using this method to clear the snow?"

"Fuck, let's hope so, Commander. That's the Captain piloting it."

Sheffield stared at the Middie in open disbelief. "Vargas?"

Red gave an open palmed shrug and a grin. "I trained with him in Gabon when he got his pilot's rating. As you say, a hot dog. He had Bécquer in abject terror every time he went up. You could see the poor guy considering his career prospects if the Captain of the *Phoenix* fried his ass in a training flight. I've heard stories about the space ace, there. Tie a string to the end of a shuttle, and he could tie any knot you wanted."

The shuttle moved cautiously along a path to the middle. With that pass completed, the shuttle gained altitude to about two hundred meters and flew back and forth in a tight pattern. Vargas inspecting his handiwork, no doubt. Then the shuttle drifted over to a central spot where all the paths he had made converged, and with a soft sigh, the shuttle settled onto the tube-grass, browned by the exhaust from the craft.

Sheffield reflected on the fifteen kinds of hell he would visit on any subordinate pilot who pulled a stunt like that on Sheffield's watch. But this wasn't a subordinate. Sheffield heaved a sigh.

"Red, let's go congratulate the Captain on a job well done."

* * *

The shuttle had what amounted to a gigantic snow blower, modeled after the ones used to clear mountain roads in the Transantarctic Mountains. Watching it trundle out of the back of the shuttle, Red realized they pretty much had to have Imprinted and assembled it over the past three days, and put it together in the shuttle. Obviously the crew of *Phoenix* had been busy little boys and girls.

It turned out a bit more assembly was needed once it trundled out of the shuttle on vast caterpillar treads. The intake was a full three meters high, more than enough to handle the snow between here and Scafeld and Lassiter's Landing. The blower towered five meters into the sky, reminding Red of the grotesquely huge trucks at open-pit mines.

Vargas deferred to Sam Buchanan when it came to driving that behemoth. Sam was the only person on the mission rated to operate a snow clearance machine that big. Or any snow clearance machine at all. Sam was from northern Greenland.

The beast was just small enough to clear the secondary roads, and tighten up the mounds of snow between the roads there weren't buildings. Sam had to move carefully on that: there were homes along the circumferences, and assuming they survived the impact and subsequent weather, he didn't want to knock them down.

The trickiest part of the operation came when Sam carefully drove the machine over some support lines of tube-grass mesh that were attached to the shuttle, which hovered some hundred and fifty meters above. He jumped out, and Vargas carefully lifted the shuttle, pulling the machine into the air and carefully placing it down on the far side of the Styx. The snow blower promptly sank into the deep snow. Vargas released the cables, letting them drop alongside the snow blower, and brought the shuttle back to the clearing.

At which point Sheffield sent word to the other modules that it was all clear and they could come out. True to his word, Vargas was done by 0900.

Colonists piled out of the modules like bees, whooping and cheering. Several just simply rotated in place, heads thrown back and arms stretched out to the sky, exalting in their freedom. Others stared in fascination at the mounds of snow, a rare sight on Earth and even rarer on Hoyl. Beneath their feet, the tube-grass was brown, a result of the shuttle's back-blast. But at the edges, it was still green and healthy as it emerged from the snow.

On the far side of the Styx, the steelwood trees still stood, and much of the lesser vegetation. Neither the shock wave nor the blizzard seemed to have done major harm.

Overhead, Zhar-Ptitsa turned his merciless glare on the snow.

If there was one thing Hoyl seemed capable of, it was recovering quickly from catastrophes.

More and more, the colonists were beginning to realize the implications of that.

Chapter 31 Growing Suspicions

RED WAS DELIGHTED TO FIND HE HAD THE DATA from the ROVER's test flight after all. Jim and Sylvie kept it and uploaded that same day after the electronic twingies from the strike had died down and they had a stable connect with *Phoenix*. Now all he had to do was return to the shed, rouse the flyer, and resume testing.

There were just two problems; the shed was flattened, and the ROVER wouldn't rouse.

It wasn't lost. Red knew where it was to the millimeter. But it was probably buried in snow, and the batteries were dead. At least, that's what Red hoped, and it simply hadn't been fried or crushed by the blast. When the snow melted—and it was doing so very quickly—they could wait for the solar panels to collect some juice and try rousing it again. If that didn't work, they would have to hike out and get it. Red wondered if he could convince Ian Mann that it was worth a brief flight in the shuttle.

It left the kids with nothing to do, but they didn't seem to mind. They had some project of their own they were working on at home.

Sheffield was doing a little strutting. Of the six hundred structures in Avalerion, only three suffered major structural damage. There was significantly more damage to objects in the interior of the structures from the blast and overpressure, but Sheffield didn't consider that to be a failing on the part of his design. Nor did anyone else, and he was being hailed for the durability of his buildings. Somehow, Voss' involvement in the design seemed to have vanished.

On the ship, Dan Vargas was wondering how best to press for a controversial course of action. He was a captain, not a tyrant, and not a god, despite what the midshipmen might think. He saw only one course of action open for the *Phoenix* and her people: pack up and leave Hoyl, and resume the search for a home in another system.

He couldn't just order it. Once off the ship, he had no more say in the affairs of the colonists than the colonists themselves felt he should have. He also knew it would split his own crew right down the middle, with as many fiercely opposing him as those willing to obey him. He didn't fancy leaving Hoyl with half the complement, leaving hundreds of people to their own devices on a world that would surely kill them sooner or later.

Tim Simmons had laid it out for them with unassailable logic. Hō-ō One, Hoyl as it was now known, was at best an ephemeral world. It couldn't have existed for more than fifty thousand years, and prospects were bleak for its existing that much longer. "It shouldn't even be here at all," he complained. "The whole moon is essentially a kinetic dynamo, more or less borrowing its own magnetic field from the mother planet. That has to introduce a huge rate of orbital decay."

Anything over fifty thousand years, and it would be tidally locked by now. The slowing rotation of the planet was a clock that allowed Simmons to calculate back to a time when it was spinning too fast to sustain itself. It had to be younger than that.

Etienne Sorlund had chimed in with his own bad news. "The average depth of the oceans is over seventy thousand meters. It's very nearly fresh water. These oceans are brand new, geologically speaking, and all that water didn't come with the moon. It's all or almost all a result of ice falls, chunks from the Hō-ō rings that have struck this moon, over and over and over. Big strikes, maybe as often as once a year. We calculated how much ice might have arrived via the night show, the shooting star gallery that's so popular, and it can only account for ten percent of the water on the planet. So the rest came from bigger strikes. Perhaps much bigger strikes. There are ice balls in those rings up to two hundred kilometers across, fifteen thousand times the mass of what hit us last little summer."

Aaron Kessler was next. "We knew there were a lot of crater sites on the land. We think the Boitumelo archipelago is a gigantic meteor strike, less than ten thousand years old. But we've been surveying the oceans, and we have a sense of the ocean bottoms. The whole planet is one big field of meteor craters. If you took away the water, it would look a lot like the back side of Earth's Moon. What happened last week was a minor event by this world's standards. It explains why the plant life we see is so much more durable than the environment would seem to demand. We had been wondering why a semi-tropical forest had trees that were flame-resistant and able to cope with severe cold, and now we know. The weather must routinely go berserk in the aftermath of these ice falls."

Trapp was last. "Some of the colonists are already talking about starting families. Once that begins to happen, they aren't going to want to pack up and move, especially since hibernation is likely to kill or maim their children. I would guess there's already a sizable number down there who feel invested enough by all the work they've done that they'll stay and take their chances, even without *Phoenix*."

Sorlund had one more bit of bad news. "As Tim implied, Hoyl doesn't have a molten core. It's nickel-iron, and the reason it has a magnetic field is only because it is deep within Hō-ō's magnetic field, and has a resonant shield of its own." He nodded to the physicist, who nodded back. "However, magnetic fields on gas giants are notoriously fickle, and sometimes just vanish for no reason at all. Worse, it happens frequently by cosmic standards, about every thousand years or so for a planet of Hō-ō's size and configuration. We could all wake up one morning and find that we're dead man walking, that we got lethal doses overnight."

This came as news to Trapp. "Would that explain why the moon is so cool?"

Sorlund pondered. "It would make a difference of maybe a half a degree. But the lower oceans are all solid ice. Some of the guys think Hoyl isn't a moon at all, but a gigantic comet."

Vargas thanked everyone and dismissed the group. He didn't feel there wasn't any remaining doubt about what needed to be done. There was, however, lots of doubt about how to do it.

He would have to go down to Hoyl and meet with Sheffield face to face. If he called him up as a subordinate, Sheffield would rebel. Vargas had never seen anything from Sheffield that could be really called mutinous, even when angered, but Vargas knew the early warning signs, and knew Sheffield had fallen in love with the place.

If need be, Vargas could leave Sheffield to his fate. But he didn't want to lose half his crew and a chunk of his passenger complement with him.

* * *

Rebekah was beginning to wonder if she would ever taste a vegetable from her garden. Between the blast from the Ice Fall and the wild weather that followed, the gardens were totally destroyed—again. Now she was going to have to rethink livestock, since Red had mentioned to her that such Ice Falls might actually be common. She couldn't think of a way to tell a herd of sheep to cover their ears. She didn't want to raise goats only to see them die in massive shock waves.

In less than fifty days it would be the autumn equinox. In about ten more days it would be daylight less than half the time, because of the eclipses. Nobody had any idea what Earth plants would make of that. The grow lights that had been in place were destroyed, and while she expected replacements within the week, she was asking herself if it was worth the wasted resources.

As if foreshadowing, it was late in the week, and evening was early. As she often did, Rebekah sat in front of her cabin in the mild evening air, untroubled by insects, enjoying the subtly sweet scent of the tube-grass. The sky sparkled with micrometeorites, a sight she no longer found friendly and relaxing. To the east a crescent Hō-ō was rising, a fat ocher rainbow. The white line of the rings, thinning as the equinox approached, was like an arrow, with Hō-ō as the bow. Only now the arrow appeared aimed at Hoyl.

Was it worth the struggle to stay on this dangerous and strange world? She wasn't one to run from a challenge, but she was beginning to feel there were just too many problems on this world to be overcome.

Even before Ice Fall, Red had been talking about moving on. She had dismissed it, in part because Red loved to explore, and a single world might be too small for his sense of wonder; his eyes widened to a far grander scheme than mere continents and oceans could provide. She knew he would be much more restless without his ROVER to play with, and hoped he got it back. This world, she hoped, was strange enough to keep him engaged.

She would have to ask him how he felt in the wake of Ice Fall. Would he say it was a sign it was time to move on, or would he see it as a challenge and dig his heels in?

Rebekah realized she might want to decide that herself before asking him. It wouldn't be a fair question otherwise.

Tomorrow she would replant, and go through the motions. The lights would arrive, and they would erect them. The canopy had stood up, but still needed a thorough inspection to ensure it hadn't taken damage from the weight of the snow, some of which was still slowly dripping through as the mass melted. Rudy Harlen had shaken his head admiringly and told her the canopy was supporting over six tons per square meter, a strength unheard of on Earth. In fact, he had added, on Earth it would have been eight tons per square meter, all that snow.

She heard a faint sound, a peep, from somewhere in front of her, beyond the edge of her porch light. Peering into the dark, she listened intently. A faint motion caught her eye. It looked as if some of the tube-grass had been disturbed. Just a faint rustle, tiny. It might have been the wind. Except the katabatic breeze that kept them comfortable eased up at night. The air was still.

She cautiously and quietly arose, and tiptoed over to where the tube-grass had moved. Moving slowly, she pulled out her data pad, set it to flashlight mode, and flicked it on.

There was nothing but tube-grass.

Perhaps it had been just the wind after all.

Even though there was no wind.

* * *

Vargas had taken up eating meals in the main mess hall, now that there were enough people awake and active that he didn't feel like a BB on the floor of Saint Paul's in there. The Velcro floor made it possible to walk, if awkwardly, and the rotating gym was right next door, perfect for before- or after-meal exercises.

There was also the fact that eating with just a select handful of people, let alone by himself in his cabin, left him dangerously isolated.

Finally, the people on board *Phoenix* were the very best and brightest Earth could produce, chosen after years of painstaking tests and trials from a pool of five million, a base that itself attracted the most adventurous and intelligent people. It would be madness not to socialize with such a fine group.

Of course, the Captain thought as bin Laden sat down across from him, the system didn't promise perfection. Ian, sitting next to bin Laden, seemed genuinely happy to see the tall, thin Egyptian, and Vargas entertained a hope that perhaps the annoying Binnie wanted to talk to Spencer.

Vargas noted that both men were wearing tube-grass tunics. They were hard to tell apart from the 'official' ships wear, except for a discrete image of Hoyl on the left sleeve. The regular tunics, while light and comfortable, were also somewhat fragile and wore out fairly quickly. The new tunics were lighter, and nearly indestructible. Various pastel versions of the same garb had been showing up among the civilian population. Vargas wasn't going to wear a modified ships' uniform, but already had several off-duty articles of clothing made from the material, including his ship-socks, which served in lieu of shoes and allowed him to walk on Velcro.

Binny held up a thumb drive for Spencer's inspection. "Doctor, I interviewed seventy three people, most of them civilian. I tried to spread it among various points of view as I could."

Spencer took the proffered data. "What did the interviews reveal?"

"I'm honestly not quite sure, Doctor. Part of the problem is that I don't really have a baseline."

"Well, you know that people who had fundamentalist tendencies were detected and eliminated from consideration for the *nu Phoenicis* program right away."

Bin Laden nodded. "That's as it should be. It's a mindset extremely poorly aligned for the emotional and intellectual demands of this sort of mission. But of course someone can be very deeply religious without being fundamentalist."

To Vargas, who had been following the conversation with increasing bafflement, this was the final straw. Dealing with bin Laden during training, he had found himself wondering how the man had passed the psych screenings. He couldn't get a single sentence out without a "if it is Allah's will" or "blessed be the Prophet." He used it in lieu of "Ser" when addressing Vargas. Legal, but annoying.

Except he wasn't doing that now. Bin Laden, possibly feeling the Captain's eye tracks, glanced over at Vargas and actually winked at him.

But Spencer was speaking, oblivious to the furtive little exchange. "And of course, you don't know if they are in your sample or not. Hm. How did you get around the right-to-privacy concerns?"

Bin Laden looked like he was expecting the question. "I kept no record of the names of the people I spoke with, and what you have there is a transcript with personal, identifiable remarks eliminated or masked. None of the interviewees know who any of the others were,

"They're numbered, of course, and I imagine that you can correlate them with your own data from interviews you conducted during elimination and training tasks."

Spencer "That sounds like it will meet medical ethics. Or my ethics, out here on the wild and woolly frontier."

By now utterly baffled, Vargas spoke up. "What is this about, if I may inquire?"

Bin Laden and Spencer blinked at each other. "I'm sorry, Captain," the psychiatrist said, spreading fingers in a placating gesture. "I was under the impression that Doctor Trapp told you about our religiosity study."

"That's what this is about?" Vargas was surprised, and it probably showed on his face.

Spencer continued, "Mister bin Laden here has been conducting the survey. He was one of the first to suspect a change in the attitudes among the crew, and he raised the issue with us that it might be subsequent to hibernation problems."

Bin Laden added, "I've been calling it 'hibernation secularism.' And my apologies, Captain; I thought you already knew. I didn't mean to be impolite."

"Hm. I'll forgive you the oversight if you answer a rude question from me."

"Fair enough, Captain. Ask away." Bin Laden's eyes had a mischievous twinkle.

"I'm accustomed to you using religious interjections in your statements to me, of the sort one associates with practitioners of Islam. Have you become more secular since we left Earth?"

"More secular? No, not especially. I am a non-believer, and have been since I was twelve. An infidel, if you will. So not more secular, but perhaps a bit wiser. I have decided it is folly to annoy people without cause."

"I see. I think I see." Vargas reflected on the nature of human interactions for a moment. Farnsworth seemed to have a bit of an Irish brogue when speaking to Sheffield, and didn't Rebekah Cohen seem to sprinkle Yiddish phrases in her dialogue when bin Laden was around? Not all of humanity's resentments and foibles had been left behind.

"Hmm. One more rude question, if I may..." He arched an eyebrow.

"Certainly, Captain. I am at your disposal."

"Commander Isaakson said you requested a name change for your ground suit, and felt it required my permission. Which I granted, by the way. But why 'Zadeh Ladin'?"

Bin Laden smiled. "For my Burqa, you mean?" His eyes twinkled.

"I just wanted the man to match the attire, is all."

OK, Vargas thought. Be mysterious. "So what did you glean from your interviews?"

Bin Laden sobered. "Nobody seemed particularly religious. Some still professed faith, but had no interest in conducting or even attending religious ceremonies or functions. I asked about any formal religious affiliations, and the answers overwhelmingly, started out, 'I used to be a. . . '." Bin Laden shrugged. "I appears Abraham's little god of the desert could not survive a trip to the stars." He raised his palms to the 'ceiling'. "Not my imagery, by the way. Rebekah Cohen came up with that."

Vargas looked at the non-com with some wonder. This had turned out to be a more entertaining meal than he expected.

"I trust you gentlemen will tell me what the results are once the data is collated."

"Yes Ser," the two men chorused. Vargas found himself almost missing the "If Allah Wills."

Chapter 32 Things That Grow On Hoyl

BY THE NEXT LITTLE SUMMER, the snow was receding rapidly. Ian Mann and André Morley had reconnoitered the shoreline to the east of them. The damage was spectacular. The alluvial shelf with the canyons that Mann had seen after that first storm was gone, and the lower reaches of the tube-grass were actually torn and tattered. Aware of just how strong the stuff was, Mann tried to imagine the titanic forces that had done that.

They flew around the tall cliffs that were the facing out from the Boitumelos at the ocean edge, marveling at the spots where cliffs of solid nickel-iron had simply broken away and fallen into the water. Morley estimated the wave height there to be half a kilometer, moving at perhaps six hundred kilometers an hour. He surmised that the preceding troughs had actually sucked the rock loose.

There was debris in the water everywhere. The ocean currents in this place were beyond belief anyway, clocked at speeds on the surface of up to seventy kilometers an hour, and far more chaotic and churning than those of Earth. Piece of vegetation floated in random clumps and when they passed the great polar mountain chain to the other side, they found forests had been swept clean of all understory for up to three kilometers inland. Only tube-grass and steelwood trees seemed to withstand the onslaught.

"I guess we know why this place doesn't have much in the away of alluvial plains," said Morley, who had been puzzling over that. "If they get super tsunamis like that on a regular basis, they get washed away before they can fully form."

Ian pointed to a raft of plant debris. "What's going on over there?"

"What do you mean?"

"Something's splashing."

"What?" Even as he spoke André slowed the craft and banked, dropping for a closer look.

The water was actively churning, motion visible were water appeared in gaps in the floating plant mass.

"I'll be go-to-hell," André said. "Those are fish."

"Or something close enough to never-mind," Ian rejoined. He glanced at the camera next to him to make sure it was running. *"Phoenix*, are you getting this?"

To his surprise, Captain Vargas responded. "Copy, Shuttle Three. Aquatic animal life. Well, that answers that."

"Ser. We'll try to get a bit closer, but we don't want to injure or scare them."

"No, stay where you are and just use the zoom. We have to assume they could possibly be intelligent. Standing orders, mister."

"Ser, all due respect, but they're fish."

There was a pause. "André, is Ian Mann with you?"

"Ser?"

"Ian, tell him."

André, safely out of camera range, rolled his eyes. Ian nodded sympathetically. "The Captain means that any life form capable of interacting proactively with its environment must be treated both as potentially hazardous and potentially intelligent. So we hang back and watch them, and especially look to see if they are watching us. Uh, does that cover it, Ser?"

Vargas sounded amused. "Not the way the book phrases it, but entirely serviceable, Mister Mann."

"Understood, Ser." The thing of it was that André did understand, fully. He knew that anything that needed to move fairly quickly in water pretty much had to be fish-shaped, and appearance and even size weren't indicators of intelligence. Octopi, while not human-level intelligent, were indisputably intelligent.

With lenses at full zoom, the men peered, trying to discern what was happening. The water was churning pretty hard, suggesting hundreds, perhaps thousands of the creatures. André spoke without moving his eyes from the scene. "That one plant looks like a hoseberry bush—probably tore loose when the tsunamis receded. There's a creature right next to it, and if the leaves are ten centimeters long like our hoseberries are, then that animal is about a meter in length. It's eating the leaves."

Jim Hartnell spoke. "Interesting. Do you see anything to indicate they are amphibious?"

Ian grinned. The xenobiologist must be beside himself with joy. He hadn't had anything in the way of professional challenges from either Disappointment or Hoyl. "Well, they have their top parts where their mouths are up out of the water. At least the ones we can see do. I think there's a lot more under the surface."

"How far from shore are you?"

"Less than half a kilometer."

"Shallow water?"

"No, deep." Ian punched up an isobar contour map of the ocean on his pad. He spoke up. "About ten thousand meters deep."

"Not much of a continental shelf."

"This world doesn't seem to have those. Some areas don't have any intermediate regions at all; the land slopes sharply into water, and keeps right on sloping for thousands of meters."

Vargas spoke up. "Do you see any sign that they are aware of your presence?"

"It's hard to tell, Captain. If they have eyes, they aren't evident. They seem engrossed in eating. As you can see, they've got lots of teeth."

Hartnell: "Those look like fish-catching teeth. Pointed, sharp, inclined slightly inward. Why would they be eating land vegetation?"

"Maybe they're eating something in the vegetation. Small land animals that lived in the hoseberry, perhaps?"

"Interesting thought, Mister Mann. Jim?"

"That begs the question. If it's the same plant, how come we don't see these no-see-ums in our hoseberry plants.?"

Nobody had an answer for that.

In the *Phoenix* at the God Console, Vargas raised Red Farnsworth. "Red, what's the status on your ROVER?"

"Still missing in action, Captain. We were planning to try to raise it this afternoon. The snow's melting quickly now. I have my hopes."

"We need it sooner than that. Requisition two brawny fellows to dig it out and bring it to you. How fast can you get it operational?"

"I would have to look at it. If the carapace wasn't crushed, possibly today. Um, Captain? Is there a rush?"

"We have a couple of men cruising near off shore south east of the Boitumelos. They were looking at the extent and nature of the debris from the tsunamis. They are presently looking at this." Vargas forwarded the live feed from Mann and Morley to Red.

Vargas hid a grin as the silence stretched. He couldn't resist enjoying shocking the voluble midshipman into silence.

Finally Red spoke. His tone was neutral, almost flat. "Those look like salmon."

"If you say so." Vargas wasn't sure what a salmon looked like, but Hartnell was nodding his head vigorously. "We need to get the ROVER out there for close-ups before they disperse."

It was a wonder the roar from the shuttle hadn't made them disperse. Red considered. "Captain, you want me to take our only ROVER, which greatly resembles a dragonfly, and have it hover above the surface of water that is filled with voracious large fish?"

Vargas sighed. "Red, if they eat it, I'll buy you a new one."

"Deal. Give me an ETA on the shuttle when it's there, and I'll round up Spencer's kids."

They hadn't tested to see how well they could control the craft line-of-sight routed through *Phoenix*. Well, now they would find out if it worked.

* * *

Red had done a pretty good job of resurrecting the shed, even if he did say so himself. Of the structure itself, the only important parts missing were the roof and ceiling, and he planned on getting replacements in a day or so. Most of the tools and equipment had been lying within ten meters of the shed, and any not in that circumference were gone, never to be seen again. He did a quick inventory. He had nearly enough spare parts for a second ROVER, although the gadget's brain, the CPU and data box, couldn't be replaced. Not for a week at least. All Red could hope was those were intact, along with the carapace. If he had those, he could be airborne within hours.

Next, he called Jim and Sylvie. Jim was at the Landing, learning logging operations. Sylvie was at home. She paused, obviously torn between coming in and some project at home. "Sylvie, we need to be in the air within the hour. The Captain himself is pushing for this. We found animal life in the Bering Sea."

She looked wonderstruck, but nodded. "I'll be there."

Red returned to his work, hoping that whatever was going on at home wouldn't affect her work. Boyfriend, maybe? She was the underage daughter of one of the line officers. It would take a brave crewman to date her.

The two showed up as the same time as the shuttle, which worked out perfectly. Two crewmen – brawny, just as the captain promised – hauled the ROVER out of the shuttle cargo. "It was under a meter of snow," one of the crewmen explained. "The trees protected it, though. It looks fairly intact."

Red examined the device. One of the wings was broken, along with a leg that wouldn't retract. Both were replaced in moments, and Jim ran the diagnostics. Red and Sylvie eyeballed the rest of it, and they proclaimed it good to go.

Red glanced up to see Sylvie flash a hand signal at Jim. Four fingers, thumb pulled in. Four something. Jim grinned, gave an enthusiastic thumbs up, and saw Red looking at him. Red-faced, he returned to his inspection.

Under other circumstances, Red might have asked, "Four what?" He was a naturally curious sort. But now was not the time.

If he had asked, Mickey might not have died the following week. But he didn't, and Mickey died.

"Reserve fuel?"

"One hundred percent." If it was over the water when at Zharset, it would at least be able to return to land for the night.

"Captain, we're on our way. ETA two hours fifteen minutes."

"Very good." Vargas ordered the shuttle to resume its original mission. He didn't want it to scare off the salmon, or whatever they were.

But when the ROVER got there, the debris had scattered, as had the creatures. Just the heaving, uneasy waves of the Hoyl Ocean were there to mark the spot.

* * *

With all of Hoyl's cropland measured in in less than two hundred square meters, Rebekah didn't need to devote more than a few hours a day to her chosen career. The crops had no infectious diseases or blights to guard against, and no insects or other animals competing for a higher spot on the food chain. Even weeds were an insignificant problem.

Rebekah knew it couldn't last. Blind evolution would eventually produce microorganisms that would live, parasitically or symbiotically off the crops, and slowly the farmer's curses would all return. For now, the only things she had to guard against were things that used to be the farmer's friend; sunlight and rain. Sometimes Rebekah missed wheat blight, boll weevils and crickets. She also wanted to sit down with Ian Mann and Ann Forster and discuss the possibilities of combining the genes that make the local vegetation so incredibly hardy with Earth plants. She didn't know if *Phoenix* had the resources for a project that vast, but the library contained every detail of the immense botanic battle to undo the immense damage GMOs did to the biosphere two hundred years ago.

The neighborhood was a little deserted these days, come to that. Red Farnsworth, her neighbor on one side, was involved in his ROVER project, vicariously exploring the highlands on the far side of the Boitumelos, scouting mining possibilities and arable land around the pole. On the other side were Doctors Spencer and Spencer. Ian and Maureen were both up on *Phoenix* these days. Ian was involved in some kind of ongoing confab with the Captain and line officers. Maureen was with some of the bioengineers, coming up with possibilities for farm animals that could withstand Zhar Ptitsa's glare. On the other side of them were the Spencer teens, Jim and Maureen. They worked with Red on the ROVER project, so they were gone most of the time, too. On the other side of Red's home was Rudy Harlen, but the taciturn engineer seemed uninterested in social discourse. Rebekah wondered how a loner like him got selected.

Before Ice Fall, it was a common practice for people to gather in the cool evenings and enjoy the nightly meteor showers, and when it was eclipsing Hoyl, the lightning show on Hō-ō, which made the giant dim red planet resemble a Japanese lantern with fireflies in it.

The practice had faded because it reminded people of the danger of another Ice Fall. But Rebekah was a *moshav* farmer; she believed that to fully live life, one had to appreciate the beauty and majesty in the things that threatened you, or you lived a life of bleak fear. Farmers learned that or died. Rebekah felt a nearly genetic imperative to enjoy the nightly light shows.

Rebekah sensed, rather than saw, a flicker out of the corner of her eye. Something in the tube-grass. She remembered her incident from the little year before. She had very nearly dismissed it as a mind trick, perhaps even a flash-dream.

Moving as slowly and stealthily as she could, she rose from her seat and pulled out her data pad and unrolled it. She set it to flash camera mode. One pinch in the corner, and the screen would go to full brightness, and more importantly, the camera would begin recording what was in the field of light.

Moving slowly allowed her eyes to adjust from the porch light to the nearly full darkness. From hunting for specimens on Earth, she knew to look for movement and shape, rather than color or sound. Whatever it was, it was small and furtive, she sensed that. So it was likely that even if it wasn't the green of the surrounding tube-grass, it would be a corresponding shade of gray or brown, something that would blend right in and fool any creature that couldn't see in full color in the dark. If it could move, it probably wasn't shaped like tube-grass.

She had no interest in trying to capture it, or do anything other than get a quick look. She knew the policy about alien life: it might be dangerous, and it might be intelligent.

She stopped and listened carefully. It was soon enough after Zharset that there was still a residual katabatic breeze, she studied it, learning the rise and fall of the sounds of its passage through the tube-grass. To her left, there was the faintest of squeaks, perhaps the sound of one tube being pressed against another by something moving past it.

She turned slowly and listened. She took an excruciating step forward. A second step.

There! She heard a rustle, and aimed her data pad. Bright light flooded the region, stroboscopically brightening as the camera whirred. Something small and gray with a pink appendage.

"Lose something, Becky?"

Startled, Rebekah dropped her data pad. Released, the light went out, leaving her blinking in the sudden darkness. "Who's there?" she demanded.

"It's me, Rudy. Do you need any help?"

Of all the damn times for the man to decide to be sociable! Later, Rebekah wondered why she didn't just tell him she dropped something. She even had a hair clip in her pocket that she could have slipped out and "found" after a couple of moments, sending Harlen on his way.

But she was startled, and said instead, "There's something moving in the tube-grass. I think it may be a small animal of some sort."

Harlen unpacked an object he had been carrying over his shoulder, which, Rebekah saw with some dismay, was a laser cutter. "Where is it?"

"Over there somewhere. You're not going to shoot it with that thing, are you?"

"Only if it attacks." He was breathing hard.

"Rudy! Don't be ridiculous," Rebekah hissed through her teeth. "It's tiny, whatever it is."

"Wasps are tiny compared to us. They can kill, though."

A minute passed, and then a second. Rebekah wondered how long Harlen could hold that laser cutter like that. The things weren't light, and with the mass mostly at the business end, not meant to be held like a rifle. She could see his upper arm beginning to quiver. She hoped it was just the awkward weight of the device that made his arm quake like that.

To her left, there was a sudden motion. She chucked her data pad at it, hoping to scare it off. At the same instant, the laser cutter flashed, burning a sharp edged ellipse in the tube-grass. But it wasn't where Rebekah had just tossed her data pad, to her relief. Were there two things?

Harlen was talking into his data pad. "Commander Sheffield? Could you please come to quadrant B-11 in Avale-rion? I've just shot something."

Sheffield's voice was sharp. "You shot someone? Who? Is this Rudy Harlen?"

"I just shot an animal of some sort."

There was a pause. "Stay right where you are. Do not move, do not fire again unless you are in danger. Is anyone with you?"

A glance. "Yes. Becky Cohen."

"Rebekah? Are you OK.?"

"Yes, Commander. But I don't know what Mr. Harlen shot. I can't see anything."

"Right. Don't move. Don't touch anything. I'll be right there."

Red, living next door, was first on the scene. He brought an ROV cam and tripod, and rapidly set it up to illuminate and record the site. He did so in utter silence, but Rebekah could see he was livid with rage. She knew Harlen wasn't one of his favorite people anyway, and didn't imagine this was going to cement their relationship. Once set up, Red kept glancing at Rebekah, obviously wanting to pepper her with questions, doubtlessly wondering what her role was in all this. She gave her head a slight shake, hoping that would convey that this wasn't her idea.

Moments later, Sheffield himself came running up, puffing slightly. He was only about a hundred and fifty meters away, and probably ran at full speed. Rebekah hid a smile, thinking that at his age, Sheffield should be grateful for the light gravity and oxygen-rich air.

He pulled out a flashlight of his own and held it at the ready. "OK, Mister Harlen, what did you shoot?"

"I'm not sure. It was a creature, maybe fifty centimeters long. Grey, and it had pink tentacles."

Sheffield gave Harlen a level glare for a moment. He turned to the scorched area and began scanning. "Mister Farnsworth, would you examine that side?"

* * *

Red began looking along his side of the oval. He wasn't entirely sure what he was looking for. Body parts? Fur? Scales?

Tentacles? He doubted a full-power blast from the laser would have left much. It could cut through tube-grass mat, in fact that why Harlen probably had one in his possession, and a critter the size of a medium small dog wouldn't have much of a chance.

He scanned, stopped, peered. "Um, Commander?" He shone his light on a pink tubular object, about two centimeters long. "I think I found a tentacle."

Chapter 33 A Showdown at Tombstone

SHEFFIELD GLOWERED. "*Peromyscus leucopus*? What the hell is that when it's at home?"

Vargas shook his head. "It's the American white-footed mouse."

"Mouse?"

"Mouse. From Earth. As you might imagine, Commander, I have people searching *Phoenix* from stem to stern, looking for any signs of infestation. I would dearly love to know how a colony of mice could have escaped the attention of everyone on board this ship for twenty-seven years."

Sheffield shook his head. "So that idiot took a laser cannon and shot a mouse."

"I suppose we're lucky the tip of the tail somehow survived. It could have been worse. If nothing remained, we would be grappling with the issue of how to punish Harlen for killing the first alien creature we encountered. As it is, there's no regulation against killing mice."

"There is that, I suppose. I take it there's absolutely no possibility the genetic match is incorrect. This is an Earth mouse?"

Vargas nodded. "Unless mice have conquered the universe, in which case we all apologize to Douglas Adams and go insane."

"Who?"

"Never mind. I've got people from housekeeping, from stocks, from quartermaster, from the kitchens, and they are all swearing up and down there is absolutely no sign of infestation on board the *Phoenix*. No Charlie has ever seen a mouse. Given the decontamination measures we all went through and the far more severe ones the ship went through before departure, I don't see how any mouse could have come aboard. Of course, mice do the impossible. Scientists went and visited the site of the Apollo 16 landing site on the Moon and found a desiccated mouse carcass in the LEM lander. They can go anywhere men can go."

"If they have a supply of food and water that can last them twenty-seven years. . . " Sheffield tapped his upper lip. "No. If they had that type of food supply, they would have had a population explosion and someone would have found the carcasses. Somebody maybe snuck them aboard as pets?"

"That at least is in the realm of possibility, but I can't imagine why anyone would. But you are thinking the same thing I am, aren't you?

Sheffield nodded. "I'll ask around, see if anyone here is raising mice."

"If you find them, ask them why in the hell they're doing that, OK.?"

"Ser."

* * *

For Rudy Harlen, the Great Mouse Hunt was a social disaster. While no camera had caught the actual shooting, Rebekah's had caught him reporting to the Commander that he had shot a gray creature a half a meter long with tentacles. Copies of that showed up on every data pad in camp.

Rudy had a particularly rough time with hibernation syndrome, and was still hit hard by flash-dreams, experiencing three or four a day. Most people had one or two such events, and found them interesting, or at worst irritating. Rudy found them frightening. One featured attacks by large faceless creatures. It would repeat itself for a week at a time, and left him in a simmering stew of unease and fretfulness.

Worse, he felt that he was only half the engineer that he had been back on Earth. Calculations that he could easily do in his head he now had to laboriously enter and check on his data pad. He kept having to look up everyday items such as angle of repose, or cosines—not just the formulae, the basic theory underlying them and why they were necessary.

He felt like a fraud. But when he tried to confront that feeling, his thoughts always veered toward anger at the people who put him in hibernation knowing it would damage him, and the sloppy leadership of the ship that had them effectively stuck on a planet not meant for human life.

The mouse incident grated. Rudy was honest enough to realize his embarrassment was self-inflicted. He resolved to do something to exculpate himself. Maybe he could find out where the mice came from, and failing that, at least learn what they were doing.

To that end, he began gathering equipment.

* * *

Red wondered if Jim and Sylvie were beginning to lose interest in the ROVER project. It had been several little years since the discovery of the "fish", and the ROVER had swung away from the promising jungles of the trans-Boitumelo lowlands and gone up the slopes of the giant crater, where it was hoped it would find mineral deposits.

Lasering chunks of rock and making spectrograph analysis of the vapor was boring work, made more tedious by the lack of promising results. Worse, they were encountering a lot of down time. The craft wasn't rated for night flight, and with the big fall equinox coming, in little winter daylight was only a couple of hours, and weak at that. Half the time was spent simply looking for a safe place to put down for the night. When light conditions were good, the winds would come up, and the ROVER would be grounded by the erratic and powerful gusts that swirled around the vast mountain ridges. And it was limited in the areas it could go, hugging south-facing slopes in order to maintain line-of-sight with *Phoenix*, which at this latitude was very low in the sky. As a result, there were days when one or both of the kids didn't show up at all. Red wasn't inclined to complain; he wasn't paying them, and usually there was barely enough going on to justify his own presence. The wild and barren slopes had no plant life, let alone animal life. No, not even a mouse, still the only land animal discovered on Hoyl.

With the ROVER on extended away status, there was no need to huddle inside the noisy and uncomfortable shed, so Red hauled the control equipment to his own home. This was another reason why he wasn't upset with the kids for no-showing. If he did need help, all he had to do was call three houses down the street, and one or both would be there within minutes. Not that he needed to call all that often. If they were finding other ways to fill their time, Red couldn't blame them.

He was putting in his time devising a ROVER that could make an uninterrupted flight to the Southern Continent. It would have to survive the scorching temperatures at the equator, and he was working on a carapace that would allow it to put down on water, and considering grapple claws that would allow it to "sleep" at night by clinging to the trunk of a tree. In reality, he could probably just ask the Captain to authorize a shuttle flight to the southern continent to drop a ROVER off, but for Red, the challenges of the design were their own justification. He kept busy that way, aware that a bored Red was a dangerous Red.

Red hadn't been around teenagers much since he was one himself, but he could tell the Spencer kids had some project going on that they weren't talking about. He hoped without conviction that perhaps they were working on possible improvements to the ROVER.

He found himself spending more and more time in Rebekah's company. Everyone else still seemed traumatized by Ice Fall, but he shared Rebekah's continued enjoyment of the Light Show. They devised a silly but engaging project, measuring the length, period and frequency of the lightening bursts on Hō-ō, and then running them through the ship's decryption program, looking for meaning in the apparently random bursts. So far the system had determined that they were, in fact, random bursts. It did, however, get them a complimentary call from an amused-sounding Captain Vargas, who noted that they had devised a path of exploration that everyone on board had totally missed, and that Simmons and the rest were watching their results with considerable interest.

Red suspected that the people on the ship where bored, too. Not Simmons, of course; moving one billionth of a percent across the diameter of the universe had made it an entirely new universe to Simmons, who was perfectly happy to inspect measurements to one hundred significant digits. As for Vargas, Red knew how bored he must feel. During the first watch they had shared after leaving Dry Dock, Vargas had spoken at length of his dream of clearing forest and starting a homestead. He wanted to reach a point where he could leave the ship in permanent orbit and come down and spend the rest of his life exploring and farming. Red finally asked how he planned on combining those two avocations, which seemed to conflict with one another. Vargas had simply smiled and said he hoped he would know which path to take when the road forked, and never look back.

* * *

For Rebekah, the third time seemed to be the charm. Her crops had already lived long enough to transition from seedlings to young mature plants, and she had hopes of a food crop within three little years. Too small a crop to be of significant use to the colony, but an immense step forward nonetheless. She was getting considerable fulfillment from all her little green babies.

Red was a good-natured man, and didn't envy her this. But he knew, in his heart of hearts, that he was getting bored.

And a bored Red was a dangerous Red.

* * *

Dan Vargas wasn't bored. He was intensely restless. He felt the pressures of leadership, particularly the loneliness. Julie's presence made an impossible demand merely an unpalatable one. But he wasn't bored.

He poured over the results of what the on-board crew had nicknamed the "Red Rover Program" double checking for signs of the minerals needed to make *Phoenix* deep-space-worthy again. Without the assurance that *Phoenix* could travel to the next star, there was no serious hope of persuading the colonists to pack up and move on.

Worse, the same problems that made *Phoenix* an unacceptable risk for interstellar flight also made it unacceptable for interplanetary flight. The thrusters couldn't move the behemoth ship to Disappointment, and the shuttles, while they had the fuel to do it, didn't have the resources to keep a crew of even two alive for the minimum of six weeks such a trip would entail. Disappointment may only be fifteen light minutes away, but as far as the colonists were concerned, it might as well be in Andromeda.

Disappointment had the mineral wealth needed. Hoyl remained a question mark.

In the meantime, he had Simmons and his team paying unbroken attention to the rings of Hō-ō. Simmons had protested, with justification, that they couldn't possibly identify the millions of objects that were large enough to be a threat to the colony, and even if they could, the chaotic jostling of the objects in the ring made reliable orbital projections meaningless. Given the same scenario as the last Ice Fall, the best Simmons could promise was two hours warning—and he wasn't willing to guarantee that.

And Daniel Vargas was often lonely. Julie was usually down in Scafeld, and while not as busy as Dan, happier, although she professed her undying resolve to be reunited. Dan didn't doubt that, but it did little to make his Spartan cabin a warmer place on the ship.

The Great Mouse Hunt, while entertaining, hadn't turned up so much as a single mouse turd. The crew had entertained themselves imagining all the myriad places a mouse might hide in the vast ship and inspecting them. He heard that there was something being offered to the first crewman to kill a mouse called the Rudy Harlen Prize, which apparently involved a golden mousetrap and some illegal ship hooch. Somewhat more positively, Dan offered a week off at Avalerion for what he deemed the most inventive plausible hiding place a mouse might find. The humor of the situation helped. A bit.

Frustrated, Dan Vargas fell endlessly with his ship through the skies of Hoyl and watched the universe recede.

* * *

Rudy had spent a fairly productive day with Commander Sheffield and Cyril Voss planning the Styx Bridge. Vargas had told Sheffield that he could go ahead and build it, provided he used only native materials. No ship raw materials, in particular any metals, were to be used. Rudy was ecstatic at the opportunity to show what steel-wood and tube-grass could do. The bridge need only traverse ten meters of not very deep water, but he resolved to build a structure that would inspire awe. He had the enthusiastic support of Sheffield and Voss, who had no doubt a credible bridge could be built with those two remarkable materials.

The day had been spent countersinking test pylons on the Avalerion side of the Styx. Rudy envisioned a single-tower suspension bridge, ten meters wide, and capable of allowing the giant snow blower to traverse the span. As the tube-grass reformed around the pylons, it would act as a surrogate bedrock. It had been Rudy's idea to drill holes at the bottom and about half a meter up, allowing the tube-grass root mat to intertwine with the pylons. In the meantime, a modest, meter-wide footbridge permitted easy pedestrian travel between Scafeld and Avalerion.

Rudy was becoming the system's leading authority on tube-grass root. The stuff fascinated him. It had an utterly unique DNA, different from anything found on Hoyl, or Earth for that matter. That it was on Disappointment and somehow sequestered radon until it broke down into polonium, and then sequestered that until it broke down into lead, amazed him no end. He was on the teams that discovered the hyper-osmotic properties that allowed it to absorb water and propel it into a chamber with water pressure thousands of times higher. This was why the Styx didn't flood during the super cell rainstorms.

He had been planning to monitor its behavior at night anyway, and now he had the equipment ready.

He was in a good mood when he returned to his home. Then he saw the tombstone.

It wasn't very big, perhaps a hundred and fifty millimeters, but it was right next to his front door where he couldn't miss it. Perplexed, he bent down to read the script laser-etched into the face of the tombstone.

"In Memory of Mickey, a Mouse who was murdered savagely and died nobly in the performance of his mousey duties. May he rest in atomic pieces."

Suddenly in a cold fury, Rudy straightened up and glared around him. His eyes lit on Red's house, a few spaces down.

It could have been anyone in the settlement. Rudy knew that. Stones were plentiful over on the Scafeld side, and anyone could access a cutting laser to shape and inscribe the rock.

A thought struck Rudy and he went out and examined the tombstone. Silvery, vaguely planar...Rudy went over and poked at his data pad, compared the images to what he held. He wasn't a geologist, but it sure looked like he was holding a chunk of Chalcocite. Copper sulphide, it was high on the list of items Vargas had the colony searching for. If it came from Scafeld or the Landing. . . Rudy shook his head, Copper was high on the list of materials they so desperately needed, and not much had been found save in the Boitumelos at ten thousand meters and above. Mining it would be a daunting task. They had been scouring the planet, and if Red, who had been doing the exploring, had picked up a piece of copper not fifty meters away without knowing what it was. . . Rudy grinned. If that were the case, he would get Red back for his prank.

Picking the tombstone up, Rudy went in and examined his gear. An assay of the mineral would have to wait until morning, and he probably wouldn't have an excuse to go over to Scafeld for a few days. But he was a decent amateur mineralogist, and once he knew the exact composition of this stone, he would know exactly what to look for.

He poured himself a beer and settled in his recreational alcove, most of his rage diffused. He knew that damned mouse incident would dog him for the rest of his life if he didn't do something about it, and in that instant, it came to him. What were the mice doing in the tube-grass, anyway? Were there any on the other side of the stream? Could mice eat tube-grass? It wasn't edible for humans, but mice could eat things humans couldn't.

He was already an expert on tube-grass. He was about to get some expertise on copper ore deposits. And now he had a third vocation. He was going to become an expert on mice.

He took a sip of his beer and looked at the tombstone again. OK, he had to admit it was pretty funny. But he was going to find out what the mice were doing, and more important, what they were going to do, and be remembered, not for a stupid mistake, but for sound study and reasoning.

And he wouldn't even have to blast any mice to kingdom come to do it. The thought caused Rudy to laugh, a sound that would have surprised his neighbors.

He felt the best he had since they had left Earth.

* * *

Red was the first to discover what a Hoyl hurricane was like. He was exploring Mount Edward IX, on the southwest side of the Boitumelos, and was rounding an innocent looking outcropping when his craft was caught by winds of incomprehensible strength. On slow-motion replay, Red could see the wings disintegrate in the blast, and the craft plummeted helplessly, bouncing down the rocky slope. When it finally came to rest, the camera was miraculously still recording, and Red could see enough of the ROVER to realize that it was a total.

For a horrid moment he wondered if there had been another Ice Fall. He was able to turn the camera skyward with some difficulty, and it showed the cliff edge, with streams of what he took to be white ribbons. It took him a few moments to realize that he was looking at ice, or water vapor. Contrails from shocked air passing over the edge of the rock. No wonder his poor ROVER had been torn apart.

He called *Phoenix*. Keeping his voice deliberately calm, he asked, "Any weather around the Boitumelos I need to know about?"

Morley answered. "There's a big one on the southeast side, Red. I would call it a hyper hurricane, so stay well away from it. But you should be OK where you are."

"Where I am? Where's that supposed to be?"

"Mount Bécquer. Am I mistaken?"

Damn. He had left Mount Bécquer three hundred and fifty kilometers behind on an impulse decision to check the escarpment along Edward IX. Sylvie had been supposed to relay the revised itinerary up to the ship's climatological section. Damn the girl. . .

No. Damn him. He should have checked to make sure it had been done. It was, after all, unknown territory.

"Is the storm any threat to the colony?"

"No. It'll spend itself on the Plug. We should be fine."

Except for the ROVER, of course. Red ended the call and called Vargas. He would need a new dragonfly, but he had a few design revisions he wanted to run past Janice and the Captain first.

* * *

As if Red's day wasn't bad enough, his data pad flashed the news that copper had been discovered in, of all places, Scafeld. The implications weren't hard to catch: he had been on an odyssey of thousands of kilometers, and one of the minerals he was looking for, one of the most important ones, had been literally below his feet.

Rudy gave a presentation from his home. He cautioned that it wasn't a big find, and that the copper ore might be little more than 'scatter' from a previous ice fall, but there were at least several hundred tons of good quality copper ore to be found at the site.

Red nodded approvingly. He didn't like being beaten to the punch—who did? But it was too important for such petty resentments. Besides, he had already teased Harlen with that silly tombstone. As far as he was concerned, that squared things.

Rudy went on to say that his attention was brought to the Scafeld site when an amateur mineralogist dropped off a sample at his home several days ago. Examining it, he determined it was, in fact, copper, and a couple of days investigation led to the Scafeld find. He placed the rock in question on his test for the camera. Clearly visible on the front was an inscription, starting, "In Memory of Mickey, a Mouse. . . "

For a few moments Red forgot all about the destroyed ROVER.

Later, when he went out to join Rebekah for the Light Show, Rudy spotted him, and gave him a cheery smile and a wave. Red responded with a greeting his father had taught him, one to be used only on supporters of the rival Manchester City football club.

Rudy's smile slipped. Apparently he noticed that Red was not pleased. Good.

* * *

Two little years later, the Big Autumn Equinox arrived. The equinox would occur shortly after dawn following a "long night" a solar eclipse. Nobody thought to have any particular ceremonies marking the occasion; nobody attached any religious or spiritual significance to the event, and since Hoyl was in late little winter, it wasn't really an equinox on that moon. Just for the gas giant itself.

It was a memorable day.

Chapter 34 A Game Of Cat And Mouse

THE DAY BEFORE, AS THE EARLY AFTERNOON ZHAR PTITSA was 'setting' behind Hō-ō, Red got the welcome news that the engineering committee had approved his blueprints for ROVERII, complete with flotation carapace and tree grapples. In the winter, weather and luck permitting, he was going to explore the southern continent. He was afraid that Rudy Harlen might vote against it and scupper the deal, but apparently he couldn't find any flaw in Red's plans.

Jim and Sylvie sat in their home and discussed approaching the Captain the day after the ellipse, after the Hoyliday. They had decided it was time to come clean and admit they had committed some fairly serious rule violations.

Julie Steinberg was preparing to take the afternoon shuttle down to Avalerion following the eclipse and had just about convinced Dan to come along for a break. The Captain was ready for a break, and things were generally pretty quiet.

The calm ended about a half hour after the eclipse began, when Rudy happened to glance at his lawn monitors to see if there was any mouse activity in the tube-grass. He would see one once in a while, scurrying about its business, but he hadn't detected any patterns to tell him where they were coming from and where they were going. He particularly wanted to know what they were eating. It wasn't the tube-grass, he was pretty sure. He'd never seen one of the constant nibblers gnaw on a stalk. So someone was feeding them.

He stared, transfixed, at what he saw on the screen. Between the residual light from Hō-ō and his porch illumination, the little drama was playing itself out in natural color.

It wasn't what the mice were doing that transfixed him, although it was pretty significant in itself. It was the unexpected company that was watching them. Rudy glanced to ensure this was all being recorded. This was going to blow everyone away.

* * *

The Spencers and Doctor Trapp had joined Captain Vargas and Julie Steinberg for dinner in the bridge mess. Trapp had developed the habit of spending a little year on *Phoenix*, and the next little year at Avalerion, and was going down on the shuttle with Vargas and Steinberg the next day. On a vessel where a doctor was rarely needed, Vargas decided he could risk having the entire medical staff on the ground at once. Adelena Conti was licensed as a nurse and midwife, and while the mission had yet to experience a pregnancy, she had enough practical experience to oversee sick bay.

The discussion would have appalled Red. Alan and Ian were arguing strenuously that robotic exploration was all fine and good, but the colony really needed to get a shuttle full of people down there on the ground, because nothing beat hands-on exploration. "Look how much more we learned about Mars once the first manned landing occurred," Trapp said.

"Alan, we learned a lot about Mars before that mission went. Even in the early twenty-first century, we knew how much radiation the astronauts would have to absorb. We knew what temperatures they would experience, we knew where they could drill for ice, and we knew Mars had no pathogens or other life that could hurt them. Red's dragonfly is going to do the same thing for us. I would like to have a solid grip on what potential dangers awaited before sending any of my people in."

"OK, I see that, but this isn't Mars. Even that dragonfly thing can get there in a week, we know there's air, and we came prepared for unknown dangers on a strange, but habitable world. Why not just send a shuttle down with a landing party?"

"It's very simple. . . " Vargas' data pad flashed red. He gave the table an apologetic glance, and tapped the pad. "Yes, Mister Harlen?"

"Captain, I have major news regarding the mice."

From down the table, Vargas heard Trapp mutter, "Oh, gods, I hope he hasn't shot another one." Resolutely keeping a straight face, Vargas replied, "Can this wait until morning?"

"Captain, please. Watch this. It's less than two minutes long." The image changed to a ground level camera shot into tube-grass. The grass was green, but the sky suggested it was night time. Out of courtesy, Vargas switched the display to holo-gram so everyone at the table could view it.

After a moment, a mouse came into view with the curious hopping gait the mice seemed to like in Hoyl's lower gravity. It stood on its hind legs, sniffing the air, and then grabbed a stalk of tube-grass and began chewing.

"Pause it," Vargas commanded. The image froze. "They can eat tube-grass?"

"I think he's just sample nibbling the way mice do, Captain."

Vargas thought rapidly. This three hundred square kilometer field of tube-grass was a handful of known places on Hoyl where it grew. It also grew on Disappointment, but was fantasti-cally toxic there. And it was too valuable a resource to permit unchecked predation.

"Captain, there's more."

"Go on."

The image resumed, and the viewers saw the tube-grass be-hind the mouse slowly parting. There was a flash of motion, and the mouse was pinned beneath one paw. It had time to emit one anguished squeak before the cat bit off its head. The cat, appar-ently aware of the camera in some way, looked up and stared di-rectly into the lens. It's face had a distinctive circle of white around one eye in an otherwise black face, an unusual marking.

Spencer was on his feet, staring at the image with his jaw hanging open.

"Tipsy?" he said.

Slowly, Vargas turned away from the giant image and to the psychologist. "Doctor Spencer, are you saying you *know* this cat?"

"Yes. It was our family pet in England. We gave it to the shel-ter fifty four years ago."

"Fifty years ago. That's quite a spry cat. Did you take the cat to the shelter yourself?"

Maureen and Ian exchanged a glance. "Jim, our elder, did." Maureen said.

"To put up for adoption," Ian added.

"It looks like there was a change of plans," Vargas said.

The image of Tipsy picked up the mouse carcass and turned and moved out of camera range. Julie leaned forward. "Mr. Harlen, could you replay that last bit? The last ten seconds? Freeze when the cat has its side to the camera."

Tipsy strode backward and deftly placed the mouse's head back on its shoulders. Then tore it off again, eyed the camera, picked up the body, and turned to. . . and stopped in mid stride.

"There, you see?" Julie was pointing at the cat's midriff.

"See what?" Vargas wasn't quite sure what Julie was pointing at. He heard Ian gasp.

"Distended nipples. That's why the kitty's belly seems to be drooping. And notice she didn't play with the mouse. She attacked, dispatched it, and carried it off. If you've ever owned a cat, you know they like to play with their prey."

Vargas had never had a cat, but was familiar with the concept. He also knew that there was one reason for distended nipples. "Are you saying that cat is pregnant? There's more than one cat?"

"I'm saying that cat is a mommy, and she's weaning her kittens. Soon she'll have them out with her, and be teaching them to catch mice."

Vargas gave Ian a long, level stare. It wasn't the murderous glower Lassiter once got, but it was definitely a sign of a displeased Captain. After a moment, the psychologist gripped his wife's hand and nodded slightly.

"Commander Sheffield."

"Ser?"

"Dispatch a group of men to the residence of Jim and Sylvie Spencer. Place them under house arrest, and seize and secure any animals you may find in the premises. Also look for scientific equipment that may be used for cloning." A thought struck Vargas. It could be the same individual cat. "Or hibernation pods suitable for small animals."

There was a pause on the other end. Sheffield said, doubtfully. "House arrest, Jim and Sylvie Spencer. Seize animals and equipment. I'll do it immediately, Ser."

"Very good."

Vargas signed off after thanking Harlen, and glanced up to catch a glimpse of the stricken expression on Maureen Spencer's face. This was definitely going to put a crimp in the festive air of the dinner. "Maureen, I don't think there's much we can do to the kids other than yell at them for gross negligence. But I have to get this situation contained as soon as possible."

Trapp spoke up. "We have a more serious problem. That mouse may have been eating the tube-grass."

"Thank you doctor. That was my next call." He paused for a minute, brow furrowed in thought. "Mister Bissont, what is your location?"

There was a pause. "I'm in Avalerion, Ser."

"What do we have at hand that can kill mice but won't hurt tube-grass?"

For such a strange question, Bissont's response was admirably quick. "That would be just about anything that can kill mice, Ser. I'm not even sure a nuclear blast would kill tube-grass. Coherent light and extreme heat or cold seem to be the only things that stop it permanently."

"OK, let me rephrase that. What do we have that will kill mice but not present a significant hazard to the colonists?"

"Ah. That's a bit trickier. Do we know the range of the infestation?"

"No. I'm assuming it's limited to the immediate area of the colony, though."

"We could always establish a perimeter and place a toxin along that perimeter. It would have to be renewed every few days and after each rain storm because the tube-grass will just absorb it, chelate it, and send it off to sea."

Trapp spoke. "Excuse me, Mister. Did you say 'chelate'"

"Ser. We think that's what it does. Radioactives, toxins, anything. It's a natural ground cleanser." Trapp looked startled.

Vargas considered. "What about mice within the perimeter?"

"Hm. That's a bit more problematic. Poisoned bait, perhaps?"

Vargas wondered if the damage was already done. Humanity's war against mice had gone on for millennia—and the mice always at least held their own.

Vargas glanced up to see Ian and Maureen giving him stricken looks. Both were quite capable of grasping why Vargas was so concerned for the plant.

"Ian, Maureen, I am willing to leave the exact manner of discipline or punishment in your hands, with one proviso."

"Establish their guilt and negligence?"

"OK, two provisos. That, and show them footage of the mice swarms that plague Australia. Make sure they understand that they may have done immense damage to the ecology, and have threatened the very existence of the most valuable resource we've found on this world."

He glared at Ian. "If they had done anything like this back on Earth in environmentally sensitive zones such as Hawaii, they would have been looking at prison and huge fines. Plus who knows what kind of lawsuits. We haven't got a government here yet, and what they did is outside of my jurisdiction as captain of this ship. I could charge them with smuggling proscribed materials, but we don't have a brig.

"I realize you both have a sense of what the gravity of the situation is, but let me spell it out for you. Mice can reproduce at an unbelievable rate, and are subject to population explosions. A pair of mice got loose in northern Australia back in the nineteenth century, and in the centuries since, they have had mice-swarms; the grain has a bountiful year, and the mice subsequently have a population explosion. The following year there is a shortage in the food supply, and they go swarming out in all directions seeking food. Billions of them. They can destroy entire crops overnight. They go everywhere, get into everything. There's so many of them that the people wind up abandoning their homes and farms because they go to bed at night and in the morning find there's a dozen mice that have climbed into bed with them. Human babies are in physical danger because a swarm of mice can attack and eat a baby. It's a nightmare."

"Your children have released mice into an environment where there may be an unlimited food supply. I'm hoping against hope that mouse was just desperate and sampling the tube-grass, and they can't really eat it. Because with an unlimited food supply and no natural predators, we're going to have mice swarms. Forever."

"Make them understand what they've done. And if they did do it, I want them to write and sign an apology to the colony. Even if we manage to eliminate the mice, they recklessly put the colony at risk. Any questions?"

There were none.

* * *

Sheffield glared at Jim and Sylvie. "I want you both to know," he ground out, "that if it was up to me, your asses would be back in hibernation and the rest of us would forget you were even there. But our Captain happened to get the happy news that you may have severely damaged the colony while he was having dinner with your parents, and that apparently softened his heart. And perhaps his head.

"So he has told me that your parents will be disciplining you. I would dearly love to persuade them to ignore any and all child-abuse laws they were raised under. Unfortunately, they probably love you, although I'm sure they are wondering why about now."

Both the Spencers sat perfectly still, heads down. He watched as the boy gulped, and hoped the girl was at least as scared.

"Now, what I need to know, so I can tell the Captain and your parents, is why you did this? What on Earth made you think the welfare of this colony could be improved by unleashing a plague of mice?"

Jim muttered something.

"What was that?"

Jim looked up at Sheffield. Sheffield didn't like the sullen glare the boy wore. He had to resist an urge to slap it off the boy's face. "We needed cat food. We couldn't requisition meat without raising questions. Grain, however, we could get; all we wanted. So we needed to convert the grain into meat."

"Why mice? Why not. . . I don't know. Hedgehogs? Cats eat hedgehogs."

Sylvie spoke defiantly. "And hedgehogs eat insects. Should we introduce flies and mosquitoes to feed the hedgehog?"

Sheffield had to remind himself they were underage civilians. "OK, but why not just tell someone you had a cat and needed meat?"

"If we told you, what would you have done?"

Sheffield almost sputtered. Damn the girl! He would have confiscated the cat and probably had it euthanized. But he couldn't say that. "It isn't that hard to get someone in stores to do you a favor. All you have to do is come up with the right bribe." It was common practice on large ships, and Sheffield himself availed himself of it from time to time. In return, he pretended not to know about the various stills both on *Phoenix* and in Avalerion, or that there was an agricultural patch outside of Lassiter's Landing where they were growing weed. Bending discipline a bit for good morale was a time honored military tradition. Unfortunately, these kids didn't have the background needed to realize that. As long as evidence of a cat wasn't pushed in his face, the kids would be getting away with it.

Sheffield's data pad flickered. "Let them in," he said.

The door opened, and Captain Vargas, Julie Steinberg and the Spencers were there. Ian and Maureen ran to their children. Sheffield was gratified to see they didn't coddle them, but simply asked if they were alright. Both kids gave noncommittal shrugs. The shrugs said clearly, "There's a crazy guy over there who wants to throw us in hibernation and throw away the key, and the Captain looks like he might enjoy watching, you guys think we're the biggest assholes on the planet and you're probably right, but other than that, we're just peachy-keen, ma."

Spencer caught the eye of each of his children in turn, and gave each a long, level stare. To Sheffield's gratification, he didn't seem happy with what he saw. "We will be discussing this at length. I thought I could trust you."

Both visibly flinched.

Spencer turned to Sheffield. "May I see the cat?"

"Cats. Plural. Right over there in that box."

Spencer looked startled and moved toward the crate. He glanced at the door. "Captain, could you. . . ?" he waved at the door.

Vargas rattled the knob and nodded. Secure. Sheffield wondered why the captain was just standing back. Obviously some decision had been reached that didn't involve him. He felt a surge of resentment at this captain who so managed to be high-handed and hands-off all at the same time.

Spencer lifted the lid and peered in. "Kittens? How many?"

"Four," Sylvie answered. They're three and a half little years old."

Ian ran the numbers. "Just weaning, then."

The mother cat languidly stood, and sniffed Ian's cupped hand. Then, with a chirp, she head butted the hand and purred, loudly.

Ian glanced toward the captain. "Well, I had been thinking they cloned the cat from Tipsy, but no. This is Tipsy." He reached in and picked up the unprotesting cat. "Yeah, you remember me, don't you?" He gave the cat a fond look. "You're having quite an adventure in this go-around, aren't you? Here you are, the oldest cat in the universe, the nearest Tom is fifty light years away, and you just had babies. Not many other cats can claim that, let me tell you." He suddenly frowned. "The nearest Tom *is* fifty light years away, right?" He glared at the teenagers. "There aren't any other cats you aren't telling me about?" Both shook their heads miserably.

Tipsy seemed unimpressed, but happy to see Ian. She curled in his arms and settled in.

"Right. So the last time I saw Tipsy here, you two were taking her to the Bristol Shelter to have her put up for adoption. Obviously, something went awry. Who's starters?"

"We got there, and they did a physical on her like they do, and the chap turned to us and said, 'This molly's pregnant. We can't have her then, can we?'"

Sylvie cut in. "Dad, we were besides ourselves. We didn't know anyone else who'd take her, especially what with her being preggers and all, and the only alternative was the pound.

One fortnight, and they gas her, kittens or no. I couldn't do that."

Even Sheffield nodded sympathetically.

"So you somehow sneaked her into hibernation. How?"

Jim pointed to the end of the table Sheffield was sitting at. There was a metal capsule, about a meter long and a quarter that wide. "They have hibernation chambers for cats. At the college. And for mice, as well. We got them there."

Ian's tone was sharp. "The college doesn't sell those, or give them away. Did you steal them?"

"No! We. . . got a little inventive with the truth."

"Humph. How inventive?"

"Well, we walked out of there with the chambers with the College's knowledge and consent."

Maureen heaved a knowing sigh. "What did you tell them?"

Sylvie spoke up. "It was my idea. I told Professor Higsby that we were going into space on an experimental flight, and wanted to know if he would like to have some experimental subjects on board so he could measure how they did in weightlessness. Nobody ever did test the chambers in weightlessness, you know."

Trapp looked thunderstruck. He opened his mouth to say something, and closed it.

"Higsby? Head of Biological Studies?"

"Yeah. You know, they really should have mandatory retirement, and the hell with tenure. Higgy should have stepped down. . . well, at least five years earlier." Maureen shook her head. "I had him as advisor for my post-doctorate thesis, and it was a nightmare. The man could barely tell a horse from a cow." She gave her children an arch glance. "And I made the mistake of ranting on about it in places where little pitchers have big ears. You decided to scam the old man, didn't you?"

"We promised to let him know the results as soon as we took the animals from hibernation and could test them." Sylvie said.

"We kept that promise, too," Jim added, "We had *Phoenix* broadcast them back about two months ago."

"Hm. Earth should get those results in about fifty years. Old Higsby will be. . . I guess one hundred and eighty years old. I'm sure he'll appreciate the results." Maureen chuckled.

"You didn't tell him where you were going, or that you were on the *Phoenix*, did you?"

Sylvie said, "Actually, we did. And to be fair, I think he understood how long it would take. But he seemed to think it might have scientific value, and said that it might make us better scientists and keep us out of trouble."

Sheffield shook his head. "Well, let's hope it made you better scientists, at least."

Trapp spoke up. "It may have scientific value, too. At least, indirectly. Remember we keep wondering why hibernation disorientation wasn't happening during the Earth tests? I think Sylvie just gave us a promising lead on that. None of the tests were done in micro-gravity. They were all Earthside."

"We had to do the thing with Tipsy, three rounds of sleep/wake," Jim said. "The first time, she just sat there and mewled piteously."

"Interesting," Trapp mused. "We tested hibernation on cats. They didn't respond like that. Of course, we didn't have them in hibernation for twenty six years, either. Or in zero gee."

"It bears further investigation, to be sure." Vargas turned to the teenagers. "So how did you get the animals on board?"

"In our duffels. Jim's was just long enough to accommodate Tipsy, and the solar panel was taped to the outside of his duffel so ambient light would power it."

"That wouldn't be enough power," Vargas objected.

"We didn't have readouts engaged. Nobody was there to read them anyway, and it's ninety percent of the power drain for a capsule."

"OK. And the mice were in Sylvie's duffel."

She nodded. "All in one chamber, twenty four of them, twelve of each."

"OK. One final question. Why did you set them loose?"

"We didn't intend to. Several mice got out about two little years ago, and we got three of the four back. The three came back in looking for food, and were starving. The fourth one got shot."

"So you formed the impression they couldn't eat tube-grass."

"We tried feeding it to them. They wouldn't eat it."

Trapp looked over at the mouse cage musingly. "That's what I would expect to hear. The stuff has a totally alien DNA, and I would be surprised if any Earth life could consume it and gain any nutrients. That's a pretty sturdy cage. May I ask who built it?"

"Does it matter, Doctor? He didn't know what it was for."

Trapp gave the cage another look. He had trouble imagining what else it could be used for other than to keep small animals, but decided not to press the matter. Word would get out eventually, he was sure.

"Captain, are we sure that mouse was actually eating the tube-grass?"

"The one, er, Tipsy decapitated? No, we don't know that. Mice will sample nibble. Jim, had that particular mouse been fed tube-grass before?"

"No, he was part of the third generation. That was the first time he saw it."

"And last. Thank you, Tipsy." Vargas looked around the table. "Does anybody else have any questions? No? Jim, Sylvie, do you have anything you want to add?"

Sylvie looked up through her eyelashes. "We're sorry?"

"We really are" Jim added. "We had a second escape, ten mice, three days ago, and we were going to tell you tomorrow."

"I wish you had made that particular choice when you first landed. Just by bringing the cat on board *Phoenix*, you negated weeks of sterilization procedures and millions of pounds of work. You've contaminated the biological structure here; even if we never have another escapee, which is highly unlikely, and even if mice can't eat tube-grass, they've left droppings which have whatever bacteria the parent mice may have been carrying. In theory, you might have even brought plague along."

Trapp shook his head in vigorous negation, but Vargas ignored him. "I understand your motivations, and there's no doubt in my mind that your intentions were benign. But you could have endangered the entire mission, and all for a pet cat. That's inexcusable.

"We agreed, all of us, in light of the fact that we have no formal authority or government in the settlement, that I would be the final arbiter of what your punishment should be. Your parents would devise it, but I do keep right of veto. Do you both acknowledge that you smuggled live animals aboard *Phoenix* against all regulations pertaining thereto, and that you were unable to contain said animals when you enlivened them here?"

Both Spencer kids nodded.

Vargas glared. "Speak up!"

"Yesser."

"Are there any mice that you can't account for beyond the ones that are here?"

"Six remaining," Jim relied in a small voice. "Two male and four female."

"Very well, My judgment, then. You are both sentenced to work 24 hours per little year cleaning and maintaining the community recycling plant. You will work out the specific times with the plant overseer, Mister Lassiter.

"You are wholly responsible for the care and feeding of the mice. They will be put in a structure that they cannot escape, and they will be the property of the scientific staff for experiments. As for the cats, we'll figure out what we can provide in the way of cat food. We have meat in stores on board ship, but it is not an unlimited supply, and I don't want people to go without for the sake of some stowaway cats. But they can't live on mice. I would have thought you knew that. But you will be responsible for their feeding and care."

Out of the corner of his eye Vargas could see Sheffield glaring, face red with anger. He wanted to build a stockade and give the kids at least a little year in there to reflect upon their sins.

Later, Vargas wished the hearings had been slated for just one day later. By then, nobody would have cared about what

Spencer called "cat and mouse games." Even Sheffield was no longer thinking about the unexpected pets by then. But he would remember that he had been angry at the Captain for what he saw as weak and indulgent leadership, and the corrosive influence of that would remain. The next meeting would have become irrelevant; the cat-and-mouse one meaningless. Almost.

Chapter 35 Should We Stay Or Should We Go?

ONCE IAN SPENCER'S FAMILY HAD LEFT, relief writ large on their faces, Lassiter, Simmons, Nate Harlen, Sorlund, Isaakson and Brülow joined them for a second, and in Vargas' mind, more important conference.

Sheffield had been surprised when he saw that nearly all the line officers had accompanied Vargas down from the *Phoenix*. Given that, the scheduled second meeting seemed inevitable. As usual, the high-handed captain had not bothered to include him in what was going on.

Vargas looked around. "Um, this might take a while. Commander, would you summon someone to see to food and refreshment for everyone who might want some?"

Great, Sheffield thought. Now I'm his butler. But he had a crewman come in and in short order, snacks and refreshments were on the table.

Vargas reached into his travel pouch and pulled out a bottle and presented it to Sheffield. "Compliments of the Captain, Number One, for the superb job you've done establishing the colony."

Sheffield looked at the bottle, and his jaw dropped. It was a brandy, fifteen years old when they pulled out of Dry Dock. Irreplaceable now. He summoned his aide, and had him provide the good Commanders' crystal and pour shots for everyone. Now somewhat mollified, he resumed his seat and waited for what he suspected was news he didn't want to hear. He knew social lubrication when he saw it, the polite term for a bribe.

"Right. We've been putting a lot of study into Hoyl. Even though our ground explorations have been, of necessity, somewhat limited, we've learned a lot about this strange world." Vargas pretended to study his notes for a moment, checking the order.

"I know you all know this already, but let me recap some of the salient physical properties. Rotation is 23 hours and 36 minutes. Gravity is 77% of Earth's. Oxygen is 26%, which normally would be an unsafe level, but is mitigated by the altitude we live at. There is no known land animal life—other than what we've brought, of course, but there is aquatic life of some sort. Plant life abounds, and with the exception of tube-grass, is of a nature that would not be considered extraordinary if it appeared on Earth. We know that some varieties of plant are edible.

"We've discovered two remarkable resources on this world. There are the steel-wood trees, some of which, I'm told, may be two thousand years old. The wood is of excellent quality for construction. The other resource is tube-grass, which can be spun into immensely strong, flame-resistant fibers and thus into cloth of extraordinary strength and durability. Those two products alone have made our sojourn here worthwhile.

"We have experienced considerable physical and emotional dislocation living on this world. Nearly all of it is unsuitable for human life, due to the extreme heat of the lower altitudes. We are compelled to cover ourselves to protect against the rays of Zhar-Ptitsa during daylight hours." Vargas self-consciously flapped his sleeves, to the amusement of the watchers. "The days are too short, and the Zharrises and Zharsets are erratic, and it is causing problems for our Circadian rhythms. As a result, people, especially people here on the ground, are finding that they are touchy, grouchy, and finding it difficult to focus. Depression is becoming pandemic. This is probably aggravated by the aftereffects of hibernation syndrome. Even with the eclipse periods, people find themselves short on sleep, and while we've been able to mitigate the effects of the full Hō-ō with artificial lights, it represents yet another limitation on the suitability of this place to our needs.

"The fact that the surrounding forested terrain survived the shock wave and blizzard that resulted from the Ice Fall, combined with the disturbing equinoctial storms like the one that destroyed the ROVER suggests that the mere fact that this region has vegetation does not mean the weather is as mild as that found on Earth. We also know that tube-grass can survive an Ice Fall and blizzard, as ours has, and that only persistent sub-zero cold can stop its spread, or temperatures persistently above about seventy five. Our meteorologists are concerned that winter storms here may be so fierce as to make the colony unsustainable. Closer examination of the vegetation shows that it can handle extraordinary transitory extremes of wind, temperature, and precipitation. The Ice Fall proved that beyond doubt.

"We suspect that Hoyl is resource-poor. The core is nickel-iron, and appears to be solid. Without tectonic movements, it's unlikely that much in the way of heavy elements other than nickel or iron will be readily accessible.

"This, in turn, means we are utterly depending on the magnetic field of Hō-ō to protect us. Our own field is a resonant result of the larger magnetic field in which we are embedded. And Ho-o's field, like that of most gas giants, is not reliable. We have measured 'flickers' in the field, and we believe it reverses fairly frequently, and we should not depend on it to protect us from corneal mass ejections or cosmic rays.

"Not only is Hoyl limited in what it can offer us, but it threatens to kill us at any given moment. Mister Simmons has been studying the makeup of Hoyl in light of the Ice Fall, and taken a much closer look at the rings. Mister Simmons has drawn the disturbing conclusion that Hoyl is struck by a projectile of the velocity we experienced an average of once a year." Shocked gasps echoed around the table. "Those are Hōvian years, of course, but still. . . "

Vargas shuffled his notes, letting everyone consider what had been said while he prepared the big blow. There was probably nothing he had said other than the frequency of Ice Falls that came as any particular surprise to any of the people around the table. They had all heard these facts before, although he suspected nobody had heard them all put together like that.

"Most of you will recall that when we were trying to determine some sort of time-keeping system, we discovered that the rotation of Hoyl was slowing. Initial measurements suggested that Hoyl might be tidally locked in fifty thousand years, but Mister Simmons and his people have been able to refine their measurements, and believe the time of tidal locking will be. . . " He glanced at Simmons.

"Thirty-two thousand, one hundred and forty-three years, and three hundred and eighty-eight days. Hōvian years, that is."

"Call it fifty thousand Earth years. Now, most of you don't consider that particularly relevant to your daily lives, beyond the fact that it made a standardized calendar and time-keeping system based on Hoyl's movements impossible. But it begged a question: if Hoyl's rotation is slowing that rapidly, what was the fastest speed it could have possibly had and survived as a planet? In other words, how fast could it spin before losing its atmosphere, its oceans, or even coming apart from centrifugal force? And given its current rate of slowing, how long ago was that? Mister Simmons?"

"Our models now show that this world cannot possibly be more than thirty thousand years old, and probably about twenty thousand."

"Thank you. I should note that Mister Simmons has put in hundreds of hours of very hard work, along with his people, to come up with those two short answers.

"Obviously, the *nu Phoenicis* system is older than that, billions of years, certainly. Hoyl is a piece of space junk that just happened to fall into orbit around Hō-ō." Vargas looked at the utterly still faces that were looking back at him. "In our home system, there are moons of some of the gas giants that we believe had similar starts. We figured that out because the orbits were highly elliptical, or outside the plane of the ellipse.

"Hoyl's orbit is not elliptical, or outside the plane of Ho-o's ellipse. We are squarely over the planet's equator, immediately outside the rings. Pretty amazing, huh? Orbits do tend to, excuse me, gravitate to equatorial planes over time, but Hoyl has less than half a percent eccentricity in relation to the planet. That's far less than any of her several-dozen naturally occurring moons. Hō-ō's ring has a 'braid' in it that is gravitational turbulence caused by Hoyl's orbit. So it has been in this orbit for at least..." Vargas gave Simmons an expectant look.

"I estimate from the 'braiding' that Hoyl has been in this orbit not longer than three thousand years."

"So here we are, on a world that cannot possibly be more than three thousand years old. On Earth, humans had already reached the hunter-gatherer stage, made jewelry and other body decorations, wore clothing, devised religions, and domesticated crops, if not animals. It was early in human history, but a blink of the eye for Earth. Earth needed a billion years just to get an oxygen atmosphere. And another two billion before plant life on land began.

"Yet we have a world that three thousand years old, and has vast, mature forests, deep oceans, an oxygen-rich atmosphere, and is in a perfect orbit to be hit frequently by flying icebergs, adding to the already large amount of water. It was solid when it got here—some of Simmons people think it was actually a large comet–but it hasn't been here long enough for friction from tidal stresses to liquefy the core.

"This permits only one conclusion. This place cannot possibly exist. And yet here we are.

"Hoyl is a construct. It is artificial. It is here because someone, for their own purposes, put it here. This world is someone's project, and we are trespassing on it."

There was utter silence for a moment, broken by loud laughter from Sheffield. Vargas stared at him, puzzled. He expected a variety of responses, but that wasn't one of them.

"Oh, Captain," Sheffield finally gasped. "I can't believe that you would pull the 'Blind Watchmaker' on us!"

"The what?"

Sheffield was still laughing. It struck Vargas as a bit theatrical. Nate Harlen spoke up.

"He actually means 'the Watchmaker argument'. It's a teleological argument, that any mechanism of sufficient complexity requires a conscious creator. It's used to assert that the universe had an intelligent creator."

"Where does 'blind' come into it?"

"It doesn't, Captain. 'The Blind Watchmaker' is a book from a couple of hundred years ago that refuted the Watchmaker allegory. Richard Dockings. Or maybe it was Dawkins."

"Mister Sheffield." Vargas waited patiently for his second-in-command to stop laughing and respond. He spotted Spencer peering at Sheffield with some concern, and wondered what the psychologist was making of this response. "Mister Sheffield?"

Sheffield's paroxysm was subsiding. He held up a hand, palm out, to ask for patience and nodded his head. He good a deep breath and stared at the Captain.

"Damn you, Vargas, I knew you were going to pull this. I figured you were planning this from the time you realized your authority as Captain was pretty much meaningless here on the ground."

"I'm not following what you're saying, Commander. If you're claiming I'm exerting unearned authority here, I'll point out that I'm not giving orders, but merely laying out the details of our situation."

"And yet you're here to tell us that we have to undo all the work we've done here and obediently get back on *Phoenix* and go who-knows-where because the world might end in twenty thousand years? No. That's not going to happen. People are invested here, they are building a home. Do you really think you can scare them by inventing alien overlords who want their property back?"

Vargas looked perplexed. "Alien overlords? No, I'm saying that this entire world is an artificial construct, and very clearly a work-in-progress. And my own gut feeling is that our role in a project like this is that of contamination. In effect, we may be doing what we just punished Ian's kids for doing a few minutes ago and contaminating a bioregion."

"Alien overlords." Sheffield's tone was flat.

"OK, so you don't believe this world is artificial. I hope you'll take a closer look at the work Simmon's team has done. I have, and the conclusion is inescapable. Those forests. . . " Vargas hooked a thumb over his shoulder in the direction of the Styx "are there because someone planted them. They didn't evolve in just a thousand years. Lieutenant Commander Sorlund has been analyzing the samples that your people have been sending up. Mister Sorlund?"

"Ser. Carbon-14 dating suggests nothing that's older than about three thousand years. Nobody has discovered anything that could even be remotely considered a fossil, despite the lack of plate tectonics. We go to ponds and probe, and the muck on the bottom is never more than a couple of inches deep. It's like this place has no paleological record at all."

Vargas nodded his thanks. "Commander, the Americas used to be notorious for people who believed the world was only six thousand years old, and that a divinity created all life forms as they are in one fell swoop. They actually amassed enough political clout to get governments that shared their beliefs in power before the whole thing collapsed under its own absurdity. I did a paper in high school on how patently absurd their beliefs were, and how they would cling to them no matter what.

"So it's with no small sense of irony that I assure you that this world is only three thousand years old, and it was fabricated by someone. I don't know who the fabricators are, or even if they would be inclined to be willing to suffer our presence if and when they return, but they can create entire worlds. They have a technology far ahead of ours.

"But they may not show up for another twenty thousand years. It may be that Hoyl was put into this orbit on the outer edge of the rings for the purpose of accumulating water. I would note that if there is one thing this world does not lack, it is water. Indeed, Mister Simmons mentioned in his report that in about twelve hundred years this spot might be under water because the constant ice falls are raising the water level by up to three meters a year. Nearly all those shooting stars we see are ice, you know. Big ice falls only make up a fraction of what hits this moon.

"I don't need alien overlords to explain why we shouldn't settle here. The last Ice Fall was fifteen hundred kilometers away and it nearly pulverized us. Eight dead and thirty injured out of a population of three hundred. As I recall, you were among the injured. If things like that hit every year, how long before one hits that's only five hundred kilometers away? Or hits you squarely?"

"Captain, how do you propose to get the modules back up to *Phoenix*?"

Vargas paused. Sheffield had, not surprisingly, identified a big reason *Phoenix* couldn't just fly away. The modules were designed to return to low orbit and recouple with the ship, but such an endeavor required vast amounts of fuel, more than they were likely to produce for some time yet. Without the modules, and more importantly, the equipment stored in them, a trip to another star would be far more difficult, not to mention colonization. Food supplies, while not depleted, were low enough that they would have to depend on hydroponics for the trip.

"Commander, we both know the fuel situation. And of course there is the fact that we still need to bring the parts for the main engine back up to triple redundancy before we fire it up again. If I gave the impression I wanted to leave tomorrow, I apologize. I had nothing of the sort in mind, and regard ourselves lucky if we can depart in two Hōvian years. And I will be sweating and keeping my fingers crossed the entire time we're here. If we are the last of humanity, and no, don't try to wave that way, because we both know Earth may have managed to destroy itself in that last war, then we've got all our eggs in one fantastically fragile basket."

"And if people down here don't want to leave?"

"Then *Phoenix*, complete with modules, would leave without them."

"And if you were prevented from taking the modules?"

"Commander, you are walking a very fine line. Are you seriously proposing to try to take parts of *Phoenix*?"

"I don't want a standoff. What I want is assurance that if the day comes that *Phoenix* leaves and some of us wish to stay behind, you'll at least leave enough behind that we can shelter and maintain technology. I'll note that it took only five hundred years from the industrial revolution to interstellar travel on Earth. Those who stay behind, if we have the copy of the library and the Imprinter, can build an interplanetary shuttle to get the materials needed from Disappointment to build another star class ship."

Vargas nearly laughed, but reconsidered just in time. Building a *Phoenix*-class ship would be well beyond the scope of five hundred people, no matter how well trained and equipped. But in several generations, three thousand people could build one using the existing plans. It wasn't impossible.

"Assuming you keep your level of technology, of course. One Ice Fall could eliminate that if it took out the Imprinter and library."

"Hasn't humanity lived under that Damoclean sword all along?"

Vargas nodded. He took a minute to consider Sheffield's position. Spencer and Trapp had worked with him in training on various personnel scenarios, including a situation similar to this, where the complement would be divided between staying at *nu Phoenicis* or moving on. The best answer, it seemed, was compromise. "Commander, I make this offer. When the time comes to leave with *Phoenix*, we will leave you two modules for shelter and to protect the database and the copy of the Imprinter, plus one shuttle, and in return, you cooperate in working to make it possible for *Phoenix* to leave."

Sheffield looked hard at Vargas. His gaze, while not trusting, was not hostile. He had expected the Captain to try to assert his shipboard authority, and Vargas had sidestepped him. Nor was he perturbed about having only two modules. He and Voss were working on what Voss called a "paint roller" designed module, in which a tubular framework of steelwood would be literally rolled over a large patch of tube-grass mat, making a cocoon that was very nearly soundproof and blast proof. Voss thought they could have several dozen of them within a year. "Very well, Captain, I think we have an accord."

Later, Vargas smiled, remembering that Sheffield has attended the same sessions with Trapp and Spencer that he had. He had expected Sheffield to demand half the modules, a concession Vargas was not prepared to make. He would have settled for four.

Sheffield, dossing down for the long night, remembered the session himself, and also smiled. He was hoping to get just one module and a shuttle. Both then realized that each had reacted and behaved exactly as they should, and perhaps prevented a lot of trouble.

But as the meeting broke up and Sheffield moved toward the door, Vargas saw that Spencer was still looking closely at Sheffield, and the psychiatrist clearly didn't like what he saw. He would have to ask him about that later.

He never did.

Part 4

The Long Night

Chapter 36 The Long Night

IT WAS THE START OF A LONG NIGHT. The next day's Zharrise, Hō-ō would be eclipsed, and so it would remain dark until 2pm, or one hour before Zharset, the following day.

The colony, and even the ship regarded these types of periods as 'down time', 'the gentle night' or the Hoyliday. It was seen as an opportunity to rest, or recreate, or if so minded, to work on projects, but in a more casual setting.

* * *

Captain Vargas and Julie Steinberg retired to the housing referred to as the King's Suite by Sheffield for an informal honeymoon. Dan had vowed not to emerge until the next Zharrise, some forty four hours later.

* * *

Jeanine Barney finished her analysis of the soil samples of Disappointment. She expected to find lots of uranium-238, assuming that the material on the surface of the soil was pitchblende. However, repeated tests showed that the earliest element in the decay chain was thorium-230. Careful evaluation came up with an inexplicable result. None of the radioactive material could be more than one hundred and fifty thousand Earth years old. Something had dusted the planet in thorium 230, and they were seeing the natural progression an eye blink later in cosmological terms. Something tickled the back of her mind. They had found thorium in the Boitumelo range, well above where the effective atmosphere ended. Wasn't it also a thin cover on nickel-iron rock?

It didn't explain why the planet was radioactive in the first place, but it demonstrated that in another one hundred and fifty thousand years or so, it would be safe to live on. Sooner, if tubegrass, with its odd chelating properties, was widespread.

She would grab Simmons in the morning and see if he had any ideas why anyone would cover a world in thorium 230. It had a half-life of seventy-seven thousand years. Someone with a lot of patience might have done it.

* * *

Red thought about going to the Imprinting module to see how the parts for ROVERII were coming along. Then he remembered he had promised Rebekah he would show her some of the constellations that were the same here as on Earth. He had kept carefully quiet when she said that she only knew the Dipper and *nu Phoenicis*, wondering how a farm girl with a double Ph.D. and the brights to make it onto the *Phoenix* could manage not to learn the constellations. It didn't occur to him that she probably knew them better than he did. He was happy to share knowledge—and other things—with her. Besides, he had some juicy gossip to share.

* * *

Rudy Harlen realized that, distasteful as he might find it, he was going to have to talk to Red Farnsworth. He knew Farnsworth was working on building Charlies that could help with farming and other settlement tasks, including harvesting tube-grass root. He had finally come up with a subroutine that would allow the devices to notice and kill mice. Several people had told him that mice were naturally inquisitive, and would taste anything that looked like it could be edible, and it was unlikely they could actually eat tube-grass but he had his doubts about that. He had spotted four mice in the tube-grass, and two of them had been nibbling at the stalks. According to common lore, they should have starved or returned home by now. Of course, "home" had a cat and four kitten being taught to hunt, and so for a mouse, being outside and ravenous might be a preferable alternative. But Farnsworth's Charlies could make nearly ideal mice catching devices. He knew Farnsworth didn't like the idea of killing mice, but he had an compromise in mind: a cage the Charlie could dump drugged mice into for return for humane disposal. Contrary to what Farnsworth claimed, Rudy didn't derive savage glee from killing mice. Farnsworth, maybe, but not mice.

* * *

Alan Sheffield leaned back in his cot with a satisfied sigh. He had little doubt that Vargas had backed off on any plans to order Sheffield to abandon Hoyl. If Sheffield could convince enough colonists to make this their home, he might have to abandon the idea of taking the *Phoenix* and leaving. If it happened soon enough, before people got too settled in their ways and a bit stultified in their thinking, he might introduce a referendum to change the name of the world. He hated "Hoyl." But he would work hard to help Vargas and whoever wanted to go with him to leave. Then, and only then, could he call this place "Home."

* * *

The only two worried about the future of the colony that evening were Doctors Trapp and Spencer. They strolled in the calm coolness of the evening, and discussed the growing visible rift between the Captain and his Second-in-Command.

Spencer negated the suggestion that Vargas resented the role of colony leader that seemed to be going by default to Sheffield. "I don't think the Captain wants control of the colony. I think he only questions if this is the right place to have a colony."

"You don't think he might have other motives for that?"

Spencer shrugged. "I don't think so, but then, I agree with him. I don't think this is a suitable world for humans to colonize."

Trapp sniffed at the air, strangely scentless, and listened to the eerie silence of a Hoyl night. *Not a creature is stirring,* he thought. *Except us, and we're alien visitors.*

Spencer had other thoughts. "Alan, do you remember the meeting we had with the Captain on your first awakening?"

"Um, I listened to recordings of it."

"Remember he wanted to look into cyberimplants to address hibernation syndrome?

Trapp rubbed at his beard and looked uncomfortable. "I remember it second-hand, as it were. It seemed an ill-considered option."

"I think we had our answer to the long-term effects of hibernation syndrome right there. He was sharp enough that even with impaired functions and confusion, he could dig up references to an esoteric banned technology from three centuries ago, and recognize it as a possible answer to the crisis."

"Yeah, but good heavens. Cyberimplantation? He'd have had a mutiny on his hands if he had proposed it to the crew!"

Spencer briefly looked uncomfortable, and then realized Trapp was dealing with one emotionally taboo subject by switching to another taboo subject. "We had our answer then, but we didn't realize it. Hibernation syndrome doesn't affect intelligence, at least not for very long.

"But it does affect judgment. And that's hard to measure, except in the abstract.

"I think it's affecting all of us to one degree or another. Including Vargas and Sheffield."

"Assuming that's the case, what would you propose we do about it? Or maybe I should say, what you propose that I, as Chief Medical Officer, do about it?"

Spencer actually chuckled at that. "Relax, Alan. I'm not asking you to declare them unfit for duty. But will you join me in persuading them, when things calm down a bit, to undergo some more hibernation re-immersions? It really does seem to help."

Trapp's beard moved up and down in the faint light. "Certainly. When things calm down."

* * *

Red returned to Charlie Central, as he thought of his new module, and considered Harlen's request for a mouse-catching Charlie. It wouldn't be difficult to fabricate such—indeed, mouse abatement robots dated back to the twenty-first century. The trick was to make sure they were selective. Like most Mantech undergrads, Red knew the story of the fellow who came up with the first mouse algorhythm, and put it in the control board of a small but very determined robot armed with a mallet. Not much on subtlety.

The robot was programmed to hunt by color, movement, and size. He left it on in his kitchen and retired for the night. The following morning, he came down to see if his creation had killed any mice, but decided to grab a quick cuppa tea and glance at the Guardian headlines first.

Unfortunately, he was wearing grey socks, and like most people, unconsciously wiggled his toes while sitting and reading.

The robot broke his big toe and it had to be amputated.

* * *

Nobody happened to be looking at Disappointment. There was no particular reason why anyone should. Even Jeanine, pondering the oddities of Disappointment soil, had no reason to look toward the planet.

Even if they did look that way, they wouldn't have seen what only a Hoyle-class space telescope could have caught: a bright purple streak across the face of the planet that pulsed three times, moving at an unbelievable speed, and then vanished.

On Hoyl, it was a quiet start to the long night.

Chapter 37 Catch a Falling Star

TUBE-GRASS ALE WASN'T EVEN REMOTELY ALE, and it only had a few drops of tube-grass nectar in it. Red had joked in training that the crew would figure out how to make hooch out of any native vegetation before anyone even knew if it was safe to consume. In this case, that was very nearly true. Food techs on *Phoenix* had declared the Hōvian plant to be non-radioactive, unlike its deadly variation on Disappointment, but were still testing for other potential toxins when someone tasted the oily residue that formed on the rubbery stalks in the early evening and discovered it had a strong, but pleasant citrus-like taste, sweet and tart at the same time.

There wasn't anything corresponding to grain to be found, but one ground-hugging plant that grew near Lassiter's Landing had a rather tasteless root bulb that was deemed edible and, it turned out, was quite happy to ferment in sugar and yeast with a little bit of heat.

The result tasted a bit like vodka and lime juice, reasonably palatable and possibly unlikely to cause convulsions, blindness, stomach cramps or dementia if taken in moderation.

When word of the beverage made it up to *Phoenix*, Doctor Trapp issued a cautionary memo advising one and all that the full properties of the plants were unknown, and adding that even if it behaved just like a regular alcoholic beverage on Earth, everyone needed to be aware that it could exacerbate symptoms left over from hibernation, such as flash-dreams and the twingies. He noted that some of the mental impairments people experienced on first and second awakenings could reoccur, and urged everyone to approach the beverage with caution.

Trapp did his best to keep the memo as light-hearted as possible. He knew that most of the colonists would heed the advisory, at least to begin with, but that the crew, most of whom had military backgrounds, were another matter. Trapp knew full well the effect of a lecture on sobriety, deportment and personal safety from a brass hat such as himself, and hoped he hadn't given tube-grass ale too big of a boost in popularity. At least some of them would discuss it with Julie Steinberg or Ian Sheffield, both of whom were more approachable, and, more to the point, located at hand in the settlement.

Popularity turned out to be self-limiting, since the stuff left a nasty hangover, and people with a genetic predisposition toward alcoholism had been weeded out. Trapp decided the stuff wasn't a severe threat, but to further limit any potential popularity resolutely kept a blind eye turned to the marijuana plants inconspicuously located in the hydroponics areas. It was already known that weed eased the twingies and kept people more relaxed. And technically, it wasn't illegal even on Earth, since *Phoenix* was an RESS vessel, and in the Royal Union marijuana was legal.

So Rebekah wasn't surprised when Red turned up with a container of tube-grass ale. She hadn't tried it herself, but the stuff had been around for about six little years now, and aside from some legendary hangovers, it didn't seem to be harming anyone. Red took a leaf and rubbed it between his fingers into the glasses. "Mint," he explained. "Hoyl grown, not hydroponic."

Rebekah cheered and tapped her glass against his. After all the false starts, she was finally enjoying something from the garden. And the mint was a nice addition to the taste.

The pseudo-evening of the Hō-ō eclipse was warm and still. The katabatic breeze off the ice cap had stilled as it always did when the temperature dropped below twenty, and that prevented temperatures from dropping below freezing. It was, Red reflected, a nearly ideal climate, if you ignored the super cells that struck once every five days or so. Red was from Manchester; there was much in the climate he could forgive.

Hō-ō hung in the southern sky, a guttering charcoal briquette. Lightning created red flashes here and there. Overhead, the stars were bright and clear, stiller and sharper than he was accustomed to seeing on Earth.

The seasons were very slowly turning. A bit over a hundred and eighty days ago when they first arrived, summer solstice was approaching, and Hō-ō hung directly overhead during the "full moon phase" and drove men mad with her baleful light. Or at least made them twitchy and irrational. Now, between the ambient lights of the settlement and that Hō-ō was nearly one third under the horizon, it was a calming and restful sight.

Red peered. *Phoenix* sometimes lay between him and Hō-ō, and sometimes you could make out the ship silhouetted against the perpetual lightning flashes on the gas giant. He kept meaning to take some time-delay zoomed images, and get a picture of the ship with multiple flashes behind it. Maybe at end of the eclipse he could capture the mysterious bands of rose-colored light that flew across the surface of Hō-ō just after Zhar-Ptitsa was occluded. Give Vargas and Julie a honeymoon memento copy, maybe. Red smiled at the thought. A Captain who was getting some was a mellow Captain, and that made for a happy crew.

Behind and above him was the open night sky of Hoyl, with a lot more stars than you could see from the surface of Earth. The air was free of pollutants and the dim lights of the tiny settlement didn't wash out the sky. He pointed. "There's *nu Phoenicis*."

Rebekah angled her neck to look along the proffered direction, and looked confused. "How is it we can see it from here? Aren't we in *nu Phoenicis*?"

"It's missing a star compared to what we saw on Earth. Our star. Zhar-Ptitsa. The rest of the constellation is still there, further on out. A couple of the stars have shifted because of our nearer perspective, but you can still recognize it."

"Of course. A constellation isn't a place, it's just a direction. We're just at the first stop along that direction. So Sol would be in the opposite direction, which would be. . . under the horizon, right?"

"Fraid so. We never see it from this latitude."

"Hm. *Nu Phoenicis* is a northern constellation on this world. So our plane of the eclipse is. . . "

"About a hundred thirty five degrees from that of the solar system. It's why the Milky wave moves sideways across the night sky. Say, I thought you said you didn't know much about the stars."

Rebekah grinned. "Part of our training, remember? I was just giving you an excuse to come hang out."

Red felt abashed, an unfamiliar feeling for him. The stuff he was telling her was part of the education all the colonists got, since it was assumed they may have to explore on a planet that didn't have GPS set up yet. Still, it was an invite. . .

"So I shouldn't tell you the dull red lump on the horizon is Hō-ō?"

"Not if you want your next drink administered orally. Look, there's Roadrunner."

"Where?" Red scanned the southern sky for the tiny Hōvian satellite, confused. Roadrunner should have. . . he double checked on his data pad. . . set twenty minutes ago. What was Rebekah looking at?

"It's there. Just coming from in front of Hō-ō now."

Red caught a glimpse of something, a pinpoint moving to the east against the southern stars. He double checked his data pad. "That's not Roadrunner. One of the shuttles, probably."

"Well, it's setting now." Rebekah decided it wasn't worth pursuing. "Have you heard anything about the big confab the big brass were having?"

"Yeah. The kids got reamed out for the cat and mouse games they played, but got slapped on the wrist as punishment. I guess his nibs didn't want to alienate his head shrink by banning them or something like that. Sheffie wasn't happy; he wanted to ream them." Red was kindly disposed toward the Spencer kids right then. They had done him a major favor, keeping him in the dark about their little home project. If he'd been implicated, he would not have gotten off so lightly. No relatives who were officers, and he was a bit too old to try and convince the higher ups that he was youthful and impetuous. At the same time he was annoyed that he hadn't figured it out for himself. The kids weren't exactly championship poker player material, after all, and he knew they were up to something.

Damn. What was that Rebekah saw? He only caught a few moments before it set, enough to know she saw something. He was pretty sure none of the shuttles were in low orbit. The mystery nagged at him. "Rebekah, I'm going to nip down to the landing area and see if all the shuttles are there. Want to come?"

"Sure. It's a nice night for a walk."

They strolled down to the landing area, where, as expected, four shuttles sat. He unrolled his data pad, checked to make sure Lassiter was awake, and hailed him. "Gord, now many shuttles are up on *Phoenix*?"

"Just the two of them. Why, you need one, Red?"

"Nah, just doing a little inventory."

Next, Bissont on *Phoenix*. He confirmed both shuttles were docked for the long night. All the shuttles were accounted for. He checked the time. Nearly a half hour had passed. If it was in low orbit, it would reappear in anywhere from fifteen minutes to an hour.

Red decided to wait to see if it reappeared before bugging Simmons with it. He wouldn't have bothered, but every tracking device on board ship was watching the rings to make sure there wasn't another Ice Fall and this looked like it was between *Phoenix* and Hoyl, where the ship wasn't looking.

They went back to Rebekah's patio, and she carefully killed all the lights inside so they wouldn't miss the mystery object if it rose in the west. Since all the shuttles were down, it was probably a rogue chunk of debris from the rings that had just happened to fall into an orbit around Hoyl. It would be fun to twit Simmons by calling him up and telling him that the two of them had eyeballed an orbital object that all his elaborate equipment had missed.

They sipped their tube-grass ales and gossiped about the planned spring venture to the trans-Boitumelo plains. Red had spotted tube-grass there, and a fair bit of new flora before the ROVER made its ill-fated venture into the high mountains. Rebekah and Red had both volunteered, and Sheffield was expected to publish a roster in a few days.

An hour passed, and Red was about to conclude that it was just a high-altitude meteorite they saw, when Rebekah shouted, "There it is!"

"Shh. You don't want to scare it."

"You really are a mental case, Red. What are you doing?" Red was tapping his data pad.

"Timing its traverse. That way we can tell Simmons where to look."

"It's getting smaller. Is it moving away?"

"No. It's moving more between us and the sun, and the part we see in daylight is getting smaller. It should wink out entirely just before it starts traversing Hō-ō."

"Oh. Of course. Red, it's acting like it's round."

"How do you mean?"

"The way the light is dimming. It's steady. If it was irregular shaped, the dimming would be a up-and-down thing, if it was rotating."

"Hm. Could be. Your eyes are sharper than mine. Of course, a lot of the objects in the rings are round. They melt, clump up as water, and refreeze. A globe is the most logical shape."

The object winked out, indicating that it was now occulted by Hō-ō, and Red checked the time, and noted the right ascension and declination of the object, both at emergence and occultation. Now he had something Simmons could use. He contacted the physicist.

Simmons, sounding bored, turned his medium range radar on the object. "It's probably just a chunk of ice off the rings," he said. "It decided to fall into orbit instead of hitting us. Must be our lucky day." He paused, checking his echoes. "Good sized chunk of ice, that. About forty meters across, I make it. I didn't see it come in. Where'd it come from?"

"It might have been there for a while, Tim. You said yourself that nobody's paying much attention to low orbit."

"We did do a scan for objects when we first got here, part of determining if anyone was home or not here. It didn't show up."

"Well, now you can plot it and we can at least get an idea of when it's going to hit us."

"Yeah, I'm glad you spotted it. It's right over you now and about a third the way across Hō-ō from your viewpoint. I don't guess you can see it. . . damn."

Red and Rebekah saw a bright spark, and then a steadily pulsating blue glare. The object moved directly to the south, leaving a luminescent trail behind it. Red, confused, assumed it was a shooting star.

"Red, did you see anything unusual just now?"

"Um, no, Just a shooting star. Why?"

"The radar says. . . hang on. Let me run a diagnostic. I'm getting impossible readings from the display."

The steak winked below the horizon, and Red and Rebekah exchanged puzzled glances. Red was scanning the western edge of Hō-ō. "It should come out in about fifteen minutes, right about there." He pointed.

"You know, Scotty was talking to me the other day, and she said she would really like to flush out the water in the ship's hull before the captain took it anywhere. I guess after twenty-eight years of cosmic rays it's gotten a bit nasty. I think a forty meter globe of ice might be just what she needs. Now, how do you corral something like that and get it up where the ship can use it?"

"Well, it's easier to move the ship to the ice." Red grinned. "If bin Laden were here, he would tell you sometimes the mountain really must go to Mohammad."

"Oh. Of course. Um, about thirty-three thousand tons. Mm, That will make quite a splash when it lands. Maybe we should call Scotty and tell her to get it while she can."

Simmons cut in. "Red, that shooting star you saw. . . what direction was it going?"

"Due south. Just about exactly between your position and us."

"My equipment checks out. But it just told me that your object just made a hard right turn into polar orbit. It went straight from equatorial to an inclination of ninty degrees."

For once, Red was at an utter loss for words. Rebekah said, "Your equipment must be wrong. That's simply not possible."

"I wish I could just say that a similar sized object just happened to cross the path of the first object that was already in polar orbit, and the first object, for whatever reason, was destroyed. That's only fantastically unlikely.

"According to my readouts, and thanks to the gods that I recorded this, is that the object slowed about eighty kilometers per second, taking about a half second to come to a complete halt, and then accelerated at the same rate into polar orbit."

"Call the captain. We've got company."

"Huh?"

"Think about it. Nothing natural could do that. It's a ship of some kind." One that doesn't bother with orbital dynamics, inertia or gravity, Red thought. Let's hope they're friendly. "We saw it, we'll back you up."

"A ship. . . " There was a pause, and Vargas voice came on. "Yes, Mister Simmons, what is it?" The tone was slightly testy, and Red remembered that Julie was with him.

"Captain, we have a bogey."

"Say again?"

Rapidly, Simmons described what his instruments showed, and included the on-the-ground reports from Red and Rebekah.

"Mister, are you saying this object accelerates at thousands of gravities?"

"I know what it sounds like, Captain, but that's what the instruments are reporting. I checked them."

Vargas reflected. Red was notorious for the occasional prank, but even Red would hesitate to call the Captain when the Captain was not only off the bridge, but on his honeymoon, for a joke. And Simmons certainly wouldn't. He had to assume the reports were real.

"Very well. Mister Simmons, you still tracking it?"

"I'm afraid not, Ser."

"Humph. Let me know the instant it reappears. Can you get 360 horizon scans going just in case it doesn't come over the north pole?"

"Yes Ser."

"Red, I want you to go to Scafeld. I'm going to scramble Sheffield and some people, and I want you on board."

"Ser. Um, Can Rebekah Cohen come along?"

"Does she have any specialized training for this?"

"Do any of us, Captain? But she was the one who spotted the bogey first."

While a puzzled Julie blinked sleepily at him, Vargas smiled grimly in the darkness. No, he thought, none of us have specialized training for this.

"Very well, Mister Farnsworth. She may bring extra perspective to what we face."

In the calm cricketless cool of the pseudo-evening, Red and Rebekah exchanged a high five.

Chapter 38 The Doctors Consult

"DOCTOR, I HAPPENED TO SET ASIDE SOME OF THE BRANDY the Captain was kind enough to offer us. Would you like to stroll out to the edge of the settlement and get a look at the night sky? I know your opportunities have been limited. And Hō-ō in eclipse is pretty impressive."

"I would like that, Ian. Oh, and we're off duty. No titles."

The two doctors took folding chairs and paced the several hundred meters to the edge of town. Once there, they flipped open the chairs, and Trapp opened his carry-all, which contained a box with a flask and two shot glasses. Spencer grinned. "I always admire a man who comes prepared to line officer meetings."

"Years of practice. They always have libations at these things, and if it's an Admiral like Vargas, it's going to be pretty good hooch. I make a point of sampling. For medicinal purposes, naturally."

"Of course. Are we going to discuss the meetings?"

"We are. What are those flickers on Hō-ō?"

"Lightning. The planet is one big thunderstorm. I've seen some that were bright enough to cast shadows."

"Impressive."

"Simmons told me that some of the really big ones expend more energy in less than a second than *Phoenix* used to get us here."

"I'll defer to his field of expertise. It's a pity we can't make use of that energy."

"We do. It's what creates our magnetic field."

"Ah. So the cosmic rays don't fry us. Very well then. And it looks pretty."

The men conversed in an idle manner. Trapp, it turned out, was curious about Hoyl. He had learned a lot about it second hand, but that didn't convey the scents, or the unsettling silence, or even how big Hō-ō was, even on the horizon. As he watched, a pulsating flash streaked down the face of the planet and below the horizon. "What was that?"

"What was what?"

"Never mind. Ian, I don't mean to tell you how to handle your kids. . . "

"You do, but I'm happy to hear you out."

"Good. Please impress on them the gravity of what they did. If they had caught Jim sneaking, er, Tipsy on board the launch would have been delayed three weeks while they decontaminated the ship. And if she had fleas, make that six weeks."

"I already let them know that the Captain didn't give them more severe punishment because he really couldn't. I'll also point out that if the ship had been forced to stand down from launch readiness because of that cat, we all would have been caught in the nuclear blast."

"I didn't think of that. You're right, of course. Um, do they know what we're going to have to do with Tipsy and her litter?"

"Well, they know they're going up to the ship for a full range of medical tests."

"Which they won't enjoy. Hopefully I won't find something. . . " his voice trailed off, unsure how emotionally attached Spencer was to his cat.

"You'd have to dissect. Jim figured that out on his own. Neither of us have mentioned that to Sylvie yet."

Trapp took a sip. "Why borrow trouble? I honestly doubt it will come to that. You say the cat had all her shots?"

"Current as of fifty years ago." Both men chuckled.

"That said, I liked how Vargas handled it."

"So did I. I also think he saw Sheffield coming a mile away, and outwitted him at every turn."

"And Sheffield thinks he got the best of the negotiations. He got half what the Captain was going to offer if pressed."

"I'm keeping an eye on him. He's getting more brittle, more temperamental."

"Sheffield?" At Spencer's nod, he continued, "He's got a short fuse these days. The Captain's doing better. I think Julie's been good for him. Still, the Captain did outwit himself at one turn."

"Oh? How so?"

"Well, before the meeting, he confided to me that he was going to go easy on your kids because they were suffering from hibernation syndrome, and would never had pulled such a stunt if their judgment hadn't been affected by it."

Spencer blinked at Trapp. "But the kids came up with the scheme back on Earth."

"Before they went into hibernation, yes. Vargas seems to have missed that point, somehow." Trapp smiled. "Not that you'll complain, of course. They're your kids."

"It might just be the pressures of getting the colony organized."

"And it may be that he's realizing it's all for naught. You saw Sheffield's approach in the meeting. He all but accused the Captain of lying."

"He might as well have." Spencer smiled, remembering how Vargas nearly punched him at first wakening. "The Captain, at least, seems to have his equanimity in place."

"Good thing, too. If we stay, I don't think Sheffield is suited to role of colony leader. Why do you suppose he negotiated for so little to remain with the colony?"

"Well, part of that was that tube-grass module scheme. That effectively means he has unlimited modules. With the imprinter, he could actually build more shuttles if he wanted. I think it even has the schematics for the fifth-generation interplanetary jobs they were about to use on the trips to Mars. Who suggested the tube-grass modules to Voss, anyway?"

"Um, I think it was Maureen. With the cat crisis, I haven't had a chance to ask her. She knows someone who has access to someone who has access." Spencer smiled mirthlessly. "Sheffield doesn't believe in sharing credit. That's OK in the military, where morale is imposed. It's a bad trait in a civilian leader, though."

"Indeed. Unfortunately, it's a trait useful in order to become a leader. Any sense as to how many colonists would resist leaving at this time?"

"Well, I have to be pretty vague. I haven't really talked to people about that. Remember, we're supposed to look surprised when someone broaches the topic. At this point, not many. There's two hundred and twelve people down here plus another hundred and ten who rotate in and out, duties split between here and the ship. I would say that thirty or thirty-five would follow Sheffield right now. It was higher before Ice Fall, of course." Spencer unconsciously waved his glass, causing the ice cubes to clink.

"If Ice Falls didn't exist, how many?"

Spencer shook his head by way of non-answer.

"OK. The Captain thinks this place is a construct, and sooner or later the owners are going to show up. I think he's right. How does that affect the number who might stay?"

"Well, people aren't prepared to believe superior alien intelligences are coming to kick us off the planet tomorrow, and that might have actually cost him support. Had to be said, though. This place is so obviously a construct." Spencer shrugged. "I don't know. People will need to make up their minds."

"That might be a problem."

"Yeah. We estimate that dissent of a third of the people could spark strife. Ice Fall has put that on the back burner for now, but if people decide the Captain is being paranoid about aliens, that might cost him support even among people who think we should go already."

"And if little green men do show up tomorrow to kick us off the planet?"

"Heh. How many of those brandies have you had, anyway?"

* * *

Commander Sean Sheffield had to struggle to keep the skepticism out of his voice. "A bogey, Captain? From Earth?"

Vargas paused. He hadn't considered that. If Earth survived the war, after fifty some years of rebuilding. . . no. It was still twenty-six light years away. "I don't think so, Commander. Its characteristics make that very unlikely."

Sheffield considered the mere existence of a bogey to be very unlikely, not to mention one hell of a coincidence. The very evening that the captain had threatened him with galactic overlords coming to reclaim what was there, and presto-change-o, those galactic overlords just happen to show up? Sheffield wasn't sure whether to be angry or concerned for the captain's mental health.

"Mister Farnsworth and Rebekah Cohen are on their way over to your side now. They'll probably have Mister Mann piloting. Add whoever you think is appropriate, get the shuttle in readiness for orbital flight, and await further instructions. I'm not sending you up until we have some idea what we're dealing with."

"Your forbearance is appreciated," Sheffield said dryly. He considered himself lucky Americaners didn't get irony. "What, exactly, are these characteristics?"

"It can make a ninety degree change in orbital trajectory, apparently nearly instantaneously. It appears to have essentially unlimited delta-vee."

"Unlimited. . . Captain?"

"Just. . . follow the orders as given. I realize how incredible it sounds, but I've got two eyewitness accounts on the ground and supporting evidence from *Phoenix*. Um, one moment, Sean."

Vargas switched channels. "Mister Simmons, any sign of our bogey?"

"No Ser."

"Let me know as soon as it appears."

Vargas switched back. "Commander, if it suits you to think I'm in error, that's fine. But for now, assume there might be something to it, and realize that if there is, it could be extremely important. Do you have a problem with that?"

There was a definite pause. "If there is something there..." Vargas noticed the emphasis on the word "is", "...should we initiate contact?"

"No. Just observe. Unless they try to speak to us first." In the dimness of the honeymoon cabin, Vargas found himself wishing nearly anyone one else on the crew was in charge of this.

An hour and a half passed, and it did not appear. Vargas gave it another half-hour, and had Sheffield's crew stand down. The bogey did not reappear that night.

* * *

A half hour after the bogey vanished below the southern horizon, Vargas contacted Lieutenant Susan Bartlett in coms with an odd request. He wanted a full daily copy of the ship's log copied to the library immediately, four hours ahead of schedule, and wanted both print copy and permanent sealed backup recording delivered to his cabin and black boxed soonest.

For Dan Vargas, it was possible evidence of humanity's first interaction with an alien intelligence. It needed to be saved for posterity. If nothing came of it, they could have a few laughs over it one day.

Susan, had heard a rumor about an hour ago that the ship had been on the verge of being ordered to general quarters earlier in the evening. Clearly something was up. She'd heard chatter about a UFO, and assumed the Captain's directive had something to do with that. She didn't believe in UFOs herself, but had to admit that on this crazy moon, anything was possible. She was glad to be stationed on *Phoenix*, where night came at the usual dependable time.

A comms person in the RESM prior to winning a spot aboard *Phoenix*, she knew that black boxing a backup was something a Captain did when he felt action was imminent, and wanted a 'note in a bottle'—a record of events leading up to the ship's destruction that was put in an immensely strong capsule with its own transponder. Only the admiralty knew how to open it. And the Captain, of course, since the code to open it involved another code, spoken in the Captain's own voice and known only to him. Hopefully *Phoenix* wasn't in imminent danger of being under attack. The average Admiral's corvette had more firepower than did *Phoenix*. There were orthodox churches that were more maneuverable .

There wasn't much hope of anyone from the admiralty showing up here in the next fifty years or more. What made her more nervous was the possible assumption by the Captain that *Phoenix* might be in danger of being destroyed. Susan knew that it was a mistake to try to read the Captain's mind, except when it was utterly necessary to the job at hand. In such circumstances the subordinate had better be fucking perfect at the art of brass hat divination. In this case, it was pretty easy; don't waste time speculating on why the Captain wanted it. Just drop everything and do it right now.

The backup took four minutes. The print out and indestructible backup took another minute. Susan than took the indestructible backup and took it to the Captain's cabin, punched a code in his door entry. The door didn't budge, but the entry box changed color from green to flashing amber. She held the indestructible backup in front of the touch pad and let it consider the object. A moment later, it turned green and flashed three times. The contents of the backup were now in the black box, and nobody on board except Vargas could retrieve it.

Two hours later, when her shift ended, Susan looked into the ship's log to see what happened during that hour and a half. There was nothing improper about her actions; the formal ship's log was open to anyone who wished to read it. The officer's log was more restrictive, although as an officer she would also have access to that. The captain's log was only accessible to the Captain, the second in command, and the CMO and CTO.

She spent an hour playing the log. There was absolutely nothing extraordinary in the voice traffic, and instrumentation logs showed only one oddity: ship's radar had gone off line for an hour, apparently for calibration operations. That wasn't due for another three days. But that was under Isaakson's command, and none of her business.

Tired, and annoyed that she hadn't ferreted out anything interesting, Susan retired for the night, and hoped the next day might be more interesting. She would get her wish.

She didn't look at remote accesses to the ship's log, or who availed themselves of it. That, after all, was perfectly routine. People ground side or off-duty often queried the ship about anything from duty roster to tomorrow's menu in the mess.

And there was nothing at all in the remote log to raise eyebrows.

Chapter 39 Aliens and the Art of Command

AFTER AN HOUR, JULIE CONCLUDED THAT DAN wasn't going to be back for a while, and from her porch she could see and hear activity that was higher than normal for Avalerion. Whatever had called Dan away was stirring things up, and she was tired of waiting.

Maureen Spencer and Asuka Tsuchishima were at the intersection, talking.

"People on board ship have been speculating right along that this moon was constructed by somebody," Asuka was saying. "Even the Captain thinks that. And Maureen, just think—if this place does belong to somebody, and those somebodies are friendly, we will see a whole new range of plant and animal life. Including intelligent life."

"I would probably have to wait. See what their approach is toward their animals. Even on Earth you can be jailed for being disrespectful to an animal in some places. We would have to explore their attitudes very carefully before we started doing tests." Maureen gave a broad grin. "Even in my native Devon, you were damned careful in how you spoke to people's cats and dogs. I lost one customer because I didn't address her cat by her full name."

"That's the sort of thing that leaves me wondering who the aliens are. She actually switched vets for such a silly reason?"

"Oh aye, and what's more, she took the poor thing to one of those dreadful assembly-line veterinarian hospitals instead. The person at the admissions counter might use the cat's full name to the woman's face, but I promise that once in past the swinging doors, that cat has no name. It's just a list of symptoms and a fix-it ticket."

"Mm."

"Mm, what?"

"Well, if there are aliens, and they built this world, and maybe some of the others in this system, would we be anything more than an animal with a fix-it ticket?"

Julie held up a hand in a tentative greeting. "Hi. What's going on?"

Asuka gave her a surprised look. "You do not know?"

Julie heard the faint emphasis on the word 'you.' She didn't mind if people thought of her as the Captain's squeeze behind her back, but it was annoying that they would assume she was privy to all of the Captain's thinking—or would say anything if she was.

"Not really. What's this about aliens?"

Maureen said, "Someone spotted an object in orbit. It showed signs of being under power. I take it you weren't with the Captain when they contacted him?"

"No. I came out, um in, just in time to hear him order a scramble. For the shuttle crew, anyway. I don't think he sent the ship to general quarters."

Maureen smiled. More juicy gossip was lost to bathroom breaks. . . or created there. "He didn't say what it was?"

"Just that there was an object that required investigation."

Asuka gave a slightly condescending smile. "I forget that you are not a line officer."

Nor are you, bitch, Julie thought. Remembering Asuka-san's many kindnessess from during her recovery, she kept her response cordial. "Is there any solid evidence that it's a ship, or is this just hen house chatter?"

Asuka's eyes narrowed slightly, but she also answered in more pleasant tones. "Nothing solid. Two people who were drinking, and some preposterous readings on the ship's radar."

"Preposterous?" Julie hoped it took more than that to haul Dan out of their honeymoon cabin.

"What I am told is that the object was in low equatorial orbit, and suddenly and instantly switched to a polar orbit."

Julie looked across the open expanse of the colony. "It seems quiet now."

"I wonder if it might be some prank. Perhaps staged by some of the Captain's people, to persuade us to leave this place."

That seemed pretty devious for Dan, Julie thought. He had told her of commanding officers he had served under who routinely used subterfuge and divide-and-conquer to control the underlings, and how it invariably wrecked morale. Dan was openly contemptuous of such command tactics. "I can't imagine the Captain doing something like that."

"Captain Vargas, no. But suppose some of his crew were eager to buttress his position?"

Julie considered that. On board ship, the majority of the people wanted to gather up the settlement and leave for a new star system. Here on the ground, she understood, opinions were more divided. "The Captain seemed puzzled by the information he had been given when he ordered the shuttle fleet to scramble. If this were some sort of ruse, then the people doing it were tricking him. I would say that fooling the Captain is a risky business, even if it's being done supposedly for his benefit. Wouldn't you agree?"

Asuka just smiled, but Maureen nodded. "He really seemed surprised by the call?"

Julie thought about the empty bed that lay accusingly behind her. "Yes, he was surprised. So was I."

* * *

Commander Sheffield sat at his console in the make-shift office that he used as pro tem town leader and pondered the readouts from the *Phoenix*. There was an artifact on the radar screens at about the same time that Farnsworth drunkenly mistaken Hoyl's moon, Roadrunner, for an alien invasion. He smirked mirthlessly to himself, and then ran the recording again, this time noting the time and velocity.

He tapped the numbers into his data pad, which obligingly spit out the answer immediately. In order for an object to make a right turn like this one had, it would have undergone lateral acceleration of at least eight thousand gravities. There wasn't a substance known to man that could handle that, let alone any kind of space ship.

Vargas wanted to move on. The Captain didn't think this planet, with the steelwood trees and incredible tube-grass root fiber, was safe to colonize. He had decided this with less than one percent of the land mass unexplored, and Sheffield couldn't help but think that here in the colony, Vargas would just be a math teacher and soccer coach, and didn't want to give up the glory of captaining the *Phoenix*.

It was one thing to present a list of problems the colonists faced and suggest that they were enough to justify bugging out. It was quite another to scare people with alien monsters based on the most ludicrous of evidence.

Sheffield felt genuine concern. None of them had been wholly themselves after hibernation syndrome, but the Captain was obviously becoming unraveled. People would think him insane, or a fool, if he tried to use this as a pretext for abandoning Sheffield's colony. He must not be given the chance to do that to himself. He deserved better, and so did the colonists.

Calling up his access as second-in-command of the *Phoenix*, Sheffield's fingers danced over his data pad screen.

* * *

Red was still peering to the north when Vargas came up and slapped him on the shoulder. "Whatever it was you saw isn't coming back tonight. Let's call it a night, shall we?"

Red looked miserable, almost defeated. "Captain, I. . . "

Vargas held up a hand. "Shh. Ship's recordings back you up. You did see something, and you did the right thing calling it to my attention. It's not your fault that the little green men turned out to be unreliable." He gave Red an easy grin and saw the Middie visibly relax. He addressed the shuttle crew. "Everyone, go home. Stay on your toes. Hopefully by morning we'll have some answers."

Sheffield stepped out of the building that served as the office/hanger for the shuttles. He saw the crew members sauntering away, and gave Vargas a surprised look.

"Giving up on First Contact already, Captain?" Sheffield approached with an overly casual saunter and a wide smile that Vargas found vaguely disturbing.

Vargas chuckled, a man without a care. "I'm not sure what people saw, myself. Did you talk to Red and Rebekah?"

"I did. I smelled alcohol on their breaths. Nothing wrong with that, of course. They were off duty. But it leaves me wondering if may have mistaken a shooting star for a UFO."

"Red himself said they considered that possibility, but dismissed it when they heard back from Simmons. And neither of them seemed impaired to me."

"We should have had Julie check their blood alcohol level."

Vargas didn't like the implied smear against his middie, or the assumption his wife would go along with such a morale-buster. He wasn't about to take it even from his second-in-command. "Doctor Steinberg is off duty. If you had any questions, you could have contacted Doctor Trapp. Or Doctor Spencer. He's qualified to run that test. And before you do, I suggest you consider that you are calling the judgment and veracity of two of your crew people into question without real cause. "

"I imagine Doctor Spencer would be perfect for the task," Sheffield said, ignoring the rest of the response. "Tell me, Captain; I could see scrambling the crew for an object that had anomalous acceleration characteristics. But based on the word of two possibly intoxicated people, and physically impossible readings from the ship's radar?"

"You don't believe it?"

"With all due respect, Captain, I don't." Sheffield's expression, which had bordered on amused detachment, turned serious. "I just checked the ship's records, Captain. There are no anomalies."

"Are you trying to tell me the ship's radar didn't report what it reported?"

"No, Captain, I'm telling you that for the period in question, the ship's radar wasn't engaged at all. It seems to have been down for the seventy-four minutes in question."

Vargas felt his face tighten in anger, clamped down viciously. "And when did you check this?"

"Just now, Captain. It will be in the log."

Captain Vargas gave Sheffield a level stare, wondering how such a thing was possible. He didn't doubt that the number two had tried and failed to access the records. He flipped out his data pad and queried the ship.

There was a ninety minute gap in the radar record. It showed the radar had been shifted from scanning the rings—at the exact time it actually was, Vargas noted—to maintenance mode for unspecified reasons. It stayed there for ninety minutes, and then resumed scanning the rings. It had come back on less than thirty minutes earlier.

Vargas rubbed the side of his nose, regarding his data pad and thinking furiously. Few people had the access codes to excise any part of the ship's records at this level. Four people, in fact. Isaacson, Nate Harlen, the Captain. . .

. . . and Sheffield. Keeping his face as immobile as he could, Vargas considered the possibility that the Second-in-command had doctored an official ship's record. He could even come up with a rationale. Sheffield had made it clear he didn't want *Phoenix* to abandon Hoyl. Would he go that far?

Sheffield's next words gave Vargas the answer.

"Oh, Captain? Next time you report a UFO, don't base it on a clear equipment malfunction like a reading of a ship turning at eight thousand gravities. I'm sure you can get people thinking about alien visitations without something that absurd."

Vargas gave Sheffield a level stare. "Thank you for your input, Commander. I'll consult with Simmons come morning to find out what the ship actually did record."

Sheffield nodded, and excused himself. Vargas knew he would glance back, and did what he imagined Sheffield would want to see: an aghast captain staring in disbelief at the gap where his only real evidence had been stored. Sheffield glanced back, and the last of Vargas' trust in him died with that glance.

Vargas was checking something else. Sheffield had accessed records, just as he said. During that time, he may have zipped through the readings, looking for anomalies. Or he might have erased them without looking. Vargas suspected he hadn't looked. The record that should have said that wasn't there, either. But the time was there, and Vargas was interested to see that he had accessed the system after Lieutenant Susan Bartlett had made a copy to the library. He looked quickly to see what the library version said, and was unsurprised to see it had been overwritten by the data stream while Sheffield was accessing it. Quick checks of the ship's log and captain's log showed they had been similarly overwritten. There was no longer any room for doubt; Sheffield had deliberately altered the records.

But Sheffield wouldn't know that Vargas had also made a backup to the black box. Sloppy. He must have been counting on Vargas to be sloppy.

Come Zharrise, some twenty hours from now, he would return to *Phoenix* and pull the record.

He felt the growing anger building within him, and realized he should avoid Sheffield for the rest of the long night, too.

Well, he was on his honeymoon. He had an excuse.

* * *

"So, Dan. This UFO. What did Red and Becky see? Really."

Vargas laughed for the first time in several hours. He had returned to the honeymoon suite with a thundercloud over his head, a dark mood strengthened by the fact that Julie wasn't there. He proceeded to violate a self-rule taught to him by Rafael, his father, and poured a drink for himself. Drinking alone was a red light in a captain, but Vargas wanted to have some of his anger dissipated before Julie got back from wherever she was.

When she returned, he discovered she wasn't in the mood. Well, he couldn't blame her, really.

Absently checking the time a little while later, he was shocked to realize it was still only five in the afternoon. Hoyl time was difficult to adjust to. They were desultorily watching a movie, and Dan was finding it harder and harder to stay in his dark mood. Humanity had just found strong evidence of intelligent life. Surely that was more important than a surly second with a morale problem.

He suggested a walk around the perimeter of the settlement so they could enjoy the eclipse night and the cool air. Julie agreed, and they pulled on sweaters, apparel they hadn't needed since leaving Earth. They had been warned that it got chill during the long nights of the eclipse, sometimes approaching zero. Vargas had been relieved to see the honeymoon cabin had a heater. No matter how much first-hand knowledge he had to the contrary, he tended to equate 'settlement' with primitive living conditions. In the meantime, he was happy to be dressed in his usual off-duty apparel, instead of the Zharsuit, which, although comfortable, looked vaguely silly. Admiral Bolitho didn't sashay around in bonnet, veil and dress, did he?

They had walked out a hundred meters past the last semicircle of buildings, which was when Julie asked what Red and Rebekah had seen.

It took about forty five minutes for Dan to tell the whole story, concluding with the mysterious vanishing of the ship's records. Julie's mouth was a straight line when he finished.

"Dan, I do not want to eat with that man. Not after that."

"Not very diplomatic for a Captain's wife," Dan grinned. The grin vanished at the expression on her face. "Right. Well, there's no formal dinner scheduled. Sean and I discussed that before we came down, and it was agreed that our honeymoon would be free of normal ship's ceremonies. So he didn't feel obliged to throw a dinner for the Admiral."

"The Admiral."

"You didn't know? That's my formal rank when I'm off the ship. That's what I retired as."

"You got demoted to run the ship?"

"No. A captain on board his own ship can order an Admiral around. But off the ship, the admiral outranks the captain."

"Let me see. On *Phoenix*, Captain Vargas outranks Admiral Vargas. Down here, Admiral Vargas outranks Captain Vargas. Is that right?"

"That's right."

"You must have some interesting conversations with yourself." Julie gave him a sly smile, and Vargas belatedly realized the Lieutenant Commander he had married would be fully aware of the ancient naval custom.

"My dear, there's a right way, a wrong way. . . "

". . . and a Navy way!" she chorused with him and they both laughed.

"Anyway, I don't have any formal obligations to Sean, nor he to me, for tonight. And I suspect he's just as anxious to avoid me as I am to avoid him right now. He has to know I realize he altered the records. I just need to figure out why."

"'Sean'. I'm amazed you can speak of the man in such a friendly tone."

Dan snorted. "When I first saw that the records were erased, I was ready to keel-haul him. On a giant space ship, that would be no small punishment. My first thoughts were that he was at the least insubordinate, and at the worst committing treason. I started to calm down a bit when I realized I couldn't identify who he might have committed treason against."

"Isn't it insubordination? Doesn't he owe you loyalty?"

"He does, and up until now he's been exemplary as my Number Two. It may even be that he still is."

"How?"

"Well, see it from his perspective. He sees a captain who scrambled a shuttle crew based on nothing more than the word of a couple of drunks, and some radar artifacts that were, on the face of it, showing physically impossible behavior. He also knows this Captain is wedded to the notion that this moon is an artificial construct, and the owners might show up tomorrow to reclaim it, which he considers. . . unlikely. . . at the very least. He may even wonder if hibernation syndrome had a bigger effect on me than anyone supposed. The best way to defuse a situation in which his Captain may do something rash and ill-advised is to knock the props out from under the Captain's fantasy. So he simply zorched the radar readings—improperly, but from his viewpoint, essential to the welfare of the ship. And he's probably meeting with Red and Rebekah right now to try and shake them loose from their stories."

"I can't imagine either of them accepting an order to lie about something they reported to their Captain?"

"I should hope not. But he wouldn't order them to lie; he would just instill doubts in their minds, convince them that they were mistaken, and it was just a shooting star or a rogue burst of lightning on Hō-ō that they saw.

"I am convinced that he doesn't believe there was a UFO. I noticed in the duty roster he ordered a complete analytic breakdown of the radar facility. It'll take it off line for a day, but ensure we know if it malfunctioned at that point or not. He believes it malfunctioned. Period. And without the reports from Red and Rebekah, I would agree that he was probably right."

Julie considered this. "If it didn't show any anomalies, what then?"

"He believes us?" Vargas chuckled and shook his head. "He's going to be in a rough spot."

"So why didn't you order that first?"

"I would have by now. But because I do believe Red and Rebekah did see something, and it behaved the way it did because it's found a way to circumvent inertia and gravity, I didn't want to take our radar off line under the circumstances. For all I know, they're hovering just below our horizon, debating what to do about us."

"You really believe aliens are invading this moon?"

"We're standing right here, aren't we?"

Julie laughed. "Point. I meant other aliens. But is that type of technology possible? Instant acceleration to near light speed"

"Not that we know of. But look; we know this planet is a construct, maybe three thousand years old. Someone very deliberately moved it here. A planet. God only knows where they moved it from. Simmons thinks Disappointment might be similarly artificial in origin, that it was the last planet they brought in before this one."

"Why move it here?"

Dan shrugged. "Maybe they need a hot-climate planet as well as a moderate one? I don't know. But to move entire planets you need some sort of way of overcoming inertia. Even if Hoyl has a solid core, it's hard to imagine any way of moving it from one orbit to another without it breaking apart. It just can't be done. Planets are far more delicate than eggs because of their mass and scale. If you tried to move the Earth even a tiny bit the entire crust would shatter. But it's equally clear that someone did it. They moved a planet, and they moved it a long way. So why should I be surprised if they can beat inertia? They must have been able to do that just to make Hoyl exist as we know it.

"Another idea I had is that they know we're here, know about radar, and hell . . . they can probably evade it at will. Even if they didn't spot the settlement, *Phoenix* is pretty hard to miss. They want us to know they are here, and give us some idea of what they can do. I think that it's entirely up to them what we learn about them. If they want to show us things, lack of radar won't matter. If they are hostile, presence of radar won't matter."

Julie took a few minutes to assimilate this.

"Getting back to Sheffield, do you really think he's trying to protect you?"

Vargas sighed. "Not really, but it's a possibility, and I owe him the benefit of the doubt. I think mostly he doesn't want his case for staying on Hoyl to be destroyed. But whether out of legitimate concern or malice, he did deliberately destroy ship's records, and I am going to put that down his throat when the time is right."

"How are you going to do that?"

With a tight smile, Dan told her of the black box in his cabin, and his efforts to get a permanent and unassailable back up. "We'll stick around to watch the solstice Zharrise as Hō-ō moves out of eclipse, and then head up to *Phoenix*. I'll hit him with it the next day."

"I would love to see the expression on his face when you do that."

"Just remember, loyalty is a two-way street. I owe it to him to have a way to save face if he was merely wrong."

"That's why I love you, Captain Vargas. I believe you mentioned dinner?"

"I did. And Sean did say yesterday that he would respect my request for no formal dinner, but would make sure the kitchen had something special. I understand a turkey dinner with fine red wine awaits us."

"Genuine turkey? We have such a thing?" Most of the crew and colonists didn't eat meat routinely or at all, but fish and fowl were considered exotic delicacies.

"Captain's ship functions stores. Along with all the trimmings, including cranberry sauce. And the wine is the finest Greenland vintners can produce."

"Wow. I think I'm going to enjoy being the Captain's wife. And maybe Sean isn't such a bad guy, after all."

"That's my hope. Having you as captain's wife is my dream."

It was about twenty days before Vargas looked in his black box for the records. By which time, they didn't matter, beyond confirming Vargas' doubts about his Number One.

Chapter 40 Like a Rainbow

CAPTAIN VARGAS DIDN'T STRIKE MIDSHIPMAN RED FARNSWORTH as the sort of brass hat who made subordinates pay for his mistakes. Sheffield might, but the Captain had placed his hands upon him and blessed him. If he had to do it over again, he still would have reported the streak.

Sheffield explained that it was just an artifact of the ship's equipment. "We have the radar down for a full system check," Sheffield said. "And you and Simmons will have it noted in your records that you brought this to our attention before we experienced a possibly critical fail. For that, my thanks."

"Commander, Rebekah and I did see a streak. What about that?"

Sheffield frowned slightly. "Tell me, Red. Is it really unusual to see a shooting star in Hoyl's night sky? I've probably seen three dozen tonight, and I wasn't even looking. And it was just sheer dumb luck that you happened to spot that meteorite just at the right time and roughly in the same place as where you thought that orbiting object might be." Sheffield chuckled. "I might have called the Captain himself if I were in your shoes. And been right to do so. Going on the information you had, you and Simmons did the right thing. On that, the Captain and I agree."

Red know the object he saw was orbiting, not flaming out in the atmosphere, but he let the matter drop and graciously accepted the Commander's kind words, but as he stepped off the footbridge on the Avalerion side, he found his doubts growing. Fulsome praise wasn't Sheffield's style, and it felt phony.

He hadn't mentioned to Sheffield – or the Captain, for that matter – that the object was blue, rather than white. Also, it pulsed, and Red thought he saw plasma circles behind it like those *Phoenix* supposedly trailed when her fusion engine was engaged. Or did his imagination tack those on?

He got home, and was unsurprised to see that Rebekah's place was still lit. He went over and knocked.

"So what are you going to do?" she asked after he filled her in on what transpired after she left.

"Talk to Simmons, I guess. I'll see if André will check his duty roster and see when he might next be down here?"

"André? What's he got to do with this?"

"He has a legitimate reason to check the roster. I have a feeling Sheffield's going to be watching for me to do that."

Ye gods and little fishes, Rebekah thought. Paranoia strikes. "I would have that you would be worried about Vargas. He's the Americaner."

Red shook his head. "The Captain isn't the one acting like he's got something to hide. Sheffield is. In any event, until we get some of resolution on this, I don't want to get caught in whatever it is going on between those two."

"When will you see André?"

"Hm. Let's see. Eclipse ends about 1400 hours tomorrow. That gives me about an hour and a half of daylight where it would be reasonable for me to contact him about weather forecasts or whatever. I hate Hoylidays. You can't get anything done."

"Do you think this will get resolved?"

"Oh, yeah. One way or another.

"Eventually."

* * *

Vargas was anxious to return to *Phoenix*, but knew that for appearance's sake he should stay until the end of the eclipse. In person, he had never seen the spectacular sideways Zharrise that marked the end of the eclipse which included the mysterious waves of light that coursed across the face of Hō-ō minutes before the actual emergence of the F8 star. As a result, time crawled.

It didn't help that there wasn't much to do in Avalerion during the Long Night. There were various group gatherings going on, and Dan and Julie sat in on a couple of them. It was Julie who first noted a vague sense, if not desperation exactly, then foreboding. Odd that she hadn't noticed it before, she thought. But the settlement was just at the equinox, which on Earth meant that daytime and nighttime were evenly split. Here, the life giver Zhar-Ptitsa was already below the horizon two thirds of the time already, or hiding behind Hō-ō, and in forty days, it would simply not rise above the horizon at all. This would be followed by a hundred and forty days of perpetual night, well beyond the extreme seen on Earth at the Poles. Nobody was sure what the weather would be like. It wouldn't get viciously cold, rarely going below freezing, but the botanists and André Morley had warned them that based on what they had learned as a result of Ice Fall, the local vegetation was capable of surviving incredibly powerful storms. And storms of the sort that destroyed Red's ROVER were sweeping further and further north, and worse, forming along the "sheltered side" of the mountain spine of the continent.

When she mentioned this feeling to Dan, he paused, eyes focused on the middle distance, and recited, "Blow, blow, thou winter wind. Thou art not so unkind; As man's ingratitude; Thy tooth is not so keen, Because thou art not seen, Although thy breath be rude." He smiled down at Julie. "Shakespeare. One of his sonnets."

"Oh, Captain, my Captain. You're making my heels round. Recite some more Shakespeare!"

"Freeze, freeze thou bitter sky, That does not bite so nigh As benefits forgot: Though thou the waters warp, Thy sting is not so sharp As a friend remembered not."

"OK, let me try one. Mph. OK, got it. 'I awoke today and found the frost perched on the town. It hovered in a frozen sky, then it gobbled summer down. When the sun turns traitor cold, and all the trees are shivering in a naked row, I get the urge for going but I never seem to go' How's that?"

"I don't know that one. Midsummer's Night Dream?"

"No, an Americaner song, about five hundred years later. 'Urge for Goin' by Joni Mitchell."

"I'll have to listen to it when we get back to the ship." Vargas tapped a memo into his data pad.

They looked in on pottery-making classes, on lectures on known properties of the plant life around Scafeld, and watched some overenthusiastic tuba players doing twenty-third century

Pahrump rap music. Vargas confided to Julie, "Music to cure constipation by."

Julie's choice of Mitchell's quote bothered him. Suppose they couldn't leave this place? If they couldn't find the raw materials they needed, what then?

Dan clicked his data pad. A half hour until end of eclipse. He waved a hand and said "dim" and the interior lighting in the cabin went down. As the settlement grew, the custom was to dim all the lights as a courtesy to those who wanted to watch the light-waves fan across the face of Hō-ō. They weren't exceptionally bright, and it didn't take much ambient light to drown them out.

"Ready?"

"Let me visit the bathroom real quick."

Dan shook his head. Women. Those visits always took about ten minutes, so he looked up Joni Mitchell on his data pad and listened for a bit. He was surprised he hadn't heard of the Saskatchewan-born singer before.

A purple flash lit the translucent tube-grass mat walls of the cabin. Dan cocked his head, trying to imagine what might have caused it. He had the data pad retract the ear buds and went to the front door. Even with the music, he would have heard something if it had been an explosion. He looked out. There wasn't much to see. Most of the homes arrayed around had already dimmed their lights, and it was still, silent, and cold. Back lit by the door, Dan exhaled, and saw his breath condensed in front of him. He turned back in to get a sweater and gloves.

He was just pulling on the gloves and Julie was coming out of the head when the light show began. A series of flashes, purple at first and then expanding to encompass the whole spectrum tattooed the walls of the structure, flickering and sweeping.

Julie pulled her chin in. "Police cars?" she said.

"No police." No emergency vehicles per se here. He pulled open the door to see bands of light, all colors of light, sweeping across the plain and over the settlement. He looked up to see the source.

Hō-ō had grown a band of flashing, strobing, multicolored lights. He gawked at the sight, wondering what on Earth he could be looking at. Unbidden, an ancient movie, "Close Encounters of the Third Kind" sprung to mind. Was this the latest manifestation of the visitors?

His data pad signaled, and without looking, he tapped it. It was Etienne Sorlund, on the bridge. "Captain, look at this! This is unbelievable!"

Vargas tore his eyes from the giant planet and looked at his screen. It was Hoyl, with a bite of light on the right side, and waves of rainbow patterns sweeping across the darkened face of the moon from left to right. It looked like someone had hung a giant prism in front of the moon. . . ah. He looked up at the sky. The flashes of light were creeping along the ring of Hō-ō as the sun advanced on the other side. The rings that were made of globules of ice and water. The rings that of course would put out spectrums of light when Zharlight hit them.

The rings that, twice a year, were exactly edge on to Hoyl, and in perfect alignment with Zhar-Ptitsa.

People were pouring out of their homes now, and looking about themselves in awe. Belatedly, Vargas set his data pad to 'record'. He glanced up at Hō-ō. The edge of the planet was starting to brighten, a sign of the end of the eclipse. The running coruscation of lights had extended along the ring further into the darkened face of the planet. There were wisps of cirrus in the night sky, and they caught and reflected streaming rainbows of their own, animated snakes of color across the sky.

Vargas glanced around and spotted Sheffield, who was staring at the ring and mouthing the word "Wow!" over and over. Vargas sidled over. "Sean," he whispered, "you told me the eclipse ending was something to see, but I never expected anything like this."

"I've never seen it like this before, Captain. This is magnificent."

Vargas took a look around. What had to be everyone in the colony was out now, and they all had their data pads out, capturing this. Movement caught his eye and he saw a cat streak through the legs of various people and into the commons building. He didn't have time to see if it was Tipsy or one of her kittens. Probably Tipsy. The kittens were still pretty young.

Sheffield's eyes were moist. "This is why I love this place, Dan. What does Earth have to compare with this?"

Vargas shook his head and said nothing. For a moment, the two men could forget their differences.

A bead of brilliant light sparkled on the side of Hō-ō, and Sheffield pulled his visor down and gestured to Vargas and his wife to do likewise. The bead sharped, grew light streaks. Suddenly a swiftly-moving succession of bands moved across the face of the planet, salmon pink rushing through the darkly sanguine orb. "There," Sheffield pointed. "That's what I brought you here to see originally."

"What are they?"

"Nobody knows. Simmons says he can't think of any property of optics that would cause it, and a couple of the exobiologists are convinced that it's some sort of organic display."

"Organic? Alive?"

"Not necessarily. A chemical reaction of some sort. Although they can't explain why it would only happen at the end of an eclipse. Nothing on Hō-ō cares where the planet's shadow falls."

"Maybe there's something about the light that makes it possible to see it only right then, and they are actually there all the time."

"That would make. . . " Sheffield broke off. Günter Brülow was shouting and pointing toward the shuttle parking area. The trio turned as one to look.

Even two hundred meters away, it looked huge. An orb, easily twenty-five meters tall hovered over the landing field. As they watched, it slowly dropped, in eerie silence, until it rested on the tube-grass. Vargas could see it was behind the shuttles, so it was even bigger than he first thought. It reposed on the air, effortlessly and in utter silence.

Vargas glanced at Sheffield. The man had something that looked like despair in his eyes.

"Well, Captain, let's go meet your alien overlords."

Chapter 41 Like a Stray Kitten

BY THE TIME THE CAPTAIN AND SHEFFIELD made it to the landing field minutes later, it was a bright and sunny late afternoon. Hō-ō, now forgotten, crossed the sky next to Zhar-Ptitsa as a thin purplish crescent.

In full light they could see the orb was pure white, with absolutely no markings. There was no sign of ports or hatches. From ten meters outside the circumference of the object, it looked immense and inconspicuous at the same time, a giant Ping-Pong ball. The colonists and crew had surged up behind Vargas and Sheffield, and with a quick aside to Sheffield, several crew members were tasked with getting the crowd to back off a bit. Vargas overheard Red saying to one especially inquisitive colonist, "Let's not frighten the nice galactic overlords who can accelerate at a bajillion Gs and float a ten million ton object a few centimeters off the ground, yeah?"

Grinning despite himself, Vargas crouched for a better look. Sure enough, the bottom of the orb was a dozen or so centimeters over the tube-grass, which didn't appear to be affected by the (presumably) huge mass hovering directly over it. Could the object be nothing more than a balloon? Vargas doubted it. "Red," he called over his shoulder, "Could you set up camera angles so we can see all sides of this thing? If the occupants decide to come out and say hi, we're going to look awful silly if we're standing on the wrong side."

Sheffield leaned over and whispered. "Should we get a shuttle up so we can see what the top half is doing?"

"No. They may see that as provocative. I'm just hoping they aren't real nervous and see a small group of unarmed people as dangerous."

"Are we unarmed? Is anyone carrying?"

Vargas scanned the crowd and spotted Rudy Harlen. The mouse-slayer had his arms crossed, but was looking up at the alien craft with a big incredulous grin. "I don't think anyone's armed. Rudy isn't, and if he isn't, a doubt anyone is." Rudy had to be feeling a bit vindicated, Vargas realized. Aliens really did exist. And they were a bit gnarlier than mice.

"Not that weapons would do any good," Vargas added.

"Nuh."

The two men waited. The minutes passed.

Vargas said, "This is getting a bit anticlimactic. I'm going to go up and knock."

Sheffield let his eye travel the extent of the orb, obviously looking for reasons why this might be a terrible idea. After a pause, he replied, "Please knock gently, Ser."

Slowly, with his arms out to the side in what he hoped was a stance of open friendly harmlessness, he walked under the object to where the hull curved down far enough for him to reach. He turned and looked at Sheffield, who glanced up and then at his data pad and nodded.

Reaching up with his gloved hand, he tapped on the hull, or tried to. The surface of the hull was soft and slightly yielding. Vargas frowned and tried again, using his knuckles. The soft surface absorbed the blows soundlessly. Vargas placed the flat of his right hand against the object and pressed. He lifted his hand away and briefly saw an indentation in the shape of his hand which faded rapidly. He moved over a couple of meters, and tried again. Same result. Another four meters, same result. The whole thing might have been encased in silly putty.

Shaking his head, he trudged back to Sheffield. "Well, that was a no-go." He explained what he had discovered, briefly pressing his hand on Sheffield's shoulder to demonstrate how hard he had pressed to leave the brief imprint in the hull surface. A light on Sheffield's med monitor started flashing. Both men started at it in astonishment.

"Ser, you're contaminated. Gloves. Take them off. Carefully."

Rubbing his hands like a card shark, Vargas was able to remove the gloves without touching the outer surface.

Glancing around, Sheffield spotted Matthew Bissont and murmured into his data pad to the toxicologist. Now standing clear of the slightly unhappy Captain, Sheffield spoke briefly to Bissont, gesturing toward the shuttles. Bissont scurried off, and returned a few moments later with waldos – similar to the trash pickers a youthful Dan used on public service park cleanup details—and a dark bag. He came over, set the bag down with the top open, and using the tongs, carefully lifted the gloves into the bag. Next, he approached Vargas with a wand and ran it around him. "Seen worse, Captain," was his verdict. "When you're done making history with First Contact, take a very long hot shower, burn those clothes, and you should be fine. Captain, I'm sorry, but I need your tunic, too."

"But I'm not wear. . . damn. OK, here you go."

"Thorium?" asked Sheffield.

"That would be my guess, Ser."

Vargas gave the orb a thoughtful glance. "How far back should we be?"

"Don't touch it and you should be OK for a short visit. Um, don't go inside, in case it's radioactive inside, too."

"Is that possible?"

Bissont shrugged. "You're asking the wrong guy, Ser. For all I know, thorium is like sunshine to them. Or maybe they just like the taste."

Vargas didn't think either sounded very likely, but had no intention of entering the craft until they knew something about the occupants. Both entry and the occupants were moot until something opened on the orb.

"Still nothing?" he asked Sheffield. He glanced over at the Commander, who shook his head. He became aware that a substantial number of the colonists were grinning at his skivvies. "OK, maybe they don't like the crowd. Let's get everyone to move back a hundred meters and see if that makes them a bit less bashful."

The crowd of colonists moved back with some reluctance.

An hour passed. During that time crew members came up with replacement tunics and gloves for both men. Even in winter, Zhar-Ptitsa was dangerous to exposed skin. At the end of the hour, Zhar-Ptitsa was crowding the horizon, with Hō-ō in close pursuit. Some of the colonists, concluding that there was nothing to see, drifted away.

Vargas and Sheffield stood about twelve meters back at the arbitrary location they had chosen, between the orb and Avalerion, exchanging desultory remarks. The orb itself did not move, did not change, and made no noise.

Zhar-Ptitsa set on a painfully short day. Sheffield murmured to Vargas, "We've got about fifty minutes until the end of twilight."

Vargas nodded. "At that point we might as well go back. Detail some people to stand guard, and keep a running video and wide-band surveillance." He unfurled his data pad. "Mr. McDonald, is that thing trying to communicate at all?"

Davis' voice came back. "It broadcasts at various frequencies, but there's no modulation. Some of the frequencies would be suitable for radar or sonar. Most are just unused bands—by us, anyway—that are broadcasting static."

"Everything being recorded for deeper analysis later?"

"As you ordered, Ser."

"Very good. Simmons?"

"Ser. Nothing to report in low orbit. Shall I do deep space scans as well?"

"Do it. Are you picking anything up from the orb itself?

"No Ser. From *Phoenix*'s vantage, it is silent."

Sheffield finished deploying watchers, and glanced over. "Maybe meeting new aliens is no big deal to them. Something that happens every ten days or so."

"Maybe, but it's a big deal to us." Vargas' exasperation rose to the fore. "Why won't they at least acknowledge us?"

"Ser, there's a port opening about seventy degrees on your left!"

The two men glanced over. "Let's go!"

Vargas and Sheffield strode around to the opening—it was only about a meter tall and half a meter wide near the 'equator'—and waited. Taking a quick glance at Vargas, Sheffield assumed the same stance: erect but relaxed, arms at the side but a bit away from the hips, palms forward. It wasn't a stance he would want to hold for long, but it made sense. We are peaceful. We are friendly. We aren't going to eat your thorium.

"Something wrong, Commander?"

"Sinuses, Captain." His tone changed. "Captain, I see movement!"

"I see it too. OK, it's show time."

A form appeared. It stepped out of the port and apparently onto thin air. Two other forms followed it. They gently began to descend, with no noise or visible signs of what was holding them up. Vargas eyed the trajectory and calculated they would land about five meters in front of them, which struck him as ideal. Ideal for humans, anyway. Hopefully these guys would find it in their comfort zone.

They landed, and both men, despite themselves, gawped. They were tiny, perhaps eighty centimeters tall. They had four legs, wide-stanced, a bit like a spider, and four arms, quadilaterally symmetrical. They appeared to be wearing space suits. The strangest part was the 'head'. The upper third of the creatures was a black tube, perhaps seventy five millimeters in diameter, with a rounded top. There was no sign of eyes or any other sensory organs.

One of the creatures was holding a device that looked quite a bit like a data pad. It didn't appear flexible however. The creature held it out in front (back? Side?) of him and didn't appear to be interacting with it, although it was impossible to tell if the creature was looking at anything, or could look at all.

The creatures stood stock-still for a couple of moments in the gathering gloom. Vargas hoped MacDonald was getting some good tight shots of these things for later study.

Finally, Vargas spoke. "Greetings. My name is Daniel Vargas, and I welcome you to the moon we call Hoyl. We are human, and we are happy to meet you."

Then he waited. The theory was that even if none of the aliens spoke English, they would at least be recording this and would analyze it themselves. If nothing else, if they ever learned English, they would at least know that the intentions of the humans were peaceful.

No response. Minutes passed. Vargas murmured out of the side of his mouth to Sheffield, "I'm going to try to approach them. Stay where you are. One might be less threatening."

"I don't think we can threaten these guys," Sheffield breathed back. "Just with the technology they've shown us, I don't think we can even touch them."

"Probably. But they don't know what our technology is, and might assume the worst. I'm going to move very slowly." He glanced over his shoulder and saw Julie standing at the front of the crowd next to Red Farnsworth, her face white in the gloaming. He gave a little wave. His arms were feeling very tired.

He moved toward the trio of aliens, moving his right foot forward very slowly through the tube-grass, praying he didn't trip and fall on his face. He finished the step and waited. No response.

He took another step and waited. The aliens seemed oblivious to his presence. They were so still he wondered if they were just probes, sent out to record for the actual aliens inside the ship.

Taking a full minute for each tiny step, he drew nearer and nearer. He was nearly a meter away from the aliens, and debating whether he should try crouching down so he might appear less intimidating, when gravity suddenly abandoned him.

He felt like he was in micro gravity, a familiar feeling on board ship, but unexpected here. His feet drifted up off the tube-grass, and he felt himself being gently propelled backward. He wound up at his original position next to Sheffield, and was slowly dropped. He was still moving backward as gravity returned, and his heel caught and he went back on his ass, arms swinging wildly.

Sheffield turned and extended an arm, never taking his eyes off the aliens. "Are you alright, Ser?"

"Yes." Angrily, Vargas resisted the urge to brush at his ass. He was unhurt, but felt humiliated. "They set me aside like a stray kitten."

He glared at the aliens. "What the hell is it with you people?" he blurted.

Sheffield gave him a shocked look, and that was the only response he got. Belatedly, he realized that the outburst was going to look awful to humans, never mind what the aliens thought. He was glad King Edward IX would never hear of this. The King clearly considered Vargas to be humanity's last great hope as ambassador to the stars. Vargas felt he was underperforming at this point.

Without warning, the aliens began rising slowly in the air. As Sheffield and Vargas gaped at them, they rose to the level of the port, and without turning, drifted back in. The port closed, becoming seamless in a process that made Vargas' eyes water.

"I think they're preparing to leave, Captain."

Vargas turned and strode toward the crowd. "Back! Everyone back! It's going to take off!"

The crowd jostled backward, confused. Vargas, now running, wondered what the blast would be like, and if any of the colonists would survive being this close to a spaceship taking off. Instinctively he looked for Julie. . .

She was right where he had last seen her, next to Farnsworth, and they were both looking up. Feeling completely flummoxed, Vargas glanced over his shoulder at the ship.

Which wasn't there.

He looked up. In the now-rapidly darkening sky, he could barely make out the white dot that was the ship, and then it was invisible. It hadn't made a whisper.

Sheffield came up alongside him. "What the fuck. . . "

Sheffield suddenly remembered his youth in Manchester, and the power of bluster that had carried him through many teenage confrontation with the local yob footies. He turned to Vargas with a wide grin and said, "Well, Captain, I guess we showed them. . . ."

A violet flash caused both men to look up, just in time to see a blue streak cross the sky and vanish. Almost a minute later there was a loud crack, and then a distant, tinny-sounding sonic boom.

"Well," Vargas mused, "that's one way they're better than us. At least they waited to clear the area before firing up their main engines."

Sheffield gave him a frankly curious look. "Of course, we weren't shooting at them."

Chapter 42 Do You Like The Neighbors?

PHOENIX REPORTED THE CRAFT MOVING TOWARD Disappointment, which came as no real surprise to anyone. An awed Simmons reported that the craft would reach the planet in about a half hour.

Nobody could agree on any single element of the alien visitation—there were even some people who insisted it hadn't happened at all—but among those that did believe, there was one recurring surmise: the alien ship had something to do with Disappointment.

This was based on the similar factoids that both the ship and Disappointment had a thin covering of thorium. Nobody could come up with a coherent explanation for that, and Simmons remarked, tongue in cheek, that maybe the aliens just liked thorium. As theories went, it was better than most.

News of how the aliens had simply brushed the Captain off made the rounds quickly amongst those who hadn't seen it. The captain's own simile, gossip-expanded to "I was set aside the way you would remove a kitten from your keyboard" became irretrievably wedded as a descriptor, and was greeted with responses ranging from amusement to outrage. Those who were outraged either because of the way the Captain was treated or because the Captain didn't seem particularly outraged. Vargas himself considered it a problem in communications, rather than a studied insult.

It gave rise to one theory. The visitors weren't aliens, according to this theory, but robotic servants. Someone posted a cartoon of an alien approaching Red's ROVER and saying, "Take me to your leader" to illustrate the notion. It would explain the utter indifference the three entities had shown, and might even explain their peculiar architecture. People equated them to the early robotic explorers of Mars. Vargas, hearing this, wondered if his First Contact had been with an alien Charlie.

Most folks were excited, the colony leaders concerned. Whether they were actually robots, or, in the unfortunate Sheffield sobriquet now sweeping the settlement called them, 'the Galactic Overlords', they were definitely aliens, and their presence meant some plans had to be drawn up.

By 5pm the word went out that Vargas and Sheffield would be holding a public meeting at 7:30. At 7:30 the meeting hall was packed, with every single colonist there.

Vargas sat quietly and watched the people file in. According to Sheffield there were about two hundred and thirty scattered among Avalerion, Lassiter's Landing, and Scafeld. There were another seventy-five on board the *Phoenix*, which meant that nearly four fifths of the people who had traveled all this way to *nu Phoenicis* dreamed on in hibernation, unaware of the strange new world over which they hovered.

Vargas was surprised at the crowd, not because he didn't think anyone would care, but because people could watch it at home, just as the personnel on board *Phoenix* were.

At precisely 1930, he stood, and used Command Presence to still the babble. After thirty seconds, he had the silent rapt attention of the audience.

"Good evening. I won't waste your time trying to explain what happened this afternoon. By now you all know that we had a rather remarkable visitation.

"Instead, I will tell you about discussions we have been having on board *Phoenix* over the past few little years. Or 'weeks' for those of you struggling with the local calendar." A few chuckles, some rueful, scattered around the audience. "Prior to the visitation today, and even before the sighting last night, most of the command officers of *Phoenix* were of the opinion that the moon Hoyl was an artificial construction, and furthermore, we were trespassing on someone else's property."

Swiftly, Vargas explained the scientific data they had amassed that let them to the conclusion that Hoyl could not be anything other than an artificial world, and why most of the line officers regarded this as making the place unsuitable for permanent settlement. The deliberations hadn't been particularly secret, and Vargas didn't see any surprised expressions.

He went on to describe what little was known about the alien's technological capacities. Mention of eight thousand Gs acceleration did draw gasps, along with the estimate, provided by Simmons just an hour earlier, that the craft approached 99.9C as it sped away.

Right on schedule, Gordon Lassiter raised his hand. "What do we know about their military technology?" It was a reasonable question for Lassiter to ask, and provided Vargas with a segue he wanted.

"Mister Lassiter, we don't know that they even have a military capacity. What we do know is that we have next to none. We have a relatively small personal armory that was included against the possibility of hostile native life forms. Lacking such, most of the armory remains on *Phoenix*. The ship itself has no significant weaponry. It was decided early on that a craft that requires eighteen hours to change the direction it's facing by 180 degrees wasn't well suited for dogfights." There were several chuckles from the crowd. "Especially against ships that can accelerate at thousands of Gs," he added to a rising tide of laughter.

The laughter subsided, and he continued, "We didn't come to fight. We came to settle. I'm sure you all remember the lectures we got during training. If we got to this system and found it occupied, we were to try to establish friendly communication, and ask if there was any place in their solar system where we might settle. If they said no, we were to move on. In any direction other than toward Earth, since my own government insisted that the location of Earth never be revealed. I think they were being a bit paranoid."

"Ya think?" rang out from someone in the crowd, and Vargas gave a rueful smile. "They had in mind that any entities we encountered might be implacably hostile. As most of you know, the mission planners dropped that requirement over Americaner objections. We are to exercise our own best judgment."

"My own feeling is that with the beings we encountered, it's going to be a while before we start swapping home photos. We don't even know how they communicate among themselves, or even if they have to. And we have no idea how to communicate with them."

Susan Bartlett raised her hand for attention. "What if we cannot communicate with them?"

"Then I sincerely hope that when they have something to say to us, they do so non-violently. I believe all intelligent species must be able to communicate, and if there are more than one intelligent species, then they must learn to communicate between, or amongst themselves. I don't know how they communicate, whether by telepathy or holding up Rorschach cards or what, but they communicate. They must. We have to find it."

Ruby Harlen was next. "Sheffield tells me that you just want to pack up and skedaddle. Is that correct?"

Vargas signed inwardly and guessed that he wasn't the only one who planted questions in the audience. Sheffield had, as well.

"That isn't quite the way I would put it. As the Commander knows, it is my position that this world is not suitable for permanent settlement. That was already my position before our friends showed up today. To that end, I believe we should direct our efforts to putting *Phoenix* into a condition where it is again capable of interstellar flight. That means securing raw material to replace damaged or missing ship elements, determining a suitable system as a new destination, and getting everyone on board who wishes to go."

"Abandoning the rest of us." Harlen's voice was flat.

Vargas managed an easy smile. "I would hardly call it abandonment when there's a standing offer for anyone who wishes to come with us to hop on board. Asuka?"

The exobotanist stood up. "Captain Vargas-sama, if the *Phoenix* leaves, we will probably never see her again." Vargas nodded. The next solar system known to have terrestrial planets was thirty eight light years away. "And Earth doesn't know we're here on Hoyl. What are our options if these aliens do consider this their property and want us off?"

Out of the corner of his eye he saw Sheffield looking down and shaking his head. Obviously this wasn't one of his planted questions. "Earth won't know we were ever here for another half century. And then only if anyone's listening." Vargas waited for Asuka to digest that. "We knew we were on our own when we left Earth, Asuka. And yes, when *Phoenix* leaves, it probably will be for good. You will be on your own, with no hope of rescue. I know that for many of you, the preference is to stay. You have that right. But I want you all to understand what it may entail. We won't be able to help you, and nobody can. And if your presence angers the..um. . . Overlords, then you'll have to count on their mercy."

Harlen shouted out, "Suppose we stop you from taking *Phoenix*?"

Vargas gave the man a long, level, humorless stare. "*Phoenix* is my command. If you propose to take her, you will have a fight on your hands."

Harlen blinked, startled. Clearly he hadn't thought it through. Vargas recalled that the man had made some vaguely mutinous talk in the first days of the mission, and wondered, not for the first time, how this hot headed fool got on the crew.

At his side, Sheffield bolted to his feet, red-faced. "That is enough of that sort of talk!" he snapped. "That adds nothing to this discussion!"

"What's it to be, Mister Harlen?" Vargas spoke with dangerous softness. "Are you going to continue advocating mutiny?" He had a sudden memory of having had this same discussion with this same man as *Phoenix* raced outward to the orbit of Mars.

Harlen shook his head. "Captain, I apologize and retract my ill-reasoned comment." He sat down. Vargas and Sheffield exchanged a quick glance. They might be adversaries over the fate of the colony, but in some odd way he was still the loyal second officer. Vargas glanced at the expression on Harlen's face and felt unease sweep through him. The man had backed down. For now. His expression wasn't that of a man who misspoke and regretted the blunder.

"Commander, since you're already standing, would you like to address the group?"

"Thank you, Captain. If you're finished. . . ? Fine. I'll note that the visitors gave no indication that we were trespassing, and didn't seem upset at our presence. We're not sure they were anything more than a survey group that may well have been simply collecting data on terrestrial planets. They left from here to Disappointment, and for all we know, may have spent and couple of hours there doing the same thing, and then moved on to Cueball and done the same thing there. And from there, gone to the next star system on their list. They may have had no more interest in Hoyl, or us, than a data entry clerk has in you when he types your name in on his computer. Nothing happened today to suggest to me that we have to abandon Hoyl."

"That's absurd!" one of the colonists shouted.

"Is it, Mister Edgers? I'll give you an example of absurd. Captain Vargas came to me and told me they had come up with a theory up on the ship that the planet was artificial, and that one day the owners would show up and reclaim their property. Lo and behold, the very next day aliens show up, for the first time in human history. What a coincidence!" He turned to Vargas with a friendly grin, "I was frankly very skeptical at the original reports that we had a visitor, and I hope the Captain will understand why, in good faith, I wondered if the 'visitation' wasn't just too much of a coincidence to be believed."

Vargas nodded. That was one element in Sheffield's response that was utterly clear to him.

"That's an absurdity at a level only the French could love. I can only conclude that the universe likes to mess with us.

"Now, if they were just a survey team of some sort, they will go on about their mysterious business and we humans will never see them again until they make their way around to the Solar System. That's my opinion.

"Now suppose the Captain is right, and they are the actual owners of this place, and will be back at some point to reclaim their property?

"It's not an unreasonable conjecture. I'll be the first to admit that. Certainly it would strain credulity and abuse all scientific logic to try to pretend that Hoyl came to exist the way it is through natural means. I'll remind people that back on Earth, in the twenty-second century there were religious cults in Europe and Asia that believed the Earth was only a couple of thousand years old, and created in just one week. This is a similar situation, only in reverse. Earth has indisputable evidence showing that it has to be at least four and a half billion years old. This world has indisputable evidence that it cannot possibly have been here more than thirty thousand years. Yet it has sophisticated and widely varied plant life, something that Earth required two billion years or more to develop. Or longer.

"Only an idiot would try to claim that Hoyl was anything other than an artificial construct. The evidence is overwhelming, approaching proof. The only puzzle remaining to me is that we didn't realize it two days after we first began orbiting this moon."

Vargas nodded. He had wondered the same thing.

"Where we differ is not on the nature of Hoyl, but the nature and intentions of those who created this world. The Captain, exercising precautions that a man in his office must take, believes they may be antipathetic or at the very least disinclined to the idea of us remaining on this world."

"If today's entities were those builders of Hoyl, then we already have evidence that our presence is of no particular concern to them. Given their technology, they could have rid Hoyl of a human presence with no more effort than brushing crumbs off your lap. Obviously, they didn't.

"Suppose they do have reservations about us being here, but were simply unable to communicate those concerns to us? But didn't want to simply eradicate us? That suggests strongly to me that when and if we open methods of communication with them, we might be able to negotiate for a small part of this world for us to call our own, preferably this locale.

"Now, I know what our mission orders say: if a world is inhabited, we are to ask politely if there is a place we can stay, and if the answer is no, to move on. Those order didn't cover this explicitly, but can be accommodated to our situation. If the aliens have an opinion on our presence, we can negotiate. But I didn't travel forty-seven light years just to be chased off by a hypothetical imponderable."

Sheffield sat down and gave Vargas an expectant look. Vargas looked around the room. He remembered the estimate that perhaps a quarter of the colonists wanted to stay no matter what, and wondered if that had changed any today.

"The commander is correct when he says my concerns are based on hypotheticals and imponderables. That is a part of a Captain's job, I'm afraid." A scattering of chuckles greeted this.

"Given the demonstrated technological abilities of our visitors, it's a hypothetical that we must take very seriously. As Commander Sheffield himself says, they could probably eliminate all of us without effort, so we need to take steps not to needlessly antagonize them. I'll remind everyone again that we have no military capability whatever.

"But it is a hypothetical, this guessing game as to what the aliens want, and to what lengths they will go toward that end. But the fact is I felt—along with most of the line officers of the *Phoenix*—that we should make moving on to a new world our top priority before the visitors showed up."

Vargas had outline notes on his data pad, but didn't need them. Counting off on his fingers as he spoke, he mentioned the emotional and psychological unsuitability of Hoyl to humans, the very limited area on the planet that could support human life at all, the difficulties of cultivation under the wildly variable Zharlight, the fact that outdoor livestock could not live under the burning gaze of the star ("Our sheep and goats would be blind in a week, if they didn't die of acute sunburn first"). He mentioned the difficulty of coherent time-keeping they were facing, from the slowing rotation to the utter inability of anyone to come up with a calendar that people could live by. Finally, he mentioned the frequent nature of the Ice Falls.

"This place can support human life, barely. But it is not a suitable home for humans, and eventually, humans would die off out here. We must find a home—a true home, one where we might reasonably expect our great-grandchildren to be able to walk unprotected under a noon-day sun, where death doesn't rain from the sky every year, and the light of the moon doesn't drive people mad."

Rebekah Cohen signaled for his attention. "You mentioned we have no military capability. But isn't it true that the Imprinter files include the schematics for a lot of advanced weaponry?"

Vargas looked around, spotted Lassiter. "Gordon, you can describe the weapons cache, if you would be so kind. . . "

"Certainly, captain." Lassiter stood, rubbing his hands on his thighs. "We have three sorts of weapons in the data; personal, such as rifles, shotguns, bows and arrows, the sort of things you might use for hunting or against dangerous wildlife; military, such as laser cannon, rocket launchers, and pain rays, and special classified. That last includes nuclear weapons, torpedoes, and others. Anyone can requisition personal weapons; the line officers can disburse military, and the classified are, as it says, classified, and encrypted, and only the captain's log has the codes.

"Of course, *Phoenix* is not credible as a warship. Top acceleration of less than two gees, and incapable of turning in the space of a day. Given the raw materials, we could build ships that could fight in space, but would be utterly ineffectual against the known capabilities of our visitors. It's pointless to launch an SDM-28 at them when they can easily dodge or outrun it, or worse, watch as it explodes harmlessly two meters off their bow. At that point, our only hope for survival would be that they didn't take it personally.

"This is just my opinion, but I think it's madness to even contemplate military action against these beings." Lassiter abruptly sat.

Vargas looked around. "Would anyone like to rebut Mister Lassiter?" Even Rudy Harlen was silent, looking down at the floor.

He felt awkward in the face of the utter silence, even though it was what he was hoping for. Looking around, he saw a lot of people nodding. There was nothing to cheer about, but people were reacting calmly.

Sheffield stood slowly, weighed down by something more than his age and Hoyl's three-quarters gravity. "I realize we've given people a lot to assimilate tonight, especially coming on the heels of today's events. So we're not going to come to a decision tonight. I propose we all take a little year to think about it and discuss it amongst ourselves, and have a meeting ten day's hence, and maybe then we'll have some idea of what direction we all need to take—or directions, come to that." He lifted an eyebrow at Vargas, who nodded. "In that case, I pronounce this meeting adjourned. Go get some sleep, if you can."

Chapter 43 The Exploration Resumes

TWO DAYS LATER, RED RECEIVED WORD FROM JEANINE Barney that the Imprinter was in the process of building ROVER II, and the Captain had authorized three more copies of it to be made. To Red's joy, all sides of the controversy over what to do about Hoyl agreed that no matter what, the moon had to be explored. The Captain wanted raw materials so the *Phoenix* could be made interstellar-ready. Sheffield wanted to find other areas humans might live. Boitumelo mentioned tube-grass root and steelwood.

Who knew what other wonders were out there? Rebekah had given him that selling point to drive the argument home; if the beings that made this world put tube-grass and steelwood trees on it as being utterly indispensable, what else might they have put on this world that was equally valuable?

The third generation ROVER resembled his little dragonfly lying dead in the northern mountains the way a shuttle resembled the Mercury capsules that had taken men into space. Ten meters long and two wide, it was essentially an unmanned shuttle. Unlike the shuttles, it was designed to repose on water. It carried four ROVERS that had been the modest second generation model Red had originally requested. When *Phoenix* was being designed, this was the version considered for the ship, but eventually was consigned to the memory of the library and the Imprinter's recipe book. It was Jeanine Barney who remembered it was there.

It could gather dozens of plant and mineral samples and bring them back to the base units, where they would be stored, along with data pertaining to location, altitude, temperature and other factors. High resolution cameras would record the locations visually, and monitor any animal life they might encounter.

Red noted, but carefully did not mention, that he had bigger tasks and more responsibilities than most of the officers. It did not, however, escape the Captain's notice.

"Red, I realize you can't do this with just the Spencer kids, so you're authorized to get up to eight people to work under your command. If the best people include some of my officers, I'll put them on detached status and they'll answer to you.

"Now, what else do you need?"

For once in his life Red was speechless. Just a few weeks ago his project had been viewed, quite condescendingly, as a vanity project designed to keep a Midshipman and two teenagers out of mischief—and it hadn't even succeeded at that. The teenagers got into mischief anyway, and ROVER's inglorious end on the slopes of the Boitumelos had left Red wondering if the project would even be continued.

Now he was head of the biggest project, in terms of people and materials as well as sheer scale, on the moon.

The kids were rehabilitating themselves, taking care of the cat population. Red wondered if some or any of the cats would be on *Phoenix* when it left. He rather hoped so. He didn't think of himself as a 'cat person' but Tipsy and the Mouse Police were awfully endearing.

He spent the next two days conferring with Gordon Lassiter, Madelyn Isaakson, Adelena Conti, Susan Bartlett and Ian Mann over where to look for what types of life. Asuka Tsuchishima signed on, along with André Morley. André in particular was a valuable addition since he could help avoid storms like the one that killed the first ROVER. Such storms were getting more frequent in the northern hemisphere.

Before the Imprinter started disgorging the parts needed to assemble the ROVERs, Red already had over one hundred volunteers. He found himself delegating training sessions for those without ROVER wrangling experience, and formed a small committee to figure out where and when the ROVERs should go.

The Northern Hemisphere, above thirty degrees north was ruled out. The ROVERs could function in full dark, but nobody knew what sort of weather the machines might encounter. Winter was coming.

One ROVER would explore the southern tip of the main continent, which extended all the way to sixty degrees south. Another three would explore the continent of King Edward Island, this world's version of Australia. One of the three would do a low flyover of the south pole where, it was believed, a small archipelago of islands existed under the perpetual cloud cover. Red resolved to pull unaccustomed rank and fly that one himself.

Sheffield recognized that the small shack the ROVER team had been operating from wasn't going to do it, and Red's HQ was moved to the new module-sized tube-grass structure at the center of Scafeld. He would share space with the library, which took up only about four cubic meters. One of the late summer improvements had been a footbridge over the River Styx. It wasn't the full-fledged traffic bridge Sheffield wanted, but it made casual trips from Avalerion to Scafeld easier, since it no longer required a shuttle. Red welcomed the five minute walking commute.

Four ROVER channels were set up so anyone on the ground or aboard *Phoenix* could watch—and comment upon—the activities of the ROVERs. Red had a hunch it would be a popular viewing site, especially in about five more little years, when the colony was in perpetual darkness and weather would effectively put the colony in hibernation.

It was, for Red, the project of a lifetime. He couldn't wait for it to begin.

* * *

Sheffield gave Vargas a look of stymied annoyance. "That idiot Harlen put me in a bind. He made it sound like dissent equated to challenging your authority with that nonsense about seizing the *Phoenix*."

"I don't suppose it's going to stop you from raising the issue anyway."

"As *de facto* colony leader, I have to ask it on behalf of those who cannot ask the question themselves."

"And you know what my answer has to be, then. The line officers of the *Phoenix* have the sole power to determine the suitability of a planet for colonization, and it presupposes that the majority of colonists would still be in hibernation at the time of the decision. Have you read the contract the colonists had to sign?"

"Yes. In all matters pertaining to the running of the ship, you are the sole and uncontested final authority. If they are on the ship, they are subject to your command. But surely the people who drew up that contract didn't envision this situation, where we are effectively stranded at a planet that can support human life, with no word on when *Phoenix* might be shipshape for a trip to the next star, and no immediate overwhelming element that makes the planet unsuitable for life. I don't see how you can handle it in any other way that would be fair."

"Commander, fairness doesn't enter into it. If I were to do as you suggest, I would be asking hundreds of people to make fateful decisions without adequate information. Wouldn't that be unfair, too?"

"Two little years would be all it would take to make that decision."

"Commander, you were in the Royal European High Navy for twenty years, were you not?"

"That's correct, Captain. Like you, retired as a captain, given brevet promotion to Admiral."

"When does the Captain of a vessel give plebiscite authority to the passengers and crew?"

"Um, never, Captain."

"Isn't that what you're asking me to do?"

"Not exactly. I'm suggesting that the sleeping colonists be given the same choice in the matter as the ones on the ground as to whether they stay or go."

"And the crew? Including yourself?"

At Sheffield's silence, Vargas continued, "You're familiar with some of the tales of mutiny on the high seas, right?" Sheffield's expression froze, and he added hurriedly, "I'm not accusing you of mutiny, Mister Sheffield; I wish to make a point."

"The Captain is not going to throw the Bounty at me, Ser?"

"The Captain is not. For one thing, I am disinclined to invite comparisons to Captain Bligh. I had other stories in mind."

"Such as?"

"The problems the Navy had with desertion in the 18th and 19th centuries in places such as Tahiti and Polynesia." Vargas cast an appraising eye at the cabins huddled against the empty expanse of tube grass. "Granted, those places had a few things Hoyl couldn't offer, such as alluring women, friendly natives, good food and a stable climate. The Royal Navy was a pretty grim life for swabbies, and it's not surprising that some of them jumped ship and went native. Ships' captains quickly realized that the only way to keep the desertion rate at low levels was to hunt down and severely punish the deserters."

"I know all this, Captain."

"I'm sure you do, Sean. Do not put me in the position of those bygone captains who had to hunt down deserters. I'll not permit that."

"Nor will I ask it." Sheffield shook his head angrily. "What will you say to the colonists who were never given the opportunity to look at Hoyl and judge for themselves?"

"Ideally, I'll have something better to offer them. As it stands, everything we know about Hoyl is in the ship's library, and if they are curious, they can read, and judge for themselves."

"Your mind is made up on this, then?"

"It is, Commander. Tell me, are you planning to join the colonists who stay behind?

Sheffield remained silent. Vargas waited, searching his face for a clue. Finally, he said, "Will you promise that you will not incite any members of the crew to desert?"

"That's a promise I'm more than willing to make, Captain. If any crew members wish to remain, I promise to have them discuss it with you personally."

"Fair enough. If we lose some of the colonists, I can live with that. One question they will have to ask themselves is if they can live with their decision, knowing that once *Phoenix* leaves the Zhar Ptitsa system, it is an irrevocable decision?"

"Captain, it's my intent to make sure everyone understands the full implications of that decision. The worst thing that could happen to our colony would be if we had people who didn't realize that the decision was a permanent one, either way."

"Very good."

For a moment, both men felt a peace and a resolution were possibilities.

* * *

Etienne Sorlund had time on his hands. A ship in synchronous orbit had little in the way of demands on a chief navigations officer, and a world that was less than fifty thousand years old wouldn't have much that would be of interest to a paleobotanist. Or paleo-anything.

So he did analysis of soil brought back from Disappointment. Microbial life rarely fossilized, but it did create characteristic changes in the mineral composition of the soil.

Sorlund called up the array of soil samples available and frowned. He'd been hoping to find some where the tube-grass grew, but Sheffield and his team hadn't brought along a cutting laser and so didn't have any way of punching through the dense root structure. Of course, just walking on tube-grass there had exposed them to dangerous levels of polonium contamination.

He studied the ship's orbital maps of Disappointment. Tube-grass was found all over the place, on all continents and at all climes. Sorlund pondered that. Given the nature of the plant, and its ability to crowd out all over forms of life, it was a wonder it hadn't taken over the planet. It didn't appear to propagate through seeds and pollen, and the only way they could start a new colony was through cuttings. And the cuttings didn't do well, usually dying out within a few weeks. The stems rarely got more than ten centimeters in height. Compare with the patch where Sheffield's team had gotten contaminated, where it grew up to a meter tall.

Mysterious stuff, Sorlund thought. What does it like in the soil? Does it photosynthesize? Disappointment had a day/night cycle and annual seasons that were much closer to those of Earth than Hoyl.

So little was known of either world. The colonists still had no idea if steelwood dropped their leaves in the autumn and were dormant for the winter or not. The leaves looked deciduous, but were unusually waxy and thick. The thick bark and relatively stubby branches might suggest it was a cold-climate or arid-climate tree. Here, though, it was believed to be moist year round, and rarely below freezing.

But at least the DNA of the steelwood tree looked somewhat familiar. It could have evolved on Earth. It seemed to have the same building blocks. Unlike tube-grass.

Sorlund examined orbital shots of some of the areas of Disappointment tube-grass. It wasn't until he spotted some at the base of a large hill that he spotted a trend. All the tube-grass patches had conventional growth on all sides, but on one side, the growth was considerably less.

The tube-grass patches migrated. Sorlund pulled up photos of tube-grass patches as seen from the ground and the shuttle. He could see it infiltrating various types of forests on one side, and seedlings and saplings emerging from bare ground on the other. He pulled up shots of the Hoyl patch and compared by eye. The stands on Disappointment were far taller and more luxuriant, a deeper shade of green and up to a meter tall. It had been assumed that it liked the climate better, but this was holding true in areas that had surroundings ranging from tropical rain forest to desert. On Disappointment, it seemed, tube-grass liked all climates. But the relatively mild one on Hoyl (discounting, for the moment, the super cell rains the area got) didn't seem to appeal to the plant.

He realized that the 'trail' the roaming colonies of tube-grass left weren't straight lines. Some made detours around mountains and water. Some hit rivers and veered from one side to another. Others veered for no apparent reason at all.

He rubbed the side of his nose, pondering this. Tube-grass exhibited tropisms. It followed something essential to its well-being, just as many plants on Earth did. Sometimes it was individual plants, such as flowers that opened and closed at sunrise and sunset, or even turned to follow the sun across the sky, like sunflowers did. Those were all examples of tropisms. Colonies of plants would grow toward or away from water, sunlight, soil acidity, nutrients, or hillsides depending on their needs. Tube-grass did the same thing.

Sorlund had already put in about thirty days on the question of what tube-grass wanted from life when he happened to glance at the records from Sheffield's final test site, the one where they were contaminated by polonium.

In his notes, Sheffield had groused about being unable to punch through the tube-grass root, and how they had taken samples from the cardinal points around the tube-grass colony. Sorlund clicked through the notes, looking to see what the soil samples revealed. Three of them showed a thin layer of thorium 230. Extremely fine grain, about one millimeter deep. The fourth one, to the north, didn't.

With mounting excitement, Sorlund found the corresponding colony on a satellite image, and zooming in, examined the surrounding plant life. It was hardwood forest, with a reasonably slow regrowth rate, so it made the direction of travel of the tube grass colony fairly obvious.

The colony was moving south. There was a thin layer of thorium 230 on the ground on three sides, but not on the side where it had been.

Initial premise: tube-grass liked thorium, followed it, and did . . . something . . . with it. He couldn't even begin to imagine what, but where the tube-grass had been, the thorium was gone.

To his immense frustration, that was the only record of thorium and tube-grass he could find in Sheffield's data. Scientifically, it wasn't anything more than a single data point. Any scientist fool enough to write a paper based on that would be laughed out of the seminar. It was, for all of that, a data point, and possibly an important one.

Tube-grass was, like Hoyl, probably designed by someone. Disappointment seemed to be a sister world to Hoyl in terms of vegetation, so it was possible that it, too, was a constructed world, perhaps not much older than Hoyl. Disappointment was, in most areas, covered in a thin, fine dusting of thorium 230. There was no conceivable reason why anyone would want to do that, but they had a plant that (maybe) ate thorium 230, saving it as radon and then polonium, until it finally degraded to lead. How or why, he couldn't begin to guess. There seemed no way this could have occurred naturally.

Why would anyone contaminate a planet like that, and then plant an entity to dispose of the contamination?

It made no sense at all. He would have to talk it over with some of the other scientists on board. They might just decide he was crazy, but then, wasn't this whole star system crazy?

He had a flicker of something half-remembered, and looked to see what the substance was on the alien craft that contaminated the Captain's suit.

Somehow, he wasn't surprised to learn that it was a very thin layer of ultra-fine dust. In fact, it was thorium 230.

Chapter 44 Red's Awkward Morning

LIKE NEARLY ALL OF THE COLONISTS, Red suffered from insomnia. Part of it was the day/night cycle that Ian Spencer once said was "best viewed from a 'Tilt-a-Whirl." Doc Spencer had once suggested to Red that the aftereffects of hibernation probably played a role with the sleeping problems: the twingies made everyone a little bit hyper, and the flash-dreams made them a bit apprehensive. Spencer had offered an antidepressant; Red had declined, with thanks. He instinctively felt that the forced gaiety of pills would be a bad blend with the twingies. Spencer looked like it wasn't the first time someone had told him that.

Jim Hartnell had pondered releasing migratory birds on Hoyl, and felt it would be a cruelty, that the poor birds would be deeply confused and disoriented by the subtly different sort of magnetic field that encompassed Hoyl, and had mentioned that on a more subtle level, the magnetic field might have an effect on the human psyche.

It was stuff like that what left Red wondering if humans were really meant to go to the stars. Hell, after three centuries they only had the most tenuous of toeholds on Mars and the Moon, and those were right next door, relatively speaking.

None of this passed through Red's head when he woke up, saw that it was still only 0430, and groaned, realizing it would be seven hours before it began to get light. He had hated the short winter days in Manchester; Hoyl was going to be far worse.

Feeling twice his age, he climbed out of his cot and sternly ordered his coffee maker to provide him with a pot of coffee capable of toppling empires. While the machine mulled over the maximum dose of caffeine a human of Red's age and weight could handle, Red unfurled his data pad and logged into the main ROVER computer at the new module.

Or tried to. The computer wasn't responding. Some idiot probably kicked the plug out, Red thought. He checked the ship's log for news, and there wasn't much. There usually wasn't a lot.

There had been a rumor making the rounds that the Captain and Sheffield had been at odds over waking the twelve hundred or so people who were still in hibernation. Red's source didn't know which party favored which side, but Red could make an informed guess. He was glad that Vargas had prevailed. The colony was already bored out of its mind and dispirited at the long dark season to come. Adding another twelve hundred motivated and trained people and giving them nothing to do would do nothing for morale. Some people had even spoke of going back into hibernation for the next hundred and fifty days or so until there was a decent amount of usable daylight again.

André Morley, safe and warm and dry aboard *Phoenix*, had sent an advisory that a massive hurricane in the western sea could result in heavy rainfall and some wind for the colony. André had cheerfully added that winds at the eye wall were about four hundred kilometers per hour, but were expected to decrease as the storm moved over the mountain ridge that formed the spine of the western hemisphere of the continent. Rain and hot: André warned that temperatures could climb to forty during the rain.

Oh, joy.

By 0500, Red decided there was nothing for it; he might as well go down to the office. He paused to ask his data pad what phase Hō-ō was in, and stepped out into the cool morning. He glanced expectantly over to Rebekah's hut. It was still dark. All the huts were, although Red was willing to bet that half of them had people lying on their backs staring up at dark ceilings and wishing to hell they could get back to sleep.

Walking softly along the dimly lit pathways, Red walked the short distance to the new module. The rear bay door was open, but that wasn't unusual. Red made a note to himself to post a memo telling people to keep it closed if André's storm turned out to be feisty; there was equipment in there that wouldn't take well to getting wet. Ever since mice had been introduced into this innocent world, Red had forbidden all food and drink in the module, reasoning that the best way to control mice was by not attracting them in the first place. The ROVERs and the controlling console weren't the only important things in there;

the library was there, too. The adjoining module had the Imprinter. Without those, the colony probably couldn't survive.

Red turned to the console, and stopped, puzzled. It was turned on, and the readout suggested it could send and receive. Red flipped out his data pad, and tried logging in. The little machine obliged without a complaint.

Red shook his head at the perversity of the universe. "Hell, I needed the walk anyway" he chuckled, and sat down.

The routes for the ROVERs had been set. Privately, Red doubted that any of the itineraries would last two days past arrival that their respective destinations. There would be just too many people pointing at screens and shouting, "Look! Look! Oh, we have got to check that out!" for the ROVERs to maintain any kind of preordained flight path.

At least that's what Red was hoping. Publicly, he made a point of howling in rage every time someone suggested deviation from orthodoxy. He saw it as his role to keep the distractions down to the point where useful work of any kind could be done. He just hoped he didn't intimidate someone who saw something possibly very important into remaining silent. He'd already had to sit down with Sylvie and get her to reassure her older brother, who had seemed to lose some of his self-confidence in the wake of the Great Feline Revolution. The poor kid was still convinced Sheffield wanted to feed him to the composter. With Sheffield, that wasn't necessarily a bad assumption to make.

Red heard a faint rustling behind him. He turned and looked. The front of the module faced the Styx, toward Avalerion, and he could see the faint glow of the settlement lights. Some of the homes were lit as people got up for the 'morning'. But the inside of the module was dark. There was no reason not to have lights on; it wasn't like they were going to attract moths. But Red's Celtic soul quailed at the thought of wasting electricity. With a self-disgusted shake of his head, Red reached over and slapped the lights on. People would be along within the hour, no point in giving them excuses for tripping and falling on their noses.

He turned his attention back toward the screen, and a moment later, heard a rustle behind him again. His hands froze above the keyboard and his head tilted, as he tried to identify the sound. Nothing.

Again, he turned back to work, and again experienced another distraction. This time it was the status lights for data transfer. Normally they would sporadically flicker as data moved amongst the colonists, the computer center, and *Phoenix*. But the lights were on steadily, indicating a big data stream. Red looked at the lights with some irritation. *Phoenix* did backups every night, but it was supposed to be between midnight and 0200, so as to not interfere with regular activities. While it was running, he couldn't save anything. He put a call in to Madelyn Isaakson.

"Ser, when will you be done with the retrieval on the CPS1249? I came in early to get some work done, is why I'm asking."

Isaakson sounded surprised. "We're not doing a backup, Mister Farnsworth. Pull up your routing screen and tell me what it says."

Red keyed in the command, and got a template error. Frowning, he tried again, with the same result.

"Ser, what is a 'template error'? That's what I'm getting when I try to access routing."

"That's odd. Usually it means that someone has successfully accessed data without the proper pass codes."

"Is that possible, Ser?"

"Sure, but the nearest hackers are forty seven light years away. There's nobody on board or down there who would need to do such a thing. I'll run diagnostics and see if I can find out what's really happening. Between you and me, Red, I suspect it's a system fuckup. We'll all be happier if we get it fixed before any of the line officers notice it, won't we? So kindly log off, and I'll run the diagnostics now. It shouldn't take more than fifteen minutes."

Red tapped his data pad to acknowledge and logged out. It was a nuisance, but a minor one. He could keep working on his data pad for the time being. Red suspected Isaacson was the de facto Number One on the ship these days, and he didn't mind getting on her good side.

Rustle.

Red looked up. A dead stalk of tube-grass flipped back and forth from behind the main computer chassis.

There was no wind.

Red stood, slowly, resisting the impulse to pat his right hip where, in an earlier life, he had once carried a firearm. He crept silently toward where the bent tube flicked back and forth, and jumped when it suddenly skittered out into the passage. A flicker of motion at the edge of the console caught his eye, and he saw a little black paw batting around the corner, seeking the tube-grass.

Red chuckled and eased out of the crouch he had involuntarily dropped into, expecting a fight. He was just glad nobody was around to see that. Especially Rudy Harlen, Mouse-slayer.

He rounded the corner, and a medium-sized kitten looked up at him in alarm, and stepped back a few paces. Dropping into a friendly, low crouch, he offered a cupped hand to the kitten. "Hello, Tsarina," he cooed, "Have you come to pay me a visit?" He wasn't as surprised as he might have been. The kids let the kittens out at night since there was nothing to threaten them, and it was only a matter of time before they discovered the foot-bridge and crossed the Styx.

The kitten paused, recognizing Red's scent, and carefully approached in mock fight mode, an arched-back sideways skittle. Red chucked her under the chin, and the kitten – about two little years past weaning now – chirped a welcome. Moving slowly, Red scooped up the kitten and gave her a head bump. Chuckling at his own reaction to the kitten's play, he turned to resume work.

And then frowned. There was some equipment behind the computer chassis that he didn't recognize. He felt some irritation. The Commander had been specific that aside from the library, he wouldn't have to share space with anyone for the duration of the project. If someone was trying to use his space for storage, he would kick some ass.

Still holding the kitten, he sidled around the chassis for a better look. It was big, nearly two and a half meters tall . . . it looked familiar.

He blinked in disbelief. It was identical to the aliens—or whatever they were—that had visited almost a little year earlier. Only it was about three times as tall as those were. He went up and tapped on the side. "Hello? Anyone in there?" There was more than enough room to conceal a practical joker. He wondered if the dark tube at the top had a hidden camera, hoping to catch Red running screaming out of the module, howling about giant aliens. Well, Mrs. Farnsworth didn't raise no fools.

He stepped back and peered at the device, frowning. The detail and articulation were, as far as he could tell, perfect. The bottom legs looked like they could move, and the arms had multiple articulations. The black tube, the utterly neutral gray of the carapace. . . someone had done their homework. He tried knocking on it again. It was solid.

A practical joke was fine, but this was obviously designed through the Imprinter, and Sheffield would not be amused at the waste of material and resources. Somebody must have put a lot of work into this, Red thought.

That's when he saw the cable leading from the 'alien' to the computer chassis. It didn't look like a regular transfer cable, but there wasn't much else it could be. Red suddenly knew why he was being shut out of the main system. This was no longer a joke. He remembered Madelyne saying nobody could have a reason to hack the main system, but pretty obviously someone did. He reached out to pull the cable out.

And something grabbed both his arms, and pulled him back from the cable, gently but with great strength. Tsarina, in danger of being dropped, scrambled up onto his shoulder, digging in painfully.

The device had grabbed Red and pulled him away from the cable. Red felt his sphincters threatening to let go, and his eyes widened. "Oh, holy fuck. . . " he breathed. This wasn't a mock up someone did as a joke. There was a real, live alien in his office, and it was holding him in a vice grip.

A third arm came around, and Red flinched, closing his eyes. When nothing happened, he cautiously opened them, and, looking to his side, saw that Tsarina was standing with her hind legs on his shoulder and her forepaws on the alien's hand. The 'hand', featured eight fingers and was much longer than a human hand.

Even more remarkably, Tsarina was bumping her head against the palm of the hand and purring loudly in an ecstasy of welcome.

Red knew he was in Scotland. He knew this because everyone had green skin and spoke Swedish. His tricycle was broken, and he had to get it fixed so he could get back up to *RESS Pinafore* and return his kipper to Captain Rudyard Kipling. . . .

Oh, fuck me, Red thought. Of all the goddam times to have a flash-dream. Tsarina had stopped stropping against the alien's hand and was looking at Red. She dropped back, balancing somewhat precariously on Red's shoulder.

The alien extended a finger to Red's head. He involuntarily pulled his head back, but there was nowhere to go. The alien had him by both arms, and he was too far from the carapace to kick—even if he knew what to kick at. The finger touched Red's forehead. . .

Red knew he was in Scotland. He knew this because everyone had green skin and spoke Swedish. His tricycle was broken, and he had to get it fixed so he could get back up to *RESS Pinafore* and return his kipper to Captain Rudyard Kipling. . . .

"What the hell. . . " Red stared wildly. He'd never heard of anyone have the same flash-dream twice in a row like that. Even the ones that first came out of hibernation as utter basket cases only had a dozen or so a day, each one unique. Never twice in a row.

The alien was motionless. With no body language or other cues, Red couldn't tell if it was thinking, or shut down, or waiting instructions.

It reached to Red again.

Red knew he was in Scotland. He knew this because everyone had green skin and spoke Swedish. His tricycle was broken, and he had to get it fixed so he could get back up to *RESS Pinafore* and return his kipper to Captain Rudyard Kipling. . . .

"All right, goddammit!" Red snarled. "I have crazy dreams! We all do! Now will you knock it the fuck off?"

The machine had gone still again. A flicker of motion caught Red's eye. He turned his head to see a smaller version of the alien, this one the same size as the ones that the Captain had tried to address, scuttle out of the module on its four legs in a spider-like motion, and then lazily lift into the sky.

Two aliens. Red hadn't even seen the small one. Drawing on emotional resources he didn't know he had, he managed a weak grin. "Got any more of those back there . . . ?"

For a few minutes nothing happened. The alien didn't seem to mind Red looking around, although Tsarina blocked his view to the right. He wondered if the data console was still showing full activity. He suspected it was. Craning his neck, he could see the cable. There didn't appear to be any more aliens back there.

The small one returned, holding a small box with some characters and circles on it. It handed the box up to the larger one, who used both its other hands to place it on top of the computer console. Red could see some advantages to that anatomy.

Reaching toward Red, who didn't flinch this time, it held its hand cupped, the way Red had when he greeted the kitten a few minutes earlier, and to Red's amazement, Tsarina stepped daintily from his shoulder onto the alien's hand. This was a kitten that normally fled in terror from Charlies.

The alien, seemingly with great care, moved its hand directly above the box, and with its remaining hand, pressed one of the buttons on the box. It then lowered its hand that held the kitten, and then pulled it back to itself.

Tsarina stood calmly in midair, apparently weightless. She began rotating very slowly as a random air movement caught her flank. She didn't seem to mind.

Red stared at the cat in utter disbelief. Tsarina stared back with detached feline equanimity. Red had seen videos of cats in zero gravity. They didn't handle it well unless they had Velcro or something they could use to attach to a 'floor'. In fact, they usually went berserk.

The alien retracted the cable, and then, apparently reconsidering, reattached it. Red thought he saw a light flicker inside the tube that was the top of the alien.

Once again, the alien touched Red's forehead. Red closed his eyes.

Red dreamt.

* * *

Red floated in space, looking down on a planetary system that he understood to be Zhar-Ptitsa's. The identities of the star and its planets were all different from what he knew, not words, but fit each, perfectly.

Hō-ō flew around the sun at a dizzying rate, with its rings bobbing slightly and a cloud of moons racing about it.

Out of the outer reaches of the system, a huge comet appeared, circled Zhar-Ptitsa once, and fell into an elliptical orbit around Hō-ō. The non-verbal appellation for it was, more or less, 'another future' or perhaps, 'a becoming'.

As he watched, the orbit became less eccentric, and shifted closer to the ring. He then understood that the vast comet was being steered in some way.

Its orbit became a nearly perfect circle, right on the fringe of the rings, and it sparkled as dozens, and then thousands of Ice Falls struck the comet. The snow and ice melted, and the seas formed, and rose. After thousands of revolutions, the remaining land areas of the comet abruptly turned green in some areas as vegetation suddenly spread, the oceans stopped rising, and Red found himself looking at the familiar image of Hoyl. Slowly, Hō-ō made a single revolution about Zhar-Ptitsa and Hoyl spun about it. Then it began to change.

He moved back several light seconds, and saw that the orbit of Hoyl was again becoming more elliptical. Further and further out from Hō-ō the moon swung, roughly bisecting the orbital path of Hō-ō itself. Something was 'pumping' it, in a matter not dissimilar to a kid pumping himself higher on the swings. Over thousands of revolutions, it got wider and wider, and at the end of each apogee, it would seem to hang suspended. The time it took for Hoyl to orbit Hō-ō nearly took the same time of Hō-ō to orbit Zhar-Ptitsa.

Then on one swing ahead of Hō-ō, it didn't fall back, but instead lifted into a slightly higher orbit around Zhar-Ptitsa. Red wondered how it was being propelled, but the dream images didn't tell him.

Then the orbit around Zhar-Ptitsa became more elliptical, the semi-major axis becoming three times that of the transverse axis, with the outermost nodes intersecting the orbit of Disappointment.

Then the ellipse fattened, becoming less eccentric, until Hoyl was in the same orbit as Disappointment, trailing about sixty degrees behind. Red floated effortlessly closer to the planet. The shapes of the continents were roughly the same, but he could see that the oceans were much lower, about ten thousand meters. The land was barren, with no vegetation at all. With a shock, he realized the planet's tilt had changed, and what had been the Sheffield highlands were now closer to the equator than the north pole, and the height of the mountains was greatly reduced. They looked like normal mountains now, with a big lake in the middle. Vaguely, Red wondered why he was surprised the world had tilted on its side. If they had the power to move it into an orbit four hundred million kilometers further out from Zhar-Ptitsa, what was to stop them from changing the axial tilt?

Lines of green began spreading around the land areas, and Red was by way of understanding that these were colonies of tube-grass, wandering about the landscape, eating the poisons from the soil and converting them to polonium, and then radon. The tube-grass would die, and it, along with the lead deposits remaining, would wash out to sea.

Red knew in a dream-knowing that this process, which would take tens of thousands of years, would begin in a few little years, perhaps only twenty days. And to stay on this already chaotic world would become even stranger and more chaotic in the near future.

* * *

Then the alien detached, and the two . . . creatures? Machines? Rolled to the module door. The large one released Red, who staggered back against the wall of the module.

Red watched as they both exited, and, as the small one had done before, lifted into the sky without noise or visible propulsion.

He followed them out and looked up they were both drifting lazily up to an orb that was floating noiselessly overhead.

The hatch closed, and with a faint 'poot' sound, the orb rapidly dwindled into the sky.

A wail brought him back to reality. He turned to see Tsarina thrashing wildly above the console. He strode over and reached into grab the cat.

That was a mistake. Tsarina grabbed on to him with every claw she owned. "Wowowowow!" he shouted and pulled the arm back, cat firmly attached. The instant she sensed gravity, Tsarina pulled loose, hit the floor, and propelled out the door at an appreciable fraction of the speed of sound.

Red examined his punctuated arm, decided that he wasn't in immediate danger of bleeding to death, and went to sit down. About half-way down, his legs gave out and he fell into the chair.

He spent a couple of minutes shaking and pulling in oxygen. Finally, with a bit more composure, he looked around. The mysterious box was still on the console, and his arm was still bleeding. There was no sign of aliens or cats.

He thumbed his data pad. Sheffield appeared on the screen. He frowned at the Middie. "Red, do you know what ti. . . "

"Sheffield, get your ass to the ROVER module immediately!"

"Mister, you better have an explanation. . . "

"DO IT! Code FIVE!" he slammed the connect closed, and called Isaakson. "Ser, did you get in to the library down here?"

Isaakson poked screens. "I'm in now. I couldn't find out why we were shut out, though."

"I think I found the problem. Do you see anything odd?"

"Nnnooo. Wait. Yes." Isaakson stared at screens. "OK, yes, I found something very odd. Um, Red, can you stand by down there? I'm calling the Captain." She paused and gave Red a sharp glance. "Why? Did you experience something unusual?"

Isaakson could only stare, astonished, as Red began laughing hysterically.

* * *

It took ten minutes for Sheffield to make his way to the module, where he found the Spencer kids disinfecting and bandaging Red's arm. He glared down at his midshipman. "What happened to you?"

"Kitten attacked me. Also, I had Visitors."

Sheffield's expression showed he could hear the capitalization of 'Visitors'. He stared at Red, his anger forgotten. "You mean from. . . " he pointed skyward.

"A large one and a little one. Apparently they come in at least two sizes."

"Did they say anything?"

"Not exactly." Red gave a rapid summation his encounter with the two aliens. He omitted was that they seemed to be able to make themselves understood to a cat. Red knew he had no proof of that, and knew how mental it would sound. Better to kind of ease Sheffield into that. He was just about to start talking about the library and the zero-g machine when they were interrupted.

Sheffield's data pad chirped and flashed red. "Yes, Captain?" The message was in privacy mode, so Red and the Spencer kids could only watch as Sheffield's face turned stony cold. "All of them, Ser? At once?"

He listened some more. "Ser. I'll do that right now. In the meantime, please God Console my data pad and Mister Farnsworth. Something has occurred here that you need to know about immediately. Code Five."

He crowded in next to Red and called up the library. Shielding the screen with his body, he tapped in the code that gave him administrative access to the vast data base. A stream of data started flowing up the screen in six columns. It moved far too quickly to read any of the other columns but one was seemingly unchanged as the machine scrolled: the date and time each file had last been accessed. That had happened twenty-three minutes ago.

"Red, did your aliens come anywhere near the computer?"

Hadn't Red just told him that? He was rattled, and not certain. "Yes Ser. The big one had a data cable plugged in. I tried to stop it, but it restrained me."

"Wonderful." He winced, gave a weary grin. "Well, let's make the Captain's morning for him."

"Captain, I've just taken a report from Midshipman Red Farnsworth. Apparently he discovered an alien interacting with the ship's library about a half an hour ago."

Privacy mode notwithstanding, Red and the others could hear Vargas' reaction. Sheffield pulled the ear bud out and rubbed his ear, grimacing.

* * *

Vargas set a record getting the shuttle down to Scafeld. He flew it himself, and nearly tore the vanes off he went into such a steep dive. A large group of colonists milled around the module entryway, and he had to muscle his way through.

He stopped, blinking. During the intervals he had contact with the ground on his trip down, he had been apprised of the zero-g box, but he was unprepared for the sight of a midshipman floating casually in the air with no visible means of support.

Sheffield reached behind a nondescript dull gray box when he saw the Captain and turned a knob. Red eased to the ground and was standing normally.

Vargas looked from Red to Sheffield. Both men looked flushed, excited, and almost happy. Sheffield especially should be in a state of paranoid rage over the data leak. "Right. You two, in here with me. You, you, and you. . . "he pointed to three crewmen at the front of the crowd, "keep this lot back away from the module." He raised his voice. "People, I realize this has been an extraordinary morning, and obviously we have a lot to discuss. I need to find out exactly what has happened here myself. Until then, please be patient. I will fill you in. I promise."

Vargas looked at Jim and Sylvie. "Did you two see any of this? Where you involved in any way?"

Sylvie replied. "We found Red sitting in his chair. His arm was bleeding and he seemed a bit . . . loopy, so we bandaged him up and got him some coffee."

"And that's the extent of your involvement?" At their nods, he said, "OK. You two please wait outside with the rest. I'm sure Red thanks you for your help."

Red wore a non-committal look and the kids, looking disappointed, walked out. Sheffield carefully closed the hatch. The ambient sound level dropped, and with it, the carnival sense.

"OK. Red, how badly were you hurt, and did the aliens hurt you?"

"My arm? I got that from a cat. The wounds are minor."

"A cat. I see. Right. Why don't you tell us what happened here, as best as you can remember, in a nice, linear fashion."

Red told the story, beginning with why he happened to be there so early in the morning and going through to when he called Sheffield, this time including the observations about Tsarina's behavior, and his own apparently induced vision.

"It wasn't like a dream, or even a flash-dream. It seemed so real that, floating in space like I was, I felt like I should be fighting for breath."

"And then you came back to reality, and they left. Did they take anything with them?"

Red concentrated. "Not that I saw, Ser. Of course, they may have pockets or storage boxes or something I couldn't see."

"And this vision. . . you're certain they implanted it?"

"Captain, I can't imagine why I would have had that sort of thing happen on my own. My flash-dreams are like everyone else's, I guess. Surreal, brief, often nonsensical. This had a sense of purpose, of. . . well, exposition. It felt like I was been advised, warned, explained to. And I remember it all clearly. Unlike with dreams."

Sheffield interjected. "Captain, if I may? Red, you're aware that the Captain plans to move on from this system as soon as it's practical to do so. Some of the colonists want to stay on after *Phoenix* leaves. What was your stance on the issue?"

Red looked started, and then abashed. Turning to Vargas in an apologetic tone, he said, "Captain, I was going to ask your permission to stay. I just couldn't leave the ROVER project. . . "

Vargas nodded. He had wondered if the Middie was considering such thoughts, and even understood why he might. He may have even given permission.

"I believe Red's story about that, Captain, even though it just about guarantees that nearly everyone will want have to leave now. Do you see what I'm getting at?"

Red interjected. "You know how you just know things in dreams, like you know you're in a certain place, even though nothing around you looks familiar?" At both officers' nods, he continued, "It was like that. In the vision, I got the very strong sense that operations to move this world would begin in a few little years. And even though the dream didn't say one way or the other, my own feeling was that it would be for the best if we weren't here at the time."

"Twenty days, eh?" Vargas rubbed his chin. "Well, we can start lifting modules as you replace them with your tube-grass constructions, Sean. I . . . wow. Twenty days? That's all?"

"And they apparently have the entire contents of our library, Captain. They know everything about us, including where we come from."

"Are we sure they accessed the library? I remember when we copied it from the ship to here, it took about six days."

"It could be done if they went through the data at the speed of light."

"None of our computers can do that."

"Not by an order of magnitude. But I remember during training they told me that the data storage on the computer was on a molecular basis, each molecule in an on or off state, and that lined up, they would be about half a million kilometers long."

"So light could pass them in a bit over a second and a half."

"Right. One point six seconds. Which is exactly the amount of time it took for them to access every file in the library. Over a quintillion a second."

Vargas shook his head. "Laws of physics don't seem to matter to these entities. For all I know, they knew everything there was to know about us before they pirated our library. And we know nothing at all about them. We don't even know if they are life forms or machines, do we?"

"Captain?"

"Yes, Red?"

"We know they gave us fair warning. And it may be trivial, but they seem to like cats."

"What about that box thing there? It really blocks gravity?"

"It really does. But frankly, Captain, it's as big a mystery to us as the aliens are. It doesn't seem to have a power source, and we don't know how to open it up and look inside, even if we dared. The casing is seamless."

"Aside from levitating cats and midshipmen, what else can it do?"

"We don't know, Captain. Frankly, I would like to remove it well away from the colony before experimenting."

"Point taken, Commander. Is it possible this is how they can accelerate to near the speed of light at millions of gravities acceleration?"

Sheffield and Red looked at one another. It hadn't occurred to either of them.

"Captain, Madelyn Isaakson here."

"Yes."

"I've been checking the library against the on-board mirror. No signs of anything missing or any damage."

"Good." Vargas had been worrying about that.

"But there is a new file there, one that uploaded to the library about two minutes after everything was accessed. It's huge, about seventy terabytes."

"Really?" *Phoenix*'s schematics took up less room than that.

"Yes Ser. And here's the really weird part.

"It's in Imprinter format."

Chapter 45 Chimps With Machine Guns

TIM SIMMONS WOULD HAVE THREATENED to hold his breath until he turned blue. He had been getting increasingly restive, effectively stuck on *Phoenix* whilst working on a model to try and explain the existence of Hoyl, and simultaneously helping maintain a watch for future Ice Falls.

As a physicist, there was simply no way he could miss out on being one of the first to experiment with the inertia box the aliens had left them.

He wanted to take a look at the vast Imprinter file that was on the ground version of the library. He wanted to upload it, but both Madelyn Isaakson and Jeanine Barney put their feet down and absolutely refused to let that file anywhere near the ship. Since Captain Vargas backed them on that, his only option would be to go ground side. He wasn't complaining.

He had a hunch that the Imprinter file contained the instructions to create another inertia box. Maybe dozens of different types of those magic boxes. And who knew what other technologies might be hidden in there?

Perhaps the Captain thought that if anyone on board the *Phoenix* could dope out the inertia boxes was Tim, or perhaps he saw something in Tim's eyes. In any event, Tim found himself with Davis MacDonald, a shuttle, and the box about fifty kilometers from the settlement. Tim reasoned that if Davis' considerable electronics and physics acumen didn't help, perhaps the part-time minister could bring a little good juju to the operation.

Davis had no such delusions. He reasoned they would be ahead of the game if they didn't accidentally jump into orbit, or find six other amusing ways of blowing themselves up.

Red wouldn't let them plug the file into the Imprinter until they knew a little bit more about it, but he was willing to accede to their equipment requests.

Tim wanted to know if the gravity waves or whatever they were could be focused, and what sort of range they had. So he asked Red if he had any ideas for small, highly visible objects that could be tethered to a meter or so of fishing line, the other end of which could be tied to tube-grass to anchor it. Red pondered it for a minute, and then turned to the Imprinter console with a wide grin. "Got just the thing!" he announced.

A minute later, an object popped out of the small feed tray. Red hefted it, handed it to Tim. "Does this fit your specifications?"

"Hm. Perfectly." Tim grinned. "You know, if our scientific findings from these tests don't make us scientific immortals, this certainly will. May I have another 249 of these?"

The three men, with help from the Spencer teens, spent an hour tying line on the objects.

Tim and Davis got out to the test site about six hours before sunrise, and spent a tedious time tying each object to a stand of tube-grass, each about five meters from its neighbor. By the time they were done, they were in the center of a circle with a radius of sixteen meters. Tim tied the inertia box to himself and Davis looped fishing line through the landing struts of the shuttle and tied those to the tube-grass. There was a steady little breeze of about two km/hour, which was exactly what Tim was hoping for.

By then it was light enough to tell a white thread from a black one, enough that the cameras mounted on the shuttle would catch the results and send them to the colony and to the ship.

"Ready, Mister MacDonald?"

Davis gave his line a slight tug. "Ready, Mister Simmons."

Tim turned what Red had assured him was the power switch. He felt gravity go away. The slight breeze caught him and he felt the line tighten.

He looked around. A small army of yellow rubber duckies with fluorescent orange beaks, bright blue eyes and big eyelashes were rising from the tube-grass and bobbing masslessly in the tiny air movements. So was Davis. So was the box. Only the shuttle remained attached to the ground. And it had been nailed there.

Davis was choking with laughter. "That has to be the most mental thing I've seen in my life," he gasped.

Tim tried clapping his hands. It felt and sounded the way a clap should. So he still had mass. He had been wondering about that. It was just someplace else as far as what lay outside the range of the box. He felt no tug when he drifted to the end of the fishing line, and didn't rebound. Did he still have inertia?

He wished he could see what happened when the breeze interacted with the edge of the no gravity zone. He could feel it on his cheeks.

He reeled the box in towards him and inspected the controls. None of them were marked in any way. Some looked like they were simple off-on switches, others looked like rheostats. Selecting one at random, he slowly turned it, looking around, trying to gage the effect. Davis' voice came over his data pad. "Some of your duckies fell into the tube-grass on the far side of the shuttle. Why didn't the shuttle itself move? You gave it some slack, right?"

"Right." Bending a leg, he brought himself close enough to the tube-grass to reach out with a foot and torque himself around the face the shuttle. "That did something, Simmons."

Simmons peered into the darkness. "What?"

"Your, ducks dropped like a scythe went through them. And, um, the ones that had fallen are starting to bob back up. It looks like you found a way to focus and direct the beam or whatever it is. Um, it looks to be about fifteen degrees wide. Hard to tell, of course. I wish we had more rubber ducks. Now there's something I never thought I would say as a professional."

"Very droll, Mister MacDonald." The Captain sounded amused. "Mister Simmons, how are you calibrating this?"

"I made little marks on all the settings that look adjustable to show their original positions. I'm noting the changes on my data pad. That setting was on the top control, which I moved to the one o'clock position."

Vargas spoke. "I don't know how the aliens could use that thing without markings of some sort. What could they see when they look at it that we can't?"

"Captain, that's a helluva good point. Davis, brace yourself. I'm turning this off."

Tim dropped the brief distance to the ground, set the box down carefully, undid his tie-down, and ran into the shuttle. He emerged a few minutes later with what looked like an old style flashlight.

He bent over the box, twisting so his body was between it and the glare from Zhar-Ptitsa. He clicked on the flashlight. At their various locales, most of the colonists watched through Simmons' helmet cam. Some of them realized what Tim was doing and started whispering to their neighbors who were still puzzled.

Davis spoke. "What do you have it set to?"

"Forty nanometers."

"Try one hundred."

"OK. Ah! Yes! Captain, everybody, this thing does have control settings. They fluoresce at 100 nanometers, a fairly standard black light setting. Um, the rotary controls all have characters around them, and it's the same characters on most of them. I think we just found their numerics!"

"Congratulations, Mister Simmons. You just gave us a Rosetta Stone."

"Perhaps. Davis, the names seem to get longer as you go counterclockwise."

"OK, yes. Look at that first character at the top. It makes up the second half of the third character, and repeats twice at the end of the fifth character. I bet that's their zero."

"And the other half is a one. Or no, it isn't. It's different on the fifth one."

"But it starts the sixth and seventh ones. It isn't just one—it denotes the significant digits to the left of the decimal. That's their 'hundred', and the first one was their ten. That would be their thousand. Yeah, it's binary notation. Base 16 counting."

"Captain, we cracked it. We have their numbering system. Let me get my pad. . . can the camera pick up the characters?"

"Very clearly. Hold it still. I imagine most of the people watching are capturing it for further study. Mr. Simmons, look at the knob at the top, the one you turned. The sequence is different on that one."

"Yeah, I see it. The top is zero, I think, and it is ascending in each direction."

"What about those two characters on either side? Might they be 'plus' and 'minus'?"

"Well spotted, Captain. I think they are. When we get it fired up I'll try turning it one notch back the other way and see what it does. It may produce a tight beam in the opposite direction."

"Carry on, then. Everyone else, if you have comments or suggestions, send them directly to me, and let MacDonald and Simmons do their work. I've several people here who can help evaluate, and if everyone starts sending their ideas to them, they won't make much progress. But we do want to hear your ideas."

Vargas found his mail receiver beeping continuously. Obviously everyone had an idea of some sort. Unable to sort them by merit, he settled for passing along the ones of the most immediate use and saving the rest.

* * *

The two men worked through the brief day, and at their request, a second shuttle flew out with some hastily built floodlights so they could continue working in the dark period, which was 15 hours a day.

By morning they sussed out the alien characters for up, down, left, right, front and back. They felt they might have the words for intensity and duration, frequency and amplitude, and they had the counting system entirely. Eight controls, all with 16 or 32 settings, plus some that seemed to be simple off/on controls. Two others seemed to be rheostats.

What they didn't have were the concepts for what the values did. Most of the controls seemingly did nothing at all.

When they finally ran out of steam, they simply dossed down in the shuttle, protected from the light of the full Hō-ō by the floodlights.

As he fell asleep, Simmons reflected that this was exactly why he wanted to go to the stars in the first place.

*** *

The next day, Simmons had a bold proposal. Rather than return to camp, he wanted to turn the inertia box on, and use a couple of the small stabilizing thrusters on the vanes of the shuttle to propel the craft straight up. Normally, this wouldn't even cause the craft to lurch on the ground; the thrusters were miniature air pressure versions of the thrusters used to control trim. Even in orbit, all of them firing at once in the same direction would impart only a few centimeters per second delta vee.

One of the discoveries they had made the day before was that not all the weight of an object vanished; only 99.99+% of it. The shuttle, when encased in the inertia field, still had an apparent weight of about four kilograms. A grinning MacDonald had demonstrated by lifting the shuttle over his head by one of its landing struts. He then brought down the house by telling his rapt audience that now he would like to try it with the field turned on, to see if the shuttle was any lighter.

Simmons theorized that the thrusters might lift the shuttle several hundred meters into the air, depending on air resistance. He wanted to measure the rate the shuttle fell, or even if it did. He promised to have the main thrusters ready to fire immediately if the rate turned out to be Hoyl's standard 7.6 meters per second squared. Nobody had any idea what might happen if an object inside the field collided with another object. Nobody knew if weight was gone, what the role of mass was.

It took Vargas a half hour to OK the scheme. Simmons surmised the Captain had talked to everyone seeing if anyone could come up with a reason why this was a perfectly dreadful idea. Nobody could.

Since dawn was several hours away, the two men spent the time untying and stowing the rubber duckies. The awareness that the planet had owners, who might even be watching, had made everyone a bit more circumspect about littering.

At first light, with the box strapped in place in the space between the pilot and copilot seat, controls set, MacDonald flicked it on. Gravity abruptly vanished, and the craft began rocking gently, the result of a mild breeze crossing the plain.

"Ready."

Vargas said, "Remember. Five seconds. No more, no less."

"Affirmative." Simmons and MacDonald exchanged a glance, and, watching his time readout, Simmons fired the thrusters. He heard MacDonald give an unbelieving chuckle, but had his eyes riveted to the time display. It flashed '5' and he cut the thrusters. He glanced out the windshield, and goggled. The sky was black, and he could see curvature on the horizon.

He scanned the pilot's panel, even as MacDonald began reading out the displays. They were almost a hundred and twenty kilometers up, and they had accelerated at nearly eight kilometers a second squared. By rights, they should be a thin film of strawberry jam on the floor of the cabin, and the shuttle itself should have been torn apart by the inertial forces. It was roughly eight hundred gravities acceleration. It hadn't even felt like they had moved.

Vargas' voice came over, sounding frantic: "Shuttlecraft, respond! Are you copying?"

Simmons leaned to the mike. "We're fine, Captain. All readouts are nominal. . . and shit. We're in space. In five seconds. How about that?"

MacDonald, sounding a bit shaky, said, "It was like a flight simulation routine, only 'way sped up. The ground dropped away at an incredible speed, and I could see the horizon to the west expanding until I could see the ocean. It was remarkable. Um, we're losing altitude. About point seven meters per second."

Simmons nodded. "That would be gravity. Apparently we didn't build up any inertia. Say, what's our hull temperature?" He took a frightened look out at the wings.

"About one twenty six"

"That's all? Good. We might have burned the craft up."

"When you suddenly vanished, we thought you had." Vargas gave a nervous-sounding laugh. "OK, bring her in. Use, um, conventional landing procedures. We have enough data now that we can start learning a whole new book on orbital flight theory."

Once coms were closed, MacDonald looked at Simmons. "You said our hull temperature was one twenty six?"

"Yeah. But Still. We took a really stupid chance."

"What is it now?"

"Um, the monitor is down."

"I didn't hear any wind as we took off. It should have been deafening."

Simmons considered. He had been watching the time display, but he would have heard wind like that. "OK. What does that mean?"

"I don't know, but I suggest we land about a half a kilometer out from the landing area."

* * *

The hull of the shuttle was hot, but not in the way they originally thought. Ionization had confused the electronic sensors that monitored the skin temperature. But the hull was very lightly covered in an extremely fine powder of thorium.

The shuttle set down after a conventional landing next to the Styx. Nearly all the radioactive dust blew off during that landing, making egress safe. Sheffield sent a shuttle armed with a water pump to hose down the first shuttle and pick up the two scientists. The tube-grass would probably treat it as fertilizer.

At Scafeld, the two scientists got gold-plated rubber duckies from a laughing Red, and asked if they could go to Disappointment tomorrow and get more gold, since they were running low.

The room suddenly quieted. Simmons' eyes widened. "We could, couldn't we? In the shuttle."

Sheffield nodded. He'd already thought of that. "I've had people calculating the amount of delta vee you expended to get as high as you did. And for a trip to Disappointment, we'll have to factor in relativistic numbers. I think. Would they apply in this case?"

"I think they should, Commander. You really want us to try to go to Disappointment tomorrow?"

"Are you up for it?"

The two scientists glanced at one another. "Yes Ser!" they chorused.

"Good. Take Red, here. Get him out of my hair. Rubber duckies. Fooking hell."

The mood was giddy. Everyone had just realized they had been handed the keys to the universe. All they had to do was learn to drive safely.

Only a few people felt any disquiet. The main reservation was aptly expressed by Doctor Spencer to Vargas, when he described the situation as being like "a troupe of chimpanzees who have just been given a nuclear weapon to play with."

Vargas found himself in agreement with that, to the extent that he overrode the plan to go to Disappointment, suggesting instead they simply aim for an unoccupied area within the Zhar Ptitsa system as a calibration run. After all, what had been meant to take them a few kilometers up had very nearly put them in space, and he didn't want a shuttle of his pancaking into Disappointment—or Hoyl—at nearly the speed of light because of a similar miscalculation.

Simmons opined that if they did run into a large object with shield on, they may simply come to a halt with no damage.

Vargas, less inclined to assume infallibility on the part of the boxes, imagined the amount of ergs released if an object the size of a shuttle hit at .99c. It would crack the planet.

He had a laundry list of questions for Simmons and MacDonald that quickly calmed the enthusiasm the men were experiencing. Where did the inertia/mass/gravity go? How did it 'go'? What effect did it have in other places? Where was the thorium coming from? If there was measurable thorium on the shuttle's hull after a trip of less than two hundred kilometers, how would it look on a trip nearly four million times as far? Why was there thorium? Oh, and have any of you scientists reflected on the fact that, when heated, powdered thorium burns like magnesium?

And the question that caused everyone at least a moment's pause: why would the aliens give an unknown race this sort of powerful tool?

Privately, even Vargas wanted to pump a fist in the air and shout 'yes!' He also convinced the group on the ground to delay the probe until they had a chance to see what that Imprinter file did. To that end, he had Isaakson and Red shut down all possible routes of communication between the two libraries and the two Imprinters, completely isolating the ground from the ship. He even ordered all other communications to be shut down until the Imprinter had finished processing the file at least enough for the initial step, which would be a request for raw materials.

That list, when the Imprinter screen coughed it up, was even more disquieting. The materials were all listed by atomic weight, and since the ratios were the same they were able to determine the raw materials needed. The recipe measured by the atomic level, an effortlessly attained level of precision that caused jaws to drop. The best the monkeys could do was plus or minus several billion atoms per element, which they hoped wouldn't be enough to spoil the product.

Whatever it was. The total mass required came to about eight hundred kilograms, including, somewhat disquietingly, thirty five kilograms of uranium 238.

When he heard that, Captain Vargas ordered the imprinter to be moved fifteen hundred kilometers from the colony, and for the program to be executed remotely. That much U-238 could make a pretty big bang.

Simmons noted that thorium 230 was one of the daughter decay products of uranium 238, but admitted that the amount on the ship's hull couldn't be accounted for by radioactive decay.

Finally, the inertia box weighed about six kilograms. If the Imprinter needed eight hundred kilograms to build something, it wasn't going to be the little gray box.

They used the inertia box to simply carry the Imprinter—which normally weighed about twenty tons—out onto a large mat of tube-grass root The corners of that were attached to the underside of a shuttle, the box loaded onto the shuttle along with the ingredients, and the whole mess flown to a field on the far side of the Boitumelos. It was out of line of sight not just of the colony, but of *Phoenix* herself.

If anyone thought Vargas was being overly cautious, they kept it to themselves. The U-238 by itself wasn't a threat to a ship in synchronous orbit, and little problem to a distant colony separated by a vast mountain range.

The ingredients were loaded into the hoppers. Each element was a bit above the amounts requested, since even if humans couldn't measure to the level of individual atoms, the Imprinter itself wouldn't take more than it needed of each, and might come within hundreds of atoms for each element.

The ship's computer converted all the base 16 numbers to binary, and since positioning of each element was based on the ratio among three axes, hoped the changes were enough to make the Imprinter happy.

They then all flew back to the colony, and the Imprinter was told to execute from fifteen hundred kilometers away.

Three days later, it was still running the commands. Everyone was surprised except Janine Barney, who pointed out to a bemused Captain that any computer having to laboriously follow the line-by-line instructions in a seventy terabyte file was going to take some time. Her own personal estimate was that it might take several more days.

It brought home to the Captain and Commander Sheffield that this really was an extraordinarily advanced and sophisticated technology, and they had no understanding of it at all. The mood shifted from one of impatient glee and an overwhelming desire to see what the little gray box could do to one of deep caution and even apprehension.

Vargas suspended live craft testing while they waited to see what the Imprinter produced. That it had gone four days without an error warning was a good sign, in his estimation.

Formally and informally, groups on the ground on the ship analyzed what little they knew, and hypothesized what new abilities humanity might be gaining.

Simmons had the most immediately interesting one. If the device produced a field big enough to envelop *Phoenix*—and Simmons felt it could—then *Phoenix* could rapidly attain relativistic speeds very rapidly, using nothing more than her thrusters. His calculations suggested that *Phoenix* could reach a theoretical maximum in a little under three days, ship's time.

"Point eight seven Cs in three days?" Vargas asked incredulously.

"No, Ser. Point nine-nine Cs. I don't think the gravitational anomalies we experienced using standard drive to attain eight Cs would occur."

"Be a terrible shame if you were incorrect, Mister Simmons. *Phoenix* go boom, all die, oh the embarrassment."

"It wouldn't be an optimal outcome," Simmons replied, and the Captain wished, not for the first time, that physicists had more of a sense of humor. "But we can do tests, using one of the modules."

"And if you were wrong?"

"I would die, and you would be out a module."

"You would die? Just you?"

"I wouldn't ask anyone else to test it, Captain. How could I?"

"What happens if we hit c plus one?"

"I don't think that's possible. For one thing, the universe might come crashing in on us?

"Excuse me?"

"The tests we've been running on the inertia box suggest that nearby objects gain mass or weight when the box is in operation."

"Did you say 'mass or weight'?"

Simmons nodded. "It isn't clear if both—or somehow just one—is changing. We need to test outside of a gravity field. We think that the greater the resistance the inertia box experiences, the more mass/weight is distributed outside the ship, more to nearby objects, less to objects further away."

"So in effect the inertia box and whatever it is transporting becomes its own gravitational object?"

Simmons looked uncomfortable. "You know what Newton's law of universal gravitation says, of course."

"The attractive force between two bodies is proportional to the product of their masses, and inversely proportional to the square of the distance."

"Right, and you determine the amount of attraction using the gravitational constant. That's what I expected to find. Only, nearby objects were affected less, and further objects more. Worse, they weren't attracted toward the field, as you might expect. Instead, they increased their attraction to Hoyl."

"That doesn't make sense."

"Not much of this does, Captain. The box plays with gravity, and it may warp time in some way we don't understand, or, failing that, some of the other dimensions."

"But you seem to think it's safe to use."

Simmons shook his head. "Not exactly. I would say it is unsafe to misuse."

"That, at least, I think I understand."

Chapter 46 Ticket to Ride

AND ON THE SEVENTH DAY THE IMPRINTER RESTED. Janine Barney woke to the live feed on her data pad announcing the operation had been completed with zero errors. Minutes later she was one of a group of people boarding a shuttle to see what the Imprinter had produced. Someone had sent a cartoon out the day before showing the Imprinter producing a hundred meter tall rubber ducky. Red, who had spent the past week trying to determine what the various ingredients might produce, considered it as good a guess as any.

The shuttle did a flyover of the Imprinter. Sheffield, at the controls, was still worried about the possibility of a booby trap. Cameras on the undercarriage took images of the Imprinter's output port.

"I don't see anything."

"Maybe it didn't actually make anything."

Sheffield eased the shuttle around and pulled up about fifty meters away. Everyone scrambled out and waded through the thick grass to the machine. Simmons had a Geiger counter pointed at the Imprinter. As they neared the Imprinter, Sheffield gave him a questioning glance.

"Just above background," he reported. "I suspect the extra comes from the loading bin that had the uranium."

Sheffield nodded and peered into the main output tray. It was empty. He scanned around at the foliage surrounding the machine. "You don't suppose whatever it made ran off into the woods, do you?"

"Here it is!" Janine was pointing to the small hopper.

They crowded around. Inside was a gray box, identical to the inertia box. Janine reached in and lifted it by the handle. She was able to pull it out without effort.

"OK, it made one of those. But what else did it make?"

The hoppers were otherwise empty. Janine walked to the far end of the Imprinter and checked the input hoppers. She was puzzled, but unsurprised, to see they were all empty.

Sheffield tossed the box from one hand to the other. "This doesn't weigh eight hundred kilos," he complained.

"Does it work?" Red asked.

Sheffield examined the control panel side and frowned. Janine helpfully focused a black light on it, and pointed. "Turn that to the third setting to the right, that one setting counterclockwise, and press that."

Sheffield did as instructed, and they both floated gently in the air. Sheffield peered down at the meter of air between his feet and the ground. "It works," he announced.

They had the original inertia box with them, but decided to have it as an emergency backup in case the first one failed. It didn't occur to anyone to wonder what would happen if one inertia box was inside the field of another such box, but fortunately for this end of the galaxy, the answer turned out to be "not much". They flew back to Scafeld and returned the Imprinter to its original location.

Red spent the next day running diagnostics and setting it to producing a variety of objects, and by evening was able to report to the Captain that it was performing flawlessly. There was, he told Vargas, nothing to account for the missing mass on the inertia box run.

Simmons suggested that the inertia box was always actually running, and that this might account for the diminished weight. Adding apologetically that it was only a guess, he suggested that the box drew a continuous stream of power from the same location where it sent the mass.

Mann and Lassiter, using only the thrusters, flew a shuttle to synchronous orbit height, and, using the mass/force calculations from the first shuttle flight, successfully parked the craft into actual orbit.

The following day Simmons and Harlen flew a shuttle out to the range of the orbit of Disappointment, using the main thrusters about four seconds for accelerating at each end of the trip. They carefully measured the thorium accumulations on the craft, and determined that for round trips from Hoyl to Disappointment, the accretions did not present a serious health risk. Lassiter suggested simply dipping the shuttles in the ocean upon return to simply wash the powder off. The former CTO produced the data that showed that the shuttles could handle submersion to fifty meters, and noted that they wouldn't be going deeper than was needed to roll the craft to rinse the powder away.

On *Phoenix*, Vargas met with Trapp, Harlen, Sorlund, Barney and Boitumelo to consider a further step. With access to Disappointment's treasure trove of minerals seemingly assured, *Phoenix* could be deep-space-ready in a matter of twenty or thirty days.

The question for the top officers to consider was this: What star system should *Phoenix* visit next?

The decision came quickly, and was unanimous.

Sheffield wasn't invited to the deliberations, although their existence wasn't kept secret from him, either.

* * *

Red still oversaw the ROVER project, but it was no longer the consuming passion of his life. If everything had changed for the people on the *Phoenix* mission, he had changed more than anybody. Not only did he believe he would not be exploring Hoyl's southern continent, but he didn't much care. Sheffield, sensing the mood change in his midshipman, had mentioned that he would recommend to the Captain that the as-yet unnamed continent, about the size of Australia, be named "Farnsworth." Red had merely nodded and allowed that that would be nice.

Unlike regular flash-dreams which tended to be as ephemeral as regular dreams (Red couldn't even remember the one he had while the alien was holding him) the vision of Hoyl being lifted up into Disappointment's orbit was as sharp and clear as the visitation itself was.

The vision was as clear as a vision could possibly be. The owners would be moving Hoyl, beginning in just a bit more than a little year, and while they hadn't made any threats or given any real warnings, the inference was clear; this would proceed whether humans were on the planet or not. The vision made it clear that when Hoyl arrived in its new orbit, there would be nothing living on the surface.

The colony was doomed. It would have been doomed anyway. The scale of the operation Red was shown suggested they had thousands of years before Hoyl became totally uninhabitable. But the operation was due to begin in the near future, and it wasn't clear how quickly that might prove lethal for plant and animal life on the moon, or future planet.

Red knew that, and discounted it. He would be dead in a hundred years, and hoped to die famed as the world's foremost explorer.

That was when he expected to never have a chance to add another planet to the five-planet insignia had had designed and wore since the colony was established. Was it really only two hundred days before?

But he had seen the capabilities of the inertia boxes, and knew, in his heart, that *Phoenix* would leave this system at nearly the speed of light, enveloped in the mysterious field of one of those boxes.

He was only a midshipman, but he could do the relativistic math, and it wasn't hard to realize what this new mode of travel portended.

No point in the entire galaxy was more than three weeks, ship's time, from any other point. In his life time, he could visit hundreds of planets over millions of years. The newness and variety of the universe was his for the taking.

A small, jungle-encrusted continent on a doomed planet just didn't have the allure it had a few cycles earlier.

Tonight, he would have dinner with Rebekah, who he knew was one of about thirty five colonists who planned to stay behind when *Phoenix* had left. The number had been much higher two little years ago, and Red had been among them. No more.

He wasn't looking forward to telling Rebekah. But there was still time to change her mind. New worlds, new plants, new challenges. Maybe they yet would find a world that could overcome the allure of exploration, and she and Red could settle down and have kids and all of that. Maybe there was a world where the days and nights were normal, and they wouldn't need protective gear to go out in the daylight and lights to make the landscape less eerie at night. Maybe plants and animals could thrive under an open sky, with gentle rains and a warm, life-giving sun.

He unconsciously fingered the thrupenny coin in his pocket. He had meant to bury the ancient coin on this planet, a sign of settling down on a new home, just as his great-great-grandparents had in the famines of the nineteenth century. He never had, though.

In his heart, perhaps he knew it was never to be.

* * *

It took nearly four days before they were ready to test *Phoenix* with the Inertia Box. Both imprinters had been kept busy during that time, the ground one making a third Inertia Box, and the shipboard one processing ores from Disappointment to replace equipment and material that had been lost through attrition. Food stores were a bit lower than Vargas liked to see, but given that the next journey would take two weeks instead of twenty-seven years, they were sufficient. Sheffield's claims to the contrary, Vargas had doubted that Hoyl would ever be self-sufficient on crops. Even the week after harvest, they were already consuming more from the ship's hydroponics then the land had produced. The crop was unimpressive. The corn was stunted, and the beans and peas had a funny taste. He looked down on the strange world they had called home for over two hundred days, and reflected that he wasn't going to miss it very much. With quite some time before the big winter solstice, the northern reaches were in perpetual darkness now, and even Sheffield had come up to the ship from time to time just for a glimpse of some Zharlight. It was a brief glimpse, since a shuttle equipped with the box could launch at will and be at *Phoenix* in less than five minutes, no matter what the orbital postions. Vargas still clung to a hope the people who wanted to stay – about twenty of them – might change their minds and come with *Phoenix* when the time came to leave.

The first journey was relatively short. *Phoenix* would use thrusters only to travel out to about the orbit of Cueball. One of the shuttles had already gone there, and the two men had even considered landing on the small icy planet just to say they had. But it was nearly a third the diameter of its orbit around Zhar-

Ptitsa from them, and going there would have quadrupled the length of time the experiment would take.

Firing thrusters, *Phoenix* could approach c in less than three days. Vargas was amused to learn the ship was now far more maneuverable than even the shuttles when the field was turned on.

Firing the main engine could put them at near c in about eight tenths of a second. Nobody was comfortable with that.

Vargas liked the idea that if attacked by hostiles, *Phoenix* could simply vanish like a soap bubble. Vargas grinned at the thought. The ship would seem, to an outsider, to have simply vanished. The ship at least now had one effective defense in case of hostile receptions. They could run away, very fast.

Mindful of that, Vargas sent a directive to Etienne Sorlund to work up a program to fire the main engines for exactly six-tenths of a second. Etienne obliged, and at Vargas' suggestion, showed it to Scotty and Madelyne before Vargas officially saw it.

That type of acceleration would be enough to extricate *Phoenix* from any situation, no matter how pear-shaped.

There were two other questions Vargas wanted answered before *Phoenix* left the Zhar-Ptitsa system. What would happen if the ship, while enveloped in the inertia field, collided with something, such as a planet? He had Scotty Boitumelo gimmicking up a dummy shuttle – one of Red's ROVERs, in fact – that they could test by aiming it, enfelded, at Roadrunner. It hit the little moon at about 300,000 kilometers an hour, and stopped. No damage to either the moon or the shuttle. Just a big cloud of dust on Roadrunner that rapidly dissipated.

Second, what happened if you shot at something that was inside a field? It interfered in some way with the electro-magnetic spectrum, causing a slight red-shift and dimming everything that came in. From within the field, Zhar-Ptitsa resembled the cooler and yellower Sol. But solid objects could leave or exit at will and without harm. But suppose someone fired at *Phoenix* just as it fired main engines. *Phoenix* would accelerate far faster than any projectile known to humans, but suppose a missile entered a field just as the engines fired? That would be considerably more difficult to test.

If they bothered to repair all the forward-oriented thrusters damaged by the nuclear explosion, they could nearly double their acceleration. Not that twelve hundred meters second squared was anything to sneeze at. One hundred and thirty gravities, more or less.

Fuel for the thrusters was a problem. They were meant to align the craft, and the designers hadn't envisioned the craft flipping nose for tail very often. Indeed, reserves had been lower than expected due to the multiple turns the craft had made for the acceleration cycles imposed at midpoint when a well-meaning doctor had put artificial gravity for disabled patients above the capabilities of the ship.

Four shuttles left for Disappointment and returned five days later with everything on the wish list needed to make *Phoenix* space worthy again. With main engine back up to triple redundancy, Vargas ordered all but two of the modules to be floated back up to the ship.

Now fully stocked, the fuel supplies would give them about ten days running time if all thrusters fired at one. In reality a quarter of them might fire at once.

New policy; anytime the ship encountered carbon-based vegetation, tank up. Running out of gas around Sirius would be dead embarrassing.

Vargas didn't just propose to explore. He now had items to trade; steelwood, tube-grass mat, even the inertia box. He started thinking in terms of how to protect this treasure.

For Vargas, it was a time of wild enthusiasm and concern over what the new technology would mean for humanity.

And humanity's dark shadow, fear.

Chapter 47 Coming Back to Earth

REBEKAH TOOK THE NEWS THAT RED WOULD BE LEAVING for the stars with resignation. She knew that the drive that led Red to *Phoenix* in the first place was the desire, not to settle, but to explore. Even if he had stayed on Hoyl, she knew, she would have led a life as a 'naval widow,' her man constantly gone on one adventure or another. She truly loved Red, and knew that she could convince him to stay, but he would spend the rest of his life looking to the stars with longing, wondering what strange new worlds he would never see.

She thought about pulling up stakes and waiting for a better world. Red had been convincing, rhapsodizing about worlds where she could work bare shouldered under the sun, raising crops and lambs, a new land of milk and honey. Many such places lay beyond the sky, Red said, far better than this doomed rock. Please come.

But the will to settle was strong in her, and she doubted Red would ever really settle. Hoyl had challenges, some daunting. Red needed challenges, but he also needed new horizons. But without an attachment to the Earth, she was rudderless, a leaf to be blown about by fitful winds.

She had another urge to stay, and bond with the land. In her belly, Red's child grew. She hadn't told Red.

Red had kissed her goodbye. He would leave for *Phoenix* in the morning, and would not return. Not on this trip.

"I will come back," he promised. "It may be in a thousand years, or ten thousand. There may be nothing left on Hoyl to show that you, or any other human, ever lived here."

"But I will stand where we stand now, and I will remember you. And I will still love you."

Awkwardly, he handed Rebekah a rolled up piece of paper. She stared at the strange object, wondering what it was.

"Read it after I'm gone. Will you promise me?" At the expression on her face, he said, "OK, I know, I know. You'll read it as soon as I'm gone. But burn it immediately afterward. I don't want anyone else to see it. I didn't even dare put it in my personal log."

Later, when her eyes had dried, she unrolled the oddly old-fashioned paper and read:

"Dear Hoyl Goyl:

'If I live a million years, I will always love you!' Some songwriter wrote that a few centuries ago and probably lived to regret it. But men have said that to women many, many times, and I plan to be the first man to live a million years. Between time dilation and new discoveries, I might outlive the sun. If I do, I will still love you.

"I wish you were coming with me, but I understand why you won't.

"First, a warning. Watch out for Sean Sheffield. He may have been a good Captain in his time, but something on this mission changed him. Maybe it was hibernation syndrome; it certainly changed all of us. But he's more brittle, less able to handle disagreement. I hope that the colony finds someone else to be the leader. I think that with too much authority, he could be a dangerous man.

"That's why I want you to destroy this after you've read it. If he knew what this said, he would be angry, and since he can't punish me for writing it, he would punish you for reading it. Waste no time. Burn it. You have plenty of other things to remember me by on your data pad. Better things, too.

"The day after my meeting with the aliens, I spoke to Ian Spencer. I figured he could listen to what I had to say, and tell me if my concerns were real, or if I was just being delusional. He told me he couldn't speak to the legitimacy of my concerns, but that there were certain markers a psychiatrist learned to watch for with patients who have unique knowledge of things, and he said I didn't exhibit those types of markers. Not the least of which was that I came to him, not with knowledge, but with doubts.

"He encouraged me to talk to the Captain and Doctor Trapp, and that's what I'm doing tomorrow.

"It's important that you know about this, too, because I think the aliens will return to Hoyl, and sooner, rather than later.

"When the alien was holding me, I felt like it would see everything inside my head, and I could see everything in. . . well, wherever it does its thinking. I don't think these things know how to lie or conceal their innermost thoughts, and I don't think they particularly care.

"They aren't malevolent, exactly. I think at first they saw us as a new, but not particularly interesting life form. They are doing some sort of census on this planet, and we were just another of the contaminants that inevitably occur on these projects. Mostly they just wanted to see if we might be useful before beginning a process that would, in time, kill us.

"They decided we weren't just animals, apparently. I think my flash-dream had something to do with that; it made me replay it several times. And then it gave me something a lot like the flash-dream, only it stayed vivid afterward. You know how flash-dreams are like regular dreams, and you can't remember what they were about a half hour later? I know they 'replayed' my flash-dream a few times, but I can't remember what it was about. Something about Sweden, I think. But the rest of it, the stuff they implanted, I remember all of that very well.

"I think when they move planets around to accrue the elements they want for each planet, they check from time to time on the life forms that show up there randomly. Some are useful, some become useful.

"And some stop being useful. They dispose of those.

"I think flash-dreams are what convinced the aliens we are more than mice or steelwood trees. But we don't normally have flash-dreams, and if that's the only thing that makes us special, they will eliminate you from the world without a moment's thought.

"So when you have children, when they are past puberty, make hibernation chambers and put them through what we all went through. Give them the twingies and the flash-dreams. It may save their lives. And this sounds demented, I know, but I think they like cats. Tsarina certainly liked them.

"When the alien gave me the inertia box, I felt a strong sense of what I can only call curiosity. Imagine giving a kitten a ball of explosive material, knowing the kitten will bat it around, and knowing that if the kitten hits it a certain way, it will explode, killing the kitten. We're the kittens, and they gave us this device, something trivial to them, just to see if we learned how to use it. I don't think it was a challenge or a warning, either. These beings simply cannot hide what they are thinking and feeling. But they are mildly curious about us.

"There's one more thing I have to say, and I'm hoping this might change your mind.

"Doc Trapp is a rotten poker player. If we had real money, I would own his ass. He's got dozens of tells. I was sitting with him and Spencer, and I asked if the brass had figured out what planet we were going to next. He looked a bit odd when I said that, so I knew that had already been decided. (Sheffield doesn't know that, by the way; I wonder why. It's like the Captain has decided he's no longer part of the crew.) So I changed the subject, and then brought it back up again, playing him, and I said that if it was up to me, our next port of call would be Earth. He kind of glanced up and off to his left, and barely managed not to shrug. Spencer caught my eye and winked, and so now I know: we're going to Earth. I think the Captain is going to announce it this evening.

"It makes sense. It'll take two weeks, ships' time, to get there. We can look in, see what's what, and figure out where to go from there.

"Think it over tonight. It may be that Earth is still intact, but will need farmers and the materials and technology we bring with us. And then after that, hundreds of new worlds. Lands of milk and honey. Maybe out there is a world that can challenge both of us. If nothing else, we'll still have each other, and we could even come back here in fifty thousand years or a hundred, and see if the aliens need us for anything. They might."

"I'll watch for you tomorrow. If you don't come, I won't be angry or disappointed, and I will always understand and support that decision. No matter what, I love you."

"Virgil, your Red Rubber Duckie."

* * *

"Captain, may I have a minute?"

"Certainly, Commander. How can I help you?" Vargas looked at the tired-looking Sheffield in his data pad, feeling a bit puzzled. Relations between the two had become so distant that he was honestly surprised if Sheffield had called simply to say good-bye. In truth, Vargas wouldn't have much minded if he hadn't.

"Captain, if I changed my mind about staying, would I be welcome on *Phoenix*?" Vargas was not surprised by the question itself, just the source. Since he had announced that the next port of call would be Earth, the number of colonists remaining had dwindled from about thirty to just thirteen, and he wouldn't be surprised if the number dropped to zero by morning. No colony would survive with eleven men and just two women.

"You would be welcome on *Phoenix*, but you would be cashiered first."

"Excuse me, Captain? Did I hear. . . "

"You did, Commander. You falsified the ship's log and tried to claim that I invented an event that the log clearly showed occurred. Falsification of official logs and impeaching of the Captain are both offenses that can strip you of all rank."

Vargas watched Sheffield's response with some interest. The man couldn't possibly be as astonished as he looked. Did he hope to bluff his way out of this?

"Captain, I don't know what you're talking about."

"The night of the first visitation. Radar tracking clearly showed the nature of the object in low orbit, and that it was intelligently guided. Two hours after that occurred, the records were mysteriously stripped from the database and replaced with radar readings of an unremarkable nature from the hour before. There's only three people who have access to do that, and I'm one of them. The other is the person who called the remarkable readings to my attention in the first place. And the third was you. Do you deny it?

"Captain, if the records show nothing remarkable happened that night, that's what the records show. I don't see where it matters now. We obviously did have a visitation."

Vargas sighed. Sheffield had just blown his final opportunity to regain his Captain's trust. "Very well, Commander." He hit a few keystrokes, and screens showing radar readout from the *Phoenix* sprung up on Sheffield's screen. "This starts just thirty seconds before the odd behavior."

Thirty five thousand kilometers apart, the two men watched as one. The "second hand" of the radar swept in a ten-cycles a second arc. A brightly lit object moved along a path typical of an object in low equatorial orbit, and then suddenly changed direction, heading toward the north pole, still at orbital velocity.

The sequence ended, and Sheffield's face reappeared on the Captain's screen. He was stony-faced and silent, giving away nothing.

"Immediately after giving the order to you to prepare a search party, I did what is required of all Captains when something utterly extraordinary occurs on their watch. I first made a permanent and indestructible recording of the incident, and then I placed a copy in the Captain's black box, and then I transmitted the recording to Earth. Yes, it will take forty-seven years to get there, and chances are slim anyone will hear it, but that was my duty, and I carried it out."

"You had your duty, too, Mister Sheffield, and you did not carry it out. Instead, you not only altered the record, but you stated to several members of my crew that in your opinion, I had invented the incident in an effort to buttress my arguments for abandoning this moon."

"Vargas, I was trying to protect you from your own folly. Any fool could see that radar reading was doctored. "

"And you assume I doctored it."

"Yes."

"And you wondered if I was incapacitated and unfit for command."

"I did."

"Did you communicate this to Doctor Trapp?"

"There wasn't time."

"There wasn't time for what, Commander? Time for me to discover you had altered the records? Time for the aliens to show up? Time for what, Commander?"

Sheffield remained silent.

A moment passed, while Vargas searched his face. "Very well, Mister Sheffield. My offer stands. We will take you back on *Phoenix*, but only as a passenger." Vargas chuckled, a cold sound. "I recommend you consider it. From what I gather, you only have eleven people who wish to stay now, and only two of them are female. You aren't going to be the first leader of a world colony; you are going to be the big dog in a small kennel, but only until one of the other dogs challenges you for the woman. You will fail."

Without a word, Sheffield signed off. Vargas sighed and furled his data pad. He had to plan a trip to Earth. Sheffield no longer mattered.

* * *

Trapp shook his head admiringly. "Two weeks. That amazes me. It took twenty six years to get here."

Spencer felt the ambiance of Trapp's office, a little bit of Earth around an alien sun. "Fifty two years, really. And the same amount of time to get back. We can't get around relatively, it seems. Plus we will spend the next month at Disappointment, stocking up on minerals. Vargas says that several tons of gold, platinum, silver and uranium, on top of what we gained on Hoyl, would probably make us welcome guests. Unless human nature has greatly changed." He chuckled.

Spencer realized he would need to start thinking in Earth calendar terms again. "Weeks" instead of "little years". Midnight to midnight would be twenty four hours. He could resume what he used to think of as a normal sleep pattern.

"I wonder what we'll find." Spencer mused.

"Well, that's the big question, isn't it?" Trapp chuckled. "Personally, I expect to find human life. Even if this was the big war everyone's been warning of for three centuries, there will be some life left. Antarctica, maybe, or Greenland. Mostly rural farmland, both of them, and nobody in their right mind would bomb that."

Spencer thought that nobody in his right mind would use a nuclear bomb on anything, but decided not to go there. "It could be another False War," he suggested. We get back and find there's billions of people, they have a full technology and then some, and who knows? Maybe they're building *Phoenix* II in a new dry dock."

"You know, that might be the most dangerous situation we could face," Trapp said. "If the Americas still exists, they might want to hang the Captain, and probably the rest of us. After all, we broke their Dry Dock."

"I don't know if the Captain is emotionally prepared to face the prospect that he may have to relinquish *Phoenix* to her rightful owners. His attitude toward her has become rather proprietary towards her since we left the Solar System."

Trapp shrugged. "I can't blame him. None of us thought we would ever have to answer to an Earth authority again." He hesitated. "He has ordered some weaponry that *Phoenix* can deploy if we get a hostile reception, you know."

Spencer sat up straight. "I haven't heard about this! What sort of weapons?"

"Well, I'm not a military expert, but they strike me as mostly defensive in nature. Lasers to cripple the guidance programs of incoming missiles, mines the ship can scatter in front of it if something is approaching too fast, that sort of thing."

Spencer relaxed slightly. "Oh. Well, I can see that."

Trapp chuckled. "He isn't planning war against the universe. In fact, when we get to the Solar System, he plans to park outside the orbit of Neptune, where we won't be noticed easily, and just set and listen for a spell. If Earth still has civilization, it will still be broadcasting in one way or another, and what's being broadcast will tell us a lot about what we're sailing into."

"If they are civilized and willing to listen?"

"The Captain plans to give them samples of tube-grass, steelwood, and the inertia box. In return, we keep *Phoenix*. He'll point out that they'll never need to build another one; with the inertia box, anything that can make it to Mars can go to Andromeda now. Then we vanish and start exploring on our own."

"Or trading, if we find other civilizations."

"Or trading, yes. There's a lot of stuff in our library that's probably of value, and we might get Manhattan Island for trinkets."

Spencer hadn't heard that simile before, but could gather the gist.

"So I understand you aren't going to hibernate?"

"No, I'm staying awake."

"Won't Julie Vargas be able to take care of routine medical stuff?"

"Certainly, especially since there's only about twenty people staying awake. You know, that surprised me. I would have guessed, when we first got here, that nobody would willingly enter hibernation again. But nearly everyone's doing it just to avoid two weeks' boredom."

"Boredom combined with intense anticipation. Did you, as a kid, wish you could get to sleep on Christmas Eve so it would be morning and you could open your gifts already? Most people are so eager to find out what happened to Earth they can't wait."

"I'm eager, too, and Maureen and the kids are hibernating."

"So why stay up?"

"I have been appointed Ye Royal Butler to her majesty, Queen Tsarina."

". . ."

"The cat. Cats, actually; we managed to snag two of the four kittens as well as Tipsy. Vargas was willing to let them on board only if I promised to feed them and devise kitty diapers for them. Took me back to my childhood, let me tell you."

"Your cats wore diapers?"

Chapter 48 Leaving Hoyl

RED WATCHED THE MAIN SCREEN IN THE MESS HALL as the engines fired. There was no sensation, of course. He still floated just above his table, tethered to the chair. The thrusters didn't make enough noise to penetrate the ship's immense hull.

For a minute, he thought the engines had failed. Nothing seemed to happen. But then he saw the terminator of Hoyl moving ever so gradually to the left, and the land below beginning to slide downward.

Were those the lights of Avalerion he saw? Or just his imagination?

The moon was now a dark mass. Hō-ō, a vast malevolent orb, slid above the top of the camera and vanished from view. New stars emerged from the cloak of the dark moon, and then steadied.

With no sensation of motion at all, *Phoenix* began accelerating at twelve hundred gravities. They were going home.

He blew the planet a kiss. He owed it that much. The coin stayed in his pocket, awaiting an eventual home.

He had his data pad, and on it, schematics for ROVER IV. This one, with its own inertia box, could explore entire solar systems. Or even galaxies.

A hand rested softly on his shoulder. Red didn't need to turn to learn Rebekah had changed her mind.

"Virgil, you already said good bye to that place. Time for the next world, and hundreds more after that."

* * *

Six days after *Phoenix* slid off the horizon and vanished forever, the first of the great equinoctial storms reached Avalerion.

Rudy Harlen sat in the tube-grass module and listened to the heat pumps whine. Despite their heavy laboring, a thin cloud of steam floated against the top of the tube-shaped shelter, and beads of condensation ran down the sides. It was a stuffy and uncomfortable forty five degrees.

Outside, it was a scorching black hell. Thunderous tumults of rain fell, in air heated to an unbearable sixty degrees, the raindrops even hotter than that. Worse, without *Phoenix* at hand, and with nobody with the expertise to translate the met charts from the satellites, nobody knew when the storm would end.

In retrospect, it should have been obvious. The storm swept up from the southeast, temporarily blocking the katabatic wind that kept the settlement cool, and bringing the weather from the superheated equatorial ocean. The true nature of Hoyl and her vivid sun had reached the colony.

There had been a couple of those damn kittens around after *Phoenix* left, but Rudy hadn't seen them since the rain started. No big loss, really. Rudy wasn't a cat person. But Sheffield had talked about getting up a search party. In this. The man was losing it.

Rudy read the note from Red Farnsworth one more time. It hadn't been addressed to him, and he was perplexed when he found it in his living room on his keyboard the evening after *Phoenix* left. It had been addressed to the Cohen woman, who had been their one remaining hope for any kind of sustainable colony until she changed her mind at the last minute and left. Red had engineered that setback, too. Someday he would pay.

He read the note three times, thinking furiously. Red was no fool, and was wise to want to hide this from Sheffield. He suspected that Rebekah had decided to do him a personal favor, and in his mind, it mitigated what he had regarded as the final betrayal of his hopes for a future on Hoyl.

He motioned to Cyril Voss and Aaron Kessler. "It's time. Go get him. He's downstairs."

A few minutes they returned, along with the remaining three members of the team. Sheffield was between them, haggard, dull-eyed, exhausted. He hadn't shaved in several days, or washed. Not that showers were any comfort in this steam bath.

Rudy motioned for Sheffield to sit, and he did so with the air of a man who has been convicted and is just awaiting the sentencing.

"It's over, Sheffield. We took a vote earlier, and all six of us have decided you aren't the leader any more. I am.

"So I have two options to offer you. You can either walk out of here and keep walking, in any direction you want. . . " Rudy smiled at his own wit as Sheffield paled, ". . . or you stay here, but under my command. What's it going to be?"

That Sheffield even had to think about it was a bit of a surprise, one that Rudy attributed to exhaustion. A walk outside right now was a scalding death sentence.

Sheffield answered, his voice a low croak. Rudy nodded.

"I think this is going to let up tomorrow," he said. When it does, we grab everything we can, we hook the modules to the shuttle, fire up the magic box, and get the fuck out of here. This world is dead."

"I don't believe that."

By way of answer, Rudy gave Sheffield Red's note. He finished, and looked at Rudy mutely.

"I think that when those things out there. . . " he pointed vaguely upward, where two orbs hovered, perhaps ten kilometers overhead, ". . . start moving this place, we're going to have thorium powder mixed in with our air. Do you doubt what Red says here? This was something he wrote to his girlfriend in case she didn't come. You think he was bullshitting her?" Sheffield shook his head.

"Right. You want a colony, so do I. But it won't be here, and it sure won't be with just seven men. So we go get some women, and there's only one place we're going to find those.

"Soon's this storm lets up, we gather our goodies, and head for Disappointment. We get what we need there.

"Then we head for Earth."

* * *

The two cats, still in the final stages of kittenhood, found themselves in a space where there was sunshine, and lots of things to climb upon and survey, and abundant tasty prey. That it was enclosed didn't bother them. The air was fresh and warm, and there were no threats. Eventually the female would come into season, and they would thrive. There were no humans about, but that didn't bother them much.

* * *

The mouse came out of its burrow cautiously and sniffed the air. The hot rains had come and gone, come and gone, come and gone. Each rain was longer than the last, and the mouse was hungry.

Desperation drove him over the footbridge and into the tube-grass, where he quickly found that the lush green vegetation was inedible.

He came back through among the buildings. He had no way of knowing it, but those building would still be standing five hundred years from now, the only sign humans had ever been here.

There had been humans, and even some cats. They were gone now. The mouse could tell that.

Emboldened, he crossed the bridge and back into the woods. At least, that was his intent.

As he crossed the bridge, something swooped from above, breaking his spine and crushing his ribcage. As he died, he knew two things.

First, that he was dying.

Second, whatever it was that had grabbed him, it was no cat.

End

www.ingramcontent.com/pod-product-compliance
Lightning Source LLC
Chambersburg PA
CBHW030923020726
47498CB00001B/83